# WE DON'T LIVE HERE ANYMORE

## COLLECTED SHORT STORIES & NOVELLAS   VOLUME 1

*The Lieutenant*

*Separate Flights*

*Adultery & Other Choices*

*Finding a Girl in America*

*The Times Are Never So Bad*

*Voices from the Moon*

*The Last Worthless Evening*

*Selected Stories*

*Broken Vessels*

*Dancing After Hours*

*Meditations from a Moveable Chair*

# ANDRE DUBUS

## We Don't Live Here Anymore

COLLECTED SHORT STORIES & NOVELLAS    VOLUME 1

Introduction by ANN BEATTIE

Series Editor JOSHUA BODWELL

DAVID R. GODINE · *Publisher*

*Boston*

This edition published in 2018 by
DAVID R. GODINE · *Publisher*
Post Office Box 450
Jaffrey, New Hampshire 03452
*www.godine.com*

LIBRARY OF CONGRESS CATALOGING-IN-PUBLICATION DATA

Names: Dubus, Andre, 1936–1999 author. | Bodwell, Joshua editor.
Title: Collected short stories and novellas / Andre Dubus ;
edited by Joshua   Bodwell.
Description: Jaffrey, New Hampshire : David R. Godine, Publisher, 2018. |
Includes bibliographical references and index.
Identifiers: LCCN 2018003815| ISBN 9781567926163 (v. 1 : softcover :
alk. paper) | ISBN 9781567926170 (v. 2 : softcover : alk. paper)
Classification: LCC PS3554.U265 A6 2018 | DDC 813/.54—dc23
LC record available at https://lccn.loc.gov/2018003815

ACKNOWLEDGMENTS

*Separate Flights*
"Over the Hill" was first published in *Sage*; "The Doctor" (© 1969 The New
Yorker Magazine, Inc.) in *The New Yorker*; "In My Life" in *Northwest Review*;
"If They Knew Yvonne" (© 1969 University of Northern Iowa), "Separate
Flights" (© 1970 University of Northern Iowa) and "Going Under" (© 1974
University of Northern Iowa) in *North American Review*.

*Adultery & Other Choices*
"An Afternoon with the Old Man" and "Andromache" first appeared in *The New
Yorker*; "Contrition" in *The North American Review*; "Cadence," "The Bully,"
and "Adultery" in *The Sewanee Review* (© 1974, 1975, 1977 by the University of
the South, reprinted by permission of the editor); "Graduation" in *New Dawn
Magazine*; "The Shooting" in *The Carleton Miscellany* (© 1974 by Carleton College); and "Corporal of Artillery" in *Ploughshares*.

# CONTENTS

# SPOTLIGHTS

*ANN BEATTIE*

ANDRE DUBUS AND I were once on book tour together. Because he was wheelchair-bound by this time, we were transported by hired car. Outside Boston, actually not so close to Boston, the car broke down. Do I remember correctly that this happened on a holiday weekend, or am I still trying to make sense of it? We sat in the back seat. Andre's friend Jack was in the seat next to the driver. There were numerous phone calls, many moments when we had, or lost, hope. We reached our publisher's voice mail. Nobody responded—well, there was *talk*, but no one did anything, as time passed and time passed. Finally, we tried to get a car by calling 1-800-RENTACAR, but that didn't work, either. A cop car pulled into the breakdown lane, assessed the situation, and raced off, light blinking. That was the end of that. Hours into this, my husband and his best friend fetched me. Andre and Jack insisted: I must go. I'd be seeing him soon, Andre said; one of the group had finally managed to summon help: a tow truck, another rental car, I don't remember. I left amid cries of "Good sport!" and "See you next week!" feeling that I should stay. (Yes, I should have.)

During this debacle I doubt I had reason to reflect on the fact that Andre and I were writers. What would that matter?

If you're busted flat in Baton Rouge, who cares that it's a *double entendre*? Off I went. My pal and I would rendezvous soon in Portland, Maine.

As it turned out, Andre didn't make it to Portland. In a coffee shop there, I overheard a young guy trying to convince a pretty woman he'd just met to go to the library reading. "He's a kind of a Raymond Carver character," he said. "And I've never heard of her." Off *Her* went, to do a solo.

When I think of Andre, an image of us in the back seat inevitably returns: the world whizzing by, everyone's bright ideas totally ineffective, the distracting and effective bleak humor that soon set in, how strange it was that a car belonging to a big company had broken down and there was no one to help us. The oddity of the situation became the prevailing reality. This isn't my segue into comparing life to fiction, then launching into a discussion of one of the best American short story writers, ever. It's just noting something in words, imagining that if there's an afterlife, Andre will be happy that I spread perplexity to readers who know (pax "The New Criticism") not to confuse the author's life with his work. We do our best, and in Andre's case, he watched keenly when he was mobile, and no less keenly when he was afflicted. He took things in straight on, and also saw from an aerial perspective. Writers or not, we're mortal, trapped in a car or trapped somewhere more spacious.

It's sort of thrilling—and maybe a bit dangerous—to have a fictional character stand alone, though this isn't an unfamiliar state to any of us; numerous works of literature focus closely, unwaveringly, on one character. We've all been alone, during exhilarating walks down woodland paths, meditating, or when everyone else has fallen asleep. We have sometimes been alone when waiting for a bus. But unless we've walked off to have a private moment, we also tend to notice that we're the only one on the street (or, in Andre Dubus's world, the last woman cleaning up the kitchen), so where is everyone else who means to board the bus? What I'm trying to get at is the surprising way Dubus does the equivalent of spotlighting a character, though his subtlety makes what he does more analogous to being in church and lighting a candle.

Once we've seen Dubus's characters alone or close up, that impression lingers. But do the characters glow (so to speak) because of inner light or external lighting? Only when we get some distance from them, and their often indelible first moments—only as the story progresses—do we get some indication. Writers usually want to find ways to animate their characters from within *and* externally, allowing us to know their private thoughts or revealing them through their interaction with others. Dubus was Catholic. It was an integral part of his identity; he often addressed the subject directly. So perhaps those private moments are analogous to the split second before a character on stage speaks, or perhaps, more aptly, analogous to a petitioner approaching a religious icon? What if we're observing a silent prayer that establishes an unspoken interaction with an unnamed force? If so, at least sometimes, might that force not be called spiritual?

Dubus's story "Over the Hill" begins: "Her hand was tiny. He held it gently, protectively, resting in her lap, the brocaded silk of her kimono against the back of his hand, the smooth flesh gentle and tender against his palm." We sense the prose's movement—it, too, can be characterized as gentle—that guides us, as the still hand seduces us into this story. After reading the opening sentences, I remained fixated on the visuals. This might be called a devotional moment. We imagine the story will either go one way or the other, but nothing in between: it will evolve mesmerically, through our senses (feel that brocade sleeve), or reverse the reader's expectations with violence.

But neither happens. Or both, as it turns out.

While the prose comes close to freezing time and forcing the scene to vibrate through our senses, the dialogue, once spoken, is of another sort—it's not beautiful, but clipped, Hemingway-esque, flat-footed, sentences that don't even aspire to be cryptic. Things change quickly, in the bar where sailors sit with Japanese women who come with a price. The main character is an unhappy man named Gale (the name carries connotations of a storm). When the woman's hand is relinquished, Gale goes to the bathroom, where there are drawings of ships, some with scrawled "obscenities," along with factual information. The image of the hand returns, conflated with hands of a different sort. Out goes the tactile, thrilling silky kimono; in comes the toilet. Along with this information: There is a "she," Gale's young wife, who—like the American girl at the end of the war in Hemingway's "Cat in the Rain"— is petulant, and wants the Japanese equivalent of the good life. Here, it has been transmuted from Hemingway to Dubus, to become "china and glassware and silk and wool and cashmere sweaters and a transistor radio." *Those* desires end with a thud—as does the litany in Hemingway's story, unless we particularly like wet kittens.

Without giving a summary of this quintessentially sad story, the violence that is the flip-side of the gentle, tranquil moment with which the story begins (we accept that love and hate are not necessarily polarities) becomes, surprisingly, something Gale directs toward himself, in a moment reminiscent of Hemingway's "Indian Camp." At the end of each story comes a moment of awareness—every new conclusion is not an epiphany—in which the reader learns the character's thoughts about mortality. Granted, one is a child and one has just left any vestiges of childhood behind. We read both writers' stories, though, in context with what we know about the ways of the world. We also take in Dubus's story with a keen awareness of how Hemingway changed the story form by making sure information subtly accrued that was at odds with things stated and observed. Post-Hemingway, a reader's attention functions like a dowsing rod, searching for subtext that reveals what's precious in proportion to how deeply it's buried.

The uneasy tension between stasis and a person's resolve to act, whether or not such action ultimately comes to pass in a Dubus story, carries an implied question of what one should or might do, versus the accommodations inherent in what one does. Dubus's stories question the status quo. Actually, they catch it and break its neck, even those times they ostensibly put it back together. Everything looks the same, but if you were to lift it, you'd feel the inherent flaw.

This might be the moment to remark on Dubus's writerly largesse. It's easy for writers to corner their characters—one way is by stacking the deck against them—yet sometimes (like being mugged in an alley) the story seems to have its own uncontainable energy and trajectory; it declares the inevitability of letting bad things happen.

Peter, the main character in "Going Under," has lost his wife. His children have moved away with her. He has relationships with younger women—some too young to finish their martinis. Ever. Here's a typical moment in which Peter, who seems neither terribly imperiled nor highly functional, has a perception that in a lesser writer's story would seem forced, probably compounded by the problem that the prose would be written in loftier language than his/her character's perceptions: "Jo was good to be with, better than eating alone; but she has not laughed since dinner, her smile is forced, and in her voice and dark eyes her ache is bitter, it is defiant; and he feels they are not at a hearth but are huddled at a campfire in a dangerous forest." What at quick glance might seem condescending—or at least Peter's tendency to only like young women depending on how they affect *him*—isn't, on closer examination, so easy to categorize. We can't just dismiss this jerk. The word "bitter"—even if it's invoked as *he* would perceive it, retaining the emphasis on him—is a word from a different realm: the realm of adult experience. Furthermore, she is "defiant." She has volition. The language changes: Peter no longer interprets as if his perceptions are interchangeable with facts; "he feels," and what he feels suggests (as the story established earlier) a tentativeness on his part, a shift in potential power. When we hear about the hearth—a word almost onomatopoetic; to say it aloud suggests breadth and warmth, even heat—we take cold comfort. This hearth carries connotations of a fairy tale. Peter would like to feel powerful; perhaps he'd like to express his condescension toward the rather random young woman, but the potential of something frightening happening enters with the allusion to a fairy tale. "Hearth" is like so many words spoken to children about a largely vanished past: gone, and therefore intended to have magical associations. The characters are "huddled" (a religious posture that is of course also symbolic). He and she are metaphorically in "a dangerous forest"—an apt analogy for life, itself. Who or what is de-stabilized here? First, the status quo. The language also produces a visceral effect; the reader would prefer the warm hearth to the unknown forest. There's no going back, though: we've been transported, propelled into new territory. Dubus's stories are so often deceptively familiar until the moment they're revealed to be a consideration of something else.

Initially, reading "Going Under," I was perplexed by Peter's histrionics: raving, in dialogue. Yet early in the story we learn (casually, in passing) that he started out as an actor. This cued me to another way of reading: his first failure was in acting (later appearing on radio). When the reader meets him, he's engaged in repetition compulsion, locked into performing—and performing badly. (No, I'm not kidding.) Here, "an Andre Dubus story" (yes, they're recognizable, but not to their detriment) deliberately teeters on farce. Wow. What a risky, admirably perverse thing for a writer to do: to give his character bad lines, and lots of them; to present moments interchangeable with your worst Broadway nightmare of having to sit still and be subjected to bombastic over-acting ("Come with me, Miranda. You love me. We'll make it. Come now, baby, come now..."). Other than the reader, the audience for this is Peter's passive, not-quite-girlfriend, Miranda, who's also involved with another man and won't make a commitment. ("I'm too young," she says sensibly, undercutting all his over-the-top, ostensible passion with three simple words.) She remains a nearly mute audience as he ups the ante, imploring her to see things his way. Gosh—ever met anyone like that?

This story also recreates, subtly cueing us through action as well as words, a potentially dangerous downside of story-telling: writers who try to hammer others (listeners; interpreters) into submission. When you get used to a writer's territory, you have certain expectations, even if they're unstated, to see those expectations reversed; this can happen even when readers are made very happy. As Flannery O'Connor pointed out about one of her stories, "Anyone is happy to see someone's wooden leg stolen."

Finally, I read "Going Under" as a serious story, though it runs the risk of being misread, in part because we identify neither with the silent, stricken Miranda, nor the bombastic, self-dramatizing Peter. Peter is desperate. "Desperate. Yes." What more information can Dubus be expected to provide? Well, this: that when Peter can't sleep, he sets out for his other girlfriend's house in the middle of the night, whistling "Summertime," George Gershwin's song from *Porgy and Bess*. Anyone familiar with the opera's lyrics knows they're sung by a man who wants to *persuade* the woman he loves to see things his way. (In retrospect, Peter's importuning "Come on" dialogue sounds similar to "You an' me can live dat high life in New York/ Come wid me ... " from the same show). Dubus is appropriating, displacing, re-creating, making comedy butt up against a serious matter: this man has no sense of self. In his conflict and stasis—in his inability to move that is so often the metaphorical straightjacket restraining free movement—Peter seems doomed to a Dante-esque ring of his own hell: "If he reaches the sidewalk, he will go around the corner of the building, to the garage in back. To reach this sidewalk he must simply traverse the lawn, walking on a shoveled walk between low white banks of snow. But he cannot go down the walk. He stands on the porch looking at the two steps and then at the T formed by the two sidewalks and at the smooth hard snow of the lawn. He starts to step onto the first step, his leg moves, it reaches the step, the other leg follows, he is standing on the step but Peter himself is not really there, whoever Peter is has been driven in panic back into the warm and lighted apartment; he is not even on the steps." This has, indeed, been a story about a person unsure of his identity, unmoored. Many writers would have concluded here, when the themes have been brought together to produce a paradoxically bleak exhilaration. Dubus does not end here. Read on. The soundtrack is provided, and the writing's as sure-footed as your own fears, stalking you.

Dubus's female characters are very well conceived, and it may be more unusual than I realize that he so consistently created and stayed so close to his female characters. But I don't want to simply assert that Dubus gives women equal time and equal potential power as men, but rather that he lets us watch fairly conventional power struggles between men and women work out unexpectedly, because there is always the inclusion of fate. Dubus's second collection, *Adultery & Other Choices* includes two examples of this:

"The Fat Girl" is almost a fairy tale, but one gone very wrong; "Andromache" is almost a prototypical tale of how military life for the men serving and their wives, but the military, ultimately, offers no clearer ability for one to triumph than engaging in something overtly reckless.

Reading "The Fat Girl," one of my favorite stories, feels as if we're spying and seeing the private moments that ruin what might go right in the life of the title character, Louise, and her relationships with her parents, college roommate, and husband. Very quickly, the reader pretty much has to take sides. And since Louise's nice roommate, Carrie, is willing to help her, it would be inhumane not to take that side—so readers think, "Yes, yes, I should be affiliated with the roommate, with the voice of reason." But that dynamic (covertly) is a love affair played out not sexually, but through one person being vigilant about what is best for another. It is as much about power as Louise's earlier struggle with her mother. But there's real affection between the roommates, and, arguably, it trumps the relationship Louise has later with her husband.

In Louise's marriage, we observe that she can get only so far with her attempts at weight loss, and then she begins to regress: "He truly believed they were arguing about her weight. She knew better: She knew that beneath the argument lay the question of who Richard was." This might seem astute—she wants it to appear that way—but I don't think we can take this as an epiphany. It makes her sound good, but is it verifiable? In the end, we see that Louise grows into a woman who wants to be alone, that she is more than willing to have her husband simply gone.

In "Andromache," Dubus focuses not on Marine officer Joe Forrest, who has died unexpectedly, but on his widow, Ellen. Dubus gives us the story's end—the outcome—at the very beginning, so there's no surprise (surprise as in *unexpected revelation*) when what happens happens. This is a good writerly advantage: to be able to let the reader know more than the characters, because the writer can take liberties with chronology, while the plot transpires as it does. It is a sneaky story: we know from the outset that Joe has died, then move backwards into another time period when we uncomfortably observe him "living." Ellen is left with the burden, but so is the reader, who has also always known.

I can see thinking of Ellen as accepting of the difficulties of being newly widowed and suddenly finding herself a civilian with two young children to fend for (she does identify them as difficulties; she's not obtuse or in denial), yet she seems to have no fail-safe if the status quo isn't maintained. But the story becomes more of a comment on military life that asks all characters to be withholding, than a story about a particular marriage. Joe and Ellen are being dictated to by the military—Joe has his role to play and Ellen has her role to play, also. But there are cracks long before Joe's death: Ellen feels condescended to; she feels slighted by the circumstances of the party; she has her confidantes, but they're too immersed in the same dynamic to really help. The story is more about "This Kind of Life" than about individuals.

Dubus goes out of his way to show us the cracks in the facades, and to show us that while two strong-willed people are behaving *appropriately*, that is no guarantee about what curve life might throw them. So I see Ellen and Joe as equal, in a way, but also as limited by context, and a bit numbed by time.

They're evenly matched, but Ellen is right: the survivors are the ones who are going to have to find a way to go on living.

I think Dubus gave his men and women comparable power because it's not about who "wins," but rather it is a reality that the struggle is undertaken again and again. The stories are about how people must make accommodations once they find out there's no winning. The external world, as Dubus sees it, is very grim—even with male and female characters who are articulate and who think they know what it is they want.

Dubus is such a master that even those times he invokes *sturm und drang*, he simultaneously casts the drama into invisible ironic quotation marks. Even when Dubus says something with his fingers crossed behind his back, his jokes are terribly serious, the stakes high, the final moments often transcendent not merely because of his prose, but because rather than expressing hopelessness, the stories lift out of moments of personal pain, sometimes to reveal imaginary, rather than real constrictions. What Dubus observes, he clearly does not endorse. His fictional world—though the reader comes to feel that if he wanted to, Andre Dubus, like Puck, could race around the earth—rooted his fiction in working class life; really, the struggle to have a life, since poverty interrupts good intentions, liquor is cheap, women were not then (are they now?) given a fair shake, and people are fallible. In these stories, the divorce rate is high, and the rate of loneliness higher. No writer has the obligation to save us from grimness (bring on Zola), but his endeavor—apparent from his first story collection—reveals a complex writer who has digested enough unhappiness that he could easily regurgitate, and of that mess—because of his wizard's ability with words—make something beautiful. There are certainly moments, lyrical moments, moments that genuinely transport the reader by simile or metaphor, but it is his ability to undercut his own talent in order to keep us in the real world that dazzles me. An example: Consider the last sentence from "The Fat Girl."

What is Dubus doing, anyway, calling one story "The Fat Girl," and another story from the same book, which alludes to a very different mythical woman, "Andromache"? He's looking straight ahead *and* from an aerial perspective, and not flinching at what's there. He's spiritually (ok, at least celestially) inclined, while knowing that his sharp eye and ear are not enough to take him where he wants to go, where he wants us to join him.

# SEPARATE FLIGHTS

*to Suzanne, Andre, Jeb & Nicole*

*The name of 'Threads of the Virgin' is applied to certain tiny threads that float in the wind and on which a certain kind of spiders ... take flight in the free breezes of the air and even in the midst of a violent storm.... But these spiders spin those floating threads out of their own entrails, delicate webs by means of which they hurl themselves into space unknown.*
    MIGUEL DE UNAMUNO
    *The Agony of Christianity*

*Save me, thought the Consul vaguely...*
    MALCOLM LOWRY
    *Under the Volcano*

# WE DON'T LIVE HERE ANYMORE

*Pity is the worst passion of all: we don't outlive it like sex.*
GRAHAM GREENE
*The Ministry of Fear*

*Come see us again some time; nobody's home but us, and
we don't live here anymore.*
A FRIEND, DRUNK ONE NIGHT

## 1

THE OWNER of the liquor store was an Irishman with graying hair; he glanced at Edith, then pretended he hadn't, and
said: 'There's my ale man.'

'Six Pickwicks,' I said. 'And a six-pack of Miller's for the
women.'

'You hardly find a woman who'll drink ale.'

'That's right.'

We leaned against the counter; I felt Edith wanting to
touch me, so I stepped back and took out my wallet. Hank had
wanted to pay for all of it but I held him to two dollars.

'Used to be everybody in New England drank ale. Who
taught you? Your father?'

'He taught me to drink ale and laugh with pretty girls.
What happened to the others?'

I was watching Edith enjoying us. She is dark and very small with long black hair, and she has the same charming gestures that other girls with long hair have: with a slow hand she pushes it from her eye; when she bends over a drinking fountain, she holds it at her ear so it won't fall into the basin. Some time I would like to see it fall: Edith drinking, lips wet, throat moving with cool water, and her hair fallen in the chrome basin, soaking.

'World War II. The boys all got drafted before they were old enough to drink in Massachusetts, see? So they started drinking beer on the Army bases. When they came home they still wanted beer. That was the end of ale. Now if one of your old ale drinkers dies, you don't replace him.'

Outside under the streetlights Edith took my arm. In front of the newsstand across the street a cop watched us get into the car, and in the dark Edith sat close to me as I drove through town. There were few cars and no one was on the sidewalks. On the streets where people lived most of the houses were dark; a few blocks from my house I stopped under a large tree near the curb and held Edith and we kissed.

'We'd better go,' she said.

'I'll bring my car to the Shell station at twelve.'

She moved near the door and brushed her hair with her fingers, and I drove home. Terry and Hank were sitting on the front steps. When I stopped the car Edith got out and crossed the lawn without waiting or looking back. Terry watched me carrying the bag, and when I stepped between her and Hank she looked straight up at me.

We talked in the dark, sitting in lawn chairs on the porch. Except Hank, who was always restless: he leaned against the porch rail, paced, leaned against a wall, stood over one of us as we talked, nodding his head, a bottle in one fist, a glass in the other, listening, then breaking in, swinging his glass like a slow hook to the body the instant before he interrupted, then his voice came, louder than ours. In high school he had played halfback. He went to college weighing a hundred and fifty-six pounds and started writing. He had kept in condition, and his walk and gestures had about them an athletic grace that I had tried to cultivate as a boy, walking home from movies where I had seen gunmen striding like mountain lions. Edith sat to my right, with her back to the wall; sometimes she rested her foot against mine. Terry sat across from me, smoking too much. She has long red hair and eleven years ago she was the prettiest girl I had ever seen; or, rather, the prettiest girl I had ever touched. Now she's thirty and she's gained a pound for each of those eleven years, but she has gained them subtly, and her only striking change is in her eyes, blue eyes that I fell in love with: more and more now, they have that sad, pensive look that married women get after a few years. Her eyes used to be merry. Edith is twenty-seven and her eyes are still merry, and she turned them bright and dark to me as I talked. When Hank and Edith left, we walked them to the car, hugging and pecking them goodnight as we always did; I watched Edith's silhouette as they drove away.

'Come here,' Terry said. She took my wrist and pulled me toward the back door.

'Come where.'

'In the kitchen. I want to talk to you.'

'Would you let go of my wrist?'

She kept pulling. At the sidewalk leading to the back door I stopped and jerked my arm but she held on and turned to face me.

'I said let go of my wrist,' and I jerked again and was free. Then I followed her in.

'From now on we're going to act like married people,' she said. 'No more of this crap.' I went to the refrigerator and got an ale. 'Just like other married people. And no flirting around with silly adventures. Do you understand that?'

'Of course I don't. Who could understand such bullshit.'

'You're not *really* going to play dumb. Are you? Come on.'

'Terry.' I was still calm; I thought I might be able to hold onto that, pull us out of this, into bed, into sleep. 'Would you please tell me what's wrong?'

She moved toward me and I squared my feet to duck or

block, but she went past me and got ice from the refrigerator and went to the cabinet where the bourbon was.

'Why don't you have a beer instead?'

'I don't want a beer.'

'You'll get drunk.'

'Maybe I will.'

I looked down at my glass, away from her face: in summer she had freckles that were pretty, and I remembered how I used to touch her in daylight, a quick kiss or hug as I went through the kitchen, a hand at her waist or shoulder as we walked in town; that was not long ago, and still she reached for me passing in the house, or touched me as she walked by the couch where I read, but I never did; in bed at night, yes, but not in daylight anymore.

'Why don't we talk in the morning? We'll just fight now, you've got that look of yours.'

'Never mind that look of mine.'

The pots from dinner were still on the stove, the plates were dirty in the sink, and when I sat at the table I brushed crumbs and bits of food from the place in front of me; the table was sticky where I rested my hands, and I went to the sink and got a sponge and wiped the part I had cleaned. I left the sponge on the table and sat down and felt her fury at my cleaning before I looked up and saw it in her eyes. She stood at the stove, an unlit cigarette in her hand.

'You and Edith, all these trips you make, all these Goddamn errands, all summer if someone runs out of booze or cigarettes or wants Goddamn egg rolls, off you go, you and Edith, and it's not right to leave me with Hank, to put me in that position—'

'Now wait a minute.'

'—something's going on, either it's going on or you want it to—'

'Just a minute, wait just a minute—two questions: why is it wrong for Edith and me to go get some beer and Goddamn ale, and what's this position you're in when you're alone with Hank, and what is it you're *really* worrying about? Do you get horny every time you're alone with Hank and you want Daddy to save you from yourself?'

'*No*, I don't get horny when I'm alone with Hank; I only get horny for my Goddamn husband but he likes to be with *Edith*.'

'We've been married ten years. We're not on our honeymoon, for Christ's sake.'

Her eyes changed, softened, and her voice did too: 'Why aren't we? Don't you love me?'

'Oh hell. Of course I do.'

'Well what are you saying, that you love me but we've been married so long that you need Edith too, or maybe you're already having her? Is that it, because if it is maybe we should talk about how long this marriage is going to last. Because you can move out anytime you want to, I can get a job—'

'Terry.'

'—and the kids will be all right, there's no reason for you to suffer if marriage is such a disappointment. Maybe I've done something—'

'Terry.'

'What.'

'Calm down. Here.' I reached across the table with my lighter and she leaned over to light her cigarette, cupping her hands around mine, and under her flesh like a pulse I could feel her need and I wanted at once to shove her against the stove, and to stroke her cheek and tousle her hair.

'Terry, you said those things. Not me. I have never wanted to leave you. I am not suffering. I'm not tired of you, and I don't need Edith or anyone else. I like being with her. Like with any other friend—man or woman—sometimes I like being alone with her. So once in a while we run an errand. I see nothing threatening in that, nothing bad. I don't think married people have to cling to each other, and I think if you look around you'll see that most of them don't. You're the only wife I know who gets pissed at her husband because he doesn't touch her at parties—'

'The other husbands *touch* their wives! They put their *arms* around them!'

'Hank doesn't.'

'That's why she's so lonely, that's why she likes to tag along like your little lamb, because Hank doesn't love her—'

'Who ever said that?'

'Hank did.' Her eyes lowered. 'Tonight while you two were gone.'

'He said that?'

'Yes.'

'Why?'

'I don't know, he just said it.'

'What were you doing?'

'Well we were talking, how else do you tell people things.'

'When people talk like that they're usually doing other things.'

'Oh sure, we were screwing on the front porch, what do you care?'

'I don't, as long as I know the truth.'

'The *truth*. You wouldn't know the truth if it knocked on the door. You won't even admit the truth about yourself, that you don't really love me—'

'Stop that, Terry. Do not say that shit. You know why? Because it's not true, it's never been true, but when you say it like that, it is. For a minute. For long enough to start a *really* crazy fight. Do you understand that?'

She was nodding, her cheeks looking numb, her eyes frightened and forlorn; then I felt my own eyes giving her pity, washing her cheeks and lips with it, and when I did that her face tightened, her eyes raged again, and too quick for me to duck she threw her drink in my face, ice cubes flying past my head and smacking the wall and sliding across the floor. I rose fast but only halfway, poised with my hands gripping the edge of the table; then I looked away from her and sat down and took out my handkerchief and slowly wiped my face and beard, looking out the back door at the night where I wanted to be, then I brushed at the spots on the burgundy sweatshirt she had brought home for me one day, happily taking it from the bag and holding it up for me to see. Then I stood up and walked quickly out the back door, and she threw her glass at me but too late, the door was already swinging to and the glass bounced off the screen and hit the floor. Somehow it didn't break.

I crossed the lawn, onto the sidewalk that sloped down with the street; a half block from the house I was suddenly afraid she was coming, I felt her behind me, and I turned, but the sidewalk was empty and lovely in the shadows of maples and elms. I went on. If there was a way to call Edith and she could come get me. But of course not. I could go back and get my car, the keys were in my pocket, I could start it and be gone before Terry came running out with a Goddamn knife, if I drove to Edith's and parked in front of the house and looked up at the window where she slept beside Hank she would know, if I waited long enough watching her window she would know in her sleep and she would wake and look out the window at me under the moon; she would tiptoe downstairs and hold me on the damp lawn. I came to a corner and went up another street. 'Edith,' I whispered into the shadows of my diagonal walk, 'oh Edith sweet baby, I love you, I love you forever.' I thought about forever and if we live afterward, then I saw myself laid out in a coffin, the beard and hair lovely white. I stopped and leaned against a car, dew on its fender cool through my slacks. Natasha and Sean and I looked at Terry in her coffin. I stood between them holding their small hands. Terry's smooth cheeks were pale against her red hair.

When she told me she was pregnant she wasn't afraid. She was twenty years old. It was a cold bright Thursday in January, the sky had been blue for a week and the snow in Boston was dirty and old. We went to a bookstore on Boylston Street and bought paperbacks for each other, then we had steamers and draft beer in a dim place with paintings of whale fishing and storms at sea and fishing boats in harbor on the walls. For some reason the waiters wore leather tunics. In those days Terry always seemed happy. I can close my eyes any time and remember how I loved her and see and feel her as she took my hand on the table and said: 'After today I'll be careful about eating, and if I promise not to get fat and if I get a job, can I keep our baby?'

Now I started walking home. We were, after all this, the same Jack and Terry, and I would go to her now and touch her and hold her; I walked faster, nodding my head yes yes yes. Then going into the dark living room I felt her in the house like the large and sharpened edge of a knife. She was asleep. I crept into the bedroom and lay beside her, at the edge of the bed so we didn't touch.

Natasha and Sean woke Terry early for breakfast but I stayed in bed, held onto sleep through the breakfast voices then their voices outside, while the sun got higher and the room hotter until it was too hot and I got up. I went straight to the shower without seeing anyone. While I was drying myself she tapped on the door.

'Do you want lunch or breakfast?'

Her voice had the practiced sweetness she assumed when she was afraid: strangers got it, and I got it after some fights or when she made mistakes with money. For an instant I was tender and warm and I wanted to help her with a cheerful line (Oh, I'll have you for breakfast, love; just stick a banana in it and hop in bed); but then sure as time is a trick I was sitting in the kitchen last night, and the bourbon and ice were flying at me.

'I don't know,' I said. Through the door I could feel the tone of my voice piercing her. 'What do you have?'

'Just cereal if you want breakfast. But if you want lunch I could get some lobsters, just for you and me; the kids don't like them anyway.'

'No, I have to hurry. I'm taking the car in.'

*Linhart*, I said to my face in the mirror. *You are a petulant son of a bitch. Why don't you drag her in here and whip her ass then eat lobster with her.* She was still waiting outside the door; I pretended not to know, and went about drying myself.

'I could go to the fish market and be back and have them done in thirty minutes. Forty to be safe.'

'I have to get the car there at twelve.'

'You *have* to?'

'If I want the work done, yes.'

'What's the work?'

'Oil and grease.'

'That doesn't take long.'

'They're busy, Terry. They want it at twelve or not at all. They don't care how badly you want a lobster. But if you want one, get it now before I leave.'

'I don't want one by myself.'

'What, you mean it won't taste good?'

'Oh, you know what I *mean*,' in that mock-whine you hear from girls everywhere when they're being lovingly teased. I started brushing my teeth.

'Cheerios or Grape Nuts?'

'Grape Nuts.'

She went away. When I came dressed to the kitchen the table was set neatly for one: a red straw place mat, a deep bowl which had the faint sparkle of fresh washing, a spoon on a napkin, a glass of orange juice. She was upstairs with the vacuum cleaner. Over in the sink were the children's breakfast dishes, unwashed; beneath them were last night's dishes.

Terry is the toy of poltergeists: washer, dryer, stove, refrigerator, dishes, clothes, and woolly house dust. The stove wants cleaning and as she lifts off burners the washing machine stops in the wash room; she leaves the stove and takes another load of dirty clothes to the wash room; it is a white load, bagged in a sheet, lying on the kitchen floor since before breakfast. She unloads the washing machine and, hugging the wet clothes to her breasts, she opens the dryer; but she has forgotten, it's full of clothes she dried last night. She lays the wet ones on top of the dryer and takes out the dry ones; these she carries to the living room and drops in a loose pile on the couch; a pair of Sean's Levi's falls to the floor and as she stoops to pick it up she sees a bread crust and an orange peel lying in the dust under the couch. She cannot reach them without lying on the floor, so she tells herself, with the beginnings of panic, that she must do the living room this morning: sweep, dust, vacuum. But there are clothes waiting to be folded, and a new load going into the dryer, another into the washer. Going through the kitchen she sees the stove she has forgotten, its crusted burners lying on greasy white porcelain. In the wash room she puts the wet clothes into the dryer, shuts the door, and starts it, a good smooth sound of machine, the clothes turning in the dark. In fifty minutes they will be dry. It is all so efficient, and standing there listening to the machine, she feels that efficiency, and everything seems in order now, she is in control, she can rest. This lasts only a moment. She loads the washer, turns it on, goes back to the kitchen, averts her eyes from the stove and makes for the coffee pot; she will first have a cup of coffee, gather herself up, plan her morning. With despair she sees it is not a morning but an entire day, past cocktail hour and dinner, into the night: when the dinner dishes are done she will have more clothes to fold and some to iron. This happens often and forces her to watch television while she works. She is ashamed of watching Johnny Carson. The breakfast dishes are in the sink, last night's pots are on the counter: hardened mashed potatoes, congealed grease. She hunts for the coffee cup she's been using all morning, finds it on the lavatory in the bathroom, and empties the cold coffee over the dishes in the sink. She lights a cigarette and thinks of some place she can sit, some place that will let her drink a cup of coffee. There is none, there's not a clean room downstairs; upstairs the TV room is clean enough, because no one lives there. But to climb the stairs for a sanctuary is too depressing, so she goes to the living room and sits on the couch with the clean clothes, ignores the bread crust and orange peel whispering to her from the floor. Trying to plan her work for the day overwhelms her; it is too much. So she does what is at hand; she begins folding clothes, drinking coffee, smoking. After a while she hears the washer stop. Then the dryer. She goes to the wash room, brings back the dry clothes, goes back and puts the wet load in the dryer. When I come in for lunch, the living room is filled with clothes: they are in heaps on chairs, folded and stacked on the couch and floor; I look at them and then at Terry on the couch; beyond her legs are the bread crust and orange peel; with a harried face she is drinking coffee, and the ashtray is full. 'Is it noon already?' she says. Her eyes are quick with panic. 'Oh God-damnit, I didn't know it was that late.' I walk past her into the kitchen: the burners, the dishes. 'Jesus Christ,' I say. We fight, but only briefly, because it is daylight, we aren't drinking, the children will be in from playing soon, hungry and dirty. Like our marriage, I think, hungry and dirty.

While I ate the Grape Nuts, Natasha and Sean came in, brown arms and legs and blond hair crowding through the door at once, the screen slamming behind them. Natasha is nine; she is the love child who bound us. Sean is seven. Looking at them I felt love for the first time that day.

'You slept late,' Sean said.

'That's because you were up late, you guys were fighting,' Natasha said. 'I heard you.'

'What did you hear?'

'I don't know—' She was hiding whatever it was, down in her heart angry words breaking into her sleep. 'Yelling and swear words and then you left.'

'You left?' Sean said. He was simply interested, not worried. He lives his own life. He eats and sleeps with us, comes to us when he needs something, but he lives outside with boys and bicycles.

'All grown-ups fight from time to time. If they're married.'

'I know,' Sean said. 'Where's Mom?'

I pointed to the ceiling, to the sound of the vacuum cleaner.

'We want to eat,' he said.

'Let her work. I'll fix it.'

'You're eating,' Natasha said.

'I'll hurry.'

'Is that your lunch?' Sean said. 'Grape Nuts?'

'It's my supper.'

I asked what they had done all morning. It was hard to follow and I didn't try; I just watched their loud faces. They interrupted each other: Natasha likes to draw a story out, lead up to it with history ('Well see, first we thought we'd go to Carol's but then they weren't home and I remembered she said they were going—'). Sean likes to tell a story as quickly as he can, sometimes quicker. While they talked, I made sandwiches. It was close to noon but I lingered; Natasha was stirring Kool-Aid in a pitcher. In twelve minutes Edith would be waiting at the Shell station, but I stood watching them eat, and I hoped something would change her day and she wouldn't be there. But she would. An advantage of an affair with a friend's wife was the matter of phone calls: there was nothing suspicious about them. If Edith called and talked to Terry I'd know she couldn't see me this afternoon. I asked the children if they wanted dessert.

'Do we have any?' Natasha said.

'We never have dessert,' Sean said.

I looked in the freezer compartment for ice cream, then in the cupboard for cookies, sweets to sweeten my goodbye, and there were none. Sean was right: we never had desserts because I didn't like them and Terry liked them too much; she controlled her sweet tooth by having nothing sweet in the house.

'I'm sorry,' I said. I knew I was being foolish but I couldn't stop. 'I'm a stupid daddy. I'll bring some dessert home with me.'

'Where you going?' Natasha said.

'To get the car worked on,' my voice jumping to tenor with the lie.

'Can I go?' Sean said. He had a moustache of grape Kool-Aid.

'Me too,' Natasha said.

'No, it takes a long time, then I'm going to run with Hank.'

'We don't mind,' Natasha said. 'We'll watch you.'

There is not one God, I thought. There are several, and they all like jests.

'No you won't,' I growled, and went at her with fingers curled like talons, then tickled her ribs; her sandwich dropped to her plate, she became a fleshed laugh. 'Because after we run we're going to a bar and drinking beer. It's what mean old men do.'

They were laughing. Now I could leave. Then Terry came downstairs, one of my old shirts hanging out, covering her shorts.

'I want us to start having desserts.'

'What?'

'Yay!' Sean said. 'Desserts.'

'We never have desserts,' Natasha said.

Terry stood looking at us, smiling, confused, ready to joke or defend.

'We're depriving the kids of a basic childhood experience.'

'What's that?'

'Mother's desserts.'

'Jesus.'

I wished she were the one going off to wickedness; I would stay home and make cookies from a recipe book.

'Well, I'm off.'

I kissed their Kool-Aid mouths, touched lips with Terry, and went out. She followed me to the screen door.

'Did you get enough to eat?'

'Sure. Not as good as lobster,' talking over my shoulder, going down the steps, 'but cheaper anyway.'

She didn't answer. In the car I thought adultery is one thing, but being a male bitch waging peripheral war is another, this poison of throwing gift-lobsters at your wife's vulnerable eyes, drying up her sweetness and hope by alluding to the drought of the budget. Which was also a further, crueler allusion to her awful belief in a secular gospel of good news: we were Americans, nice, healthy, intelligent people with nice, healthy, intelligent friends, and we deserved to eat lobsters the day after a fight, just as we deserved to see plays in Boston and every good movie that came to town, and when I told her there was no money she was not bitter, but surprised. She was also surprised when the bank told her we were overdrawn and she found that she had forgotten to record a check, or when someone wrote her about a bill that lay unopened in her desk.

When I got to the Shell station Edith was parked across the street. I told the man to change the oil and grease it.

'I'll go run some errands with the wife,' I said, thumbing over my shoulder at Edith. 'Then I'll come pick it up.'

He looked across the street at Edith.

'Keys in the car?'

I slapped my pockets.

'Yes.'

I wondered what twelve months of daylight would do to adulterers. In daylight it seemed everyone knew: the fat man in the greasy T-shirt nodding at me as I told him twenty weight and a new filter and grease, the women who drove by and glanced at me as I waited to cross the street, and the little suntanned boy, squinting up at me, pulling a wagon with his tricycle on the sidewalk beside her car. I got in and said: 'He knows too.'

'Who?'

'That kid. He knows where we're going.'

She drove through the city. It is built on the Merrimack, which is foul, and the city itself is small, ugly, and has the look of death, as a man with cancer does. The industry was shoes, but the factories have been closing. On the main street the glass-fronted stores, no matter their size, all have the dismal look of pawn shops or Army surplus stores. But urban renewal has started: on the riverbank they have destroyed some old gray wooden buildings; in their place a shopping center will be built, and then as we stop at the red light and look toward the river we shall see instead the new brick buildings with wide glass windows, and specials posted on the glass of the supermarket, and the asphalt parking lot with cars, shopping carts, and unhappy women. Our city is no place for someone who is drawn to suicide.

When Edith got to the divided highway I twisted around and opened the ice chest on the floor in the back. Already we had a ritual like husband and wife: it was for me to begin the drive by opening two beers, lighting two cigarettes. Today she had added something: two Löwenbraüs, two Asahis, and two San Miguels angled up at me in the ice.

'She brings such presents,' I said, and kissed her cheek.

'Cold presents from a cold woman.'

An opener was in the glove compartment, under one of her scarves that was red and soft like pants in my hand. The Asahis opened with a pop. Edith glanced in the rear-view mirror, swallowed, then took the lighted cigarette from my fingers.

'I think I'll change to Luckies,' she said, smiling.

'Sure, do that. Why not just let him babysit for us.'

We avoided naming them: we said he, she, him, her.

'He'd be glad to.'

'Well *she* wouldn't, sweetheart.'

I told her about the fight; the sun was warm on my face and arm at the window, the air smelled of trees and grass, we were driving in rolling wooded country under a blue sky, and I was too happy to care about last night. I told it quickly.

'I think he wants to make love with her,' she said.

'Why?'

'Why? Because she's pretty and he likes her and he hasn't had any strange since Jeanne. Why do you think?'

'I mean why do you think he wants to?'

'The way he looks at her. And the way he looked when we came back from getting beer last night.'

'Guilty?'

'Sheepish. Does that bother you?'

'Not me.'

'Good. We can babysit for each other,' smiling, her eyes bright.

'She blooms, she blooms,' I said. 'And in May you were so hurt.'

'In May I was alone.'

I am surrounded by painful marriages that no one understands. But Hank understands his, and I think for him it has never been painful; the pain was Edith's, and she came to me with it in May, at a party. When she asked me to go outside I

knew she had finally caught Hank, and because she is small
and her voice soft I saw her as vulnerable, and I felt she lacked
the tough spirit to deal with adultery. First I found Terry in
the kitchen so she wouldn't miss me, then start looking about
to see which woman was missing too. I told her where I was
going and she understood too that Edith had finally caught on;
she looked at me with that veiled excitement we feel in the
face of other people's disasters. In the backyard, away from
lighted windows, Edith and I sat side by side on a picnic table.

'You probably already know this, I guess Terry does too
and everybody else: about Hank and that phony French bitch
that somebody brought to our Christmas party—'

'Jeanne.'

'And they crashed that party.' She touched my shirt pocket
for a cigarette. 'I forgot my purse inside. Bumming cigarettes,
that's how I first got suspicious: he'd come home with Parliaments, I guess they lay around in bed so long he smoked all
his, and now I don't know what to do, I can't stand to see him
naked, I keep thinking of—shit: I ought to divorce him, I could
do that but I don't really want to, but why shouldn't I? When
he doesn't love me.'

She stopped. My arm was around her; I patted her shoulder, then squeezed her against my side. There was a time in
my life when I believed I could help people by talking to them,
and because of that I became a confidant for several people,
most of them young girls who were my students. People told
me about marriages, jobs, parents, and boyfriends, and I listened and talked a lot and never helped anyone at all. So now
if someone comes to me I offer what I know I can give: the
friendship of a listening face. That night I held Edith and listened and said very little. After a while she jumped down
from the table and walked toward the shadows of the house.
She was wearing a white dress. I was about to call to her when
she stopped and stood smoking with her back turned. Then
she came back to the table.

'You're good to me.'

'I haven't helped you any.'

She stood looking up at me. I got down from the table and held her, pressing her face to my chest and stroking her hair, then we kissed and she squeezed me tightly, her hands moved on my back, and her tongue darted in. We stood a long time kissing in the shadows.

'Come see me.'

'Yes.'

'Monday afternoon.'

'Are you sure?'

'Yes. Yes, I want you to. Come at one.'

Next day was Sunday, and all day while the sun was up I didn't believe Edith, and I didn't believe what I had felt holding her, but after dinner in the night I went for a walk and I believed all of it again, and that night in bed I lay awake for a long time, like a child before a birthday. After my twelve o'clock class Monday I drove to Edith's. When she opened the door I knew from her face that she had been waiting.

Now the place we were going to, the place we always went to after that first afternoon in her house, was a woods off a highway in New Hampshire: down a wide, curving dirt road, dry and dusty, then she parked in the shade and I opened two San Miguels, got the blanket from the back seat, and we climbed a gentle slope, brown pine needles slippery underfoot. I timidly held her hand. I prefer adultery to be a collision: suddenly and without thinking alone with a woman, an urgent embrace, buckles, zippers, buttons. Walking up through the trees gave me time to watch Terry taking the lunch dishes from the table, stacking them on the counter by the sink, and with a distracted, troubled face starting to wash the dishes from three meals. At the knoll's top I lay the blanket under pines and a tall hemlock and heard behind me the buttons of her shorts; I turned and, kneeling, pulled the shorts down her warm brown legs. She took her shirt off and reached back for the clasp of her brassiere; then she lay on the blanket and watched me until I was naked, lying beside her with the sun shining over the crown of a gray birch onto my face.

'What'll we do in winter,' she said.

'In the car, like kids.'

'If we have a winter.'

I kissed her eyes and said: 'When fall comes we'll make love in the car and when winter comes we'll fog the windows and make love wearing sweaters and in spring we'll be back here on this blanket on this hill.'

'Promise me.'

'I promise.'

Then I was alone thinking of a year of deceiving Terry and Hank and the others whom you don't and can't watch out for because they're faceless and nameless, but they're always watching you. I could feel Edith knowing what I was thinking.

'I promise.'

'I know you do. No, lie down, love. I want to be on top. There. Hello, love.'

I reached up for her breasts and watched her face, eyes tightly shut, lips parted, and the long black hair falling across her right cheek, strands of it in her mouth, and she tossed her head, neck arching, and the hair fell back over her shoulder. Then I shut my eyes, and my hands dropped from her breasts and kneaded the earth. For a while we were still, then I opened my eyes to the sun and her face.

'I don't want to move yet,' she said. 'I want to sit here and drip on you.' Already I could feel it. 'Can you get the beer?'

I reached behind me and gave her a bottle and watched her throat as she swallowed. I raised my head to drink from mine.

'You're much faster now,' she said.

On that afternoon in May we went to the guest room, downstairs at the rear of the house, and after an hour I gave up. We had our shirts on and I was wearing socks.

'Are you sure you can't?' she said.

'I keep listening for Sharon to come down or Hank to walk in.'

'You're sure that's all it is?'

'That's plenty enough.'

We went outside and sat on lawn chairs in the sun. After

a while Sharon woke up and came out and played at Edith's feet. I said I would see her tomorrow, at the shopping center north of town, just over the New Hampshire line; then I went home happy and Terry said: 'You must have had a good day in class.' I avoided her eyes until she turned back to the stove, then I looked at her long red hair and like singing I thought: *I will love them both.* I said I would go take a shower, and I went to our bedroom: the bed was unmade and a pair of her Levi's and a shirt were on the floor, and I had to step over the vacuum cleaner to get into the bathroom, where two wet towels lay on the floor but no clean ones in the closet, and I yelled at her: 'Could I have a Goddamn towel!' That night I read in the living room until she was asleep, and next afternoon Edith and I found this road and woods and hill, and that time it wasn't Sharon and Hank I saw with my closed eyes but Terry at home, and Edith kept working with me until finally I came in spite of thinking, it was like some distant part of me coming, like the semen itself had decided it was tired of waiting, and it spurted out just to give us all a rest. For two or three weeks I was like that, then all at once one day I wasn't, as though even guilt and fear could not survive the familiarity of passion.

Now Edith lay beside me and we drank beer going tepid and smoked lying naked in the sun.

'Don't let it get sunburned,' she said. 'You'll get caught.'

'Poor limp thing.'

'I'll keep the sun off.'

'No. I can't.'

'Yes you can.'

'I'm an old man.'

'You're my young lover. Your stomach's growling; have you eaten lunch?'

'Grape Nuts. I slept late.'

'You should live with me. I'd feed you better than that.'

'It's what I wanted. She feeds me what I want.'

'You taste like me.'

A squirrel darted up the hemlock. After a while I said, 'Wait.' I stroked her arm, then tugged it, and she moved up beside me. I was on her, in her, taking a long time, the sun on my back, sweating against her belly, listening to the monologue of moans.

'Did you?' I said.

'Yes. I want you to.'

Her tongue-moistened fingers went up to my nipples. She had taught me I had those.

'Oh love,' she said.

'Again?'

'I think so. Yes. God, yes.'

She took me with her and I collapsed on her damp belly and breasts and listened to the pounding of her heart.

'It felt like spurting blood,' I said.

'Did it hurt?'

'I couldn't tell.'

'My young lover.'

'I'm starving.'

'You have to run first.'

'Maybe I'll cop out.'

'No, you have to be strong, taking care of two women. Would you like to live with me?'

'Yes.'

'I'd like to live with you. We should all rent one big house.'

'And who'd mop up the blood?'

'There wouldn't be any blood.'

'She'd cut my throat.'

I got up and dressed and went down to the car for the Löwenbraüs, then back up the slope treasuring my hard climbing calf muscles; now I wanted to run. She was dressed, lying on her back, her hands at her sides, eyes closed, face to the sun.

'I wonder how we'll get caught,' she said.

'He'll smell you when I undress.'

'I mean Terry. If he caught us I wouldn't care, I wouldn't stop unless you wanted to. You probably would. You'd be embarrassed.'

'Maybe not.'

'You would. You keep trying to fit me into your life, but it's hard for you, and if you got caught you'd throw me out. But you're part of my life: you're what allows me to live with Hank.'

'Am I a what? I don't want to be a what.' I held up the Löwenbräu. 'This is one. It's what's going to make me belch for the first mile.'

'You're my lovely what.'

'Good old Jack, just part of the family.'

'Sure. You make me a good wife. If I didn't love you I'd have to love someone else. We married too young—'

'We all did.'

Once at a party Terry was in the kitchen with Edith and two other wives. They came out grinning at the husbands: their own, the others. They had all admitted to shotgun weddings. That was four years ago and now one couple is divorced, another has made a separate peace, fishing and hunting for him and pottery and college for her; and there are the Allisons and the Linharts. A deck-stacking example, but the only one I know.

'He needs us, Sharon and me, but he can't really love anyone, only his work, and the rest is surface.'

'I don't believe that.'

'I don't mean his friendship with you. Of course it's deep, he doesn't live with you, and best of all you're a man, you don't have those needs he can't be bothered with. He'd give you a kidney if you needed one.'

'He'd give it to you too.'

'Of course he would. But he wouldn't go to a marriage counselor.'

'You funny girl. After a long carnivorous fuck you talk about a marriage counselor. Who *are* you, sweetheart?'

'My name is Edith Allison and I'm the leader of the band. I wanted to go to a marriage counselor so he'd talk. Because he wouldn't talk just to me. He wanted everything simple: he'd been screwing Jeanne, now he'd stopped, and that was that.'

'What more did you want?'

'You know what I wanted. Remember me back in May? I still believed in things. I wanted to know where we were, what Jeanne meant. Now that I have you I know what she meant: that he doesn't love me. You love the person you're having the affair with. But it doesn't matter now, I can live with him like that, on the surface. He'll be busting out again soon. He's been hibernating with that novel since he broke off with Jeanne. Before long he'll look around and blink and screw the first thing that walks into his office.'

'Jesus. I hope somebody goes in before I do.'

'He'd probably do that too.'

'Now, now: bitchy bitchy.'

'Well, he screws his wife once in a while, so why not another man.'

'He screws you? Frigid like you are?'

'I try hard.'

'I hear you can go to St. Louis and screw for that man and woman who wrote the book. The one about coming.'

'Really?'

'Sure. They watch you and straighten out your hang-ups.'

'Let's you and I go. I'd like them to watch us. We'd make them hot.'

'You might get rid of your guilt. Do you good.'

'Why spoil my fun? Maybe you'd learn to come more.'

'What would a wee dirty lass like you have told a marriage counselor?'

'I was trying to keep from being a wee dirty lass. I'm glad now I didn't. What are you doing?'

'Touching you.'

'Isn't it getting late?'

'I don't know.'

'Can you again?'

'I don't know.'

We left our shirts on, a wrong move: they reminded us that time was running out. My back hurt but I kept trying; Edith didn't make it either, and finally she said: 'Let's stop.'

Our shirts were wet. We gathered up the bottles, the cigarettes, the blanket. In the car she made up her face.

'What'll you do with the bottles?' I said.

'I think I'll burn candles in them at dinner. And if he
notices—which he wouldn't—I'll tell him they're souvenirs
from this afternoon. Along with my sore pussy.'

'He'll see them in the garbage. You know, when he empties it or something.'

She started the car and grinned at me, almost laughing.

'And then what, Charlie Chan?'

'He'll wonder why in the hell you drank six bottles of
imported beer this afternoon.'

'Well, he doesn't deserve honesty, but a few clues might
be nice.'

'Sometimes I think—'

It was possible she wanted him to catch her; you have to
keep that in mind when you're making love with a man's wife.
But I didn't want to talk about it.

'Sometimes you think what?'

'Sometimes I think I love you even more than I think I do.
Which is a lot.'

'Which is a lot. Impotent as you are, you try hard.'

She turned the car around and drove slowly and bouncing out of the woods. At the highway she stopped and put on
sunglasses.

'Light me a Lucky,' she said. 'My last one till—?'

I thought of the acting and the lies and, right then, if she
had said we must stop seeing each other, I would have been
relieved.

'I don't know, I'll call you.'

As she drove onto the highway both of us pretended we
weren't eyeing the road for friends' cars. My damp shirt and
chest cooled in the air blowing through the window.

'My pecker aches.'

'I'm going to keep the sitter another hour and take a nap.'

'Let me give you some money for her.'

'Another time. Mother sent me some.'

'The empties are in the chest.'

'I'll go by the dump.'


Summer school was in session, and walking downtown you'd see college girls licking ice cream cones. Once I was teaching *Goodbye, Columbus* and a blonde girl with brown eyes like a deer stopped me at the door before class and said: 'Mr. Linhart, what is oral love?' She was licking a lollipop. I looked away from her tongue on the lollipop and said fellatio; when she asked what that was I mumbled in the heat of my face that she ought to ask a girl. It took me a couple of hours to know she was having fun with me. After that I tried to talk to her but she had only wanted that fun; she had a boyfriend who waited every day in the hall outside our classroom, and seeing them holding hands and walking down the hall I felt old and foolish. That was three years ago, when I was twenty-seven.

On summer afternoons there were no classes, and the buildings were empty. Most days when I climbed the three flights of stairs in the old, cool building Hank would be working with his back to the open door; he'd hear me coming and he'd turn smiling, stacking and paper-clipping the manuscript. 'Hi,' he'd say, his voice affectionate like he was talking to a woman or a child. There are several men I love and who love me, all of us married, passive misogamists, and if we did not have each other to talk to we would probably in our various ways go mad. But our love embarrasses us; we show our affection in reverse: *Where you been, you sonofabitch? Look at that bastard, he wouldn't buy a round for Jesus Christ—*But Hank only did that if it made you feel better.

'Hi,' he said.

'You can't write, you fucker, so let's go run.'

'One Goddamn page.'

'In four hours?'

'Three hours and forty-six minutes. Let's go.'

I started walking downstairs before he asked what I had

done with my day. Walking over to the gym he was quiet. By the flagpole he lit a cigarette, then flung it to the sidewalk, crumpled his pack and threw it hard, like an outfielder; it arched softly, red and white in the sun.

'You just quit.'

'Goddamn right.'

'Which time?'

'For the last time.'

'You won't make it.'

'You watch. They're pissing me off. They're trying to kill me.'

'They have no souls.'

'Exactly.'

'So they're not trying to kill you.'

'Not the cigarettes. I mean the fuckers that make 'em.'

There were tennis players in the locker room. We had lockers next to each other and I glanced at him as he pulled up his jockstrap then gym shorts.

'Jesus, don't you ever get fat?' I said.

'I'm fat now.'

He pinched some tight flesh at the back of his waist.

'Bullshit,' I said.

I rarely believed that Edith preferred my flabbier waist and smaller cock. But sometimes I believed it and, when I did, I felt wonderful.

'You smell like beer, man.'

'I had a couple.'

'I'll carry you in.'

'Watch me go, baby.'

On the clipped grass behind the gym we did push-ups and sit-ups and side-straddle hops, then started jogging on a blacktop road that would take us into the country.

'Five?' I said.

'I oughta do ten. Run off my Goddamn frustration.'

'A page a day's not bad.'

'Shit.'

It was a hot, still day. We ran easily, stride for stride, past the houses where children waved and called to us and women looked up from their lawns or porches. I belched a couple of times and he grinned and punched my arm. Then the houses weren't close together anymore, the country was rolling and we climbed with it, pounding up the blacktop, not talking as we panted up hills, but going down or level we talked: 'Goddamn, there's that lovely orchard.' 'Hold your breath, mothuh, here comes the hog stench.' 'Jesus, look at that cock pheasant.' Then he was all right, he had forgotten his work, he was talking about shooting pheasants in Iowa, walking through frozen cornfields, the stalks lying brown in the sun. We ran to the top of a wooded hill two and a half miles from the gym and started back, still stride for stride: it would be that last two hundred yards when he'd kick. We ran downhill through sudden cool shade between thick woods; in fall the maple leaves turned orange and yellow and scarlet, and it was like peeping at God. Then on our left the woods stopped, and the hog smell lay on the air we breathed as we ran past the cleared low hills and the barn, chickens walking and pecking in front of it, then past the hog pen and the gray shingled house. A white dog came out from under the porch, barking; he had missed us on the way up, and now he chased us until he was almost at our legs, then we looked back at him and yelled 'Hey white dog!' and he trotted away, looking back at us over his shoulder, sometimes stopping to turn and bark. Running has taught me that most dogs are cowards. But there used to be a Doberman pinscher living on this road: he loped after us so quietly that we never knew he was there until we heard his paws on the road and we'd yell and turn on him and crouch to fight, watching him decide whether he wanted to chew on us. He always looked very detached; that's what scared us. Then he'd trot back down the road, dignity intact; we were glad when last year he moved away. All the other dogs were like the white one at the farmhouse. Past the farm there were trees again, pines motionless in the still air, and then to the right, up a long green hill, the apple orchard.

'You're a little screwed up this summer,' Hank said.

'Do I look it?'

'Yep.'

'Should've taught summer school.'

'Maybe not.'

'Thought I wouldn't this year. Needed a break, I thought. Now I need the money.'

'Need the work more.'

'Bothers me. You'd think a man would do something. All that time. Read. Even think. Noble fucking pursuits. I run errands. Makes me wonder what'd happen if I didn't have to make a living.'

'You'll never find out.'

'Good. Probably mean suicide. Man ought to be able to live with himself. Idly. Without going mad. Women do it.'

'Not so well.'

'Work is strange.'

'All there is.'

'This. This is good.'

'Best of all.'

We stopped talking and right away my head was clear and serene, I was lungs and legs and arms, sun on my shoulders, sweat seeping through the red handkerchief around my forehead, dripping to my eyes, burning, and I flicked it away with a finger. At the houses near the college he moved ahead of me, a pace or two. I caught him and ran beside him for a while, then he kicked and was gone; I stretched my legs, arms swinging, breath in gasps, and watched his back ten then twenty yards away as he sprinted past the gym and slowed and walked, head going up and down for air, hands on his hips. I walked beside him. He didn't smile at beating me, but I felt a smile as though in his rushing breath.

'Competitive bastard,' I said.

Then he smiled, and I believed then he knew I was making love with Edith and he was telling me he knew, saying, *You see Edith can't touch me and you can't either, what matters here is what matters to me and what matters to me is I will write and I will outrun you and I will outlive all of you too, and that's where I am.*

He didn't smoke, either. After the shower, a long time of hot water on the shoulders and legs and back muscles, then warm then cool, we drank Heineken draft in tall frosted mugs. We were alone in the bar, then a thin bald man came in carrying wrapped fish. Adjacent to the lounge was the dining room, where people ate fish from the sea and looked out at the dirty Merrimack; if you walked out of the lounge, across the hall, you went into the fish market. Before starting to drink, Hank and I had gone in and stood in the smell of fish, looking at the lobsters in a tank. I thought of Terry, but not with guilt; I had loved and run and sweated that out of me. I stood shifting my weight from one leg to another so I could feel the muscles, and I breathed my own clean smell with the salt water and fish, and resolved not to smoke for an hour, to keep the sharp sense of smell I always had after running restored innocence to my lungs; and I loved and wanted to embrace Edith and Hank and Terry, who in their separate ways made my life good. I felt at the border of some discovery, some way I could juggle my beloveds and save us all. But I didn't know what it was.

The man with the fish sat to our left, put his fish on the bar, and ordered a Schlitz. Betty was tending bar; she was a middle-aged blonde who had lived all her life in this town. She sat on a high stool near the taps and talked to the fish man. He looked at the Heineken sign over the mirror and asked if that was imported beer; she said yes it was. He said he'd never heard of it and she told him oh yes, it was quite popular, it sold ten to one here.

'Schlitz,' Hank said, so they couldn't hear. 'Some people like it better inside the horse.'

'Did you see her before she left?'

'Yeah, I saw her.' He gave me the foxy smile I got after he beat me running.

'To tell her goodbye?'

'Remember when I went to New York to see my agent?'

'Ah. I didn't know you could lie so well.'

He held out two dollars to the woman.

'We'll have a round, and give my friend on the end a Heineken.'

The fish man looked over at us.

'Well, thank you. Thank you very much.'

'Beats that horse piss Schlitz is bottling.'

Betty grinned. The fish man was embarrassed and he started to say something, maybe about Schlitz, then he just watched her filling the mug; when he tasted it, he said: 'Well, by golly, it does have something to it, doesn't it?'

He and Betty talked about beer.

'I've never spent the night with anyone but Terry.'

'Same old thing. Sleep, dream, wake up in the morning; piss; brush your teeth.'

'Have a cigarette, lover.'

'Hell no. Every time I want one I'm going to hold my breath for sixty seconds and think of the Marlboro man and the Winston assholes and all the rest of them, and that'll do it.'

'All right, I won't till you do. But you won't be able to stand Edith. I quit once for three days and Terry smelled like an ashtray.'

'Not *all* over. It was a good scene, though, in Boston. Hotel, took her to the airport in the morning, sad loving Bloody Marys. Then up in the air. Gone. Me watching the plane. Thinking of her looking down. Gone. Back to France. Maybe I'll go see her someday.'

'You love her, huh?'

'I was fucking her, wasn't I?'

'I guess it was tough breaking it off, her right down in Boston.'

'Jack.' Grinning. 'What made you think I broke it off? Why would I do a stupid thing like that?'

'Well, when the shit hit the fan Edith said you broke it off.'

'Course she said that. It's what I told her.'

'Have a beer, you sly son of a bitch.'

I held up two fingers to Betty and she slid off the stool.

'Wait,' the fish man said. 'I'll get this one for the boys, and—lemmee see—' he pulled out a pocket watch from his khakis, peered down in the red-lighted dark '—yeah, Betty, I'll have one more, then I'll be getting home and put my fish in the oven.' Hank cocked his head and watched him. 'Don't get it started, the wife'll come home and start looking around, wanting to know where's the dinner.'

'I don't blame her,' Betty said.

'Oh sure. She works all day too, and I get home a little earlier, so I put the dinner on.'

She gave us the beer and we raised our mugs to him and said thanks. He raised his, smiled, nodded, sipped. He picked up his fish, turning it in his hands, then lowered it to the bar.

'If I'm going to fry it I can start later, but when I'm baking like with this one, I need a little more time.' He looked through the door at two men going into the dining room. 'Someday I'm going to come in here and get me one of those fish platters. I'll be about ready for one, one of these days.'

Hank was watching him.

'Did you ever want to leave with her?' I said.

'Why?'

'You said you loved her.'

'I still do. You're nineteenth century, Jack.'

'That's what you keep telling me.'

'It's why you've been faithful so long. Your conscience is made for whores but you're too good for that, so you end up worse: monogamous.'

'What's this made for whores shit.'

'The way it used to be. Man had his wife and kids. That was one life. And he had his whore. He knew which was which, see; he didn't get them confused. But now it's not that way: a man has a wife and a girlfriend and they get blurred, you see, he doesn't know where his emotional deposits are supposed to be. He's in love, for Christ sake. It's incongruous. He can't live with it, it's against everything he's supposed to feel, so naturally he takes some sort of action to get himself back to where he believes he's supposed to be. Devoted to one woman or some such shit. He does something stupid: either he breaks with the girl and tries to love only his wife, or he leaves the wife and marries the girl. If he does that, he'll be in the same shit in a few years, so he'll just have to keep marrying—'

'Or stay monogamous.'

'Aye. Both of which are utter bullshit.'

'And you think that's me.'

'I think so. You're a good enough man not to fuck without feeling love, but if you're lucky enough for that to happen, then you feel confused and guilty because you think it means you don't love Terry.'

I looked him in the eyes and said: 'Have you been talking to my mistress?'

'Mistress pisstress. I've been talking to *you* for three years. I've been watching you watching women.'

I believed him. If he knew about Edith and me, it was because he'd guessed: they had not been talking.

'Am I right?' he said.

'I worry about Terry, that's true. Just getting caught, I mean. I worry about love affairs too: the commitment, you know.'

'What's commitment got to do with a love affair? A love affair is abandon. Put the joy back in fucking. It's got to be with a good woman, though. See, Jeanne knew. She *knew* I'd never leave Sharon and Edith. Commitment. That's with Terry. It doesn't even matter if you love Terry. You're married. What matters is not to hate each other, and to keep peace. The old Munich of marriage. You live with a wife, around a wife, not through her. She doesn't run with you and come drink beer with you, for Christ sake. Love, shit. Love the kids. Love the horny wives and the girls in short skirts. Love everyone, my son, and keep peace with your wife. Who, by the way, is not invulnerable to love either. What'll you do if that happens?'

'That's her business.'

'All right. I believe you.'

'You should; it's true.'

'So why are *you* so uptight?'

'I'm not, man. What brought all this on, anyway?'

'I didn't like that look of awe in your face. When I said I
spent the night with Jeanne, and never broke up with her. I
love you, man. You shouldn't feel awe for *anything* I do. I
don't have more guts than you. I just respond more, that's all.
I don't like seeing you cramped. Chicks *like* you, I *see* it, Jack.
Hell, Edith gets juiced up every time you call the house. Other
day Sharon said she wanted a jack-in-the-box, I thought
Edith would fall off the couch laughing. Wicked laugh. Lying
there laughing.'

'Jack-in-the-box,' I said, smiling, shaking my head.

He slapped my shoulder and we drained our mugs and
left. 'Take care,' I said, passing the fish man. 'See you boys.' He
raised his mug. Going out the door Hank turned left, toward
the dining room; I waited while he talked to the hostess, nodding, smiling, reaching for his wallet. He gave her four dollars
and waved off the change.

'What was that about?'

We walked to the front door and I started to go outside,
but turned instead and went into the fish market.

'I bought him a fish platter.'

I went to the lobster tank, and an old man in a long white
apron came from behind the fish counter.

'He'll be gone before it's ready,' I said.

'Told her to give him a beer too. He won't waste a beer. By
the time he's done, there it'll be.'

'All right: cool.' I turned to the old man. 'How much are
you getting for lobsters?'

'As much as we can,' winking, laughing, then a wheeze
and a cough.

The chicken lobsters were a dollar seventy-nine a pound;
she loved to eat, she'd say *mmmm*, sucking the claws, splitting
open the tail. I asked for two and didn't watch him weigh
them or ring them up. I couldn't; it was like when they call
you in to pay for your crime: your father, your boss: the old
humiliation of chilled ass and quickened heart. They were
four dollars and fifty-two cents. I did not think about the bank
balance until I bought the wine. On the way to Hank's I stopped

at the liquor store and bought Pinot Chardonnay, Paul Masson: two-fifty. Seven dollars. Two on beer. Nine. I went next door into the A&P; Hank was waiting in the car, listening to the Red Sox in a twi-nighter. Eight at the service station: seventeen. I bought half pints of strawberry, chocolate, and vanilla ice cream, a bunch of bananas, a can of chocolate syrup, a jar of cherries, a pressurized can of whipped cream, but no nuts, there were only cocktail nuts, salted things. My children didn't know what a banana split was; I had told them the other day how the boys and I used to eat them after a movie, and if I could spend seven on Terry and me then certainly they deserved—was love no more than guilt? I have a girl so Terry should have a lover. We get lobster and Pinot Chardonnay so the kids should have this junk. The banana splits cost four dollars and twenty-eight cents. A twenty-one-dollar day, only two on something I wanted: the beer with Hank. Now I could slide back the door in my mind, look at the bank balance written there: forty-three dollars and eighty cents. I had glanced at it yesterday, I hadn't really wanted to see, but it sprang like a snake and got in my head and stayed there. Eight days before payday and a week's groceries still to buy. What now? Stop drinking? Stop smoking? So we could sit stiff and tight-faced night after night, chewing blades of grass, watching the food and milk and gas all going down down down. We had tried that once, for six weeks: nothing but red wine, a dollar and a quarter a half gallon. Nothing happened. The bourbon and gin and beer money never turned up; it jumped into the cash register at the supermarket, the service stations, it went to the utilities and telephone gangs, the landlord, it paid for repairs on a bad car, it went to people who sold bad shoes to children and to people who sold worse toys. It just kept going, and days before payday it was gone; when the last milk carton was empty, Terry put powdered milk in it and didn't fool the kids, and every day there was more space in the refrigerator and cupboard, and each day I woke wanting payday to come and hating the trap I was in: afraid of death and therefore resisting the passage of time, yet now having to wish for it.

'I spent twenty-one bucks today. What's the score?'

'Sox, 2–1. Top of the third. You broke?'

There were driving lanes in the big parking lot, but people drove through the parking spaces too; they drove in circles, triangles, squares, trapezoids, and other geometric figures, and I had to look in all directions at once.

'Not for a couple of days.'

'Here.' He took out his wallet.

'No, man. That's not why I said that.'

'Jesus, I know that. How much you need?'

'I can't.'

'Come on. Some day you'll come through for me.'

'I need about forty *bucks*, man. I'll go to the bank.'

He was holding out two twenties and Reggie Smith was catching a fly ball on the warning path.

'Edith got a check from Winnetka.'

'It won't last for shit if you support me too.' Thinking of the imported beer, the babysitter.

'We needed two hundred, so she asked for three and her mother sent five.'

'*Five?* No shit: you mean there are people in the world who can write a check for five hundred dollars and not break into tears? I'll pay it back a little at a time, okay?'

'Sure. Buy me a bottle some time. Buy me one round of *beer* some time, you cheap cocksucker.'

At his house he said to come in for a quick one. I was worried about the ice cream but he reached back and took it from the bag, so I followed him in. She was at the stove. She smiled at us over her shoulder; she had changed her shorts and shirt and had a red ribbon in her black hair. She looked as if she'd changed souls. She stirred a pot of something and looked in the oven while Hank put up the ice cream and opened two ales and a beer. Then she sat at the table and asked Hank for a cigarette.

'I quit.'

'Good luck, baby.'

I gave her one of mine, and took one too.

'Oh, a Lucky,' she said.

'See what you did. As long as he was with me he didn't smoke.'

'I like to corrupt.'

'You looked like a girl from the forties just then,' I said. 'Or early fifties. Taking the tobacco off your tongue. Except their fingernails were painted. You'd see that red fingernail moving down their tongues, and I used to love watching them.'

'Why?' Hank said.

'I don't know. I think it was watching a woman being sensual. You were a little hard on that fish man.'

'I know. Didn't seem so funny once I got in the car.'

'What fish man?'

I watched her listen to the story and I thought how she didn't know Hank and Jeanne hadn't ended till she went back to France. And whether he guessed or not he could never know what she was like out there on the blanket. Now she was just an attentive young wife, listening to her husband, her eyes going from him to Sharon with her coloring book on the floor. Still they had a marriage. He was talking to her about his day. She had got that money for them. Her dinner smelled good, and her house was clean. I felt it was my house too, and I remembered what I was like before I loved her, during that long time when I wasn't in love; I need to be in love, I know it is called romantic, it isn't what they call realistic, I am supposed to settle into the steady seasons, the ticking Baby Bens, of marriage.

'Hank, that was cruel.'

'I know. But he had no balls. Cooking, for Christ sake.'


At my back door I smelled spaghetti sauce. She was ironing in the kitchen and I looked past her at the black iron skillet of sauce on the stove. I didn't give her a chance to ask me how the day had been; I saw the question in her face as she looked up from ironing and reached for her drink at the end of the ironing board. Edith had not been drinking when Hank and I got there, and I wondered if other wives drank before their husbands came home.

'This guy gave me some lobsters,' I said, as the screen door shut behind me. 'I saved his daughter from drowning and he gave me all he had.'

'Oh let me *see*.'

She hurried around the ironing board and took the bag and looked in. I put the wine in the freezer compartment.

'Wine too?'

'Sure. And some stuff for the kids.'

I gave her the supermarket bag.

'Oh look,' peering in, taking out the jar of cherries, the whipped cream, the chocolate syrup. 'What a nice daddy.'

She took the ironed clothes on hangers upstairs, then put the ironing board and basket of waiting clothes in the wash room. I got the ball game on the radio and sat at the kitchen table with the *Boston Globe* while she looked for her big pot and found it and put it on the stove. I skimmed the news stories I couldn't believe while I told her Hank had written only a page, he had quit smoking, we had had a good run, drunk some beer, and he had loaned me forty dollars. She was happy about the money, but she said very seriously we must be sure to pay him back, ten dollars a payday till it was done. All this time I was following the ball game and getting through the news about Nixon and the war, getting to those stories I could believe: a man winning a tobacco spitting contest; a woman and her son drowning, taken into the sea by waves on the coast of Maine; the baseball news. I could also believe all stories about evil. I was accustomed to lies from the government and the press, and I never believed them when they spoke with hope or comfort. So I believed all stories of lies, atrocity, and corruption, for they seemed to be the truth that I was rarely told and that I was waiting for. I knew that my vision was as distorted as the vision of those who lied, but I saw no way out. When I finished the paper, I started to tell Terry about the fish man, but with the first word already shaping my lips, I stopped.

In a marriage there are all sorts of lies whose malignancy slowly kills everything, and that day I was running the gamut from the outright lie of adultery to the careful selectivity which comes when there are things that two people can no longer talk about. It is hard to say which kills faster but I would guess selectivity, because it is a surrender: you avoid touching wounds and therefore avoid touching the heart. If I told her the story, she would see it as a devious way of getting at her: the man's cooking would be the part of me she smothered; Hank's buying the seafood platter would be my rebellion. And she would be right. So I treated our disease with aspirins, I weaved my conversation around us, and all the time I knew with a taste of despair that I was stuck forever with this easy, lying pose; that with the decay of years I had slipped gradually into it, as into death, and that now at the end of those years and the beginning of all the years to come I had lost all dedication to honesty between us. Yet sometimes when I was alone and away from the house, always for this to happen I had to be away from the house, driving perhaps on a day of sunlight and green trees and rolling meadows, I would hear a song from another time and I could weep (but did not) for the time when I loved her every day and came up the walk in the afternoons happy to see her, days when I never had to think before I spoke. As we ate lobsters and drank wine we listened to the ball game.

And later, after the spaghetti dinner that wasn't eaten, we made love. We had watched the children, who were impatient for banana splits and so ate only a little and that quickly, sucking spaghetti, spearing meatballs, their eyes returning again and again to the door of the freezer compartment, to Terry slicing bananas, punching open the can of chocolate syrup. They were like men late for work eyeing the clock behind a lunch counter. They loved the banana splits, ate till I feared for their stomachs, then I went with a book to the living room couch, and Terry put the meatballs and spaghetti sauce in the refrigerator to be warmed again another day.

When she got into bed I pretended to be asleep but she touched my chest and spoke my name until I looked at her.

'I went a little crazy last night,' she said. 'I'm sorry.'

'Okay.'

'I shouldn't have got drunk.'

She found my hand and held it.

'Forget it,' I said.

'I've got to grow up.'

'Who ever told you grown-ups weren't violent?'

'Not with their husbands.'

'Read the papers. Women murder their husbands.'

'Not people like us.'

'Sailors' wives, is that it? Construction workers?'

'I don't mean that.'

'Maybe some people have enough money so they don't have to kill each other. You can have separate lives then, when things go bad. You don't have to sweat over your beer in the same hot kitchen: watching her fat ass under wilted blue cotton, her dripping face and damp straight hair. Pretty soon somebody picks up a hammer and goes to it. Did Hank make a pass?'

'Yes.'

'He did?'

'I said yes.'

'Well?'

'Well what.'

'What did he do?'

'None of your business.'

'All right, then: what did *you* do?'

'Nothing.'

'Come on.'

'He tried to kiss me on the porch, so I went inside.'

'Where?' Grinning at her. 'Here?'

'To the *kit*chen. To get a beer.'

'And he followed you in and—'

'Said he loved me and kissed me and said he didn't love Edith. Then I felt dirty and we went outside and sat on the front steps.'

'Dirty. Because he said that about Edith?'

'Yes. She's a sweet girl and she doesn't deserve that, and I don't want any part of it.'

'But until he said that, you felt all right.'

'We can stop this now. Or do you want to know whether his nose was to the left or right of mine?'

'Do you remember?'

'We were lying on the floor and he was on my right, so I'd say his nose was to the left of mine.'

'Lying on the floor, huh? Goodness.'

'I'd squatted down to get a beer from—Oh shut up.'

'I was only teasing.'

'You were doing more than that. You're glad he kissed me.'

'Let's say I'm not disturbed.'

'Well I am.'

She got out of bed for a cigarette and when she came back I pretended to be asleep and listened to her smoking deeply beside me. Then she put out the cigarette and started touching me, the old lust on quiet signal, and I mounted her, thrusting the sound of bedsprings into the still summer night, not a word between us, only breath and the other sound: and I remembered newly married one morning she was holding a can of frozen orange juice over a pitcher and the sound of its slow descent out of the can drove us back to bed. I could feel her getting close but I still was far away, and I opened my eyes: hers were closed. I shut mine and saw Edith this afternoon *oh love*; then I thought *she is thinking of Hank, behind those closed eyes her skull is an adulterous room*, and now he was here too and he had given me the forty dollars and it was Hank, not I, Hank who was juggling us all, who would save us, and now we came, Hank and Terry and Edith and me, and I said, 'Goodnight, love,' and rolled over and slept.

# 2

On a moonlit summer night, in a cemetery six blocks from my house, lying perhaps among the bones of old whaling men, in the shadow of a pedestaled eight-foot bronze angel, Hank made love to my red-haired wife.

At midnight I had left them on the front porch. Edith had the flu, and Hank had come over late for a nightcap; it was the day after payday and I gave him ten dollars which he didn't want to take. We drank on the front porch, but I was tired and I watched them talking about books and movies, then I went to bed, their voices coming like an electric train around the corner of the house, through the screen of my open window. I slept. When I woke my heart was fast before I knew what it knew. I lay in silence louder than their voices had been, and listened for the creak of floor under a step, the click of her Zippo, a whisper before it died in the air. But there was only silence touching my flesh, so they weren't in the house; unless making love in the den or living room they had heard my heart when I woke and now they were locked in sculpted love waiting for me to go back to sleep. Or perhaps they were in the yard and if I went outside I would turn a corner of the house and smack into the sight of her splayed white legs under the moon and the white circle of his wedging ass.

The clock's luminous dial was too moonlit to work: with taut stealth I moved across the bed, onto Terry's side, and took the clock from the bedside table: two-twenty. I waited another ten minutes, each pale gray moonlit moment edged with expectancy, until I was certain it was emptiness I heard, not their silence. And if indeed they were listening, I would cast the burden of cunning on them: I rolled over and dropped my feet thumping to the floor, and walked to the bathroom next to my room and turned on the light. I flushed the toilet, then went out through the other door, into the kitchen, the dining room, the living room, and stepped onto the front porch. The night was cool and I shivered, standing in my T-shirt so white if they were watching. His car was parked in front. Their glasses were on the steps. I picked them up: lime and gin-smelling water. Then I went to bed and waited, and I saw them under the willow tree in the backyard, the branches hanging almost to the grass, and I asked myself and yes, I said, I want the horns; plant them, Hank, plant them. I wanted lovely Edith now there with me and twice I picked up the phone and once dialed three numbers, but she would be asleep with her fever and there was nothing really to tell yet, I didn't really know yet, and after that I lay in bed, quick-hearted and alert, and waited and smoked.

At ten minutes after three he started his car. I ran tiptoe-ing to the living room window as his car slowly left the curb and Terry stood on the sidewalk, smoking; she lifted a hand, waving as Hank drove down the street. He blinked his inte-rior light, but I couldn't see him, then his car was dark, just tail lights again, and then he was gone and the street was quiet. She stood smoking. When she flicked the cigarette in the street and started up the walk, I ran back to the bedroom. She came in and crossed the living room, into the dining room and bathroom. She stayed there a while: water ran, the toilet flushed, water ran again. Then in the kitchen she popped open a beer and went to the living room; her lighter clicked, scraped, clicked shut. When she finished the beer she plunked it down on the coffee table and came into the bedroom.

'Where've you been?'

She got out of her clothes and dropped them on the floor, and lies cracked her voice: 'I woke up and couldn't get back to sleep so I went out for a walk.'

She went naked to the living room and came back shak-ing a cigarette from her pack and lit it and got into bed.

'Terry.'

'What.'

'You don't have to tell me that. I woke up at two-twenty.'

She drew on her cigarette. Still she had not looked at me.

'You bastard. Did you ever go to sleep?'

'Yes.'

'I wish I could believe that.'

'I was tired.'

'You could've brought me to bed.'

'You could've come with me.'

She threw back the sheet and blanket and got out of bed

and went fast, pale skin and flopping hair, out of the room. She came back with a beer and got into bed and covered up and bent the pillow under her head so she could drink.

'I'm lonely, that's why. I'm a woman, I'm sorry, I can't be anything else, and I need to be told that and I need to be made love to, you don't make love with me anymore, you fuck me; I sat on the steps with him and he held my hand and listened to me talk about this shitty marriage because all you ever see is the house, you don't see me, and he said let's go see the bronze angel, we've never seen it in the dark, and I was happy when he said that and I was happy making love—'

So she had really done it, and I lay there feeling her wash down me, from my throat, down my chest, my legs, then gone like surf from the sea, cold like the sea.

'—and I lay afterward looking up at her wings and for the first time since leaving the porch I thought of you and for a moment under her wings I hated you for bringing me to this. Then that went away. I wanted to go home and seal up the split between us, like gluing this shitty old furniture, I wanted to clap my hands for Tinker Bell, do something profound and magic that would bring us back the way we used to be, when we were happy. When you loved me and when I never would have made love with someone else. And all the way walking home I wanted to hurry and be with you, here in this bed in this house with my husband and children where I belong. And right now I love you I think more than I have for years but I'm angry, Jack, way down in my blood I'm angry because you set this up in all kinds of ways, you wanted it to happen and now it has and now I don't know what else will happen, because it's not ended, making love is never ended—'

'Are you seeing him again?'

'No.'

'Then it's ended.'

'Do you think making love is like *smoking*, for Christ sake? That if you quit it's *over*? It's not just the act. What's wrong with you—it's feeling, it's—'

She drank, then sat up and drank again, head back for a

long swallow, then she lit a cigarette from the one she was smoking.

'It's what,' I said.

'Promises.'

'You promised to see him again?'

'I didn't say anything. Opening my legs is a promise.'

'But he must have said something.'

'I wish you could hear your voice right now, the way it was just then, I wish I had it taped and I'd play it for you till you went to a shrink to find out why your voice just now was so Goddamn oily. You *like* this. You *like* it. Well hear: it took us a long time to get to the cemetery because we kept stopping to kiss and when we did walk it was slow because we had our arms around each other and his hand was on my tit all the time and when we got to the angel we didn't look at her, not once, we undressed and got down on the ground and we fucked, Jack, we fucked like mad, and I was so hot I came before he did; the second time I was on top and it was long and slow and I told him I loved him and you, you poor man, you sick cuckold, look at your face—Jesus Christ, what am I married to?'

'Will you stop?'

'Why should I? You ought to be knocking my teeth out now. But not you. You want to watch us. Is that it? Is that what you want, Jack?'

I sat up and was swinging at her but stopped even before she saw it coming, and my hand opened and I pointed at her eyes, the finger close, so close, and I wanted to gouge with it, to hit, to strangle, the finger quivering now as I tried not to shout beneath the children's rooms, my voice hoarse and constricted in my throat: 'Terry, you fuck who you want and when you want and where you want but do not do *not* give me any of your half-ass insights into the soul of a man you've never understood.'

Then she was laughing, a true laugh at first or at least a smile, but she lay with her head back on the pillow, throat arched, her shoulders and breasts shaking, and prolonged it, forced it cracking into the air, withering my tense arm, and I got out of bed so I would not even touch the sheet she lay on.

'Oh God: half-ass insights into the—what? The soul of a man I've never understood? Oh my. You poor baby, and it's so simple. You think you're a swinger, free love, I can fuck whoever I want, oh my how you talk and talk and talk and it all comes down to that one little flaw you won't admit: you're a pervert, Jack. You need help. And I'm sorry, I really am, but there's nothing I can do about it. I made love with Hank tonight and he wants to see me tomorrow—or this afternoon really—and when I finish this beer I'm going to sleep because the kids'll be up soon and you're not known for getting them breakfast—'

'I'll do it. Forget it, I'll do it.'

'Fine. Do that. That's one thing you can do. You can't help me with my other problem any more than I can help you with yours. See, I'm a big girl now and I knew what I was doing tonight and I don't know if I can very well say tomorrow—today—well gee Hank that was last night but this is now and gee I just don't want to anymore. I mean even you with all your progressive and liberal ideas will have to admit that even adultery has its morality, that one can cop out on that too. So I have things to figure out.'

'Yes.' I started leaving the room. 'Do what you can.'

'Oh, that's good.' I stopped at the door but didn't look back. 'That's what all my good existential friends say whenever I want advice: Just do what you can. Well, I will, Jack, I will.'

I went to the kitchen and drank an ale and when Terry was asleep I went to bed.


Next morning I woke first, alert and excited, though I had slept only four hours. Everything was quiet except birds. I got up and dressed, watching Terry asleep on her back, mouth open; I stepped over her clothes on the floor, and going through the living room picked up her beer can and brought it to the kitchen. In the silence I could feel the children sleeping upstairs, as if their breathing caressed me. I went outside: the morning was sun and blue and cool air. I drove to a small grocery store and bought a *Globe* and cigarettes. Then I drove to a service station with a pay phone and parked but didn't get out of the car. It was only five minutes of nine on a Sunday morning, and they would be asleep. Or certainly Hank would. But maybe she wouldn't, and I drove to their street: all the houses looked quiet, theirs did too, and I went past, then turned around in a driveway and started back, believing I would go on by; then I stopped and walked up their driveway to the back door and there she was in the dim kitchen away from the sun, surprised, turning to me in her short nightgown, a happy smile as she came to the door and pushed it gently so the latch was quiet. I stepped in and she was holding me tight, and I stroked her soft brushed hair and breathed her toothpaste and soap.

'Are you all right now?'

'The fever's gone. Was it fun last night?'

'They made love.'

She moved her head back to look at me and say, 'Really?'; then she was at my cheek again. 'She told you?'

'She didn't want to, but I knew, I had waked up. They went to the bronze angel.'

'Are you jealous?'

'No.' She was holding me, rubbing her cheek on my chest. Her kitchen was clean. 'They might see each other today. If they do, we can get together.'

'We'll have the kids and they'll have the cars.'

'Shit.'

Water started boiling; she let me go and turned off the fire. Then she was back.

'How are you?' I said.

'Still weak, that's all. I told you the fever's gone.'

'I mean about them.'

'Fine. I think it's fine. He'll be asleep for a long time.'

'He might wake up.'

'We'd hear him, we'd be right under the bedroom. He always goes to the bathroom first.'

'Sharon,' I said.

'She'll sleep too.'

We started for the door; she stopped and put instant coffee in two cups and poured water. Then we crept through the house to the guest room.

When I left, after drinking the coffee that was still warm enough, Sharon was coming downstairs. Before getting into the car I squinted up at the bedroom where Hank slept.

At home I didn't go in; I sat on the back steps to read the sports page. I could smell Terry's cigarette, then I heard her moving and she came outside in her robe, hair uncombed, and sat beside me and put a hand on my shoulder. I nearly flinched.

'I was scared,' she said. 'When I woke up and you weren't there. I thought you had left.'

'I did. To get cigarettes and a paper.'

'What took so long?'

'Driving around looking at the bright new morning.'

'Is it?'

I looked up from the paper and waved a hand at the trees and rooftops and sky.

'Blink your eyes and look at it.'

'Your beard's beautiful in the sun. It has some blond and red in it.'

'I got that from you and the kids.'

'I thought you had left me.'

'Why should I?'

'What I said.'

'That's night talk.'

'I know it. Just as long as you know it. I was being defensive because I was scared and when I'm scared I get vicious.'

'Why were you scared?'

'Because I have a lover.'

'Is that what you've decided?'

'I haven't decided anything. I made love with Hank so I have a lover, no matter what I do about it. You really don't care?'

She had the right word: care. So I must get her away from that. The way to hunt a deer is not to let him know you're alive.

'I care about you. It's monogamy I don't care about.'

'You've said that for years. I've waked up with that whispering to me for years. But a long time ago you weren't that way.'

'A long time ago I wasn't a lot of ways.'

'I couldn't let you do what I'm doing.'

'Are you doing anything?'

'I don't know yet.'

'But you want to.'

'If I knew that I'd know something.'

'Why don't you know it? I know it.'

'How?'

Her hand was still on my arm; I was scanning box scores.

'You stayed out there with him because you wanted to and I think you came home planning to see him today and tomorrow and tomorrow and tomorrow, but when you found out I knew about it then it got too sticky. Just too bloody sticky. To all in one night leave monogamy and then have to carry it out with your husband knowing about it, staying with the kids while you—'

'Oh stop,' her voice pleading, her fingers tightening on my shoulder. 'Shhh, stop.'

'Isn't that so?'

'I don't know. I mean, sure I wanted to, and I like Hank very much; in a way I love him, and I love you and nothing's changed that, what's with Hank is—' she squeezed my shoulder again and looking at the paper I heard the fake smile in her voice '—it's friendly lust, that's all. But it might not be marriage, living like this.'

'We're married. You and I are married. So it has to be marriage.'

'It might not be for long.'

'I wish Boston were a National League town. You mean you're afraid you'll run off with him?'

'*No. My God* no. There are all sorts of ways for a marriage not to be a marriage.'

'You're just afraid because it's new.'

'If I kept on with Hank you'd want a girl. You'd feel justified then. Maybe even with Edith, and wouldn't *that* be a horror.'

'Seems strange to me that while you're deciding whether or not to make love with a man you call your lover, you're thinking most about what *I'll* do.'

'That's not strange. You're my husband.'

'It is strange, and it's beneath you. This is between you and Hank, not me.'

She took a pack of cigarettes from the carton I'd bought and sat smoking while I read.

'Are you hungry?' she said.

'Yes.'

'Pancakes and eggs?'

'Buckwheat. Are the kids up?'

'No. I think I'll take them to the beach today. Do you want to go?'

'I want to watch the game.'

'I think I'll tell him no.'

'Is that what you want?'

'I don't know. I'm just scared.'

'Because I know about it?'

'Because there's something to know.'

She went inside. I read the batting averages and pitching records, then the rest of the paper, listening to her washing last night's pots and dishes. Then she started cooking bacon and I sat waiting, smelling and listening to the bacon, until I heard Natasha and Sean coming downstairs. We ate for a long time, then Terry lit a cigarette and said, 'Well,' and went to the bedroom and shut both doors. I could hear her voice, but that was all. Natasha and Sean were upstairs getting dressed; when Terry came back to the kitchen she went to the foot of the stairs and called them and said to put on bathing suits. 'We're going to the beach!'

'The beach!' they said. 'The beach!'

'How did you get it done?' I said.

'He answered. He'd said he would. I asked how Edith was and he told me.'

'That was the signal?'

'Yes.'

'Poor Hank. And what if you had decided to see him?'

'I wouldn't have called.'

She had been smoking a lot all morning. Now she started making a Bloody Mary.

'Do you want one?'

'No. How's Edith?'

'All right. Her fever's gone.'


For some years now I have been spiritually allergic to the words husband and wife. When I read or hear husband I see a grimly serene man in a station wagon; he is driving his loud family on a Sunday afternoon. They will end with ice cream, sticky car seats, weariness, and ill tempers. In his youth he had the virtues of madness: rage and passion and generosity. Now he gets a damp sponge from the kitchen and wipes dried ice cream from his seat covers. He longs for the company of loud and ribald men, he would like to drink bourbon and fight in a bar, steal a pretty young girl and love her through the night. When someone says wife I see the confident, possessive, and amused face of a woman in her kitchen; among bright curtains and walls and the smell of hot grease she offers her husband a kiss as he returns from the day sober, paunchy, on his way to some nebulous goal that began as love, changed through marriage to affluence, is now changing to respectable survival. She is wearing a new dress. From her scheming heart his balls hang like a trophy taken in battle from a young hero long dead.

I wheezed again with this allergy as I stood on the lawn and watched Terry and Natasha and Sean drive off to Plum Island. They had a picnic basket, a Styrofoam cooler of soft drinks and beer, a beach bag of cigarettes and towels, and a blanket. They left in a car that needed replacing. This morning's lovely air was now rent apart by the sounds of power mowers. One was across the street, two blocks down to the right; the man behind it wore a T-shirt and shorts and was bald. The one to the left was on my side of the street, behind shrubs, and I only saw him when he got to the very front of his lawn, turned, and started back. I sat on the grass and chewed a blade of it and watched the bald man. I wondered what he was thinking. Then I thought he must be thinking nothing at all. For if he thought, he might cut off the engine that was mowing his lawn and go into the garage and jam the garden shears into his throat.

Yet once in a while you saw them: they sat in restaurants, these old couples of twenty and twenty-five and thirty years, and looked at each other with affection, and above all they talked. They were always a wonder to see, and when I saw them I tried to hear what they said. Usually it was pleasant small talk: aging sailors speaking in signals and a language they have understood forever. If I looked at most couples with scorn and despair, I watched these others as mystified as if I had come across a happy tiger in a zoo; and I watched them with envy. *It can be faked*, Hank said once. We were in a bar. The afternoon bartender had just finished work for the day, his wife was waiting for him in a booth, and they had two drinks and talked; once they laughed aloud. *There are two kinds of people*, Hank said. *The unhappy ones who look it and the unhappy ones who don't.*

Now I went inside and upstairs and turned on the ball game. Hank's marriage wasn't a grave because Hank wasn't dead; he used his marriage as a center and he moved out from it on azimuths of madness and when he was tired he came back. While Edith held to the center she had been hurt, and for a few days when she started guessing that Hank was not faithful I didn't like being with them: you could smell the poison on their breaths, feel the tiny arrows flying between them. Now she had a separate life too and she came home and they sat in the kitchen with their secrets that were keeping them alive, and they were friendly and teasing again. It was as simple as that and all it required was to rid both people of jealousy and of the conviction that being friendly parents and being lovers were the same. Hank and Edith knew it, and I knew it. I had waked happy, believing Terry knew it too, and now after her one night she was at the beach with the children, and we were husband and wife again. I sat watching the game. Far off, as though from the streets behind the black and white ball park, I could hear the power mowers.

After dinner Terry came to the living room where I was reading on the couch. Upstairs the children were watching television.

'Hank came to the beach.'

'He found you? On a hot Sunday at Plum Island? My God, the man's in love.'

'He says he is.'

'Really?'

'Oh, I know it's just talk, it's just a line—he wants to see me tonight.' She was smoking. 'I wish I hadn't last night. But I did and it doesn't seem really right to say yes and then next morning say no, I mean it's not like I was drunk or something, I knew what I was doing. But I'm scared, Jack.' She sat on the couch; I moved to make room, and she took my hand. 'Look at me. What do you *really* think? Or really feel. You're not scared of this? People screwing other people?'

'No, I'm not scared.'

'Then why am I? When I'm the one who—Jesus.'

'What did you feel at the beach?'

'Guilty. Watching my children and talking to him.'

'Did you tell him you'd meet him?'

She lowered her eyes and said, 'Yes.'

'And now you don't feel like it because it's embarrassing to leave the house when I know where you're going. If I didn't know, you'd have got out with some excuse. Does Hank know that I know?'

'I didn't tell him. It just seemed too much, when we're all together. Won't you feel strange? When you see him tomorrow?'

'I don't think so. What are you going to do tonight?'

'I'm going to think about it.'

She went to the kitchen. I listened to her washing the dishes: she worked very slowly, the sounds of running water and the dull clatter of plate against plate as she put them in the drainer coming farther and farther apart so that I guessed (and rightly) she had done less than half the dishes when I heard her quickly cross the floor and go into the bathroom. She showered fast, she must have been late, then she opened the bathroom door to let the steam out. Late or not, of course she spent a long while now with the tubes and brushes and small bottles of her beauty, which was natural anyway and good, but when people came over or we went out she worked on it. I had always resented that: if a car pulled up in front of the house she fled to the bathroom and gave whoever it was a prettier face than she gave me. But I thought, too, that she gave it to herself. She closed the bathroom closet, ran the lavatory tap a final time, and came out briskly into the bedroom; lying propped on the couch, I looked over the Tolstoy book; she had a towel around her, and I watched her circling the bed, to our closet. She was careful not to look at me. On the way to the mirror she would have to face me or turn her head; so I raised the book and read while she pushed aside hangered dresses, paused, then chose something. I felt her glance as she crossed the room to the full-length mirror. I tried to read, listening to the snapping of the brassiere, the dress slipping over her head and down her body, and the brush strokes on her hair. Then I raised my eyes as she stepped into the living room wearing her yellow dress and small shiny yellow shoes, her hair long and soft, and behind the yellow at her shoulders it was lovely. When I looked at her she opened her purse and dropped in a fresh pack of cigarettes, watching it fall. She had drawn green on her eyelids.

'Well—' she said.

'All right.'

'I'll do the dishes when I get back.'

'No sweat.'

She looked at me, her eyes bright with ambivalence: love or affection or perhaps only nostalgia and, cutting through that tenderness, an edge of hatred. Maybe she too knew the marriage was forever changed and she blamed me; or maybe it wasn't the marriage at all but herself she worried about, and she was going out now into the night, loosed from her moorings, and she saw me as the man with the axe who had cut her adrift onto the moonless bay. My face was hot. She turned abruptly and went upstairs and I listened to her voice with the children. She lingered. Then she came downstairs and called to me from the kitchen: 'The movie should be over around eleven.' I read again. I could have been reading words in Latin. Then the screen opened and she was back in the kitchen, my heart dropping a long way; she went through the bathroom into the bedroom, the car keys jingled as she swept them from the dresser, and my heart rose and she was gone. After a while I was able to read and I turned back the pages I had read without reading; I read for twenty minutes until I was sure Hank was gone too, then I went to the bedroom and phoned Edith.

'"Ivan Ilyitch's life was most simple and most ordinary and therefore most terrible."'

'Who said that?'

She wasn't literary but that didn't matter; I loved her for that too and anyway I didn't know what did matter with a woman except to find one who was clean and peaceful and affectionate and then love her.

'Tolstoy. Our lives aren't so simple and ordinary.'

'Is she gone too?'

'A movie. That's what she tells me so the kids can hear repeated what she told them. A new twist to the old lying collusion of husband and wife against their children. But she also told me the truth.'

'He's going to see some Western. He says they relax him and help him write next day. I hate Westerns.'

'I love them. There's one on the tube tonight and I'll watch it with the kids.'

'We'll have to do something about these cars.'

'Maybe a car pool of sorts.'

'Dear Mother, please buy me a car so I can see my lover while Hank sees his.'

'Is she really that rich?'

'She's that rich. I miss you.'

'Tomorrow. Eleven?'

'I'll go shopping.'

'I'll go to the library.'

'You use that too much. Some day she'll walk over and see if you're there.'

'She's too lazy. Anyway, if things keep on like this maybe I can stop making excuses.'

'Don't count on it.'

'Being a cuckold's all right, but it's boring. Get a sitter and take a taxi.'

'Go watch the movie with your children.'

Terry hadn't put her beauty things away; they were on the lavatory and the toilet tank, and I replaced tops on bottles and put all of it into the cabinet. I went to the foot of the stairs and called.

'What!' When their voices were raised they sounded alike; I decided it was Sean.

'Turn to Channel Seven!'

'What's on!'

'Cowboys, man! Tough hombre cowboys!'

'Cowboys! Can we watch it!'

'Right!'

'All of it!'

'Yeah! All of it!'

'Are you gonna watch it!'

'I am! I'll be up in a while!'

I got a pot out of the dishwater and washed it for popcorn. Once Sean called down that it had started and I said I knew, I knew, I could hear the horses' hooves and I'd be up evermore ricky-tick. There were Cokes hidden in the cupboard so the kids wouldn't drink them all in one day. I poured them over ice and opened a tall bottle of Pickwick ale and got a beer mug and brought everything up on a tray.

'Hey neat-o,' Natasha said.

'Popcorn!'

I pulled the coffee table in front of the couch and put the tray on it.

'Sit between us,' Natasha said.

Sean hugged me when I sat down.

'We got a good Daddy.'

'Now Mom's watching a movie and we're watching a movie,' Natasha said.

'What movie did Momma go to?'

'I believe a Western.'

'You didn't want to go?'

'Nope. I wanted to see this one. He's going to hit that guy soon.'

'Which guy?'

'The fat mean one.'

'How do you know?'

'Because if he doesn't hit him we won't be happy.'


When the movie was over, I tucked them in and kissed them and went downstairs to Tolstoy and the couch; as I read I kept glancing at my watch and at midnight I thought how she never uses the seat belt, no matter how many times and how graphically and ominously I tell her. I kept reading and I remembered though trying not to Leonard in Michigan: he had married young and outgrown his wife and he hated her. When he was drunk, he used to say Nobody hates his wife as much as I hate mine. And one night drinking beer—he was a big weight-lifting man and drank beer like no one I've ever known—he said I've thought of a way a man can kill his wife. You take her for a ride, you see, and you have a crash helmet with you and it's just resting there on the seat between you, she wonders what it's there for, but the dumb bitch won't say anything, she won't say anything about anything and the world can fall down and still she'll just blink her Goddamn dumb eyes and stare and never let you know if there's any-thing burning behind them, then you get out on some quiet straight country highway and put that son of a bitch on your head and unbuckle her seat belt and hold onto that son of a bitch and floorboard into a telephone pole and throw the crash helmet way the fuck out into the field—

I wished the movie hadn't ended and I was still upstairs watching it with the children; the TV room was a good room to be in, the cleanest in the house because it was nearly bare: a couch, two canvas deck chairs, the TV, and a coffee table. A beach ball and some toy trucks and cars were on the floor. The secret was not having much life in the room. It was living that defeated Terry: the rooms where we slept and ate and the living room and dishes and our clothes. The problem was a simple one which could be solved with money, but I would never make enough so that I could pay someone to do Terry's work. So there was no solution. Two years ago Terry had pneumonia and was in the hospital for a week. Natasha and Sean and I did well. Everyone made his own bed and washed his own plate and glass and silver, and we took turns with the pots; every day I washed clothes, folded them as soon as they were dry, and put them away; twice that week I vacuumed the house. All this took little time and I never felt harried. When Terry came home, I turned over the house to her again, and the children stopped making their beds and washing their dishes, though I'd told her how good they had been. We could do that again now, and I could even have my own laundry bag and put my things in it every night, wash my clothes once a week and wash my own dishes and take turns with the pots, I could work in the house as though I lived with another man. But I wouldn't do it. If Terry had always kept house and was keeping it now, then I could help her without losing and I would do it. But not the way she was now.

In Michigan when I was in graduate school, she found us an old farmhouse in the country for a hundred a month, and for a while she was excited, I'd come home and find the furniture rearranged, and one afternoon she painted the bathroom orange. The landlord had paid for the paint, and for two buckets of yellow for the kitchen; he was an old farmer, he lived down the dirt road from us, he liked Terry, and he told her when she finished the kitchen he'd buy paint for the other rooms. Whatever colors she wanted. For a few days she talked about different colors, asked me what I thought the bedrooms should be, and the halls, and then a week went by and then another and one day when I was running down the road Mr. Kenfield was at his mailbox and he asked me how the painting was coming. I called over my shoulder: 'Fine.' That afternoon we painted the kitchen. I was sullen because I should have been studying, and we painted in near silence, listening to the radio, while Natasha watched and talked. When we were done I said: 'All right, now tell Kenfield you're too busy to paint the other rooms. At least now when he comes for coffee he'll see the yellow walls. And if he pisses he'll see the orange ones. Now I'm going upstairs to do my own work.'

All through graduate school that's what she kept doing: my work. When I brought a book home she read it before I did, and when my friends came over for an afternoon beer and we talked about classes and books and papers, she sounded like a graduate student. Once I daydreamed about her soul: she and Rex and I were sitting at our kitchen table drinking beer, and I watched her talking about *Sons and Lovers* and I remembered her only a year ago when I was a lieutenant junior-grade and she was complaining about the captain's snotty treatment of reserve officers, deriding the supply officer's bureaucratic handling of the simplest matters, and saying she wished there were still battleships so I could be on one and she could go aboard. And in that kitchen in the farmhouse in Michigan I daydreamed that Rex and I were ballplayers and now it was after the game and Terry had watched from behind the dugout and she was telling us she saw early in the game that I couldn't get the curve over, and she didn't think I could go all the way, but in the fifth she saw it happen, she saw me get into the groove, and then she thought with the heat I'd tire, but after we scored those four in the seventh—and he *didn't* tag him, I *know* he didn't—she knew I'd go all the way—And she kept talking, this voice from behind the dugout. And from behind the dugout she came up to my den where I worked and brought a book downstairs and later when I came down at twilight, blinking from an afternoon's reading, I'd find her on the couch, reading.

A couple of years ago in this house in Massachusetts, she put Sean to bed on the same dried sheet he had wet the night before; I noticed it when I went up to kiss the children good-night. That was two days after I had gone to the basement and found on the stairs a pot and a Dutch oven: the stairway was dimly lit, and at first I thought something was growing in them, some plant of dark and dampness that Terry was growing on the stairs. Then I leaned closer and saw that it had once been food; it was covered with mold now, but in places I could see something under the mold, something we hadn't finished eating. I got the tool or whatever I had gone down for, then I went to the living room; she was sitting on the couch, leaning over the coffee table where the newspaper was spread, and without looking at her—for I couldn't, I looked over her head—I said: 'I found those pots.' She said: 'Oh.' I turned away. I have never heard her sound so guilty. She got up and went down the basement stairs; I heard her coming up fast, she gagged once going through the kitchen, and then she was gone, into the backyard. Soon I heard the hose. I stood in the living room watching a young couple pushing a baby in a stroller; they were across the street, walking slowly on the sidewalk. The girl had short straight brown hair; her face was plain and she appeared, from that distance, to be heavy in the hips and flat-chested. Yet I longed for her. I imagined her to be clean; I pictured their kitchen, clean and orderly before they left for their walk. Then Terry came in, hurrying; from where I stood I could have seen her in the kitchen if I'd turned, but I didn't want to; she went through the kitchen, into the bathroom, and shut the door; then I heard her throwing up. I stood watching the girl and her husband and child move out of my vision. After a while the toilet flushed, the lavatory tap ran, she was brushing her teeth. Then she went outside again.

For two days we didn't mention it. Every time I looked at

her—less and less during those two days—I saw the pot and Dutch oven again, as though in her soul.

But when I kissed little Sean and smelled his clean child's flesh and breath, then the other—last night's urine—I went pounding down the stairs and found her smoking a cigarette at the kitchen table, having cleared a space for herself among the dirty dishes; she was reading the *TV Guide* with a look of concentration as though she were reading poetry, and in that instant when I ran into the room and saw her face before she was afraid, before she looked up and saw the rage in mine, I knew what that concentration was: she was pushing those dishes out of her mind, as one sweeps crumbs off a table and out of sight, and I saw her entire life as that concentrated effort not to face the dishes, the urine on the sheets, the pots in the dark down there, on the stairs. I said low, hoarse, so the children wouldn't hear: 'And what *else*. Huh? What *else*.' She didn't know what I was talking about. She was frightened, and I knew I had about three minutes before her fright, as always, turned to rage. 'What *else* do you hide from behind *TV Guides*? Huh? Who in the hell *are* you?'

'What didn't I do?' She was still frightened, caught. She pushed back her chair, started to rise. She gestured at the dishes. 'I'll do these as soon as I finish my—' and we both looked at the ashtray, at the smoldering cigarette she could not have held in her fingers.

'It's not what you didn't do, it's *why*. I can list a dozen whats every day, but I can't name one reason. *Why* do I live in the foulest house I know. Why is it that you say you love me but you give me a shitty house. Why is it that you say you love your children but they go unbathed for days, and right now Sean is lying in last night's piss.'

'I forgot.'

'Goddamnit,' and I was nearly whispering, 'that's your *TV Guide* again, you're hiding, you didn't forget anymore than you forgot those pots—'

'Will you stop talking about those pots!'

'Shhh. I haven't mentioned them since I found them.'

'They've been in your eyes! Your Goddamn nitpicking eyes!'

And she fled from the room. I stood listening: her steps slowed at the top of the stairs, calmly entered Sean's room, and then she was talking, her voice sweet, motherly, loving. Sean jumped to the floor. After a while Terry came down with the dirty sheet; she went through the kitchen without speaking, into the wash room; I heard her taking wet clothes from the washer to the dryer, then putting a new load in the washer. She started both machines. So she had forgotten the clothes in the washer too, was behind on that too; yet neither of those was true. She hadn't forgotten, and she wasn't merely behind. She was . . . what? I didn't know. For a moment I had an impulse to go through the entire house, a marauding soldier after her soul: to turn over the ironing basket and hold before her eyes the shirts I hadn't seen in months; to shine a flashlight under the children's beds, disclosing fluffs of dust, soiled pajamas, apple cores; to lift up the couch cushions and push her face toward the dirt and beach sand, the crayons and pencils and pennies—over every inch of every room, into every cluttered functionless drawer (but no: they functioned as waste baskets, storage bins for things undone). I wanted to do that: take her arm and pull and push her to all these failures which I saw, that night, as the workings of an evasive and disordered soul.

I left the kitchen as she entered it from the wash room. I went on the front porch for a cigarette in the dark. It was fall then, and for a while I was able to forget the house. The air was brisk but still, and I was warm enough in my sweatshirt; I walked down to the end of the block and back, smelling that lovely clean air. Then I went back into the house. As soon as I stepped in, it all struck me: it was there waiting, jesting with me, allowing me the clean walk in the air, the peace, only to slap me when I walked in.

I stayed in the living room with a book. After two pages I laid it aside and looked for one that would serve as well as the autumn night had; I found one, and after two pages I was right, there was neither house nor Terry. The book was *Saturday*

*Night and Sunday Morning*, and I saw myself in the book, a single man drinking gin and loving a married woman. I thought of the sleeping children above me and was ashamed; but I also felt the slow and persuasive undertow of delight.

Then I heard her singing in the kitchen. She was washing the dishes now; beyond her, from the closed wash room, came the rocking of the washer, the hum of the dryer. I didn't want her to sing. She sings alone in the kitchen when she's angry, brooding.

So I knew then I wouldn't be able to keep reading the book; she would do something. I read faster, as though speed would force a stronger concentration, would block her out. I was able to read for nearly an hour. It took her that long to clean the kitchen; the washer and dryer had stopped, but she hadn't removed the dry clothes and put the wet ones in the dryer. So when she came into the living room, a bourbon and water in her hand, all fright and guilt gone now, her face set in that look of hers that makes me know there are times she could kill me, I looked up at her, then stood and looked scornfully not at her face but past her, and said in a low, cold voice that I would go put the clothes in the dryer.

'Wait. I want to talk to you.'

We stood facing each other.

'We can talk while the clothes are drying.'

'No. Because I'm not ready to fold the others. And don't look at me like that, I'll fold them, Goddamnit.'

I sat down, got out of the position of being squared off, got out of range.

'I'm tired of being judged. Who do you think you are anyway? Who are you to judge me? I *did* forget Sean had wet last night. If you got them up one morning out of every thousand, if *you* loved them as much as you say you do—oh, that was shitty, accusing me of not loving my children, it's the way you always fight, like a catty, bitchy woman—lying inn*uen*dos—if *you* ever got them up you'd know he hadn't wet for four or five days before that, so I wasn't used to—'

'Three days. He's been telling me every morning.'

'All right: three. Anyway, I forgot.' She had finished her cigarette; she found another on the bookshelf. 'And I *did* forget those pots. I cooked in them the night you had the party.'

'What night I had the party?'

'Whatever Goddamn night it was. When you were—' she mocked a child's whine '—so depressed—you and your fucking self-indulgent bad moods—'

'What *night* are you talking about?'

'When you called up your *friends* to have this impromptu Goddamn party.'

'They're your friends too.'

'Oh sure: me and the boys. They bring their wives over because they have to; I get to talk to the wives. It's *your* party, with *your* friends, in *my* Goddamn house I'm supposed to keep clean as Howard *John*son's.'

'You know my friends like you. We were discussing the pots. The famous pots on the stairs.'

'You supercilious shit.' I smiled at her. 'I cooked in them that night, and you were in your funky mood, and you had to call Hank and Roger and Jim and Matt, I didn't even have time to clean the Goddamn kitchen, and I put those pots on the stairs, I was going to wash them when everybody went home but they stayed half the Goddamn night—'

'I recall you dancing.'

'So I forgot them that night, I probably got drunk, I don't know, and the next day I wasn't thinking about dirty *pots*. I just don't go around thinking about pots! And I forgot them until you found them. And that's the absolute God's truth!'

She went to the kitchen and came back with a fresh drink and stood looking at me.

'I hate to say this, baby,' I said. 'But you're full of shit. I can believe you forgot them that night, what with drinking and dancing. Although I don't see why you couldn't have washed them while these quote friends of mine unquote wandered in— other women do that, you know—I realize you probably had to put your face on and so forth before they came, but after they came I think you could have got someone to talk to you in

the kitchen for ten minutes while you washed a Dutch oven
and a pot—'

'Ten minutes!'

'Fifteen, then.'

'A lot you know. Would my husband have sat with me?
Hell no, he's busy flirting—'

'Oh, stop that crap. Now: I can even believe that you forgot them next morning. But I cannot and will not cater to
your lie by trying to believe that you forgot them for the weeks
they've been down there—'

'It hasn't been weeks.'

Now her voice didn't have that shrill edge; it was quieter,
sullen, and cunning.

'While you were describing your ordeal of merging the
problem of two dirty pots with the problem of enjoying a party,
I was scratching around through my file of memories—I have
this penchant for nostalgic memories, you know—and what I
come up with is this: the party was on Friday, the twenty-first
of September; today is the twentieth of October; those pots
were there about a month. Are you going to stand there drinking my booze and tell me that you did not miss those pots for
one month? Or, for one month, descend the basement stairs?'

Then she was throwing things: first the glass, exploding
on the wall behind me; I got up from the chair and ducked the
copper ashtray, but she got my shoulder with her lighter.
I started toward the kitchen, where the car key hung on a nail;
she got in front of me and choked me with both hands. 'You
crazy bitch—' I shoved hard and she fell back against the table,
bumping her hip. She came after me but I was gone, slamming the door, leaping from the top step and running across
the lawn to the car. I heard the screen door opening then I
was in the car, locking all four doors and jabbing the key twice
then into the slot and as I turned it and the car started she
grabbed the door handle; I accelerated and was gone.

I went to Plum Island and got out and walked on the
beach. The moon was out and on the water, and a cold wind
blew out to sea. I walked until I was too cold and Terry was

gone, my head clear, I was only shivering and walking. Sometimes I stopped and faced the water, taking deep breaths, the wind pushing at my back. Then I drove to a bar where fishermen and men who worked with their hands sat drinking beer with their big wives. I sat at the bar, turning the stool so my back was to the color television, and after two glasses of ale I thought surely she must hate me, and I felt good, sitting there in her hatred. I knew what she felt when she came at me with her bright, tearful eyes and shrill voice and reaching, choking hands: she wanted my death. And sitting in the bar, watching the couples, I liked that.

I remembered the night I had called my friends to come over and drink; I had been sitting on the lawn toward evening, drinking beer and watching the children play; then they came to me and sat on the grass at my feet and I stroked their heads like dogs, and talked to them, and when Terry came out I was telling them a story, making it up as I went along, and I put them in the story: When Natasha and Sean Were Cowboys, it was called; they were comic and heroic, mostly heroic, they endured blizzards, they raised a baby cougar, they captured an outlaw. While I told the story, Terry barbecued pork chops. I felt serene and loving but somehow sad. And it was that sad love that made me, when the children were in bed, call Hank and Matt and Roger and Jim.

Then sitting at that bar, watching the couples who looked past and over me at the movie or variety show or whatever, I remembered clearly the lawn, the children, the story, and my mood, and I remembered eating dinner on the lawn too: barbecued pork chops, baked beans, green salad, garlic bread—I sat in the bar seeing my paper plate in the sunset evening on the lawn, back in September. The baked beans. I saw my fork going into the pile of beans on my plate; and I remembered later, in the kitchen, Sean and I standing over the Pyrex dish and finishing the last of the beans. She had cooked on the grill and in a Pyrex dish.

She had lied. Though at first I thought she had only been mistaken. Because I hate lies so, and I didn't want to believe she would lie. But finally I told myself no: no, she lies. For the story was too good: my mood, my party, had caused her to forget her work. When confronted with the mold and stench of those pots, the urine on the sheets, she reached back for the one night she could use as an excuse.

So she avoided work and she lied. Then what does she want? I thought. What on earth does she want? And right away I knew: to be beautiful, charming, intelligent, seductive, a good cook, a good drinker, a good fuck. In short, to be loved by men and admired by women. A passive life. A receptive life.

I remember once the landlord's daughter came by, a girl of sixteen; she wanted to go into the attic, she thought she left her bicycle pump there. It was a Saturday afternoon; I answered the door and when she told me what she wanted, I thought: *A bicycle pump. My pitiful wife is to be done in by a bicycle pump.* Because the house looked as though it were lived in, not by a family, but a platoon of soldiers holing up before moving on. We had had a party the night before. She had at least moved the party mess to the kitchen, where it still was, along with the breakfast and lunch dishes; on the table, the countertop, in the sink; the kitchen floor was sticky with spilled booze; every bed was unmade; and so on. I let the girl in, and called Terry to show her to the attic; then I went out and got Sean and we rode our bicycles along the Merrimack. When we got back, Terry was standing at the sink, washing dishes.

That night *Uncle Vanya* was on NET. By then our house was in reasonable order, and Terry sat drinking beer and watching the play. Laurence Olivier played Doctor Astrov, and when he said: 'She is beautiful, there's no denying that, but ... You know she does nothing but eat, sleep, walk about, fascinate us all by her beauty—nothing more ... And an idle life cannot be pure ...' I wanted to glance at Terry but did not. She sat and watched and when it was over she said, 'Jesus,' and weaved upstairs to bed. Next afternoon we were supposed to go hear Cannonball Adderley at Lennie's; I had put the money aside on payday; we were going with Hank and Edith, but all morning and through lunch she said she wasn't going, her life had reached a turning point, the landlord's daughter (*oh her face!* she said; *she was so hurt, and so—scornful!*) and *Uncle Vanya* were too much, she would work, she would work, she would start right now by paying for being a slob, she would not go hear Cannonball Adderley. I told her she was being foolish, that if she were serious her house would need a long, thorough cleaning, and that she might as well wait for Monday morning, the traditional day for taking on a load of shit. But she wouldn't go. So I went, and told Hank and Edith that Terry was turning over leaves. I didn't have to say more; they like mysteries. Cannonball was playing at four. I got home about eight. The children were in bed, the kitchen was clean, and in the living room Terry was asleep in the warm hum of her portable hair dryer. The house was neither dirtier nor cleaner than when I left. I never asked how she spent the afternoon. I guessed she did normal surface cleaning, and spent a lot of time with the children; it's what she does when she feels guilty. For three days after that she made all the beds as soon as we got up in the morning; on the fourth day, without a word about *Uncle Vanya* or girls looking for bicycle pumps, or Cannonball Adderley, her slow momentum stopped, like a bicyclist going up a steep hill: she got off and walked the bike. Everything went back to below normal.

In that bar on the night she gripped my throat, really gripped it—and for how long would she have squeezed if I hadn't been able to push her away? She had right away shut off my windpipe—in that bar, I saw something: I saw her sitting with the *TV Guide* among those dishes, with that look of concentration which was real, yes, but it wasn't concentrating *on* something, it was concentrating away from her work. She was saying no. And I thought: Why, that's her word: No. It is what she said to the life that waited for her each morning, perched on the foot of the bed. She simply refused to live it, by avoiding work, by lying about it, and by—yes: I believed it: violence. It wasn't me she hated, me she wanted to kill: it was the questions I raised. Yet I couldn't really separate my questions from me any more than I could separate Terry from her house. She is what she does, I tell her; and I suppose, for her, I am what I ask. And that is why, I thought, our quarrels usually ended violently: because she could not or would not answer my questions about pots on the stairs and Sean lying in last night's piss. So she hit me.

And now tonight she was out with Hank and I remembered the day I found the pots and went up to the living room and told her and she went downstairs; I remembered how I stood at the window and watched the couple pushing their baby in a stroller; the girl was, as I have said, rather plain, and her breasts were a little too small, and her hips a little too wide, but I stood watching her, and that is what I wanted and what I have refused all the years to admit I wanted: a calm, peaceful life with that plain, clean girl pushing her stroller in the sunlight of that afternoon.

# 3

She came home long after midnight, an hour and twenty minutes into a new Monday, coming through the back door into the kitchen, where I sat drinking bourbon, having given up on Tolstoy, sitting and sipping now. She stood just inside the door, looking at me, shaking her head: 'Not this way, Jack. Not after ten—' Then her eyes filled, her lips and cheeks began to contort, she bit off her voice and went to the refrigerator for ice. I stood, to go to her; but then I didn't move. I stood near the wall and watched her make the drink; her back was turned, her head lowered, the hair falling on both sides of her face, and I saw us as in a movie and all I had to do now was cross the room and take her shoulders and turn her and look into her eyes, then hold and kiss her. *We can try again*, I would say. And: *Yes, darling*, she would say: *Oh yes yes*. I stood watching her. When she turned, her eyes were dry, her cheeks firm.

'I've been drinking alone in DiBurro's, for the first time in my life, alone in a bar—'

'What happened?'

'Never mind what happened. I've been thinking about love, and I want to tell you this, I want to tell you these things in my heart, but I don't want to see your face. Your cold, guilty face.' She sat at the table, facing the back door; I leaned against the wall, waiting. 'All right then: I'll move.' She turned her chair so she was profiled to me. 'Don't worry, you'll get rid of me some day, but not like this, not this sordid, drunken adultery, do you know—no, you wouldn't because you never look at me—do you know that I drink more than any woman we know? I'm the only one who gets drunk as the men at parties. I'm the only one who starts drinking before her husband comes home. So you'll get rid of me anyway: I'll become a statistic. Because, you see, I don't keep a Goddamn Howard Johnson's for you, because I read a lot and, you know, think a lot, and I read someplace that booze and suicide claim many of us, us housewives; did you know that? No other group in the country goes so often to the bottle and the sleeping pill. I guess that's how they do it, with pills. Although as a child I knew a woman who played bridge with my mother, she shot herself one afternoon, a tiny hole in the temple, they said— from a tiny pistol, Daddy said, a woman's gun—she had been in and out of hospitals like others were in and out of supermarkets—maybe there's not much difference, they're both either a bother or terminal—and she was convinced she had cancer. That's what the ladies said, my mother and her friends, but they weren't known for truth, on summer afternoons they had chocolate Oreos and Cokes and talked of little things, said trump and no-trump and I pass; I used to walk through and see their souls rising with the cigarette smoke above their heads. Oh yes, they would rather believe relentless old cancer was eating the bones or liver or lungs of their dead friend than to believe one of the zombies in their midst had chosen one sunny afternoon to rise from the dead. She's the only suicide I've known. And I've only known one alcoholic, unless I'm one, which I'm not. I drink a lot at parties and on nights like this one when my husband sends me off to fuck his friend. I don't drink at lunch or early afternoon, but at ten in the morning a real lush will talk to you smelling of booze, a nice, pleasant enough smell but awfully spooky when the sun's still low and the dew hasn't burned off the grass, like in high school Sue's mother was an alcoholic, she was rich and lovely so maybe it was all right, she didn't really need to function much anyway. She always smelled of booze, she was usually cheerful and friendly, and you never saw her glass until five o'clock, at the cocktail hour. 'So much for statistics.'

She went to the sink and poured another bourbon.

'Don't you want to stop that?'

She turned with the ice tray in her hands.

'Give me a reason, Jack.'

I looked at her for a moment, then I looked around the room and down into my glass. She poured the drink and sat at the table and I watched the side of her face.

'A man must have done those statistics,' she said. 'They sound like a fraud. Because he was treating housewife like a profession, like lawyer or doctor or something, and that's wrong, he's including too many of us; if he had done the same with men, just called them all husbands, you can bet they'd have the highest rate. Most of them I know are pretty much drunks anyway, and they commit suicide in all sorts of cowardly ways; sometimes in the bank I wait in line and watch the walking suicides there, the men on my side of the counter and on the other, those lowered eyes and turned-down lips and fidgety glances around like God might catch them dying without a fight. So they should classify us if they must classify us by our husbands' jobs: how many pharmacists' wives are too drunk to cook at night? How many teachers' wives slit their fucking throats? But that wouldn't be accurate either. We are an elusive sex, hard to pin down. Though everyone tries to. I know: I have red hair. She has that red-headed temper, Daddy used to say. I was thinking about him tonight. Once when I was ten he took me fishing. We stood barefoot on the sand and cast out into the surf for flounder. The fishing rod was very long; I had to hold it with two hands and I shuffled forward with my side to the sea, and the rod was behind me almost dragging in the sand, then I arced it high over my head and the line went out, not as far as his but better than I had done before, and he said it: 'That's better.' I reeled in praying I'd hook one, please dear God for one sweet fish. Wasn't that absurd? To think the luck of catching a fish would make me somehow more lovable? Because then it'd follow that to be unlucky was to be unlovable, wouldn't it? And I must have believed that, as a child. And while I was drinking alone tonight I thought maybe I still believe that. But of course luck isn't an element in my life now. I don't fish or play cards; but there's always skill. So should I expect my cooking and screwing to make me more lovable? Maybe. I suppose a man can't be expected to love a woman who fails in the kitchen and the bed. I'll admit that—even though I believe conversation and companionship are more important—but I'll admit that first a man has to be well fed and fucked. "Only God, my dear, could love you for yourself alone and not your yellow hair." What if I cooked badly? Or were paralyzed and couldn't screw? Because maybe then you do hate me for my house, because it's dirty sometimes—'

'I don't hate you.' She looked at me: only for a moment, then she turned away and finished her drink and rose for another. 'Terry—'

'How would you know if you hate me? You don't even know me. You say, "You are what you do." But do you really believe that? Does that mean I'm a cook, an errand runner, a fucker, a bed maker, and on and on—a Goddamn *clean*ing woman, for Christ sake? If you—*you*, you bastard—' looking at me, then looking away '—lost all discipline, just folded up and turned drunk and was fired, *I'd* love you, and I'd get a job and support us too. Maybe no one else would love you. You'd be a different man, to them: your friends and your students. But not to me. I'd love you. I'd love you if you went about at night poisoning dogs. So what is it that I love? If action doesn't matter. I love you—' looking at me, then away '—I love Jack Linhart. And I say you're more than what you do. But if you love me for what I do instead of for what I am—there *is* a difference, I *know* there is—then what are you loving when I screw Hank? Because if you love me for what I do then you can't want me to be unfaithful because if I screw somebody else it's because I love him, so either you don't love me and so you don't care or you don't know me and you just love someone who looks like me, and what you like to do is add to my tricks. Screw Hank. Shake hands. Sit, roll over, play dead, fetch—loving me like a dog. Because I'm not like that, I simply love a dog, I had dogs, four of them, they all disappeared or died or got killed, like everything else around here, like me, and I just *loved* them: fed them and petted them and demanded no tricks. No fucking tricks! But not you.' She stood up and looked at me. 'Am I right? You don't love me, you love the tricks? Is that true? My stupid spaghetti sauce, the martini waiting in the freezer when you come home in the afternoons, the way I for Christ's sweet sake look and walk and screw?'

'I love Edith,' I said, and looked her full in the face; probably I didn't breathe. Her face jerked back, as if threatened by a blow; then she was shaking her head, slowly at first then faster back and forth, and I said: 'Terry. Terry, yes: I love her. I don't love you. I haven't for a long time. I don't know why. Maybe no one ever knows why. I'm sorry, Terry, but I can't help it, I—'

'Nooooo,' she wailed, and she was across the room, dropping her glass, tears now, shaking her head just below my face, pounding my chest, not rage but like a foiled child: she could have been striking a table or wall. 'No, *Jack*. No, *Jack*—' Then she shoved me hard against the wall and I bounced off and pushed her with both hands: she fell loudly on her back, her head thumped the floor, and I crouched with clenched fists, looking down at her frightened face and its sudden pain. She rolled on one side and slowly got up.

'Come on,' I said. 'Come take it.'

She looked at my face and fists, then shook her head.

'No. No, you're right: I've hit you too much. You're right to push me down. I've hit you too much.'

She went to the sink and stood with her back to me, bent

over the counter with her head on her arms, one fist in a light rhythmic beat; after a while she turned. Tears were on her cheeks and she sniffed once and then again.

'All right. I won't cry and I won't hit you. Edith. So Edith then. All right. Jesus.' She looked around for her glass. I moved to pick it up from the floor, but she said, 'Oh fuck you,' and I straightened again. She took a glass from the cupboard and poured a long drink; the ice tray was empty. She went to the refrigerator and put the glass on top of it and opened the freezer compartment, then stood holding the door and looking in at the trays and vapor and frozen juice cans, and I thought then she would cry; but she didn't, and after a while she banged out an ice tray and went to the sink and ran water on the back of the tray and pulled the lever but the ice didn't come out; then she squeezed the dividers with her hands, then jerked back, dropping the tray and shaking a hand: 'I hate these Goddamn cutting ice trays.' She ran hot water again and worked the lever and got some cubes. Then she stood leaning against the stove, facing me across the table.

'That fucking bitch whore Edith. My fucking friend Edith. So up Terry. Alone then. I should have known. I did know. I knew all the time. I just wouldn't let myself know that I knew. How long have you been screwing her?'

'May. Late May.'

'Yes. I thought so. I thought so tonight going to meet Hank and I thought so while we high school screwed in the car, I saw you, the way you look at her like you haven't looked at me in years, and I saw you screwing her and when Hank finished I told him I wanted to be alone, just to take me back to DiBurro's where my car was. Did you love me until you fell in love with Edith?'

'No.' I shook my head. 'No. I guess that's why I lo—'

'Don't say it! I don't have to keep hearing that. I—' She lowered her head, the hair covering her eyes, then she went to her purse on the table and got a cigarette and lit it at the stove, holding her hair back behind her neck. When she turned to face me she looked down at the gold wedding ring on her finger, then she twisted it as though to pull it off, but she didn't; she just kept turning it on her finger and looking at it.

'We must have had a lot of people fooled. A lot of people will be surprised. My boyfriend.' She let her ring hand fall. 'I'm thirty years old, I've lost my figure—'

'No, you haven't.'

'Don't, Jack. I've lost my figure, I'm not young anymore, I don't even want to be young anymore, I've become just about what I'll become—' I could not look at her: I went to the refrigerator needing motion more than I needed ale, and got a bottle and opened it and went to the door and stood half-turned, so my back wasn't to her but my face wasn't either. 'But there was a time when I wanted to be young again, I never told you that, I didn't see any reason to load you down with it. I remember once nursing Sean when he woke in the night in Ann Arbor, I had the radio on in the kitchen turned down low and listening to music and watching Sean, and of course I loved him but I was almost halfway through my twenties and I'd been married all that time. Then *La Mer* came on the radio and all at once I was back five years, the year before I met you, the summer I was nineteen and all of us used to go to Carolyn Shea's house because it was the biggest and her parents were the best, her mother and father would come and talk to us in the den where the record player was, she was just a little patronizing to the girls but not to the boys, only because she was a woman; but he wasn't patronizing to anyone at all. The boys would come over: Raymond Harper and Tommy Zuern and Warren Huebler and Joe Fleming, and sometimes they'd bring cherrystones, or steamers, and Mr. Shea would help them open the cherrystones and if they brought steamers Mrs. Shea would steam them and we'd sit in the kitchen with beer or wine. We were there all the time, all that summer, and no one was in love with anyone, we all danced and went to movies and the beach, and all that summer we played *La Mer*. When it came on the radio that night in Ann Arbor I thought of Raymond getting knocked off a destroyer at night and they never found him, and Tommy got fat and serious, and Joe became an undertaker like his father, and Warren just went away; and Leslie had an abortion, then married someone else and went to live in Nebraska, and Carolyn married a rich jerk from Harvard Law, and Jo Ann married a peddler and turned dumb to survive, and then there was me nursing my baby in Ann Arbor, Michigan, and I started to cry, loud and shaking, and I thought you'd hear and think Sean had died and I clamped my teeth shut but I couldn't stop crying because I knew my life was gone away because you didn't have a rubber with you because we'd never made love before—and isn't that tender and sweet to think of now?—and I was foolish enough to believe you when you said you wouldn't come inside me, then foolish enough not to care when I knew you were about to and I went to bed that night with Natasha alive in me and next morning when I woke I knew it. Then you got rubbers but every time I knew it didn't matter; I gave up hope, but I thought if I was lucky anyway, I'd start dating others. I would make love with you but I would date others. I was twenty years old. So now you say you don't love me. You love Edith.' Her lower lip trembled, then she spun around, her back to me, and slapped the counter with both hands. 'I won't cry. You bastard, you won't make me cry. I've given you my *liiife.*' She wiped her eyes once, quickly, with the back of a hand and faced me again. 'Oh, how I *hate* your Goddamn little girl stu- dents you bring in here to babysit, those naïve, helpless little shits, what I'd *give* for their chance, to be young and able to finish college and *do* something, I could be in New *York* now, I could be *any*where but *no*. I had to get *mar*ried. I should have aborted—' Her voice lowered to almost a whisper, and she stopped glaring at me and looked somewhere to my side, her eyes fixed on nothing, just staring: 'I thought of it. I didn't get the name of an abortionist but I did get the name of a girl who'd had one, just by manipulating a conversation I got that done, but I didn't go on. Not because I was scared either. What I was scared of was being knocked up and getting married to my boyfriend. That's what you were: my boyfriend. But no, not Terry, she wanted to do the right thing. So I did. And now

Natasha's here and so of course I'm glad I didn't kill her. After you see a child and give it a name you can never think about abortion. But I've wasted my life. I knew it all the time but I didn't let myself, I was going to make the best of it, I was going to keep on being a girl in love. All right, then. You're having an affair with Edith and you love her and you don't love me. All right. I won't cry and I won't hit you. When are you leaving?'

'I don't know.'

'You might as well go today.'

'I guess so.'

'Is Edith leaving?'

'We've never talked about it.'

'Oh, you must have.'

'No.'

'So you might be like the coyote.'

It was a joke we'd had from the Roadrunner cartoons; one of us trying something fearful and new was like the coyote: poised in midair a thousand feet above a canyon and as long as he doesn't look down he won't fall.

'It doesn't matter,' I said. 'I wouldn't take her from Hank anyway, if he wants her.'

'So it's not her: it's me. Well Jesus. I've been telling you and telling you you don't love me. But I never really meant it. I never believed it at all. Was it the house?'

'I don't know.'

'No. I guess you can't know, anymore than I can know why I still love you. Jack?' Her lip trembled. 'Don't you love me even a little?'

I looked above her, over the pots on the stove, at the wall. Then I closed my eyes and shook my head and said: 'No, Terry.' Then without looking at her I left. I went to the bedroom and undressed in the dark and got into bed. I heard her in the kitchen, weeping softly.

Sometimes I slept and all night she did not come to bed and all night I woke and listened to her. For a while she stayed in the kitchen: she stopped crying and I went to sleep listening to her silence, and when I woke I knew she was still there, sitting at the table under the light. I had not been heartbroken since I was very young; but I could remember well enough what it was like and I wished Terry were leaving me, I wished with all my heart that she had come to me one afternoon and looked at me with pity but resolve and said: *I'm sorry but I must go*—I wish I were now lying in bed grieving for my wife who had stopped loving me. I rolled one way and then another and then lay on my back and breathed shallow and slow as though sleeping, but I couldn't; I felt her sitting in the kitchen and I felt her thinking of me with Edith and me divorced laughing on a sunny sidewalk with some friend, and I felt her heart's grieving, and then I was nearly crying too. I sat up, slowly shaking my head, then lit a cigarette and lay on my back, listening to her silence, then my legs tightened, ready to go to her, but I drew on the cigarette and shook my head once viciously on the pillow and pushed my legs down against the mattress. Then I heard her taking pots from the stove: footsteps from the stove to the sink, and the sound of the heavy iron skillet lowered into the dry sink, footsteps again and this time the higher ringing sound of the steel pot and then higher again of the aluminum one. She began scraping one of them with a knife or fork or spoon. She knocked the pot against the inside of the plastic garbage can and started scraping another. Then she washed and dried them and hung them on the pegboard. She ran water into the sink and I lay staring into the night as she washed the dishes. She washed them quickly, then she was moving about and I guessed she was circling the table, wiping it clean, and after that the stove. Still she was moving with quick steps, into the laundry room and out again, to the sink, and she lowered a bucket into it and turned on the water; I swung my feet to the floor and sat on the edge of the bed. When she started mopping the floor I went to the kitchen. She knew I was there at the doorway but she didn't look up: she was bent over the stroking sponge mop, her head down, toward me; water had splashed on the front of her yellow dress; she was mopping fast, pushing ahead of her a tiny surf of dirty water and soap. Finally she had to stand straight and look at me. Her forehead was dripping, her hair was stringy with sweat, and I could not imagine her with Hank a few hours earlier.

'Come to bed.'

'No. I want to clean my house. I've been a pig and I've beaten you and thrown things at you. I know it's too late for you but maybe not for me, maybe I can at least be good for my babies. Or maybe you'll miss them and want to come back and the house will be clean. Couldn't you just stay and keep screwing Edith? Couldn't you be happy then?'

'You don't want that.'

'No, I guess not.' Mopping again, bent over. 'I don't know. Maybe I could change. Go to bed, love; I want to clean my house.'

I slept lightly. Sometimes I heard Terry moving about the house, and I felt the night leave and the day grow lighter and warmer; at one warm and light time I heard a vacuum cleaner beneath my dreams. When I heard the children's voices I woke up; but I would not open my eyes. I lay on my side and listened to their voices. After a while I heard Terry upstairs, in Sean's room above me. She was walking from one spot to another; then she pushed furniture across the floor. I opened my eyes and looked into the living room: Natasha was standing in the doorway.

'You should see the house.'

'What's she doing upstairs?'

'She just fed us and cleaned up our mess and now she's doing the upstairs.'

Sean called from the kitchen: 'Is that Daddy you're talking to?' I winked at Natasha.

'Is that true you don't love Mom?' she said.

'Who told you that? The morning paper?'

'I heard Mom last night.'

'Oh? Who was she talking to?'

Sean came in, carrying a full glass of orange juice; he held it out in front of him, his forearm extended, and watched it while he stiffly walked to the bed.

'Thanks, chief,' I said, and kissed him.

'I couldn't hear you,' Natasha said. 'Just Mom.'

'Are you getting divorced?' Sean said.

'Wow. You really know how to wake a fellow up.'

Upstairs the vacuum cleaner went on. I imagined what Terry had got from under the bed.

'Natasha said you were leaving.'

'That's an idea. Where should I go? Join the Mounties?'

'I want to live with you,' Sean said.

'I'm not going to choose,' Natasha said.

'Ah me. You shouldn't listen to drunk grown-ups fighting, sweetheart. It's always exaggerated.'

'Mom said you were leaving and you love Edith and you screwed her.'

'Do you know what that means?'

'Yes.'

'What?' Sean said. 'What what means?'

'Nothing,' I said, looking at him and feeling Natasha's eyes on me. 'Just grown-up foolishness.' I looked at Natasha. 'Let's get on our bikes.'

'You haven't eaten yet.'

'Let's go to the river,' Sean said.

'We'll stop someplace where I can eat and you two can have something to drink.'

I told them to get the bikes out while I dressed. When they were gone, I called Edith to tell her I couldn't meet her. Hank answered.

'I can't run today,' I said. 'I'm sick. The flu. Tell Edith I have the flu and maybe she'll feel guilty for spreading it to her friends.'

White clouds were piled in the sky, and from the southwest gray was coming. I led Natasha and Sean in single file down our street, to the river. From our left the air was turning cooler and the gray was coming. We stopped at a small grocery store and got a quart of apple cider and stood on the sidewalk, drinking from the bottle and looking across the blacktop at the dark river.

'Is it true about you and Edith?' There was in her eyes a will to know, a look of deep interest; nothing more.

'Is what true?' Sean said. He was down there, below our voices and souls, looking at the river.

'It is and it isn't,' I said to Natasha's eyes. 'I don't know if I have the wisdom to explain it to a little girl I love.'

She took a quarter from her pocket and gave it to Sean.

'Go buy us something to eat.'

He hurried into the store.

'Where'd you get that?'

'My allowance.'

'I'll explain as well as I can,' I said. I watched her eyes. 'I don't want to abort it.' They hadn't changed.

'What's that mean?'

'To kill something before it's fully developed. Like a party you're planning. Or a baby inside the mother.'

'Oh.'

Now I remembered Terry lowering her voice: *I should have aborted*; even in her raging grief the old instinct of an animal protecting her young was there. Then I looked at the river and the lush woods on the other side, turning bright green as the gray and black moved faster over us; at the horizon the last puffs of white and strips of blue were like daylight under a tent wall; I turned from Natasha because there were tears in my eyes, not for her because she was strong and young and there was hope, but for Terry and her trembling lip: *Jack? Don't you love me even a little?* I am afraid of water; but looking out at the river I wanted suddenly to be in its flow, turning over once, twice, with the current; going down with slow groping arms, and hands opening and shutting on cool muddy death, my hair standing out from my head as I went bubbling down to the bottom. I shuddered, as much with remorse as fear. Then my wish was over. I stood alive again and breathed the rain-scented air and I knew that I would grow old with Terry.

'Mother and I have made mistakes,' I said. She was standing at my side, almost touching; I kept my eyes on the woods across the river. Seagulls crossed my vision. 'You must trust us to make things better for everyone. Your mother and I love each other. She's a good and wonderful woman, and don't worry about anything you heard last night, people are all sorts of things, and one mistake is only a small part of a person, Mother's very good, and Edith is very good, and—'

'And so are you,' she said, and slipped her hand into mine and I couldn't go on.

The sky was completely gray now and it watched us ride home; we put our bikes in the garage and crossed the lawn and as we climbed the back steps it began to rain. We stood in the darkened kitchen and watched it coming down hard and loud. Sean was touching my leg. I tousled his hair, then turned on the light. The room changed: when it was dark and we had looked out at a day as dark as our kitchen, I had felt we were still out there in the rain, the three of us, somewhere by the river and trees; I could live in that peace, from one fresh rain-filled moment to the next, forever. Now with the light we were home again; our bodies were lightly touching but the flow, the unity, was gone. We were three people in a troubled house. I touched them and went to the bedroom. Terry was putting my clothes in a suitcase. She looked clean and very tired; she had showered and changed clothes. She tried to smile, failed, tried again, and made it.

'Was it awful?' she said.

'Was what awful? Why are you doing that?'

'I thought that's where you went. To tell the kids.'

I pushed the suitcase to make room, and lay on the bed; I would not look at her.

'Unpack it,' I said.

'Why? Couldn't you tell them?'

'I don't want to.'

'I'll call them in and we'll both tell them.'

'I mean I don't want to leave.'

She stepped closer to the bed and I was afraid she would touch me.

'You really don't?'

'No.'

'Is it the kids? I mean I know it's the kids but is it just the kids? You could see them, you know. Whenever you wanted. And I'd never move away, I'd live here as long as you teach here—so if it's just telling them, we can do it and get it over with, these things are always hard, but we can do it—'

'It's not that.' I shut my eyes. 'Unpack the suitcase.'

Across the bed I felt her pain and hope. I kept my eyes shut and listened to her moving from the bed to the closet and hanging up my clothes. Then she came around to my side of the bed and sat on the edge and put a hand on my cheek.

'Hey,' she said softly. 'Look at me.'

I did.

'It'll be all right,' she said. 'You'll see. It'll be all right again.'


She slept the rest of the afternoon, then woke to cook dinner; during dinner she and the children talked, and sometimes I talked with the children, but mostly I listened to their voices and the rain outside the window. After cleaning the kitchen Terry went back to bed and slept late next morning; then she called Edith and asked her to go to lunch.

'Do you have to?' I said.

She stood in the kitchen, in a short skirt and a bright blouse and a raincoat, looking pretty the way women do when they meet each other for lunch.

'I've loved her,' she said. 'I want to keep loving her.'

The rain had stopped for a while, but now it was coming down again. They were a long time at lunch; the children were bored, so I let them watch a movie on television. It was an old movie about British soldiers in India; I explained to the children that the British had no business being there, then we were all free to enjoy watching the British soldiers doing their work. They were all crack shots and awfully brave. The movie hadn't ended when Terry came upstairs and, smiling happily, said: 'Don't you want to come down?'

'Just for a minute. I want to see the rest of this.'

I followed her downstairs and put on some water for one cup of tea. Her face was loving and forgiving and I could not bear to look at her, I could not bear the images of her in warm collusion with Edith; for I could see it all: we would gather again in living rooms, the four of us, as though nothing had happened. And perhaps indeed nothing had.

'She wants you to go see her tonight.' Her cheeks were flushed, her eyes bright, and she smelled of bourbon. 'She's going to tell Hank, she's probably told him by now, she said he won't mind—'

'I know.'

Bubbles were forming beneath the water in the pot. I held the cup with the tea bag and waited.

'I told her about Hank and me, right away, as soon as I'd told her I knew about you two, and it's all right, I told her it was like her with you, because she wasn't trying to steal you or anything, it was to save herself, she said, and—'

'I don't want to hear it.'

'You don't?'

'No. I don't know why. I just don't.'

The water was boiling, and I poured it into the cup.

'I'm sorry,' I said. 'I'm sure it was a fine afternoon with Edith.'

'It was.' I looked at her. She was watching me with pity. 'It was wonderful.'

I went upstairs. Going up, I could hear the rifles cracking. That night I went to see Edith and Hank. They were drinking coffee at the kitchen table; the dishes were still there from dinner, and the kitchen smelled of broiled fish. From outside the screen door I said hello and walked in.

'Have some coffee,' Hank said.

I shook my head and sat at the table.

'A drink?' he said.

'Aye. Bourbon.'

Edith got up to pour it.

'I think I'll take in a movie,' Hank said.

Edith was holding the bottle and watching me, and it was her face that told me how close I was to crying. I shook my head: 'There's no need—'

But he was up and starting for the back door, squeezing my shoulder as he passed. I followed him out.

'Hank—'

He turned at his car.

'Listen, I ought to dedicate my novel to you.' He smiled and took my hand. 'You helped get it done. It's so much easier to live with a woman who feels loved.'

We stood gripping hands.

'Jack? You okay, Jack?'

'I'm okay. I'll be laughing soon. I'm working on the philosophy of laughter. It is based on the belief that if you're drowning in shit, buoyancy is the only answer.'

When I got back to the kitchen, Edith was waiting with the drink. I took it from her and put it on the table and held her.

'Hank said he'd guessed long ago,' she said. 'He said he was happy for us and now he's sad for us. Which means he was happy you were taking care of me and now he's sorry you can't.'

I reached down for the drink and, still holding her, drank it fast over her shoulder and then quietly we went to the guest room. In the dark she folded back the spread and sheet; still silent and standing near each other we slowly undressed, folding clothes over the backs of chairs, and I felt my life was out of my hands, that I must now play at a ritual of mortality and goodbye, the goodbye not only to Edith but to love itself, for I would never again lie naked with a woman I loved, and in bed then I held her tightly and in the hard grip of her arms I began to shudder and almost wept but didn't, then I said: 'I can't make love, I'm just too sad, I—' She nodded against my cheek and for a long while we quietly held each other and then I got up and dressed and left her naked under the sheet and went home.

Like a cat with corpses, Terry brings me gifts I don't want. When I come home at night she hands me a drink; she cooks better than any woman I know, and she watches me eat as though I were unwrapping a present that she spent three months finding. She never fails to ask about my day, and in bed she responds to my hesitant, ambivalent touch with a passion I can never match. These are the virtues she has always had and her failures, like my own, have not changed. Last summer it took the house about five weeks to beat her: she fought hard but without resilience; she lost a series of skirmishes, attacks from under beds, from closets, the stove, the vegetable bin, the laundry basket. Finally she had lost everything and since then she has waked each day in her old fashion which will be hers forever: she wakes passively, without a plan; she waits to see what the day will bring, and so it brings her its worst: pots and clothes and floors wait to be cleaned. We are your day, they tell her. She pushes them aside and waits for something better. We don't fight about that anymore, because I don't fight; there is no reason to. Except about Edith, she is more jealous than ever; perhaps she is too wise to push me about Edith; but often after parties she accuses me of flirting. I probably do, but it is meaningless, it is a jest. She isn't violent anymore. She approaches me with troubled eyes and says maybe she's wrong but it seemed to her that I was a long time in the kitchen with—I assure her that she's wrong, she apologizes, and we go to bed. I make love to her with a detachment that becomes lust.

Now that it is winter the children and I have put away our bicycles, oiled and standing side by side in the cellar, the three of them waiting, as Sean says, for spring and summer. We go sledding. The college has a hill where students learn to ski and on weekends it is ours; Natasha and Sean always beg Terry to come with us and she always says no, she has work to do, she will go another time. I know what it costs her to say this, I know how she wants to be with us, all of us going shrilly down the hill, and then at the top a thermos of chocolate for the children and a swallow of brandy for mama and papa. But she knows that with the children I'm happy, and she always says she will go another time. We sled and shout for a couple of hours until we're wet and cold, and when we come home with red cheeks Terry gives us hot chocolate.

Last week Hank sold his novel, and Saturday night he and Edith gave a party to celebrate. At noon that day Hank and I ran five miles; the sky was blue then; later in the afternoon clouds came and by night snow was falling. When I went up to his office he had finished writing (he has started another novel) and his girl was there; she is nineteen, a student, and she has long blonde hair and long suede boots and the office smelled of her cigarette smoke. Hank has not started smoking again. He is very discreet about his girl and I think only Terry and I know; we don't talk about it, Terry and I, because she can't. I know it bothers her that she can't, I know she wishes she were different, but she isn't. Edith knows too, about Hank and his girl; they don't lie to each other anymore.

'It's not love,' she said that night at the party. We had gone to the front porch to breathe and watch the snow. 'It's marriage. We have a good home for Sharon. We respect each other. There's affection. That's what I wish you could have: it's enough. It's sad, watching you two. She loves you and you never touch her, you don't look at her when you talk. Last summer, after we stopped seeing each other, I went to the zoo that week, I took Sharon to the zoo; and we went to see the gorilla: he was alone in his cage, and there were women with their children watching him. They're herbivores—did you know that? They're gentle herbivores. I don't like zoos anyway and I shouldn't have gone but it was such an awful week, finding out how to live this time, I'd been through that in May and then there was you and then in July there wasn't, so I took Sharon to the zoo. And I looked in the gorilla's eyes and he looked so human—you know?—as if he *knew* everything, how awfully and hopelessly and forever trapped he was. It's not like watching a flamingo. He was standing there looking at us looking at him, all the young mothers in their pants and skirts the colors of sherbet and the jabbering children. Then he reached down like this and shit in his hand. He was watching us. He held up the handful of shit—' and she held her hand up, shoulder-high, palm toward me '—and then he brought it to his mouth and licked it. His eyes were darting from side to side, watching us. They were merry and mischievous, his eyes. Then he licked it again. Around me the mothers were gasping and some of the children were laughing; then they all hurried away. Murmuring. Distracting their children. But I stayed, and he looked at me like he was smiling and then he showed me his shit again and then he licked it and then he showed it to me again; he almost looked inquisitive; but by then I was squeezing Sharon's hand and looking in his eyes and I was crying, standing there weeping on a sunny afternoon in front of a gorilla, and he watched me for a while, curious at first, and then he lowered his hand with the shit and we just stood looking at each other, he was looking into my eyes, and he knew that I knew and I knew that he knew, and if he could have cried he would have too. Then I left. And after a few weeks when I was able to see someone besides myself I'd see you and I'd think of that trapped gorilla, standing in his cage and licking his own shit. And I wanted to cry for you too—not just me, because I love you and can't touch you, can't be alone with you, but I wanted to cry for you. And I did. And I still do. Or at least I feel like it, I cry down in my soul. Oh Jack—are you trying at all?'

'There's nothing to try with.'

I could not look at her eyes, for I wanted to hold her and there was no use in that now. I moved to the window and looked in; from the couch Terry looked up and smiled; she held the smile when Edith moved into her vision and stood beside me. I turned from the window. Around the streetlight the falling snow was lovely. Terry had stopped watching us after the smile; she was talking ardently with Hank and Roger, and I thought poised like that—a little high on bourbon, talking, being listened to, being talked to—she was probably happy. I raised my glass to the snow and the night.

'Here's to the soul of Jack Linhart: it has grown chicken wings and flaps near the ground.' I drank. 'I shall grow old and meek and faithful beside her, and when the long winter comes—' I drank '—and her hair is white as snow I shall lay my bent old fingers on her powdered cheek and—'

'I love you.'

'Do you still?'

'Always.'

'And live with Hank.'

'He's my husband and the father of my child.'

'And he's got a Goddamn—All right: I'm sorry. It's bitterness, that's all; it's—'

'I don't care if he has a girl.'

'You really don't?'

'Some women take up pottery, some do knitting.'

'Oh.'

'Yes.'

'I guess I didn't want to know that.'

'I'm sorry.'

'Jesus. Oh Jesus Christ, I really didn't want to know that. Course there's no reason for you not to have someone, when I can't, when I—Jesus—'

I went inside and got drunk and lost track of Terry until two in the morning, when she brought my coat. I told her I was too drunk to drive. In the car I smelled her perfume, and I thought how sad that is, the scent of perfume on a rejected woman.

'Edith has a lover,' I said.

'I know. She told me a month ago.'

'Do we know him?'

'Do you want to?'

'No.'

'We don't anyway.'

'Why didn't you tell me?'

'I didn't want to talk about it. I think it's sad.'

'It makes her happy.'

'I don't believe it.'

'Oh, you can't tell.'

'Please don't,' she said. She was leaning forward, looking into the snow in the headlights. 'I know you don't love me. Maybe someday you will again. I know you will. You'll see, Jack: you will. But please don't talk like that, okay? Please, because—' Her voice faltered, and she was quiet.

While she took the sitter home I sat in the dark living room, drinking an ale and looking out the window. In the falling snow I saw a lover for Terry. I went to bed before she got home and next morning I woke first. The sky had cleared and the snow was hard and bright under the sun. While I drank tomato juice in the kitchen Natasha and Sean came downstairs.

'Get dressed,' I said. 'We'll go buy a paper.'

'We should go sledding,' Sean said.

'All right.'

'Before breakfast?' Natasha said.

'Why not?'

'We've never gone first thing in the morning,' Sean said. 'It'll be neat.'

'Okay,' Natasha said. 'Is Mom awake?'

'No.'

'We'll write her a note.'

'Okay. You write it. And be quiet going upstairs.'

'We will,' Sean said, and he was gone up the stairs.

'What should I write?'

'That we're going sledding at nine and we'll be back about eleven, hungry as hell.'

'I'll just say hungry.'

I got my coat and filled its pockets with oranges, then went outside and shoveled the driveway while they dressed warmly for the cold morning.

# OVER THE HILL

## 1

HER HAND WAS TINY. He held it gently, protectively, resting in her lap, the brocaded silk of her kimono against the back of his hand, the smooth flesh gentle and tender against his palm. He looked at her face, which seemed no larger than a child's and she smiled.

'You buy me another drink?' she said.

'Sure.'

He motioned to the bartender, who filled the girl's shot glass with what was supposedly whiskey, though Gale knew it was not and didn't care, then mixed bourbon and water for Gale, using the fifth of Old Crow that three hours earlier he had brought into the bar.

'I'll be right back,' he said to the girl.

She nodded and he released her hand and slid from the stool.

'You stay here,' he said.

'Sure I stay.'

He walked unsteadily past booths where Japanese girls drank with sailors. In the smelly, closet-sized restroom he closed the door and urinated, reading the names of sailors and ships written on the walls, some of them followed by obscenities scrawled by a different, later hand. The ceiling was bare.

He stepped onto the toilet and reaching up, his coat tightening at the armpits and bottom rib, he printed with a ballpoint pen, stopping often to shake ink down to the point again: *Gale Castete, Pvt. USMC, Marine Detachment, USS Vanguard Dec 1961.* He stood on the toilet with one hand against the door in front of him, reading his name. Then he thought of her face tilted back, the roots of her hair brown near the forehead when it was time for the Clairol again, the rest of it spreading pale blonde around her head, the eyes shut, the mouth half open, teeth visible, and the one who saw this now was not him—furiously he reached up to write an obscenity behind his name, then stopped; for reading it again, he felt a gentle stir of immortality, faint as a girl's whispering breath into his ear. He stepped down, was suddenly nauseated, and left the restroom, going outside into the alley behind the bar, where he leaned against the wall and loosened his tie and collar and raised his face to the cold air. Two Japanese girls entered the alley from a door to his left and walked past him as if he were not there, arms folded and hands in their kimono sleeves, their lowered heads jabbering strangely, like seagulls.

He took out his billfold, which bulged with wide folded yen and tried unsuccessfully to count it in the dark. He thought there should be around thirty-six thousand, for the night before—at sea—he had received the letter, and that morning when they tied up in Yokosuka he had drawn one hundred and fifty dollars, which was what he had saved since the cruise began in August because she wanted a Japanese stereo (and china and glassware and silk and wool and cashmere sweaters and a transistor radio) and in two more paydays she would have had at least the stereo. That evening he had left the ship with his money and two immediate goals: to get falling, screaming drunk and to get laid, two things he had not done on the entire cruise because he had had reason not to; or so he thought. But first he called home—Louisiana—to hear from her what his mother had already told him in the letter, and her vague answers cost him thirty dollars. Then he bought the Old Crow and went into the bar and the prettiest hostess came and stood beside him, her face level with his chest though he sat on a barstool, and she placed a hand on his thigh and said *Can I sit down?* and he said *Yes, would you like a drink?* and she said *Yes, sank you* and sat down and signaled the bartender and said *My name Betty-san* and he said *What is your Japanese name?* She told him but he could not repeat it, so she laughed and said *You call me Betty-san;* he said okay, *I am Gale. Gale-san? Is girl's name. No,* he said, *it's a man's.*

Now he buttoned his collar and slipped his tie knot into place and went inside.

'You gone long time,' she said. 'I sink you go back ship.'

'No. S'koshi sick. Maybe I won't go back ship.'

'You better go. They put you in monkey house.'

'Maybe so.'

He raised his glass to the bartender and nodded at Betty, then looked at the cuff of his sleeve, at the red hashmark which branded him as a man with four years' service and no rank— three years in the Army and eighteen months in the Marines— although eight months earlier he had been a private first class, nearly certain that he would soon be a lance corporal, then walking back to the ship one night in Alameda, two sailors called him a jarhead and he fought them both and the next day he was reduced to private. He was twenty-four years old.

'I sink you have sta'side wife,' Betty said.

'How come?'

'You all time quiet. All time sink sink sink.'

She mimicked his brooding, then giggled and shyly covered her face with both hands.

'My wife is butterfly girl,' he said.

'Dat's true?'

He nodded.

'While you in Japan she butterfly girl?'

'Yes.'

'How you know?'

'My mama-san write me a letter.'

'Dat's too bad.'

'Maybe I take you home tonight, okay?'

'We'll see.'

'When?'

'Bar close soon.'

'You're very pretty.'

'You really sink so?'

'Yes.'

She brought her hands to her face, moved the fingertips up to her eyes.

'You like Japanese girl?'

'Yes,' he said, 'Very much.'


# 2


Now he could not sleep and he wished they had not gone to bed so soon, for at least as they walked rapidly over strange, winding, suddenly quiet streets he had thought of nothing but Betty and his passion, stifled for four and a half months, but now he lay smoking, vaguely conscious of her foot touching his calf, knowing the Corporal of the Guard had already recorded his absence, and he felt helpless before the capricious forces which governed his life.

Her name was Dana. He had married her in June, two months before the cruise, and their transition from courtship to marriage involved merely the assumption of financial responsibility and an adjustment to conflicting habits of eating, sleeping, and using the bathroom, for they had been making love since their third date, when he had discovered that he not only was not her first, but probably was not even her fourth or fifth. In itself, her lack of innocence did not disturb him. His moral standards were a combination of Calvinism (greatly dulled since leaving home four and a half years earlier), the pragmatic workings of the service, and the ability to think rarely in terms of good and evil. Also, he had no illusions about girls and so on that third date he was not shocked. But afterward he was disturbed. Though he was often tormented by visions of her past, he never asked her about it and he had no idea of how many years or boys, then men, it entailed; but he felt that for the last two or three or even four years (she was nineteen) Dana had somehow cheated him, as if his possession of her was retroactive. He also feared comparison. But most disturbing of all was her casual worldliness: giving herself that first time as easily as, years before, high school girls had given a kiss, and her apparent assumption that he did not expect a lengthy seduction any more than he expected to find that she was a virgin. It was an infectious quality, sweeping him up, making him feel older and smarter, as if he had reached the end of a prolonged childhood. But at the same time he sensed his destruction and, for moments, he looked fearfully into her eyes.

They were blue. When she was angry they became suddenly hard, harder than any Gale had ever seen, and looking at them he always yielded, afraid that if he did not she would scream at him the terrible silent things he saw there. His memories of the last few days before the cruise—the drive in his old Plymouth from California to Louisiana, the lack of privacy in his parents' home—were filled with images of those eyes as they reacted to the heat and dust or a flintless cigarette lighter or his inability to afford a movie or an evening of drinking beer.

He took her home because in Alameda she had lived with her sister and brother-in-law (she had no parents: she told him they were killed in a car accident when she was fifteen, but for some reason he did not believe her) and she did not like her sister; she wanted to live alone in their apartment, but he refused, saying it was a waste of money when she could live with her sister or his parents without paying rent. They talked for days, often quarreling, and finally, reluctantly, she decided to go to Louisiana, saying even that would be better than her sister's. So he took her home, emerging from his car on a July afternoon, hot and tired but boyishly apprehensive, and taking her hand he led her up the steps and onto the front porch where nearly five years before, his father—a carpenter—had squinted down at him standing in the yard and said: *So you joined the Army. Well, maybe they can make something out of you. I shore couldn't do no good.*

## 3

Strange fish and octopus and squid were displayed uncovered in front of markets, their odors pervading the street. The morning was cold, damp, and gray: so much like a winter day in Louisiana that Gale walked silently with Betty, thinking of rice fields and swamps and ducks in a gray sky, and of the vanished faces and impersonal bunks which, during his service years, had been his surroundings but not his home.

They walked in the street, dodging through a succession of squat children with coats buttoned to their throats and women in kimonos, stooped with the weight of babies on their backs, and young men in business suits who glanced at Gale and Betty, and young girls who looked like bar hostesses and, like Betty, wore sweaters and skirts; men on bicycles, their patient faces incongruous with their fast-pumping legs, rode heedlessly through all of them, and small taxis sounded vain horns and braked and swerved and shifted gears until they had moved through the passive faces and were gone. Bars with American names were on both sides of the street. Betty entered one of the markets and, after pausing to look at the fish outside, Gale followed her and looked curiously at rows of canned goods with Japanese labels, then stepped into the street again. Above the market a window slid open and a woman in a kimono looked down at the street, then slowly laid her bedding on the market roof and, painfully, Gale felt the serenity of the room behind her. Betty came out of the market, carrying a paper bag.

'Now I make you sukiyaki,' she said.

'Good. I need some shaving gear first.'

'Okay. We go Japanese store.'

'Where is it?'

'Not far. You sink somebody see you?'

'Naw. Everybody's on the ship now. They'll be out this afternoon.'

'What they do when you go back? Put you in monkey house?'

'Right.'

'When you go back?'

'Next week. Before she goes to sea.'

'Maybe you better go now.'

'They'd lock me up anyhow. One day over the hill or six, it doesn't matter.'

'Here's store.'

'You buy 'em. They wouldn't understand me.'

'What you want?'

'Shaving cream, razor, and razor blades.'

He gave her a thousand yen.

'Dat's too much.'

'Keep the rest.'

'Sank you. You nice man.'

She went into the drugstore. He waited, then took her bags when she came out and, walking back to her house, treating her with deference and marveling at her femininity and apparent purity and honesty, he remembered how it was with Dana at first, how he had gone to the ship each morning feeling useful and involved with the world and he had had visions of himself as a salty, leather-faced, graying sergeant major.

## 4

*—and she was gone for a week before we could even find her and even when we got out there she told us she wasn't coming with us, she was going to stay with him and it took your daddy about a hour to talk her into coming with us and you know how mad he gets, I don't see how he didn't whip her good right there, that's what I felt like doing, and it's a good thing that boy wasn't*

*there or I know your daddy would killed him. I don't know how long it was going on before, she used to go out at night in your car; she'd tell us she was going to a show and I guess we should have said no or followed her or something but you just don't know at the time, then Sunday she didn't come home and her suitcase was gone so I guess she packed it while I was taking a nap and stuck it in the car. I hate to be writing this but I don't know what else a mothers supposed to do when her boys wife is running around like that. We'll keep her here til you tell us what your going to do, she don't have any money and daddy has the car keys. Tell us what your going to do, I hope its divorse because she's no good for you. I hate to say it but I could tell soon as I seen her, theres something about a girl of her kind and you just married too fast. Its no good around here, she stays in your room most of the time and just goes to the kitchen when she feels like it at all hours and gets something to eat by herself and I don't think we said three words since we got her back—*

He returned the letter to his pocket, lighted a cigarette, poured another glass of dark, burning rum that a British sailor had left with Betty months before, and looked at his watch. It was seven o'clock; Betty had been gone an hour, promising to wake him when she came home from the bar. During the afternoon they had eaten sukiyaki, Betty kneeling on the opposite side of the low table, cooking and serving as he ate, shaking her head each time he asked her to eat instead of cook, assuring him that in Japan the woman ate last; he ate, sitting cross-legged on the floor until his legs cramped, then he straightened them and leaned back on one arm, the other hand proudly and adeptly manipulating a pair of chopsticks or lifting a tumbler of hot *sake* to his lips. After eating she turned on the television set and they sat on the floor and watched it for the rest of the afternoon. She reacted like a child: laughing, frowning, watching intently. He understood nothing and merely held her hand and smoked until near evening, when they watched an American Western with Japanese dialogue and he smiled.

Now he rose, brought the rum and his glass to the bedroom, undressed, went back to the living room for an ashtray and cigarettes, then lay in bed and pulled the blankets up to his throat. He lay in the dark, his hands on his belly, knowing that he could not take her back and could not divorce her; then he started drinking rum again, with the final knowledge that he did not want to live.

# 5

He stood in the Detachment office, his legs spread, his hands behind his back, and stared at the white bulkhead behind the Marine captain. That afternoon, as his defense counsel told the court why he had gone over the hill, he had felt like crying and now, faced with compassion, he felt it again. But he would not. He had waited two weeks at sea for his court-martial and every night, sober and womanless and without mail, he had lain in bed with clenched jaws and finally slept without crying. Now he shut his eyes, then opened them again to the bulkhead and the voice.

'If you had told me about it, I would've got you off the ship. Emergency leave. I'd have flown you back. Why didn't you tell us?'

'I don't know, sir.'

'All right, it's done. Now I want you to know what's going to happen. They gave you three months confinement today. We don't keep people in the ship's brig over thirty days, so you'll be sent to Yokosuka when we get back there and you'll serve the rest of your sentence in the Yokosuka brig. So we'll have to transfer you to the Marine Barracks at Yokosuka. When you get out of the brig, you'll report there for duty. Do you understand all that?'

'No, sir.'

'What don't you understand?'

'When will I get back to the States?'

'You'll finish your overseas tour with the Barracks at Yokosuka. You'll be there about a year.'

'A year, sir?'

'Yes. I'm sorry. But by the time you get out of the brig, the ship will be back in the States.'

'Yes, sir.'

'One other thing. You've worked in this brig. You know my policies and you know the duties of the turnkeys and prisoner chasers. While you're down there, I expect you to be a number one prisoner. Don't give your fellow Marines a hard time.'

'Yes, sir.'

'All right. If you need any help with your problem, let me know.'

'Yes, sir.'

He waited, blinking at the bulkhead.

'That's all,' the captain said.

He clicked his heels together, pivoted around, and strode out. A chaser with a nightstick was waiting for him outside the door. Gale stopped.

'Son of a bitch,' he whispered. 'They're sending me to Yokosuka.'

'Go to your wall locker and get your toilet articles and cigarettes and stationery,' the chaser said.

Gale marched to his bunk, the chaser behind him, and squatted, opening the small bulkhead locker near the head of his bunk, which was the lower one, so that his hands were concealed by the two bunks above his and he was able to slide one razor blade from the case and hide it in his palm. He packed his shaving kit with one hand and brought the other to his waist and tucked the razor blade under his belt.

He rose and the chaser marched him to the brig on the third deck, where Fisher, the turnkey, took his shaving kit and stationery and cigarettes from him and put them in a locker.

'It's letter-writing time now,' Fisher said. 'You can sit on the deck and write a letter.'

'Sir, Prisoner Castete would like to smoke.'

'Only after meals. You missed the smoke break.'

'Sir, Prisoner Castete will write a letter.'

Fisher gave him his stationery and pen and he sat on the deck beside two sailors who glanced at him, then continued their writing.

He did not write. He sat for half an hour thinking of her scornful, angry, blue eyes looking at him or staring at the living room wall in Louisiana as she spoke loudly into the telephone:

*What do you expect me to do when you're off on that damn boat? I bet you're not just sitting around over there in Japan.*

*No! I haven't done a damn thing. Goddamnit, Dana, I love you. Do you love me?*

*I don't know.*

*Do you love him?*

*I don't know.*

*What are you going to do?*

*What do you mean, what am I going to do?*

*Well, you have to do something!*

*It looks like I'm going to sit right here in this house.*

*That's not what—oh you Goddamn bitch, you dirty Goddamn bitch, how could you do it to me when I love you and I never even looked at these gooks, you're killing me, Dana, sonofabitch you're killing me—*

*Son. Son!*

*Mama?*

*She was going to hang up on you and you calling all the way from Japan and spending all that money—*

*Were you standing right there?*

*Yes, and I couldn't stand it, the way she was talking to you—*

*Why were you standing there?*

*Well, why shouldn't I be there when the phone rings in my own house and my boy's—*

*Never mind. Where's Dana?*

*In the bedroom, I guess. I don't know.*

*Let me talk to her.*

*She won't come.*

*You didn't ask her.*

*Gale, you're wasting time and money.*

*Mama, would you please call her to the damn phone?*

*All right, wait a minute.*

*What do you want?*

*Dana, we got to talk.*

*How can we talk when your mother's standing right here and you're across the ocean spending a fortune?*

*If I write you a letter, will you answer it?*

*Yes.*

*What?*

*Yes!*

*I got to know everything, all about it. Did you think you loved him?*

*I don't know.*

*Is he still hanging around?*

*No.*

*Dana, I love you. Have you ever run around on me before this?*

*No.*

*Why did you do it?*

*I told you I don't know! Why don't you leave me alone!*

*I'll write to you.*

*All right.*

*Bye. Answer my letter. I love you.*

*Bye.*

The letter-writing period ended and he handed the blank paper and pen to Fisher, who started to say something but did not.

Gale did not start crying until after he was put into a cell and the door was locked behind him and he had unfolded his rubber mat under his chin and with both hands was working it into a mattress cover and he thought of Dana, then of himself, preparing his bed in a cell thousands of miles away, then he started, the tears flowing soundlessly down his cheeks until he was blinded and could not see his hands or even the mattress and it seemed that he would never get the cover on it and he desperately wanted someone to do it for him and lay the mattress on the deck and turn back the blanket and speak his name. He dropped the mattress, threw the cover against the bulkhead, unfolded the blanket, and lay down and covered himself, then gingerly took the razor blade from under his belt, touching it to his left wrist, for a moment just touching, then pressing, then he slashed, knowing in that instant of cutting that he did not want to; that if he had, he would have cut an artery instead of the veins where now the blood was warm and fast, going down his forearm, and when it reached the inside of his elbow he said:

'Fisher.'

But there was no answer, so he threw off the blanket and stood up, this time yelling it:

'Fisher!'

Fisher came to the door and looked through the bars and Gale showed him the wrist; he said sonofabitch and was gone, coming back with the keys and opening the door, pulling Gale out into the passageway and grabbing the wrist and tying a handkerchief around it, muttering.

'You crazy bastard. What are you? Crazy?'

Then he ran to the phone and dialed the dispensary, watching Gale, and when he hung up he said:

'Lie on your back. I oughta treat you for shock.'

Gale lay on the deck and Fisher turned a waste basket on its side and rolled it under his legs, then threw a blanket over him.

'Son of a bitch!' he said. 'They'll hang me. How'd you get that Goddamn razor?'

# 6

The doctor was tall, with short gray hair and a thin gray moustache. He was a commander, so at least there was that much, at least they didn't send a lieutenant. The doctor filled his cup at the percolator, then faced Gale and looked at him, then came closer until Gale could smell the coffee.

'You didn't do a very good job, did you, son?'

'No, sir.'

'Do you ever do a good job at anything?'

'No, sir.'

The doctor's eyes softened and he raised his cup to his lips, watching Gale over its rim, then he lowered the cup and swallowed and wiped his mouth with the back of his hand.

'You go on and sleep now,' he said, 'without any more silly ideas. I'll see you tomorrow and we'll talk about it.'

'Yes, sir.'

Gale stepped into the passageway where the chaser was waiting and they marched down the long portside passageway, empty and darkened save for small red lights, Gale staring ahead, conscious of the bandage on his wrist as though it were an emblem of his uncertainty and his inability to change his life. He knew only that he faced a year of waiting for letters that would rarely come, three months of that in the brig where he would lie awake and wonder who shared her bed and, once released from the brig, he would have to return to Betty or find another girl so he would not have to think of Dana every night (although, resolving to do this, he already knew it would be in vain); and that, when he finally returned to the States, his life would be little more than a series of efforts to avoid being deceived and finally, perhaps years later, she would—with one last pitiless glare—leave him forever. All this stretched before him, as immutable as the long passageway where he marched now, the chaser in step behind him, yet he not only accepted it, but chose it. He figured that it was at least better than nothing.

# THE DOCTOR

1

In late March, the snow began to melt. First it ran off the slopes and roads, and the brooks started flowing. Finally there were only low, shaded patches in the woods. In April, there were four days of warm sun, and on the first day Art Castagnetto told Maxine she could put away his pajamas until next year. That night he slept in a T-shirt, and next morning, when he noticed the pots on the radiators were dry, he left them empty.

Maxine didn't believe in the first day, or the second, either. But on the third afternoon, wearing shorts and a sweatshirt, she got the charcoal grill from the garage, put it in the backyard, and broiled steaks. She even told Art to get some tonic and limes for the gin. It was a Saturday afternoon; they sat outside in canvas lawn chairs and told Tina, their four-year-old girl, that it was all right to watch the charcoal but she mustn't touch it, because it was burning even if it didn't look like it. When the steaks were ready, the sun was behind the woods in back of the house; Maxine brought sweaters to Art and the four children so they could eat outside.

Monday it snowed. The snow was damp at first, melting on the dead grass, but the flakes got heavier and fell as slowly as tiny leaves and covered the ground. In another two days the snow melted, and each gray, cool day was warmer than the one before. Saturday afternoon the sky started clearing; there was a sunset, and before going to bed Art went outside and looked up at the stars. In the morning, he woke to a bedroom of sunlight. He left Maxine sleeping, put on a T-shirt, trunks, and running shoes, and carrying his sweat suit he went downstairs, tiptoeing because the children slept so lightly on weekends. He dropped his sweat suit into the basket for dirty clothes; he was finished with it until next fall.

He did side-straddle hops on the front lawn and then ran on the shoulder of the road, which for the first half mile was bordered by woods, so that he breathed the scent of pines and, he believed, the sunlight in the air. Then he passed the Whitfords' house. He had never seen the man and woman but had read their name on the mailbox and connected it with the children who usually played in the road in front of the small graying house set back in the trees. Its dirt yard was just large enough to contain it and a rusting Ford and an elm tree with a tire-and-rope swing hanging from one of its branches. The house now was still and dark, as though asleep. He went around the bend and, looking ahead, saw three of the Whitford boys standing by the brook.

It was a shallow brook, which had its prettiest days in winter when it was frozen; in the first weeks of spring, it ran clearly, but after that it became stagnant and around July it dried. This brook was a landmark he used when he directed friends to his house. 'You get to a brook with a stone bridge,' he'd say. The bridge wasn't really stone; its guard walls were made of rectangular concrete slabs, stacked about three feet high, but he liked stone fences and stone bridges and he called it one. On a slope above the brook, there was a red house. A young childless couple lived there, and now the man, who sold life insurance in Boston, was driving off with a boat and trailer hitched to his car. His wife waved goodbye from the driveway, and the Whitford boys stopped throwing rocks into the brook long enough to wave too. They heard Art's feet on the blacktop and turned to watch him. When he reached the bridge, one of them said, 'Hi, Doctor,' and Art smiled and said 'Hello' to them as he passed. Crossing the bridge, he looked down at the brook. It was moving, slow and shallow, into the dark shade of the woods.

About a mile past the brook, there were several houses, with short stretches of woods between them. At the first house, a family was sitting at a picnic table in the side yard, reading the Sunday paper. They did not hear him, and he felt like a spy as he passed. The next family, about a hundred yards up the road, was working. Two little girls were picking up trash, and the man and woman were digging a flower bed. The parents turned and waved, and the man called, 'It's a good day for it!' At the next house, a young couple were washing their Volkswagen, the girl using the hose, the man scrubbing away the dirt of winter. They looked up and waved. By now Art's T-shirt was damp and cool, and he had his second wind.

All up the road it was like that: people cleaning their lawns, washing cars, some just sitting under the bright sky; one large bald man lifted a beer can and grinned. In front of one house, two teenage boys were throwing a Frisbee; farther up the road, a man was gently pitching a softball to his small son, who wore a baseball cap and choked up high on the bat. A boy and girl passed Art in a polished green M.G., the top down, the girl's unscarfed hair blowing across her cheek as she leaned over and quickly kissed the boy's ear. All the lawn people waved at Art, though none of them knew him; they only knew he was the obstetrician who lived in the big house in the woods. When he turned and jogged back down the road, they waved or spoke again; this time they were not as spontaneous but more casual, more familiar. He rounded a curve a quarter of a mile from the brook; the woman was back in her house and the Whitford boys were gone too. On this length of road he was alone, and ahead of him squirrels and chipmunks fled into the woods.

Then something was wrong—he felt it before he knew it. When the two boys ran up from the brook into his vision, he started sprinting and had a grateful instant when he felt the strength left in his legs, though still he didn't know if there was any reason for strength and speed. He pounded over the blacktop as the boys scrambled up the lawn, toward the red house, and as he reached the bridge he shouted.

They didn't stop until he shouted again, and now they turned, their faces pale and open-mouthed, and pointed at the brook and then ran back toward it. Art pivoted off the road, leaning backward as he descended the short rocky bank, around the end of the bridge, seeing first the white rectangle of concrete lying in the slow water. And again he felt before he knew: he was in the water to his knees, bent over the slab and getting his fingers into the sand beneath it before he looked down at the face and shoulders and chest. Then he saw the arms, too, thrashing under water as though digging out of caved-in snow. The boy's pale hands did not quite reach the surface.

In perhaps five seconds, Art realized he could not lift the slab. Then he was running up the lawn to the red house, up the steps and shoving open the side door and yelling as he bumped into the kitchen table, pointing one hand at the phone on the wall and the other at the woman in a bright yellow halter as she backed away, her arms raised before her face.

'Fire Department! A boy's drowning!' pointing behind him now, toward the brook.

She was fast; her face changed fears and she moved toward the phone, and that was enough. He was outside again, sprinting out of a stumble as he left the steps, darting between the two boys, who stood mute at the brook's edge. He refused to believe it was this simple and this impossible. He thrust his hands under the slab, lifting with legs and arms, and now he heard one of the boys moaning behind him, 'It fell on Terry, it fell on Terry.' Squatting in the water, he held a hand over the Whitford boy's mouth and pinched his nostrils together; then he groaned, for now his own hand was killing the child. He took his hand away. The boy's arms had stopped moving—they seemed to be resting at his sides—and Art reached down and felt the right one and then jerked his own hand out of the water. The small arm was hard and tight and quivering. Art touched the left one, running his hand the length of it, and felt the boy's fingers against the slab, pushing.

The sky changed, was shattered by a smoke-gray sound of winter nights—the fire horn—and in the quiet that followed he heard a woman's voice, speaking to children. He turned and looked at her standing beside him in the water, and he suddenly wanted to be held, his breast against hers, but her eyes shrieked at him to do something, and he bent over and tried again to lift the slab. Then she was beside him, and they kept trying until ten minutes later, when four volunteer firemen descended out of the dying groan of the siren and splashed into the brook.


No one knew why the slab had fallen. Throughout the afternoon, whenever Art tried to understand it, he felt his brain go taut and he tried to stop but couldn't. After three drinks, he thought of the slab as he always thought of cancer: that it had the volition of a killer. And he spoke of it like that until Maxine said, 'There was nothing you could do. It took five men and a woman to lift it.'

They were sitting in the backyard, their lawn chairs touching, and Maxine was holding his hand. The children were playing in front of the house, because Maxine had told them what happened, told them Daddy had been through the worst day of his life, and they must leave him alone for a while. She kept his glass filled with gin and tonic and once, when Tina started screaming in the front yard, he jumped out of the chair, but she grabbed his wrist and held it tightly and said, 'It's nothing, I'll take care of it.' She went around the house, and soon Tina stopped crying, and Maxine came back and said she'd fallen down in the driveway and skinned her elbow. Art was trembling.

'Shouldn't you get some sedatives?' she said.

He shook his head, then started to cry.

Monday morning an answer—or at least a possibility—was waiting for him, as though it had actually chosen to enter his mind now, with the buzzing of the alarm clock. He got up quickly and stood in a shaft of sunlight on the floor. Maxine had rolled away from the clock and was still asleep.

He put on trousers and moccasins and went downstairs and then outside and down the road toward the brook. He wanted to run but he kept walking. Before reaching the Whitfords' house, he crossed to the opposite side of the road. Back in the trees, their house was shadowed and quiet. He walked all the way to the bridge before he stopped and looked up at the red house. Then he saw it, and he didn't know (and would never know) whether he had seen it yesterday, too, as he ran to the door or if he just thought he had seen it. But it was there: a bright green garden hose, coiled in the sunlight beside the house.

He walked home. He went to the side yard where his own hose had lain all winter, screwed to the faucet. He stood looking at it, and then he went inside and quietly climbed the stairs, into the sounds of breathing, and got his pocketknife. Now he moved faster, down the stairs and outside, and he picked up the nozzle end of the hose and cut it off. Farther down, he cut the hose again. He put his knife away and then stuck one end of the short piece of hose into his mouth, pressed his nostrils between two fingers, and breathed.

He looked up through a bare maple tree at the sky. Then he walked around the house to the Buick and opened the trunk. His fingers were trembling as he lowered the piece of hose and placed it beside his first-aid kit, in front of a bucket of sand and a small snow shovel he had carried all through the winter.

# IN MY LIFE

I HAD MY HAIR in curlers all afternoon the day they electrocuted Sonny Broussard. Or the day before, I guess, because they did it at midnight. That seems in a way a strange time to do it, but when you think about it, it starts to make sense. Better for it to happen at night. At least I think I wouldn't want it first thing in the morning, staying awake all night, then dawn, then sunrise through the cell window and it waiting for me; I think I'd rather wait all day and see the sun set and the dark come and know now in the night I was going. But maybe that's only because I work nights and don't like mornings. His real name was Willard, he was big, and sometimes I still remember his weight on top of me and his smell of booze and nigger.

'I bet you liked it,' Charlie said once. 'I bet you twitched a little.'

'Shit. I was dry as a cracker. I just lay there and watched him with my legs like this and I was saying to myself *Dear Jesus* because I thought when he finished he'd cut my throat and that's why I wouldn't even shut my eyes.'

'Didn't he say nothing, all that time?'

'*There*. He said *There* when he finished. He said it twice. When he was leaving he stumbled, he was still pulling up his pants, and he knocked over the lamp—there used to be one over there on the dresser, a little lamp I had—and it broke and he started running. That's when I stopped being so scared and I wanted to kill him and I called the sheriff.'

Charlie is married. It seems after you get to be twenty-five there's nothing around but married men. I was married when I was eighteen, we had to, but I miscarried, and inside of two years I couldn't stand the sight of him. His name was Brumby, and I came to hate that name, and I would pronounce it hating. I'd say, 'Okay, *Brumby.*' One morning I woke up and he was gone. I went in the kitchen and there was a note on the table, with the salt shaker resting on it. I was grinning when I picked it up. It said: *I'm sorry, I'll send money. Brumby.* I laughed, I was so glad he finally took it on himself to leave. But while I was laughing there was a little frost in my insides, listening to the quiet in the house. Then I turned on the radio and put water on for coffee. While it was dripping I took a shower, humming. I went naked to the kitchen, it was summer and already the morning getting hot; a mama blue jay was making a racket in the fig tree. I got a cup of coffee and a cigarette and turned up the radio so I could hear it in the bathroom and went back and made up my face. The radio was playing hillbilly. I took a long time with my face, I felt good and free, and I prayed: *Thank you sweet Jesus, don't let him change his mind.* He left me the car. That afternoon I went to town and bought a yellow dress at Penney's; when I got home I put it on and drove up the little white shell road through the pines to the highway. The Bons Temps was a mile down the highway and I went there and asked them if they needed a cocktail waitress and Mr. Breaux hired me because I'm pretty. Brumby sent me a money order for fifty dollars and asked if I was going to divorce him, and when I got around to it, I did.

The only time I ever missed him was around dusk and I knew it wasn't really him I missed. The sun would go down and I'd have the lights but it wasn't the same. But I was lucky: I'd be fixing supper about that time and getting dressed and made up for work. I'm glad I don't work in the day, especially in winter when it gets dark early. If I worked in the daytime I'd leave a light on when I left in the morning so it'd be there

to come home to. We have Blue Law in our parish, so sometimes on Sunday afternoons I go see my sister and her husband in Opelousas or go to a movie and I always turn some
lights on first, the overhead light in the kitchen and the floor
lamp in the living room. On a good sunny day I can't even tell
they're on, the sun comes in so bright in those rooms.

They took a long time getting around to killing Sonny,
almost sixteen months after he walked in the front door (I
keep them locked now and I have a dog that barks at niggers
walking past on the road and a pistol that I at least know how
it works) and did what he pleased and stumbled out drunk.
So I had a lot of time to get over him; or it. Everybody at the
Bons Temps was nice to me while it was still in the papers.
Then I had my period. Then Earl came along: he was married,
he was a postman, and on Friday and Saturday nights he
played electric guitar in the hillbilly band at the Bons Temps.
I'd say Earl saved me in a way. I still felt different, like I had
sores or something, and I thought Sonny Broussard being a
nigger would keep a man away; but then one Saturday night
Earl came home for a cup of coffee with me and everything
was all right. I woke up wondering if he still felt the same in
the morning. He couldn't get out on week nights, so I didn't
see him till Friday and as soon as he grinned I knew it was
okay. So it was every Friday and Saturday nights for a couple
of months, and I'd watch him get up and dress fast in the cold.
In the morning I'd wake up late and lie there smoking and
looking out at the frost on the grass that was left, and the
brown earth, and beyond that the pines in the sun. Or some
mornings it was doing that slow cold rain and I didn't want to
get up and light the heaters, it was so cold, and I'd stay in bed
a long time till I felt like the quiet was going to explode; then
I'd get up and soon the bacon was sizzling and smelling. Then
his wife found out and she even wrote me a letter calling me a
hateful woman for carrying on with her man; the letter came
to the Bons Temps and I read it thinking, *Her man? Why it
wasn't even him, it was just a couple of times a week, about four
hours all told.* But that was the end of it with Earl; his wife

was waiting up for him. But I was all right then, Earl had taken care of me.

There was Vern between Earl and Charlie, while Sonny Broussard was waiting, and most of the time I didn't think about him; but sometimes I did and I wished it had come out at the trial that he had done other things too, robbery or maybe an old knifing, but he hadn't. It was just that one thing with me and I had called the sheriff, I had wanted him dead when he knocked over the lamp and ran; I wanted him dead when the sheriff and a deputy came, then went up the shell road way back up in the pines where some nigger shacks were; I wanted him dead when they caught him that same afternoon in Port Arthur, Texas; and I wanted him dead when I saw him in the courthouse. But when they said they would do it I felt funny, sort of like surprised, and scared too. Then, like I say, there was Earl and he didn't mind; and the trucker Vern that came home on a Friday night and stayed with me all day till time for work Saturday, then he was on the road again; I haven't seen him since but some day I hope to. Charlie is good to me, though. He's a big rough man and it doesn't matter if his wife waits up for him or not, he'll tell her it's none of her business where he's been. Once he stayed until the sun was coming up, and there were shadows from the pines.

They killed Sonny Broussard on a Thursday in March. In late afternoon I took my curlers out real slow, then the sun was going and I turned on the lights and put the rice on and played the radio; while I was brushing my hair I tried to picture him in the prison, they probably had every corner lighted up, and I wondered was he eating supper. I don't care about niggers one way or the other. I hated his smell and his black and his booze breath and him in me, I hated his panting and grunting over my face, and his big hands pressing mine back on the pillow. I'd never go with one on purpose. His lawyer wasn't much older than me, already getting sloppy fat and with a crewcut. He asked if I put up a fight; I said not much, I was scared he'd kill me. That was all he asked me about that.

He mostly tried to show Sonny Broussard had a clean record and that night he was dead drunk.

Brushing my hair at the bathroom mirror I thought myself pretty and I wondered how long I'd be pretty, so many days and nights go by, and I forget where they go, and I wonder if it's like that to get old, if the time will come when I dye it black over the gray and if I won't be able to remember that Vern's last name was Mackey and that I knew him between Earl and Charlie in the winter of nineteen fifty-six. Then I thought about Sonny Broussard standing there when I woke up with my heart pounding and he dropped his pants and pulled back the sheet and spread my legs like parting canes in a canebrake and I was so dry but still he done it fast, maybe a couple of minutes like Charlie is first time around, then him saying *There. There.*

I thought maybe I could tell Charlie. But for a long time he wasn't at the Bons Temps that night; even for a Thursday there wasn't much of a crowd, not even enough people to change the air, so at eleven o'clock I could still smell the dance wax. I kept looking at the door and the clock. About eleven o'clock I got nervous and it got worse, I always had a cigarette going in my ashtray at the bar. Then about eleven thirty-five I was serving a table of four, my tray was wet and the quarters and nickels sticking, but still this fellow was prying up every one of them until his pressing on the tray made it hard to hold. When he had the last nickel, Charlie behind me said: 'Jill.'

I spun around and almost grabbed him. He was bigger in his mackinaw, a big broad face with thick reddish hair.

'I thought you wouldn't come.'

'Hell yeah,' he said. He was grinning.

Then for a while I talked to Charlie at the bar and waited table; I was still nervous but happy too because he'd be with me that night. I looked at the clock at five minutes to twelve while I was waiting for Curtis to mix a Vodka Collins and open three beers. Then I brought them to the table. The juke box had stopped so I took my quarter tip and punched three

Hank Williams songs. It said one minute, and Hank was singing. I looked at the maybe twenty faces scattered about at the tables, there were some men together but mostly couples, older than me, and I watched their cigarettes and their hands and faces. I thought *Sweet Jesus.* I thought *I have felt his body and now they are going to burn it.* Then I thought *No.* Then I said it out loud, 'No,' and it was midnight.

We got home at one-fifteen and went into the kitchen that was lighted up. This time I didn't put on coffee, I said I'd drink with him a little, and I took from the cupboard the bourbon he kept there for his time with me. He was being careful, he wasn't sure how to treat me, he hadn't known tonight was the night until I went fast from the dance floor and stood beside him sitting so big on the bar stool and I put my face on his arm and said, 'He's dead, Charlie.' So now he made us some drinks, we had one in the kitchen, the next one in bed, naked under the covers, but I still wasn't sure I wanted to do anything. We were on our sides, looking at one another, propped on our elbows so we could drink.

'It was just a couple of minutes,' I said. 'That he was in me.'

'Yes.'

He was watching me, and I thought for a second how good it was that he was relaxed, not like Earl, he never hurried to leave.

'If they shot him that morning,' I said. 'Or if you'd known me then and you'd dragged him out of his shack and beat him up.'

'I would've.'

'Do you want another drink?'

'Nope.'

'Could we just lay here a while?'

'Sure.'

He put our glasses on the bedside table and lay on his back with one arm out for me and I got my head on it and lay half on my side so all of me was snug against him.

'Can you wait a while?' I said.

'There's other nights coming.'

'I've had eleven,' I said. 'I don't count him.'

'You're off to a good start.'

'One knocked me up and he was a slob,' I said.

Pretty soon I fell asleep. A long time later he woke me up and I said yes I wanted to. Over his shoulder there was pale light at the window.

# IF THEY KNEW YVONNE

*to Andre and Jeb*

## 1

I GREW UP IN LOUISIANA, and for twelve years I went to a boys' school taught by Christian Brothers, a Catholic religious order. In the eighth grade our teacher was Brother Thomas. I still have a picture he gave to each boy in the class at the end of that year; it's a picture of Thomas Aquinas, two angels, and a woman. In the left foreground Aquinas is seated, leaning back against one angel whose hands grip his shoulders; he looks very much like a tired boxer between rounds, and his upturned face looks imploringly at the angel. The second angel is kneeling at his feet and, with both hands, is tightening a sash around Aquinas's waist. In the left background of the picture, the woman is escaping up a flight of stone stairs; her face is turned backward for a final look before she bolts from the room. According to Brother Thomas, some of Aquinas's family were against his becoming a priest, so they sent a woman to his room. He drove her out, then angels descended, encircled his waist with a cord, and squeezed all concupiscence from his body so he would never be tempted again. On the back of the picture, under the title *Angelic Warfare*, is a prayer for purity.

Brother Thomas was the first teacher who named for us the sins included in the Sixth and Ninth Commandments, which, in the Catholic recording of the Decalogue, forbid adultery and coveting your neighbor's wife. In an introductory way, he simply listed the various sins. Then he focused on what apparently was the most significant: he called it self-abuse and, quickly sweeping our faces, he saw that we understood. It was a mortal sin, he said, because first of all it wasted the precious seed which God had given us for marriage. Also, sexual pleasure was reserved for married people alone, to have children by performing the marriage act. Self-abuse was not even a natural act; it was unnatural, and if a boy did it he was no better than a monkey. It was a desecration of our bodies, which were temples of the Holy Ghost, a mortal sin that resulted in the loss of sanctifying grace and therefore could send us to hell. He walked a few paces from his desk, his legs hidden by the long black robe, then he went back and stood behind the desk again and pulled down on his white collar: the front of it hung straight down from his throat like two white and faceless playing cards.

'Avoid being alone,' he said. 'When you go home from school, don't just sit around the house—go out and play ball, or cut the grass, or wash your dad's car. Do *anything*, but use up your energy. And pray to the Blessed Mother: take your rosary to bed at night and say it while you're going to sleep. If you fall asleep before you finish, the Blessed Mother won't mind—that's what she *wants* you to do.'

Then he urged us to receive the Holy Eucharist often. He told us of the benefits gained through the Eucharist: sanctifying grace, which helped us fight temptation; release from the temporal punishment of purgatory; and therefore, until we committed another mortal or venial sin, a guarantee of immediate entrance into heaven. He hoped and prayed, he said, that he would die with the Holy Eucharist on his tongue.

He had been talking with the excited voice yet wandering eyes of a man repeating by rote what he truly believes. But now his eyes focused on something out the window, as though a new truth had actually appeared to him on the dusty school ground of that hot spring day. One hand rose to scratch his jaw.

'In a way,' he said softly, 'you'd actually be doing someone a favor if you killed him when he had just received the Eucharist.'

I made it until midsummer, about two weeks short of my fourteenth birthday. I actually believed I would make it forever. Then one hot summer night when my parents were out playing bridge, Janet was on a date, and I was alone in the house, looking at *Holiday* magazine—girls in advertisements drinking rum or lighting cigarettes, girls in bulky sweaters at ski resorts, girls at beaches, girls on horseback—I went to the bathroom, telling myself I was only going to piss, lingering there, thinking it was pain I felt but then I knew it wasn't, that for the first wakeful time in my life it was about to happen, then it did, and I stood weak and trembling and, shutting my eyes, saw the faces of the Virgin Mary and Christ and Brother Thomas, then above them, descending to join them, the awful diaphanous bulk of God.

That was a Tuesday. I set the alarm clock and woke next morning at six-thirty, feeling that everyone on earth and in heaven had watched my sin, and had been watching me as I slept. I dressed quickly and crept past Janet's bedroom; she slept on her side, one sun-dark arm on top of the sheet; then past the closed door of my parents' room and out of the house. Riding my bicycle down the driveway I thought of being struck by a car, so I rode on the sidewalk to church and I got there in time for confession before Mass. When I got home Janet was sitting on the front steps, drinking orange juice. I rode across the lawn and stopped in front of her and looked at her smooth brown legs.

'Where'd you go?'

'To Mass.'

'Special day today?'

'I woke up,' I said. 'So I went.'

A fly buzzed at my ear and I remembered Brother Thomas quoting some saint who had said if you couldn't stand an insect buzzing at your ear while you were trying to sleep, how could you stand the eternal punishment of hell?

'You set the alarm,' she said. 'I heard it.'

Then Mother called us in to breakfast. She asked where I had been, then said: 'Well, that's nice. Maybe you'll be a priest.'

'Ha,' Daddy said.

'Don't worry, Daddy,' Janet said. 'We don't hate Episcopalians anymore.'

I got through two more days, until Friday, then Saturday afternoon I had to go to confession again. Through the veil over the latticed window Father Broussard told me to pray often to the Virgin Mary, to avoid those people and places and things that were occasions of sin, to go to confession and receive Communion at least once a week. The tone of his whispering voice was kind, and the confessional itself was constructed to offer some comfort, for it enclosed me with my secret, and its interior was dark as my soul was, and Christ crucified stared back at me, inches from my face. Father Broussard told me to say ten Our Fathers and ten Hail Marys for my penance. I said them kneeling in a pew at the rear, then I went outside and walked around the church to the cemetery. In hot sun I moved among old graves and took out my rosary and began to pray.

Sunday we went to eleven o'clock Mass. Janet and I received Communion, but Mother had eaten toast and coffee, breaking her fast, so she didn't receive. Most Sundays she broke her fast because we went to late Mass, and in those days you had to fast from midnight until you received Communion; around ten in the morning she would feel faint and have to eat something. After Mass, Janet started the car and lit a cigarette and waited for our line in the parking lot to move. I envied her nerve. She was only sixteen, but when she started smoking my parents couldn't stop her.

'I just can't keep the fast,' Mother said. 'I must need vitamins.'

She was sitting in the front seat, opening and closing her black fan.

'Maybe you do,' Janet said.

'Maybe so. If you have to smoke, I wish you'd do it at home.'

Janet smiled and drove in first gear out of the parking lot. Her window was down and on the way home I watched her dark hair blowing in the breeze.

That was how my fourteenth summer passed: baseball in the mornings, and friends and movies and some days of peace, of hope—then back to the confessional where the smell of sweat hung in the air like spewed-out sin. Once I saw the student body president walking down the main street; he recognized my face and told me hello, and I blushed not with timidity but shame, for he walked with a confident stride, he was strong and good while I was weak. A high school girl down the street gave me a ride one day, less than an hour after I had done it, and I sat against the door at my side and could not look at her; I answered her in a low voice and said nothing on my own and I knew she thought I was shy, but that was better than the truth, for I believed if she knew what sat next to her she would recoil in disgust. When fall came I was glad, for I hoped the school days would break the pattern of my sins. But I was also afraid the Brothers could see the summer in my eyes; then it wasn't just summer, but fall and winter too, for the pattern wasn't broken and I could not stop.

In the confessional the hardest priest was an old Dutchman who scolded and talked about manliness and will power and once told me to stick my finger in the flame of a candle, then imagine the eternal fire of hell. I didn't do it. Father Broussard was firm, sometimes impatient, but easy compared to the Dutchman. The easiest was a young Italian, Father Grassi, who said very little: I doubt if he ever spoke to me for over thirty seconds, and he gave such light penances—three or four Hail Marys—that I began to think he couldn't understand English well enough to know what I told him.

Then it was fall again, I was fifteen, and Janet was a freshman at the college in town. She was dating Bob Mitchell,

a Yankee from Michigan. He was an airman from the SAC
Base, so she had to argue with Mother for the first week or so.
He was a high school graduate, intelligent, and he planned to
go to the University of Michigan when he got out. That's what
she told Mother, who believed a man in uniform was less
trustworthy than a local civilian. One weekend in October
Mother and Daddy went to Baton Rouge to see L.S.U. play Ole
Miss. It was a night game and they were going to spend Saturday night with friends in Baton Rouge. They left after lunch
Saturday and as soon as they drove off, Janet called Bob and
broke their date, then went to bed. She had the flu, she said,
but she hadn't told them because Mother would have felt it
was her duty to stay home.

'Would you bring me a beer?' she said. 'I'll just lie in bed
and drink beer and you won't have to bother with me at all.'

I sat in the living room and listened to Bill Stern broad-
cast Notre Dame and S.M.U. I kept checking on Janet to see if
she wanted another beer; she'd smile at me over her book—
*The Idiot*—then shake her beer can and say yes. When the
game was over I told her I was going to confession and she
gave me some money for cigarettes. I had enough to be
ashamed of without people thinking I smoked too. When I
got home I told her I had forgotten.

'Would you see if Daddy left any?'

I went into their room. On the wall above the double bed
was a small black crucifix with a silver Christ (Daddy called it
a graven image, but he smiled when he said it); stuck behind
the crucifix was a blade from a palm frond, dried brown and
crisp since Palm Sunday. I opened the top drawer of Daddy's
bureau and took out the carton of Luckies. Then something
else red-and-white caught my eye: the corner of a small box
under his rolled-up socks. For a moment I didn't take it out. I
stood looking at that corner of cardboard, knowing immediately what it was and also knowing that I wasn't learning anything new, that I had known for some indefinite and secret
time, maybe a few months or a year or even two years. I stood
there in the history of my knowledge, then I put down the

cigarette carton and took the box of condoms from the drawer. I had slid the cover off the box and was looking at the vertically arranged rolled condoms when I heard the bedsprings, but it was too late, her bare feet were already crossing the floor, and all I could do was raise my eyes to her as she said: 'Can't you find—' then stopped.

At first she blushed, but only for a second or two. She came into the room, gently took the box from me, put the cover on, and looked at it for a moment. Then she put it in the drawer, covered it with socks, got a pack of cigarettes, and started back to her room.

'Why don't you bring me a beer,' she said over her shoulder. 'And we'll have a little talk.'

When I brought the beer she was propped up in bed, and *The Idiot* was closed on the bedside table.

'Are you really surprised?' she said.

I shook my head.

'Does it bother you?'

'Yes.'

'You're probably scrupulous. You confess enough for Eichmann, you know.'

I blushed and looked away.

'Do you know that some people—theologians—believe a mortal sin is as rare as a capital crime? That most things we do aren't really that evil?'

'They must not be Catholics.'

'Some of them are. Listen: Mother's only mistake is she thinks it's a sin, so she doesn't receive Communion. And I guess that's why she doesn't get a diaphragm—that would be too committed.'

This sort of talk scared me, and I was relieved when she stopped. She told me not to worry about Mother and especially not to blame Daddy, not to think of him as a Protestant who had led Mother away from the Church. She said the Church was wrong. Several times she used the word love, and that night in bed I thought: love? love? For all I could think of was semen and I remembered long ago a condom lying in the dust of a country road; a line of black ants was crawling into it. I got out of bed, turned on a lamp, and read the *Angelic Warfare* prayer, which ends like this: *O God, Who has vouchsafed to defend with the blessed cord of St. Thomas those who are engaged in the terrible conflict of chastity! grant to us Thy suppliants, by his help, happily to overcome in this warfare the terrible enemy of our body and souls, that, being crowned with the lily of perpetual purity, we may deserve to receive from Thee, amongst the chaste bands of the angels, the palm of bliss....*

Janet didn't do so well in the war. That January she and Bob Mitchell drove to Port Arthur, Texas, and got married by a justice of the peace. Then they went to Father Broussard for a Catholic marriage, but when he found out Janet was pregnant he refused. He said he didn't think this marriage would last, and he would not make it permanent in the eyes of God. My parents and I knew nothing of this until a couple of weeks later, when Bob was discharged from the Air Force. One night they told us, and two days later Janet was gone, up to Michigan; she wrote that although Bob wasn't a Catholic, he had agreed to try again, and this time a priest had married them. Seven months after the Texas wedding she had twin sons and Mother went up there on the bus and stayed two weeks and sent us postcards from Ann Arbor.

You get over your sister's troubles, even images of her getting pregnant in a parked car, just as after a while you stop worrying about whether or not your mother is living in sin. I had my own troubles and one summer afternoon when I was sixteen, alone in the house, having done it again after receiving Communion that very morning, I lay across my bed, crying and striking my head with my fist. It was a weekday, so the priests weren't hearing confessions until next morning before Mass. I could have gone to the rectory and confessed to a priest in his office, but I could not do that, I had to have the veiled window between our faces. Finally I got up and went to the phone in the hall. I dialed the rectory and when Father

Broussard answered I told him I couldn't get to church but I had to confess and I wanted to do it right now, on the phone. I barely heard the suspicious turn in his voice when he told me to come to the rectory.

'I can't,' I said.

'What about tomorrow? Could you come tomorrow before Mass, or during the day?'

'I can't, Father. I can't wait that long.'

'Who is this?'

For a moment we were both quiet. Then I said: 'That's all right.'

It was an expression we boys used, and it usually meant none of your business. I had said it in a near-whisper, not sure if I could speak another word without crying.

'All right,' he said, 'let me hear your confession.'

I kneeled on the floor, my eyes closed, the telephone cord stretched tautly to its full length:

'Bless me Father, for I have sinned; my last confession was yesterday—' now I was crying silent tears, those I hadn't spent on the bed; I could still talk but my voice was in shards '—my sins are: I committed self-abuse one time—' the word *time* trailing off, whispered into the phone and the empty hall which grew emptier still, for Father Broussard said nothing and I kneeled with eyes shut tight and the receiver hurting my hot ear until finally he said:

'All right, but I can't give you absolution over the phone. Will you come to the rectory at about three?'

'Yes, Father.'

'And ask for Father Broussard.'

'Yes, Father, thank you, Father—' still holding the receiver after he hung up, my eyes shut on black and red shame; then I stood weakly and returned to the bed—I would not go to the rectory—and lay there feeling I was the only person alive on this humid summer day. I could not stop crying, and I began striking my head again. I spoke aloud to God, begging him to forgive me, then kill me and spare me the further price of being a boy. Then something occurred to me: an image tossed up for my consideration, looked at, repudiated—all in an instant while my fist was poised. I saw myself sitting on the bed, trousers dropped to the floor, my sharp-edged hunting knife in my right hand, then with one quick determined slash cutting off that autonomous penis and casting it on the floor to shrivel and die. But before my fist struck again I threw that image away. No voices told me why. I had no warning vision of pain, of bleeding to death, of being an impotent freak. I simply knew; it is there between your legs and you do not cut it off.

## 2

Yvonne Millet finally put it to good use. We were both nineteen, both virgins; we started dating the summer after our freshman year at the college in town. She was slender, with black hair cut short in what they called an Italian Boy. She was a Catholic, and had been taught by nuns for twelve years, but she wasn't bothered as much as I was. In the parked car we soaked our clothes with sweat, and sometimes I went home with spotted trousers which I rolled into a bundle and dropped in the basket for dry cleaning. I confessed this and petting too, and tried on our dates to keep dry, so that many nights I crawled aching and nauseated into my bed at home. I lay very still in my pain, feeling quasi-victorious: I believed Yvonne and I were committing mortal sins by merely touching each other, but at least for another night we had resisted the graver sin of orgasm. On other nights she took me with her hand or we rubbed against each other in a clothed pantomime of lovemaking until we came. This happened often enough so that for the first time in nearly seven years I stopped masturbating. And Saturday after Saturday I went proudly to confession and told of my sins with Yvonne. I confessed to Father Grassi, who still didn't talk much, but one Saturday afternoon he said: 'How old are you, my friend?'

'Nineteen, Father.'

'Yes. And the young girl?'

I told him she was nineteen. Now I was worried: I had avoided confessing to Father Broussard or the Dutchman because I was afraid one of them would ask about the frequency of our sins, then tell me either to be pure or break up with her and, if I did neither of these, I could not be absolved again. I had thought Father Grassi would not ask questions.

'Do you love her?'

'Yes, Father.'

'At your age I think it is very hard to know if you really love someone. So I recommend that you and your girl think about getting married in two or three years' time and then, my friend, until you are ready for a short engagement and then marriage, I think each of you should go out with other people. Mostly with each other, of course, but with other people too. That may not help you to stay pure, but at least it will help you know if you love each other.'

'Yes, Father.'

'Because this other thing that's going on now, that's not love, you see. So you should test it in other ways.'

I told him I understood and I would talk to my girl about it. I never did, though. Once in a while Yvonne confessed but I have an idea what she told the priest, for she did not see things the way I saw them. One night, when I tried to stop us short, she pulled my hand back to its proper place and held it there until she was ready for it to leave. Then she reached to the dashboard for a cigarette, tapped it, and paused as though remembering to offer me one.

'Don't you want me to do it for you?' she said.

'No, I'm all right.'

She smoked for a while, her head on my shoulder.

'Do you really think it's a worse sin when it happens to you?' she said.

'Yes.'

'Why?'

I told her what the Brothers had taught me.

'You believe that?' she said. 'That God gave you this seed

just to have babies with, and if you waste it He'll send you to hell?'

'I guess so.'

'You have wet dreams, don't you?'

'That's different. There's no will involved.'

'What about me? It just happened to me, and I didn't use up any eggs or anything, so where's my sin?'

'I don't know. Maybe sins are different for girls.'

'Then it wouldn't be a sin for me to masturbate either. Right? I don't, but isn't that true?'

'I never thought of that.'

'Well, don't. You think too much already.'

'Maybe you don't think enough.'

'You're right: I don't.'

'I'll tell you why it's a sin,' I said. 'Because it's reserved for married people.'

'Climax?'

'Yes.'

'But you're supposed to be married to touch each other too,' she said. 'So why draw the line at climax? I mean, why get all worked up and then stop and think that's good?'

'You're right. We shouldn't do any of it.'

'Oh, I'm not sure it's as bad as all that.'

'You're not? You don't think it's a sin, what we do?'

'Maybe a little, but it's not as bad as a lot of other things.'

'It's a mortal sin.'

'I don't think so. I believe it's a sin to talk about a girl, but I don't think what you do with her is so bad.'

'All right: if that's what you think, why don't we just go all the way?'

She sat up to throw her cigarette out the window, then she nestled her face on my chest.

'Because I'm scared,' she said.

'Of getting pregnant?'

'I don't think so. I'm just scared of not being a virgin, that's all.'

Then she finished our argument, won it, soaked her small handkerchief in my casuistry. Next morning at breakfast I was tired.

'You're going to ruin your health,' Mother said. 'It was after one when you got home.'

I flexed my bicep and said I was fine. But now Daddy was watching me from his end of the table.

'I don't care about your health,' he said. 'I just hope you know more than Janet did.'

'*Honey*,' Mother said.

'She got it reversed. She started babies before she was married, then quit.'

That was true. Her twin boys were four now, and there were no other children. Bob had finished his undergraduate work and was going to start work on a Ph.D. in political science. Early in the summer Mother had gone up there and stayed two weeks. When she got back and talked about her visit she looked nervous, as though she were telling a lie, and a couple of times I walked into the kitchen where Mother and Daddy were talking and they stopped until I had got what I wanted and left.

'I won't get pregnant,' I said.

'Neither will Yvonne,' Daddy said. 'As long as you keep your pants on.'

Then finally one night in early fall we drove away from her house, where we had parked for some time, and I knew she would not stop me, because by leaving her house she was risking questions from her parents, and by accepting that she was accepting the other risk too. I drove out to a country road, over a vibrating wooden bridge, the bayou beneath us dark as earth on that moonless night, on through black trees until I found a dirt road into the woods, keeping my hand on her small breast as I turned and cut off the ignition and headlights. In a moment she was naked on the car seat, then I was out of my clothes, even the socks, and seeing her trusting face and shockingly white body I almost dressed and took her home but then she said: Love me, Harry, love me—

The Brothers hadn't prepared me for this. If my first time had been with a whore, their training probably would have worked, for that was the sort of lust they focused on. But they were no match for Yvonne, and next morning I woke happier than I had ever been. At school that day we drank coffee and held hands and whispered. That night on the way to her house I stopped at a service station and bought a package of condoms from a machine in the men's room. That was the only time I felt guilty. But I was at least perceptive enough to know why: condoms, like masturbation and whores, were something the Brothers knew about. I left that piss-smelling room, walked into the clear autumn night, and drove to Yvonne's, where they had never been.

For the rest of the fall and a few weeks of winter, we were hot and happy lovers. I marveled at my own joy, my lack of remorse. Once, after a few weeks, I asked her if she ever felt bad. It was late at night and we were sitting at a bar, eating oysters on the half-shell. For a moment she didn't know what I meant, then she smiled.

'I feel wonderful,' she said.

She dipped her last oyster in the sauce, and leaned over the tray to eat it.

'Do we have enough money for more?' she said.

'Sure.'

They were ninety cents a dozen. We watched the Negro open them, and I felt fine, eating oysters and drinking beer at one in the morning, having made love an hour ago to this pretty girl beside me. I looked at her hair and wondered if she ought to let it grow.

'Sometimes I worry though,' she said.

'Getting pregnant?'

'Nope, I never said you had to use those things. I worry about you.'

'Why me?'

'Because you used to think about sins so much, and now you don't.'

'That's because I love you.'

She licked the red sauce from her fingers, then took my hand, squeezed it, and drank some beer.

'I'm afraid someday you'll start feeling bad again, then you'll hate me.'

She was right to look for defeat in that direction, to expect me to move along clichéd routes. But, as it turned out, it wasn't guilt that finally soured us. After a couple of months I simply began noticing things.

I saw that she didn't really like football. She only enjoyed the games because they gave her a chance to dress up, and there was a band, and a crowd of students, and it was fun to keep a flask hidden while you poured bourbon into a paper cup. She cheered with the rest of us, but she wasn't cheering for the same thing. She cheered because we were there, and a young man had run very fast with a football. Once we stood up to watch an end chasing a long pass: when he dived for it, caught it, and skidded on the ground, she turned happily to me and brushed her candied apple against my sleeve. Watch out, I said. She spit on her handkerchief and rubbed the sticky wool. She loved sweets, always asked me to buy her Mounds or Hersheys at the movies, and once in a while she'd get a pimple which she tried to conceal with powder. I felt loose flesh at her waist when we danced, and walking beside her on the campus one afternoon I looked down and saw her belly pushing against her tight skirt; I lightly backhanded it and told her to suck her gut in. She stood at attention, saluted, then gave me the finger. I'm about to start my period, she said. Except for the soft flesh at her waist she was rather thin, and when she lay on her back her naked breasts spread and flattened, as though they were melting.

Around the end of November her parents spent a weekend with relatives in Houston, leaving Yvonne to take care of her sister and brother, who were fourteen and eleven. They left Saturday morning, and that night Yvonne cooked for me. She was dressed up, black cocktail dress, even heels, and she was disappointed when she saw I hadn't worn a coat. But she didn't say anything. She had already fed her brother and sister, and they were in the den at the back of the house, watching television. Yvonne had a good fire in the living room fireplace, and on the coffee table she had bourbon, a pitcher of water, a bucket of ice, and a sugar bowl.

'Like they do in Faulkner,' she said, and we sat on the couch and drank a couple of toddies before dinner. Then she left me for a while and I looked into the fire, hungry and horny, and wondered what time the brother and sister would go to bed and if Yvonne would do it while they were sleeping. She came back to the living room, smiled, blushed, and said: 'If you're brave enough, I am. Want to try it?'

We ate by candlelight: oyster cocktails, then a roast with rice and thick dark gravy, garlic-tinged. We had lemon icebox pie and went back to the fireplace with second cups of coffee.

'I love to cook,' she said from the record player. She put on about five albums, and I saw that we were supposed to sit at the fire and talk for the rest of the evening. The first album was Jackie Gleason, *Music, Martinis, and Memories,* and she sat beside me, took my hand and sipped her coffee. She rested her head on the back of the couch, but I didn't like to handle a coffee cup leaning back that way, so I withdrew my hand from hers and hunched forward over the coffee table.

'I think I started cooking when I was seven,' she said to my back. 'No, let's see, I was eight—' I looked down at her crossed legs, the black dress just covering her knees, then looked at the fire. 'When we lived in Baton Rouge. I had a children's cookbook and I made something called Chili Concoction. Everybody was nice about it, and Daddy ate two helpings for supper and told me to save the rest for breakfast and he'd eat it with eggs. He did, too. Then I made something called a strawberry minute pie, and I think it was pretty good. I'll make it for you some time.'

'Okay.'

I was still hunched over drinking coffee, so I wasn't looking at her. I finished the coffee and she asked if I wanted more, and that irritated me, so I didn't know whether to say yes or no. I said I guess so. Then watching her leave with my cup, I disliked myself and her too. For if I wasn't worthy of the evening, then wasn't she stupid and annoyingly vulnerable to give it to me? The next album was Sinatra; I finished my coffee, then leaned back so our shoulders touched, our hands together in her lap, and we listened. Once she took a drag from my cigarette and I said keep it, and lit another. The third album was Brubeck. She put some more ice in the bucket, I made toddies, and she asked if I understood *The Bear.* I shrugged and said probably not. She had finished it the day before, and she started talking about it.

'Hey,' I said. 'When are they going to sleep?'

She was surprised, and again I disliked myself and her too. Then she was hurt, and she looked at her lap and said she didn't know, but she couldn't make love anyway, not here in the house, even if they were sleeping.

'We can leave for a while,' I said. 'We won't go far.'

She kept looking at her lap, at our clasped hands.

'They'll be all right,' I said.

Then she looked into my eyes and I looked away and she said: 'Okay, I'll tell them.'

When she came back with a coat over her arm I was waiting at the door, my jacket zipped, the car key in my hand.


We broke up in January, about a week after New Year's. I don't recall whether we fought, or kissed goodbye, or sat in a car staring mutely out the windows. But I do remember when the end started; or, rather, when Yvonne decided to recognize it.

On New Year's Eve a friend of ours gave a party. His parents were out of town, so everyone got drunk. It was an opportunity you felt obliged not to pass up. Two or three girls got sick and had to have their faces washed and be walked outside in the cold air. When Yvonne got drunk it was a pleasant drunk, and I took her upstairs. I think no one noticed: it was past midnight, and people were hard to account for. We lay on the bed in the master bedroom, Yvonne with her skirt pulled up, her pants off, while I performed in shirt, sweater, and socks. She was quiet as we stood in the dark room, taking our pants off, and she didn't answer my whispered Happy New Year as we began to make love, for the first time, on a bed. Then, moving beneath me, she said in a voice so incongruous with her body that I almost softened but quickly got it back, shutting my ears to what I had heard: This is all we ever do, Harry—this is all we ever do.

The other thing I remember about that night is a time around three in the morning. A girl was cooking hamburgers, I was standing in the kitchen doorway talking to some boys, and Yvonne was sitting alone at the kitchen table. There were other people talking in the kitchen, but she wasn't listening; she moved only to tap ashes and draw on her cigarette, then exhaled into the space that held her gaze. She looked older than twenty, quite lonely and sad, and I pitied her. But there was something else: I knew she would never make love to me again. Maybe that is why, as a last form of possession, I told. It could not have been more than an hour later, I was drunker, and in the bathroom I one-upped three friends who were bragging about feeling tits of drunken girls. I told them I had taken Yvonne upstairs and screwed her. To add history to it, I even told them what she had said.

# 3

Waiting in line for my first confession in five months I felt some guilt but I wasn't at all afraid. I only had to confess sexual intercourse, and there was nothing shameful about that, nothing unnatural. It was a man's sin. Father Broussard warned me never to see this girl again (that's what he called her: this girl), for a man is weak and he needs much grace to turn away from a girl who will give him her body. He said I must understand it was a serious sin because sexual intercourse was given by God to married couples for the procreation of children and we had stolen it and used it wrongfully, for physical pleasure, which was its secondary purpose. I knew that in some way I had sinned, but Father Broussard's definition of that sin fell short and did not sound at all like what I had done with Yvonne. So when I left the confessional I still felt unforgiven.

The campus was not a very large one, but it was large enough so you could avoid seeing someone. I stopped going to the student center for coffee, and we had no classes together; we only saw each other once in a while, usually from a distance, walking between buildings. We exchanged waves and the sort of smile you cut into your face at times like that. The town was small too, so occasionally I saw her driving around, looking for a parking place or something. Then after a while I wanted to see her, and I started going to the student center again, but she didn't drink coffee there anymore. In a week or so I realized that I didn't really want to see her: I wanted her to be happy, and if I saw her there was nothing I could say to help that.

Soon I was back to the old private vice, though now it didn't seem a vice but an indulgence, not as serious as smoking or even drinking, closer to eating an ice cream sundae before bed every night. That was how I felt about it, like I had eaten two scoops of ice cream with thick hot fudge on it, and after a couple of bites it wasn't good anymore but I finished it anyway, thinking of calories. It was a boring little performance and it didn't seem worth thinking about, one way or the other. But I told it in the confessional, so I could still receive the Eucharist. Then one day in spring I told the number of my sins as though I were telling the date of my birth, my height, and weight, and Father Broussard said quickly and sternly: 'Are you sorry for these sins?'

'Yes, Father,' I said, but then I knew it was a lie. He was asking me if I had a firm resolve to avoid this sin in the future when I said: 'No, Father.'

'No what? You can't avoid it?'

'I mean no, Father, I'm not really sorry. I don't even think it's a sin.'

'Oh, I see. You don't have the discipline to stop, so you've decided it's not a sin. Just like that, you've countermanded God's law. Do you want absolution?'

'Yes, Father. I want to receive Communion.'

'You can't. You're living in mortal sin, and I cannot absolve you while you keep this attitude. I want you to think very seriously—'

But I wasn't listening. I was looking at the crucifix and waiting for his voice to stop so I could leave politely and try to figure out what to do next. Then he stopped talking, and I said: 'Yes, Father.'

'*What?*' he said. '*What?*'

I went quickly through the curtains, out of the confessional, out of the church.

On Sundays I went to Mass but did not receive the Eucharist. I thought I could but I was afraid that as soon as the Host touched my tongue I would suddenly realize I had been wrong, and then I'd be receiving Christ with mortal sin on my soul. Mother didn't receive either. I prayed for her and hoped she'd soon have peace, even if it meant early menopause. By now I agreed with Janet, and I wished she'd write Mother a letter and convince her that she wasn't evil. I thought Mother was probably praying for Janet, who had gone five years without bearing a child.

It was June, school was out, and I did not see Yvonne at all. I was working with a surveying crew, running a hundred-foot chain through my fingers, cutting trails with a machete, eating big lunches from paper bags, and waiting for something to happen. There were two alternatives, and I wasn't phony enough for the first or brave enough for the second: I could start confessing again, the way I used to, or I could ignore the confessional and simply receive Communion. But nothing happened and each Sunday I stayed with Mother in the pew while the others went up to the altar rail.

Then Janet came home. She wrote that Bob had left her, had moved in with his girlfriend—a graduate student—and she and the boys were coming home on the bus. That was the news waiting for me when I got home from work, Mother handing me the letter as I came through the front door, both of them watching me as I read it. Then Daddy cursed, Mother started crying again, and I took a beer out to the front porch. After a while Daddy came out too and we sat without talking and drank beer until Mother called us to supper. Daddy said, 'That son of a bitch,' and we went inside.

By the time Janet and the boys rode the bus home from Ann Arbor, Mother was worried about something else: the Church, because now Janet was twenty-three years old and getting a divorce and if she ever married again she was out of the Church. Unless Bob died, and Daddy said he didn't care what the Church thought about divorce, but it seemed a good enough reason for him to go up to Ann Arbor, Michigan, and shoot Bob Mitchell between the eyes. So while Janet and Paul and Lee were riding south on the Greyhound, Mother was going to daily Mass and praying for some answer to Janet's future.

But Janet had already taken care of that too. When she got off the bus I knew she'd be getting married again some day: she had gained about ten pounds, probably from all that cheap food while Bob went to school, but she had always been on the lean side anyway and now she looked better than I remembered. Her hair was long, about halfway down her back. The boys were five years old now, and I was glad she hadn't had any more, because they seemed to be good little boys and not enough to scare off a man. We took them home— it was a Friday night—and Daddy gave Janet a tall drink of bourbon and everybody talked as though nothing had happened. Then we ate shrimp *étouffée* and after supper, when the boys were in bed and the rest of us were in the living room, Janet said by God it was the best meal she had had in five

years, and next time she was going to marry a man who liked
Louisiana cooking. When she saw the quick look in Mother's
eyes, she said: 'We didn't get married in the Church, Mama.
I just told you we did so you wouldn't worry.'

'You *didn't?*'

'Bob was so mad at Father Broussard he wouldn't try
again. He's not a Catholic, you know.'

'There's more wrong with him than that,' Daddy said.

'So I can still get married in the Church,' Janet said. 'To
somebody else.'

'But Janet—'

'Wait,' Daddy said. 'Wait. You've been praying for days so
Janet could stop living with that son of a bitch and still save
her soul. Now you got it—right?'

'But—'

'Right?'

'Well,' Mother said, 'I guess so.'

They went to bed about an hour past their usual time, but
Janet and I stayed up drinking gin and tonic in the kitchen,
with the door closed so we wouldn't keep anybody awake. At
first she just talked about how glad she was to be home, even
if the first sign of it was the Negroes going to the back of the
bus. She loved this hot old sticky night, she said, and the June
bugs thumping against the screen and she had forgotten how
cigarettes get soft down here in the humid air. Finally she
talked about Bob; she didn't think he had ever loved her, he
had started playing around their first year up there, and it had
gone on for five years more or less; near the end she had even
done it too, had a boyfriend, but it didn't help her survive at
all, it only made things worse, and now at least she felt clean
and tough and she thought that was the first step toward hope.

The stupid thing was she still loved the philandering son
of a bitch. That was the only time she cried, when she said
that, but she didn't even cry long enough for me to get up and
go to her side of the table and hold her: when I was half out of
my chair she was already waving me back in it, shaking her
head and wiping her eyes, and the tears that had filled them

for a moment were gone. Then she cheered up and asked if I'd drive her around tomorrow, down the main street and everything, and I said sure and asked her if she was still a Catholic.

'Don't tell Mother this,' she said. 'She's confused enough already. I went to Communion every Sunday, except when I was having that stupid affair, and I only felt sinful then because he loved me and I was using him. But before that and after that, I received.'

'You can't,' I said. 'Not while you're married out of the Church.'

'Maybe I'm wrong, but I don't think the Church is so smart about sex. Bob wouldn't get the marriage blessed, so a priest would have told me to leave him. I loved him, though, and for a long time I thought he loved me, needed me—so I stayed with him and tried to keep peace and bring up my sons. And the Eucharist is the sacrament of love and I needed it very badly those five years and nobody can keep me away.'

I got up and took our glasses and made drinks. When I turned from the sink she was watching me.

'Do you still go to confession so much?' she said.

I sat down, avoiding her eyes, then I thought, what the hell, if you can't tell Janet you can't tell anybody. So looking at the screen door and the bugs thumping from the dark outside, I told her how it was in high school and about Yvonne, though I didn't tell her name, and my aborted confession to Father Broussard. She was kind to me, busying herself with cigarettes and her drink while I talked. Then she said: 'You're right, Harry. You're absolutely right.'

'You really think so?'

'I know this much: too many of those celibates teach sex the way it is for them. They make it introverted, so you come out of their schools believing sex is something between you and yourself, or between you and God. Instead of between you and other people. Like my affair. It wasn't wrong because I was married. Hell, Bob didn't care, in fact he was glad because it gave him more freedom. It was wrong because I hurt the guy.' A Yankee word on her tongue, *guy*, and she said it with that accent from up there among snow and lakes. 'If Bob had stayed home and taken a *Playboy* to the bathroom once in a while I might still have a husband. So if that's a sin, I don't understand sin.'

'Well,' I said. Then looking at her, I grinned and it kept spreading and turned into a laugh. 'You're something, all right,' I said. 'Old Janet, you're something.'

But I still wasn't the renegade Janet was, I wanted absolution from a priest, and next morning while Mother and Daddy were happily teasing us about our hangovers, I decided to get it done. That afternoon I called Father Grassi, then told Janet where I was going, and that I would drive her around town when I got back. Father Grassi answered the door at the rectory; he was wearing a white shirt with his black trousers, a small man with a ruddy face and dark whiskers. I asked if I could speak to him in his office.

'I think so,' he said. 'Do you come from the Pope?'

'No, Father. I just want to confess.'

'So it's you who will be the saint today, not me. Yes, come in.'

He led me to his office, put his stole around his neck, and sat in the swivel chair behind his desk; I knelt beside him on the carpet, and he shielded his face with his hand, as though we were in the confessional and he could not see me. I whispered, 'Bless me Father, for I have sinned,' my hands clasped at my waist, my head bowed. 'My last confession was six weeks ago, but I was refused absolution. By Father Broussard.'

'Is that so? You don't look like a very bad young man to me. Are you some kind of criminal?'

'I confessed masturbation, Father.'

'Yes? Then what?'

'I told him I didn't think it was a sin.'

'I see. Well, poor Father Broussard: I'd be confused too, if you confessed something as a sin and then said you didn't think it was a sin. You should take better care of your priests, my friend.'

I opened my eyes: his hand was still in place on his cheek, and he was looking straight ahead, over his desk at the bookshelf against the wall.

'I guess so,' I said. 'And now I'm bothering you.'

'Oh no: you're no trouble. The only disappointment is you weren't sent by the Pope. But since that's the way it is, then we may just as well talk about sins. We had in the seminary a book of moral theology and in that book, my friend, it was written that masturbation was worse than rape, because at least rape was the carrying out of a natural instinct. What about that?'

'Do you believe that, Father?'

'Do you?'

'No, Father.'

'Neither do I. I burned the book when I left the seminary, but not only for that reason. The book also said, among other things, let the buyer beware. So you tell me about sin and we'll educate each other.'

'I went to the Brothers' school.'

'Ah, yes. Nice fellows, those Brothers.'

'Yes, Father. But I think they concentrated too much on the body. One's own body, I mean. And back then I believed it all, and one day I even wanted to mutilate myself. Then last fall I had a girl.'

'What does that mean, you had a girl? You mean you were lovers?'

'Yes, Father. But I shouldn't have had a girl, because I believed my semen was the most important part of sex, so the first time I made love with her I was waiting for it, like my soul was listening for it—you see? Because I wouldn't know how I felt about her until I knew how I felt about ejaculating with her.'

'And how did you feel? Did you want to mutilate yourself with a can opener, or maybe something worse?'

'I was happy, Father.'

'Yes.'

'So after that we were lovers. Or she was, but I wasn't. I was just happy because I could ejaculate without hating myself, so I was still masturbating, you see, but with her—does that make sense?'

'Oh yes, my friend. I've known that since I left the seminary. Always there is too much talk of self-abuse. You see, even the term is a bad one. Have you finished your confession?'

'I want to confess about the girl again, because when I confessed it before it wasn't right. I made love to her without loving her and the last time I made love to her I told some boys about it.'

'Yes. Anything else?'

'No, Father.'

'Good. There is a line in St. John that I like very much. It is Christ praying to the Father and He says: "I do not pray that You take them out of the world, but that You keep them from evil.' Do you understand that?"

'I think so, Father.'

'Then for your penance, say alleluia three times.'


Next afternoon Janet and I took her boys crabbing. We had an ice chest of beer and we set it under the small pavilion at the center of the wharf, then I put out six crab lines, tying them to the guard rail. I remembered the summer before she got married Janet and I had gone crabbing, then cooked them for the family: we had a large pot of water on the stove and when the water was boiling I held the gunny sack of live crabs over it and they came falling out, splashing into the water; they worked their claws, moved sluggishly, then died. And Janet had said: *I keep waiting for them to scream.*

It was a hot day, up in the nineties. Someone was water-skiing on the lake, which was saltwater and connected by canal to the Gulf, but we had the wharf to ourselves, and we drank beer in the shade while Paul and Lee did the crabbing. They lost the first couple, so I left the pavilion and squatted at the next line. The boys flanked me, lying on their bellies and looking down where the line went into the dark water; they had their shirts off, and their hot tan shoulders and arms brushed my legs. I gently pulled the line up until we saw a crab just below the surface, swimming and nibbling at the chunk of ham.

'Okay, Lee. Put the net down in the water, then bring it up under him so you don't knock him away.'

He lowered the pole and scooped the net slowly under the crab.

'I got him!'

'That's it. You just have to go slow, that's all.'

He stood and lifted the net and laid it on the wharf.

'Look how big,' Paul said.

'He's a good one,' I said. 'Put him in the sack.'

But they crouched over the net, watching the crab push his claws through.

'Poor little crab,' Lee said. 'You're going to die.'

'Does it hurt 'em, Harry?' Paul said.

'I don't know.'

'It'd hurt me,' he said.

'I guess it does, for a second or two.'

'How long's a second?' Lee said.

I pinched his arm.

'About like that.'

'That's not too long,' he said.

'No. Put him in the sack now, and catch some more.'

I went back to my beer on the bench. Paul was still crouching over the crab, poking a finger at its back. Then Lee held open the gunny sack and Paul turned the net over and shook it and the crab fell in.

'Goodbye, big crab,' he said.

'Goodbye, poor crab,' Lee said.

They went to another line. For a couple of hours, talking to Janet, I watched them and listened to their bare feet on the wharf and their voices as they told each crab goodbye. Sometimes one of them would stop and look across the water and pull at his pecker, and I remembered that day hot as this one when I was sixteen and I wanted to cut mine off. I reached deep under the ice and got a cold beer for Janet and I thought of Yvonne sitting at that kitchen table at three in the morning, tired, her lipstick worn off, her eyes fixed on a space between the people in the room. Then I looked at the boys lying on their bellies and reaching down for another crab, and I hoped they would grow well, those strong little bodies, those kind hearts.

# GOING UNDER

*to Holly*

Miranda is wearing purple and waiting in the open doorway, behind her are the yellow walls of the living room and the orange couch where they have loved, her hair is nearly black, it is very long, and her body is long and slender. She is twenty-one years old; the day she was born Peter was fifteen. In her purple sweater and pants she is lovely, and he presses his face into her shoulder, her hair, he is squeezing her and her heels lift from the floor, then he kisses her and breathes from deep in her throat the scorched smell of dope. He looks at her green eyes: they are glazed and she is smiling, but it is a smile someone hung there; Miranda is someplace else. But now her eyes are making some appeal, then they move away from Peter's and when they return they are simply green again, bright again, and she nestles into his chest and murmurs, 'Only one little pipe,' and he holds her ever more tightly, crushing against her the loneliness he always feels when she lowers between them the glass wall of her smoking; the muscles of his arms and chest are taut with squeezing her, he is working isometrics against his heart, and it begins to give, it is subdued, it won't scream at her. It knows the heavy price of pushing Miranda further away.

He holds and kisses her again, and they move through the living room—her black and white photographs are on the walls; soon she will start working with color—and into the kitchen where she makes him a martini. She is not really a drinker, she has never drunk a whole martini, but he has taught her to make them and she likes to and when it is ready she tastes it, then hands it to him, and he sits at the table and watches her strong fingers peeling boiled shrimp. Her face is straining against the dope, she is trying to listen to him as he props his feet on a chair and sips the martini and unwinds. He tells her about his afternoon and the traffic driving home from Boston and she listens with exaggerated concentration; her responding smiles come a moment late and are held a moment too long.

By candlelight they eat shrimp cocktail while the sole broils, her kitchen is light blue, and from the walls hang red and orange pots and mugs; Dylan songs come from the record player in her bedroom, they eat fish and drink Chablis, she has only a couple of glasses because she is already high, he helps her with the dishes, and they linger still in the kitchen. He finishes the wine, the candles burn and drip and in their light her face overwhelms him, his blood is quick, she sees this and her smile vanishes, her face ages with passion, they rise and she leans over and blows out the candles, and they walk down the hall toward the music in the dark.

In the morning he wakes first; early sunlight comes through the window and he goes to it and looks out at the bright snow on the hemlock branches that nearly touch the frosted pane. He gets back in bed. After a while Miranda begins to wake; he feels her watching him, and he turns his head. She is staring at him, the way his children used to stare from their baby beds; he would pass the bedroom door and see Kathi lying on her back, plump fingers rubbing the satin border of her blanket, her eyes staring wide and blank as though her mind were still asleep. Miranda is the only adult he's ever seen wake that way. He is about to speak to her but she closes her eyes and is asleep. When she wakes again he brings her grapefruit juice and they lie warmly and drink.

'Let's eat lobsters tonight,' he says. 'I'll cook them.'

She looks away. Her eyes do not leave his but she looks away. It's talent she has.

'I won't be able to,' she says.

'Oh. Well, maybe tomorrow night.'

'I don't think I'll be able to then either.'

'I thought we had plans for tonight. A movie.'

'Did we?'

'I guess we didn't.'

This is the way they end up talking. Miranda has a fiancé; Peter doesn't know why. That is, he doesn't know why, having a fiancé, she began making love with him; or, making love with him, still has a fiancé. Now he knows, and she knows he does, that her fiancé is making some demand; perhaps he called yesterday and asked her to come to Connecticut today. Probably he did, and probably that pressure is why she smoked last night. But Peter can only work with probabilities, with guesses, for the centrifugal force of their evasion takes them further and further from the center of themselves. He lies quietly, feeling the weekend stretching out before him and now in the room demons are about and he turns to Miranda, his touch is gentle and she believes it is gentle, for that is what she needs now; she wants forgiveness and she believes he is giving it to her, but he is not. Not now. He has done that long ago, forgiven her in advance for every betrayal he had already decided to take. It is not forgiveness now, it is not even tenderness, his gentle fingers are wily, they don't show how desperate he is, they stroke away her fear, they draw love to her warm surfaces, joyfully she takes him and he has what he wants: the demons are gone. Yet there is more: demons gone are demons forgotten, and now he is free to watch her face and love her, and she is free too, she feels absolved, her eyes are uncluttered, they are passionate and profound, and she says: 'I love you, Peter, I love you—'

That moment carries him through the rest of the day; or it helps him do what he must do to get through a winter Saturday. He is a disk jockey and five afternoons a week his voice leaves him and goes into ears he will never know. When he was younger he was an actor. Then he had a son and named him David, and then a daughter and they named her Kathi, and he went into radio. For a while he hated his life, and at night he drank. Then after a couple of months he started feeling good. He started feeling very good. His work was not exciting, but he liked making money and bringing it home to Norma and David and Kathi. He liked having money to go see plays, and he liked not having to worry about being in one. He put on weight and made friends who came over on Saturday nights. This happy adjustment to the possibility of peace coincided with his admission that he had no more talent than thousands of others, and he would have spent his life trying to do TV commercials while he looked for work on the stage. For a long time he enjoyed those pleasures that money and family love can bring. But now his family is in Colorado and Norma is married to an affluent man and, though he sends money for the children, they don't need it.

They left last summer and on that morning he woke with a heart heavy and dead, as if waking for the funeral of his dearest friend, and he drank juice and took bacon from the refrigerator and laid three strips in a skillet, but he was trembling and his stomach fluttering and he put the slices back in the package, shoving them curved and folded under the cellophane. He would have had a drink but he didn't want their memory through the years to smell and taste again booze on their father's morning lips. Then he was faint with fear and he breathed deeply several times and got into the shower, his heart no longer grieving as if for another's death: it was his own execution he cleansed himself for, scrubbing under the hot spray, trying to feel and see nothing but his hand and the bar of soap and his lathered and dripping flesh, but he saw himself driving there and he saw them coming out of the house with love and goodbye in their faces and he raged aloud *No No No*, eyes closed and fists swinging at air and spray and then he slipped: his feet gone and arms reaching, one against the flat wet wall, the other toward the handle of the glass door, clutching at it and missing as his head struck the back of the tub and he lay gazing up at the spray that now hit his belly and groin; then he closed his eyes and waited to be knocked out. After a while he opened his eyes and touched his head. A swelling; no blood. He stood up: he was able to. He would be able to shave now, to put on clothes, to drive there, to do it all. Before leaving the bathroom he looked once at the tub where he wanted to lie bleeding while the water struck him hot, then warm, and finally cold while he slept.

The day was blue and warm, the breeze from the east: a beach day. They were waiting on the front steps of the house he had left: plump, red-haired Kathi, her eyes excited and green and troubled with love, eight years old yet Peter knew that as well as her fatherless Colorado mornings and nights and the shyness of stepfather suppers she saw every moment of his waking and preparing which now he mustered himself to conceal. His son was ten, his light brown hair over his ears and down close to his shoulders, near blond from their days at the sea, bony once but now muscles too, his shoulders broad and sloping, and his hand in Peter's was loving, but Peter could feel in it too his separate peace and he knew that because Kathi was a girl he would live in a different way in her memory than in his son's. When Peter left home, David would not help Kathi and Norma help him load the car, and when Peter went inside and kissed him, holding his turning face, he would not leave the house, so Peter went out with Kathi and Norma and kissed them both and started the car; then David came running, it was dusk and in that light he ran gray and without features, then he stooped and picked up something from the dark lawn, he was close to the window now, arm lifting as he ran, his face dear now, crying, shouting *You bum You bum You bum* and throwing something that missed as Peter fled. When they saw each other two days later the boy had accepted Peter's betrayal; he moved back into Peter's love, accepted that too, but his acceptance had about it an aura of manly decision, and Peter could feel his eyes and his touch saying: *You have chosen to go. All right. Then I must grow without you and since there's nothing I can do but accept it, I might as well do better than that: I choose it.* So on the front steps as the three of them sat, the car in the driveway to their right packed for the trip west, David's blue eyes were pained for his father and for himself, yet that pain was muted by his resolve to endure. Holding him, Peter tried very hard to be grateful for that resolve.

Then Norma came out and when she saw them she turned her head and stood wiping her eyes, then faced them and pressed Peter's hand and started for the car. He rose and pulled Kathi and David up with him. They followed Norma to the car. She turned and, looking at some point on his neck or chest, she reached for him, hugged him very hard, patted his back, whispered, 'Take care,' and had turned and was gone even as he whispered the 'You too' she never heard. She circled the car and got in and he couldn't see her face till he crouched between David and Kathi, only a glance at her profile, her fingers brushing quickly at her eyes, then he was looking into their faces, and then long hugs and many kisses, tight squeezes till they all gasped, and saying again and again, 'At Christmas you'll fly out,' then he asked who had first turn in the front seat, it was Kathi, and he picked her up and put her on the seat and buckled her in and while he was doing that David got into the back and buckled his belt. Norma had mercifully started the engine and he leaned in and kissed David and then stepped back smiling, waving, calling out to their mournful and smiling faces to have a good trip, to write him about the trip, to paint pictures of the trip, to send him pictures of the trip, giving them that final image as they drove away, their arms waving out the windows: their father standing erect and smiling in the morning sun, wishing them well.

Then he drove home through tears and again tried to

prepare a meal and again could not eat; then he lay on his bed and submitted with curiosity and hope to the rape of grief. He lay there for an hour while the faces of David and Kathi assaulted him. Then he gave up: he could neither die of a broken heart nor go crazy. He got up from the bed, smoothed the wrinkles he had made, took off his clothes, laid them neatly on the bed, put on jockstrap and gym shorts, his heart still heavy as he tied his white leather running shoes, but his blood quickening with challenge and hope; he tied a red handkerchief around his forehead to keep sweat out of his eyes and went outside, and he ran.

It is what he is doing now, wearing a nylon running suit, a wind-breaker, mittens, and a ski cap. He is now two miles from home on a road going east from his apartment. He lives in a small town, so already he is out in the country; he runs past farmhouses, country homes, service stations. There are not many cars and most of the time he has the privacy of his own sounds—his steady breathing, his feet on the wet plowed and sanded blacktop—and, more than that, the absolute privacy of his body staking its claim on a country road past white hills and dark green trees, gray barns, and naked elms and maples and oaks waiting for spring: his body insisting upon itself, pumping blood and pounding up hills. Running is the only act in his life that gives him what he pays for. It is as simple as that.

Two and a half miles from his house, at the top of a hill, he looks across the sparkling white meadows, shadowed by trees and barns, and sees the Merrimack and chunks of ice flowing to the sea. Then he turns and starts back. Sweat has turned to ice on his handlebar moustache, he is running against a cold wind that has now frozen a drop of sweat on his freeze-burning cheek, he can see the droplet of ice at the bottom of his vision, one nostril is frozen partly shut, the temperature is around nineteen but the wind hits him with a chill below zero, his jockstrap is frozen hard as a shield at his crotch, and its edges chafe his legs. He approaches a man walking, a man over sixty, beneath his clothing he is wiry, he is walking briskly on the side of the road in boots and corduroys and sweaters and mackinaw, his face is red in the cold, and somehow Peter knows he is not walking to someplace, he is walking to walk, and when Peter is close enough they smile at each other and the man says, 'I wish I could do that,' and Peter says, 'You don't need to.' The man's eyes are good ones, and Peter waves and runs on, feeling light-hearted at the sight of the old man with a smile and a fast walk and bright eyes; and against and through the cold wind he runs happily home with aching lungs.

Dusk comes to his rooms before it comes to the sky. He turns on the lights and goes outside and stands on the shoveled and icy sidewalk and watches it come. He is drinking a hot toddy. On the common across the street, where stoned kids sprawl in the warm seasons, pines and bare maples and elms cast their final shadows on the snow. Beyond the common is a white church whose lighted steeple rises above the trees, above everything in the town, and stands against the darkening sky. There is a wide strip of light to the west, but all color has gone with the sun and as he sips and shivers and watches, the light fades and dusk is here, the worst time for the lonely, when sounds are louder and silence has a shape Peter can feel as he walks through it, and when death on a cold wind touches the windows. Then dusk is gone too, night has come dark and cold, Peter looks up at the stars and tries to recall this morning with Miranda, but the memory is cerebral and nothing against the dark. He goes inside and, like his children, he is wary of turning corners and opening closet doors, and he wants to tell his children they are right, that long ago when he told them it was only their imagination he was right too but not right enough, for what they saw yet couldn't see frightened them, and it was real.

He makes another drink and turns the records over, he is listening to Brubeck and Mulligan, and he sits on the bed, looking at the yellow phone on the bedside table. His body is vibrant from his run, he feels strong and able, and he'd better be, for now the demons are here, they are moving in the room, they are waiting. They won't come and get him. Always they watch and keep their distance; when he feels strong they watch quietly, like prone dogs; when he weakens they grow restive, and he can almost hear them. He has learned the rules: they are powerless to close that final distance, they cannot seize him unless he opens his own gates. He picks up the phone and dials the area code of loss, then the numbers of where they live. Norma answers.

'Are you all right?' she says.

'Yes,' and he tightens his closed eyes and pictures her in the house in Colorado. She has not changed with the times: her brown hair is cut short, she uses lipstick, she smokes Luckies. She is wearing slacks and a tight sweater, showing the good curves of her body that finally he could no longer touch. He has not seen the house; probably he never will. The children have written to him that it is new and big and has large windows and from the kitchen window they look at mountains. Kathi painted a picture of the house and sent it to him; it seems to be a ranch house. She drew her own face grinning out her bedroom window. Beyond the house a smiling sun shone over the mountains, and a grinning dog stood on the green lawn.

He asks for the children and she says she'll get them, she leaves the phone and he listens to her calling them, he strains to hear every sound in the house, and now he is listening for smells and colors too, for warmth and light, he is listening for joy and sorrow and everything he doesn't know, and now Kathi is on one phone and David on another, and Peter's voice is warm and cheerful: 'I liked your letters and your pictures. How are you?'

'Fine.' 'Fine; how are you?'

'Good. What were you doing?'

'When?'

'Just now. When I called.'

'Watching TV.' 'Cartoons,' Kathi says. 'It's snowing.'

'Is it a good snow?'

'Yeah!' David says. 'We didn't go to school.' 'So we get three days off,' Kathi says. ''Cept tomorrow we're supposed to have skiing lessons. But maybe we won't.'

'Skiing lessons? Both of you?'

'Yeah,' David says. 'We're in the same group too.' 'It's hard to walk on them.'

'Do you like it?'

'It's neat!' David says.

'Do you like it, Kathi?'

'Maybe so. I'll see.'

'Good. You learn to ski, and then it'll be spring and then in summer we'll go to the beach every sunny day, I'm getting bunk beds to go in my living room—'

'Bunk beds?' David says. 'Neat!'

'I want the top,' Kathi says.

'We'll work it out, and I'm going to try to work mornings from six to ten instead of afternoons so we'll have the rest of the day for the beach, I'm pretty sure I can swing it, and we'll get brown as old wet driftwood—' then they are all talking about summer coming, and flying to Boston, they are talking about the beach, David wants boiled lobsters at the cheap screened picnic table restaurant near the sea, Kathi hates school, she wants summer, David doesn't mind school, he says Kathi won't make friends, that's why she doesn't like it, and when she assents with her silence (Peter can feel that silence: it is hot-faced while a chill creeps like fog over her heart) his own heart breaks, his arms yearn to hold her, to protect her, to do anything that will take her happily through her days, realizing at once that this is true and not true, for he will do anything for Kathi except submit to the death of living with and trying once more after the long killing pain to love her mother, and all he can say is, 'Try, Kathi; I was shy too; you have to try, no one will come to you, people aren't like that, they go their own ways, you give it a try, you hear.' Knowing he is saying nothing, and now they are all saying I love you, they are all smacking kisses into the three phones, his closed

eyes see Kathi and David, then they start over again I love you
I love you I love you and kisses and kisses over the wires,
through his clear night and their late afternoon snow, and
when he hangs up he does not cradle the receiver, demons
move in from the walls, he reaches over and depresses the
button and then he calls Jo. As always her voice is guarded, as
though she were a fugitive. He asks her to dinner. Her voice
doesn't change, but she accepts. Then he takes off the records,
turns on the radio so he will not come home to silence, leaves
on the lights, and flees his apartment.

Some people divorce because they hope for resurrection and
afterwards you can see in them a new energy, a new strength.
But Peter believes Jo did it with her last effort, like a suicide
stepping onto the chair and ducking her head into the noose.
    'It's been so long since I've had a good meal,' she says.
    'What do you eat?'
    'Frozen things. Things in cans. Pizza. It's rotten to do it to
the girls. Sometimes I feel guilty and I cook something and
eat it with them.'
    They have brandy and they have pulled their chairs near
the fireplace, where two logs are burning. In the restaurant
she smoked a lot and talked a lot, and she ate a large meal,
oysters on the half-shell, broiled scallops, and Peter, his back
tingling like a nervous gunfighter's (for the demons followed
him into his car, and in the chatter behind him they stalked
among tables), savored his shrimp broiled on a stick with
tomato and bacon and resting on a nest of spinach, he sipped
Chablis, putting a stake on the good meal, the bottle of wine,
and Jo was good to be with, better than eating alone; but she
has not laughed since dinner, her smile is forced, and in her
voice and dark eyes her ache is bitter, it is defiant, and he feels
they are not at a hearth but are huddled at a campfire in a
dangerous forest.
    He met her in the early fall, before Miranda. She is one of
his listeners, one of the women he talks to on weekday after-

noons, the only one he really knows. In the fall the station had a contest with one hundred winners: the wives who wrote the best letters telling why they should leave their husbands at home and go to a New England Patriot football game. *All my life I've been watching men,* she wrote. *When I was a very little girl I watched boys throwing rocks and beating each other up and racing across the schoolyard after school. When I was a teen-ager I watched them playing football and basketball, and at home they played street hockey and when the ponds froze they played ice hockey across the street from my window. I watched them drive off in cars, I watched them hitchhike to Florida, I watched them go into the service and I watched them come home strutting and winking about their adventures. I always believed when I got married it would be my turn. My husband would watch me. He doesn't. He watches football on television. If I'm going to spend my life watching men who aren't watching me, then at least once it should be fun, and I should be able to dress up and go out to do it. Maybe my husband will see me on television and then he can watch me watching.*

Peter sat with her at the game, she told him about her letter, she was pleased that he remembered it. During the game he watched her. She was excited, she was having fun, but there was a desperate quality about her fun, as though she had just been released from prison. It was the same that night, after the studio party where they drank enough to impassion their intent: in the motel she made love with a fury, but he knew it was forced, that her tightening arms, her bucking hips were turned against the fetters which clanked at her heart. The affair was short because that clanking never went away. It was in her voice: when she was pretending—and nearly always she pretended—her voice was low and flat, as if she had just waked from a deep sleep; but most of the time her voice was high and brittle with cheer, her laughter was forced and shrill, and he could hear in it the borders of hysteria. Like most unfaithful wives she was remorseless: she felt she deserved a lover. Yet it did her no good. Her heart was surrounded by obdurate concentric circles of disappointment and bitterness; she could not break through, so Peter couldn't either, and finally they broke it off and both pretended that aversion to the deceptions and stolen time of adultery was the reason.

'You always liked to eat,' Peter says.

'I know.'

'What else don't you like anymore?'

'It's not that I don't like things.'

'You can't, is that it?'

'Yes. Sometimes I take pills.'

'To cheer you up?'

'They're not *that* good. He keeps calling, he doesn't want me to go through with the divorce, he wants me to take him back. Sometimes I think I ought to. It's not worth it.'

'What's not worth it?'

She shrugs. Peter is angry, he wants to tell her that for years he hasn't thought about sin, hasn't believed in sin, hasn't used the word sin, but now he is thinking depression is a sin, perhaps the only one that many people can commit. But he takes their glasses to the kitchen for more brandy. Her house is clean; he knows that unhappy women often lapse into disorder and dirt, and walking back to the living room he feels affection for Jo, he thinks of her dusting furniture as his voice comes over the radio. He sits beside her and tells her funny stories, he clowns for her, and it is like the stage again, he is not Peter Jackman, he is a changing face, a cracking voice, he is a field of laughter, and she laughs and sometimes succeeds in really laughing, and when she does this she reaches across the short distance between their chairs and grips his arm or hand, and he regrets but cannot ignore the current in her fingers and without a word he accepts. Still he rises, hoping to leave, but when they kiss her tongue is a desperate cry on his, so he follows her creeping up the stairs past her daughters' rooms and into her bed where with a heart like packed snow he makes love and then lies stroking her face as though with a cool cloth against fever. When she is sleepy he gets up and dresses in the moonlight and she says very quietly: 'Peter?

Will you come back sometime?'

He tells her he will, and he goes out into the night.

'I want you to care,' he says.

'I can't,' Miranda says.

She is sitting on the orange couch; at another time he would be sitting beside her, but his (and her) Saturday night has riven them, though he is the only one who knows it; or he believes he is the only one who knows it. So he faces her from a basket chair across the narrow room. She is sipping tea, and she is tired. She is smoking Marlboros, one after the other. Like many girls her age, she smokes almost continually. A part of Peter admires this; he sees it as insouciance toward death. Another part of him sees it as insouciance toward life.

'What does that mean, you can't? Do you mean you can't feel anything because you just aren't able to, or do you mean you can't because you're not supposed to?'

'I'm not supposed to.'

'But did you feel anything when I told you?'

'Yes.'

'Did you like it?'

'No.'

'Then you're not free. And I'm not either. But I already know that. It's you that has to know it. We both made love with other people last night. We're supposed to care. If we can't, then we're trapped in something else.'

'I'm tired,' she says.

She puts out her cigarette and lights another. In the past few minutes he has built a cage around her and behind it her face is confused and frightened. He knows she would like to put on music and smoke dope and quietly merge with the beats and rhythms from her record player. It is late Sunday night, Miranda has an hour ago returned from Connecticut and submitted to his pleas on the phone—he had been phoning every half hour since six o'clock—and has let him come over for a drink. He is drinking bourbon, though he knows he shouldn't, for it will oil his tongue and he will talk and one of his rules with Miranda, one of the rules which allows him to keep her, is not to talk too much of how he feels, for if she knows how much he loves her (she knows), how much he needs her (she knows), she will bolt under the pressure. She doesn't actually bolt: she doesn't send him away, she doesn't walk out on him. She simply goes away inside herself, while she turns to him a smile, gives to him a hand; and that makes him more lonely than any escape by any woman he's ever known. So daily with her he lives with songs he will never sing and screams he will never scream. But tonight he is drinking, and in a fearful moment of release he decides to go to the kitchen and pour himself another, knowing as he watches it pour that he too will be pouring soon, and within his relief there is a core of anger, the contradictions tangled like barbed wire in him again, for what he feels is love and he wants to tell it to Miranda, yet at the same time he is angry because she has managed them so that he can't tell her, and now, going back to the living room with his bourbon, he wants with all his heart to carry her away and make her his wife, yet he also would like to grab her by the shoulders and shake her till she cries.

At the door to the living room he stops. He looks at her quiet and lovely profile: she sips the tea, wipes her lips with the back of her cigarette hand, the lips shaping a kiss as they press themselves dry, then she draws on the cigarette, exhales, and begins again with the tea. She knows now that he is at the door but she doesn't know he is stopping to watch her, and in that moment, when she is drying tea from her lips, he is struck with a purifying love which he knows, if he could sustain it, would save him. He sees a sad young girl who is trying to live as well as she can; who does not hurt him out of spite or malice but only so she can survive; who gives him as much of herself as she is able to and only balks when he demands more; and who has gotten him through many nights. He could not help falling in love with her; what he could have helped was what happened afterward, and he had chosen to make love with a woman who wore an engagement ring; and standing in the doorway he is about to simply say I love you, and kiss her goodnight, and then go home and let her sleep. But now, though she doesn't look at him, she is aware that he is watching her and looking at her profile he knows this and the distance of the moment is broken and he makes a final choice: he crosses the room and settles into the chair.

'Talk to me,' he says.

Her eyes raise to his, then she looks down at her hands with the cigarette and tea, and then she sips and smokes.

'You have to tell me what's happening in you. Do you think it's me you love, is that it? Are you waiting to be sure? Talk to me, Miranda. Why are you making love with me? You can tell me that, can't you? Don't you know it's painful for me when you go off for a weekend and we pretend you didn't? If we could at least talk about it maybe it wouldn't be so bad. If you'd say anything at all about what you feel, even if you'd say you loved him and you were just doing some humbug with me, even that, even if I had that definition of what I am, but you won't even say that much, you just sit there and look at your hands. And there's death in you. With your dope and your silence and your two lovers. You erase yourself. Well, you're not going to erase me too. And that's what happens when I'm lonely and I end up with Jo. And I'm not going to do that anymore. I've *been* there. Jesus, I've *been* there, Miranda—'

Sitting in the basket chair he is subtly overwhelmed, memory launches a sneak attack, his blood remembers making love with a landlocked heart, and he sits there with the ghosts of love past: the affairs with melancholy wives when he was a husband, and with each new one he believed he was in love, yet always the day came for goodbye and usually it came some time after both hearts had turned away or back onto themselves. No matter, all were goodbyes from the instant of their first hello, all were liaisons whose passions were fed by the empty cupboards of the lovers' homes; and all the time to make these couplings profound instead of privative he tried as best he could to believe he was in love, his love for Norma long dead, killed by their mutual adulteries, symptoms of a more complex distance which he has never truly understood; and with each new woman he said to himself, *She must be the last, she will be the last, she is the last,* because there was death in that repetition of lovers, each goodbye was a little death, and the affairs themselves were too because they were shallow and ephemeral and so he felt shallow and ephemeral too, his soul untapped on his march to death, a stranger between the thighs of a stranger—'Miranda.' He stands up. He wants to cross the room and take the cup and cigarette from her hands, but he doesn't dare, for he is afraid that his eyes and the touch of his hands cannot reach her. So he stands at his chair and uses his voice. 'Miranda: will you live with me?' She looks up at him and in her eyes there is a flicker of assent, he sees it, grabs it, holds on for his very life while she looks down again into her empty tea cup, her cigarette is finished too, she reaches for the pack, picks it up, changes her mind, puts it down, then changes her mind again and takes a cigarette. 'I love you, Miranda. I can't keep sharing you. I want you to come live with me. Now; tonight.' He looks around the room to see what he can pack in their cars: the photographs from the walls, the table lamps, the coffee table, cushions; from the bedroom the record player and records; he has a vision of the two of them carrying things downstairs, with each load their hearts are lighter, they ascend the stairs together for another load, their impulsiveness gives them easy laughter—'We can pack some things tonight. Tomorrow morning I'll get a truck and move the rest while you're at work. When you come home it'll be all done. This week I'll build you a darkroom, there's room in the kitchen, it's too big anyway. We'll do it. Won't we? I know I shouldn't sound like something wounded you have to bring in off the street. But I don't have time anymore to be smart—will you live with me?'

'I can't.'

'Why? You want to. I can feel it. It's not him stopping you. If you really loved him you wouldn't want me at all. So why can't you?'

'I'm too young.'

'You're not too young. You have two lovers.'

'I wish I didn't have any.'

'You mean you wish nobody asked you questions.'

'Yes. That's what I wish.'

'You can't do that, Miranda. You can't make love and not have questions. Goddamnit, Miranda—' But there is nothing to say. He has said it all, and between him and Miranda his guts hang in the air. He is adrift in those desperate spaces of vulnerability where she will never follow, there is no way for him to get back, and he yields to his old stubborn muscle, the heart, and he follows it across the room, watching himself fall to his knees and take the cigarette from her hand and put it out, then hold both her hands and look into her green, brimming eyes and say: 'Miranda, I can't do it anymore. I can't pretend I love you less, I'm not strong enough to keep pretending I'm strong, I can't keep standing around waiting and staying alive on the little you give, because you're all I've got—don't you know that? surely you *know* that—I don't have my kids, I don't have work, I have a job—Miranda: listen. I'm not as crazy as I sound. Desperate, yes. I mean I know I spend twenty-three hours every day getting in shape for that one hour when I might go under. Is that what scares you?' The tears are going down her cheeks now, and she is slowly shaking her head. 'It has to be that or nothing, Miranda. I can't go back to the other. Come with me, Miranda. You love me. We'll make it. Come now, baby, come now—' Her tears are faster, they flow over her lips and drop to her lap, but still she is shaking her head even as her hand takes the back of his neck and pulls him forward; her other hand goes around his back, his face is in her breasts, and he feels against his forehead the beating of her heart. He tries to stand but her arms hold tightly. His hands on her knees, he pushes himself up, he stands, and her arms fall away. She rises with him. Fiercely she hugs him again, and now there is a turnabout that mollifies his anguish, her silence and her tears on his cheek pull him out of himself, he is holding her, through her soft hair he is stroking her neck, his lips turn to her ear and he says: 'I'm sorry, Miranda. I have to. It hurts too much, the way it was. I have to try to survive. I'm sorry, baby—' and he hugs her very tightly, glances once at her damp face as he turns away and takes his coat and leaves.

There will be no sleep tonight. He knows it when he enters his apartment, which is lighted; from the bedroom comes Janis Joplin on the radio. He goes to the kitchen: bourbon started his evening at dusk and brought his night to its dark crescendo, and now perhaps it will allow him to wane. He makes a drink, brings the bottle to the table, sits down, and props his feet on a chair. He is about to drink but instead he pauses and listens to McCartney. He does not want the music coming down the hall from the bedroom. When it does that it only penetrates the spaces near the door, where the sink is. But over there at the refrigerator and there at the stove and here at the cupboard and counter opposite his chair and here beside him at the dark reflecting window and the wide sill where he rests his arm there is no music and when he looks at these places he sees silence. He goes to the bedroom and gets the portable radio, switching to DC when he unplugs it and listening to McCartney as he goes down the hall; on DC the reception is not as good, and he sets the radio on the counter, plugs it in, switches back to AC, and the faint static is gone. He turns out the overhead light so the room is dark except for the light coming from the hall. He sits and swallows bourbon, then lights a cigarette, his first of the day. The demons are stirring now, he feels them creeping down the hall, and in another moment they are standing by the sink to his right, and he feels like a colonel with an exposed flank. He finishes the drink and then another, but in his mind there is a relentless dagger of sobriety that will not give in to the booze. What he must do is sleep, and he takes the radio to the bedroom and gets into bed.

Right away his legs tell him it is no use. They will not relax, they will not sink into the mattress, they are restless as they are before he runs. He tries hypnotizing his toes and feet and calves, but by the time he is repeating *My knees are asleep* the calf muscles and feet are yearning again. And he cannot make his mind stop. If he could, then his muscles would follow peacefully and rest like sunning snakes, but his mind is filled with the idea and necessity of sleep, and the more he pushes with his mind the more his muscles and blood push back until the struggle gives him a sensation very much like the need to scratch. Yet still he tries to relax, he closes his eyes and breathes as he would if he were falling asleep, and for a moment it nearly works, his mind has stopped thinking sleep and has begun to drift into a dream when he realizes this and is immediately awake, his heart fast, his arms tight at his sides.

His luminous clock on the chest of drawers tells him it is eight minutes after two, and now he knows he will lie awake till four at the least, but probably five or six, and that he will wake at eight as usual and the day that waits for him will be long, his body tired, his reflexes distorted—he will be easily startled—and as dusk comes his heart and nerves will start again and he will have to devise some way to ease himself into the night, to sneak up on sleep. Angrily he throws back the covers and gets out of bed, his feet strike hard on the floor, his legs take him quickly to the kitchen and he gets ice and pours bourbon and returns to the bedroom where he turns on the radio and lowers the volume on Crosby Stills Nash and Young, then gets into bed, propping himself on two pillows so he can drink. He lights a cigarette and watches his exhaled smoke in the dark.

Before he has half-finished the drink he knows he will call Jo. But he tells himself he won't. It has never worked with Jo and he does not want to hurt another woman, not ever. He does not think he can love Jo, but he is afraid Jo can love him. And he does not want to go to her now, the way he is, for he knows he can mistake relief for love and then it will sour and there will be wounds. He must go it alone, ride out this night, hang on to its neck and mane, and ride. Besides, it is two twenty-seven, she will be asleep (he picks up the phone), he should be tougher than this (he is dialing), he shouldn't disturb poor Jo in all the ways this call will disturb her (it rings), it isn't right, he ought—On the second ring she answers. She has been asleep and there is fear in her voice.

'Jo, I'm sorry.'

'Peter?'

'I'm sorry. You were sleeping, I knew you'd be asleep, but—' He listens to tears coming to his voice, he will not allow them to crest, he stops speaking.

'What happened?' Jo says.

He doesn't answer. He is listening to his silent throat, trying to know if he can talk without crying; but he doesn't have to. Jo takes over, and in a moment which he even trusts he loves her.

'Come on over,' she says.

'I can't do that.'

He has answered without listening first and his voice is all right; or at least it doesn't break into liquid. Jo is working for him.

'Sure you can. Come on.'

'It's awfully late. You won't get any sleep.'

'I'll sleep tomorrow while the girls are at school.'

'Are you sure?'

'Come on.'

'I'll bring some bourbon.'

He turns on the light and blinks, and now his legs are put to good use, they cross the room and take clothes from the closet, he dresses and goes to the kitchen and gets the bottle. Passing his bedroom door again he sees the unmade bed and knowing he is foolishly careful he goes in and makes it, leaving no signs of decline for the demons' morale. He takes a moment to decide it is all right to turn off the radio, turns it off and the bedside lamp too, gets his coat and gloves and heads fast down the hall and out that door into the foyer, dark stairs rising at his left, and goes out the front door into the cold where, on the narrow, icy front porch, he stops.

The apartment's lawn is at most twenty feet wide from the front steps to the sidewalk. If he reaches the sidewalk he

will go around the corner of the building, to the garage in
back. To reach this sidewalk he must simply traverse the lawn,
walking on a shoveled walk between low white banks of snow.
But he cannot go down that walk. He stands on the porch
looking at the two steps and then at the T formed by the two
sidewalks and at the smooth hard snow of the lawn. He starts
to step onto the first step, his leg moves, it reaches the step,
the other leg follows, he is standing on the step but Peter himself is not really there, whoever Peter is has been driven in
panic back into the warm and lighted apartment; he is not on
the steps. His body stands spiritless and abandoned, it feels as
though it has neither bone nor muscle, it is only shivering flesh
inside clothing that doesn't belong to him. He turns away
from the dark street and the lawn and goes back into the apartment, where he catches up with himself sitting on the bed and
turning on the lamp and taking a shot from the bottle, then
corking it and dropping it to the bed and picking up the phone.

'Jo, I can't cross the lawn. It looked huge, it looked like
Nebraska. I took a step. Or two of them. I had the bourbon and
I had the car key in my hand. I couldn't get down the steps.'

'You want me to come get you?'

'You can't leave your kids.'

'I could leave them for just a minute.'

'No.'

'Don't you want me to?'

'I want to be able to move. Look, I feel better now.' He
looks around his room at things he has bought, things which
every day tell him he's at home. They seem to be telling him
that now. The room is a place he can depart from, Jo's voice
on the phone is a person he can go to. He is uncorking the
bottle. 'I think I can make it' he says, and swallows as she says,
'I'll get a fire going. We'll have hot toddies. It'll be nice, Peter.'

Clutching the bottle in one hand, keys dangling from the
other, he goes down the hall. He is whistling before he realizes he is. He is whistling 'Summertime.' In the foyer he closes
the apartment door behind him, in that closed dark space the
demons are so near that he wants to make some sound, not a

scream or sob of terror, but a growl, a shout, a sharp command, so they will know they are still dealing with a man in possession of—He is out of the foyer, he is on the porch, and he shuts the door behind him and looks at the dark and minatory sky over dark, white-splotched rooftops; across the street the common is white and smooth; black evergreens rise from it, they are tall and wide, they obscure the sky, they become the horizon until he looks past them at the white church tower with a light in the very top of its steeple, it is nearly a white light in the open, unglassed windows, up where the bell is. Beyond it the sky is without stars. He looks down at his own silent white lawn, and he crosses the porch and is on the top step and without breaking stride he is on the second step and then the walk itself, he is moving, he reaches the sidewalk that parallels the street and he turns right and reaches the corner where there is a streetlight.

He looks to his left-front, lifts his eyes to the light of the steeple, scans the peaceful snow of the common, and then abruptly turns right and is looking down a dark street and sidewalk; as he moves forward he leaves the streetlight behind him, he is passing his living room and now he approaches his bedroom window, but he keeps his eyes fixed on the dark sidewalk before him, he sees that and the huge stump that was a tree until the telephone lines came, he sees the shadowed snow piled between the sidewalk and the apartment and, in his vision to the front and in the corner of his left eye, the dark road. There is no more wind here than there was at the front of the apartment, there is no wind at all tonight, but on this sidewalk he is colder, his breath is fast as though he were walking briskly for miles; only a few feet ahead of him is the corner of the building, he will go past that to the driveway and then turn and walk up it and open the door to the garage and then get into his car—He stops. For a second (and in that second his fear stops the clock, he stands within the circle of a pause that threatens to hold him) he knows he cannot go forward but he also believes he cannot retrace his steps, cannot reach the corner he has left, believes he will stand immobile holding a whiskey bottle and car keys until someone comes to save him.

Then he is turning, he is heading fast back to the corner, too relieved to feel shame or failure, the streetlight is waiting, now the door, then he is in his warm hall and he goes directly to the kitchen. He takes off his gloves and makes a drink. He goes to the bedroom, drops his coat to the floor, and turns on the radio. Judy Collins is singing, plaintive and sweet. He sits on the bed, drinks twice, drinks again, then he calls Jo. She does not say hello. She says: 'I'll come get you.'

'Wait. Every time you say that I think I can make it. Last time I almost got to the driveway, I got as far as the kitchen. Look: hold on, will you? I'll just go take a look outside and see how things are. Will you just hold a minute?'

'I'll hold. The fire is going. I'm looking at the fire.'

'What do you have on?'

'My nightgown and a robe. They're both pink. My feet are bare. They were cold but now they're warm by the fire.'

'Are you drinking?'

'A little brandy with coffee.'

'Coffee? You'll never sleep.'

'I need to wake up some. You woke me from what they call a drugged sleep. And I just smoked my last cigarette. And you know how coffee and brandy make you want to smoke. So you have to get out of the house so you can bring me some cigarettes. There are all-night service stations with machines.'

Her voice is warm and cheerful, perhaps amused. He knows the game she is playing with him, but he needs it and it seems to be working. He imagines himself in his car, driving.

'I have some here,' he says. 'I'll bring those.'

'Good. Go see how things look outside.'

'Here I go,' he says, and drops the phone to his pillow, not all the way from his ear but lowering it first to a gentle height; he feels he must treat the phone as though Jo were in it. As he goes down the hall past the children's paintings (he averts his eyes from Kathi's happy sun and happy dog and her own happy face at the window in Colorado) he knows he won't make it. The hall itself is too long, already there is too much distance from his bedroom, the only place tonight where he can be, and what will happen if he lets himself be driven there and that room too becomes untenable? He pictures himself huddled on the bed while demons crawl the floor. He looks out the front door, but does not cross the threshold, he does not even take his hand from the doorknob, his look outside is hasty and as he sees the white lawn and dark street with its dirty snowbanks and the swath of yellow sand under the streetlight, the full dark pines and hemlocks, the stripped oaks and maples and elms of the common, and the lighted steeple beyond, he is seeing himself facing the alone and cold passage down the side of his apartment to the garage in the rear, and he is turning away and pulling the door shut behind him. Walking back down the hall he drinks and he drinks again before lifting Jo from his pillow.

'Things are bad out there,' he says. He sits on the bed and looks around him. 'Things are pretty bad in here too, they're coming with bugles. I feel like I'm in the Chosin Reservoir.'

'Peter: listen. Put your drink down.'

'Jesus.' He puts it down.

'Do you have your coat on?'

He looks at it on the floor, shakes his head, then says, 'No.'

'All right. Where is it?'

'It's on the floor. Right here.'

'Leave it there. Leave the drink on the table. Do you have your car keys?'

'They're in my pocket.'

'Take them out and hold them.' To do this he must stand up. He stands and reaches into his pocket and brings out the keys. He lets the other keys fall to the bottom of the ring and holds the ignition key at the ready. 'Now go outside as fast as you can. Don't shut your door behind you. Don't look to the left or the right. Don't wear gloves or a coat. If you stop you'll be cold. You'll be cold anyway. Get in the car and start it and drive it back to your door. Then leave the engine running and come back here and get your coat and tell me you're on your way. You woke me up and now I'm awake till breakfast and I want those cigarettes and I want to see you. Now go.'

The actor in him is dead but by no means buried and he mutters huskily into the phone, 'All right, baby,' drops the phone, and surrenders to a long glance at the drink on the table but doesn't touch it. He gets a trotting start down the hall and through the foyer, leaves the front door open so light and warmth follow him outside like mute, tactile cheers. He makes it down the walk and turns and walks as fast as he can and when he reaches the corner he is shivering with cold. He turns and heads into the dark, eyes on the sidewalk; as he passes his dark living room he feels its emptiness, but as he passes the bedroom he feels Jo in there on the pillow, she is a wing man in a World War II movie, he is blinded by his shattered cockpit, she is talking him back to the carrier, she is seeing him as he passes the last bedroom window and now the lone kitchen window and he has gone farther than before.

His fingers are stiff and he jams them in his pockets, the right hand still clutching the key, and he has passed the rear corner of the building, he is approaching the driveway, with a sense of victory he turns and goes up the driveway, he knows there are two trials still ahead: stepping into the garage and then getting into the car. But he has momentum and he believes he can make it, his boots are crunching on the packed snow of the driveway, to his right is the dark rising bulk of the building where others sleep, the garage is white before him, the closed door is waiting for his hand. He is there and his cold hand closes on the black handle and he pushes upward, it is good to use his arm and shoulder, to deal with something as direct and physical as thrusting a garage door upward. The door goes up on its rollers and disappears above him. He knows better than to pause. He moves quickly into the dark garage, his teeth are chattering as he slides behind the wheel of the Volvo, his shivering fingers miss the ignition slot, then he finds it and inserts and turns and the engine starts as he notices (wise Jo, she must have gone crazy a few times) that the chill in his back is so severe that it has overwhelmed the other chill he would have felt on a night like this: the chill telling him that if he looks in the rear-view mirror he will finally see the face of a demon.

He has no time for demons now, no warm space in his body where fear of them can live. As he backs out of the garage, twisting to his right to look out the rear window, he is thinking only of the coat and gloves on his bedroom floor. He drives to the corner, leaves the engine idling, and trots up the sidewalk and through the door and down the hall. He puts on his coat and gloves, picks up the phone, and says: 'I'm on the way.'

'*Good,*' Jo says, and he is down the hall and out the door. He drives through the small empty town, he stops shivering, he warms beneath his coat and in his gloves, the car warms and he turns on the heater. From the radio Joan Baez serenades and celebrates his drive past locked and front-lighted stores and one bundled policeman checking locks.

She hugs him at the door and takes him to the fire in the living room and, still holding him, gives him a maternal and possessive smile that, on a saner night, would frighten him. Looking at her he begins to think that maybe she never has gone crazy, that maybe by instinct she knew what to do with him, the way they always know what to do when someone is sick or hurt. He gives her the cigarettes, she gratefully lights one, and asks if he wants a hot toddy. He says he does. She unbuttons his coat, slips off his scarf, goes behind him and takes his coat off.

'Sit here by the fire,' she says. 'I'll make the drinks.'

She takes the bottle and leaves. He sits and watches the fire and props his feet on a leather hassock. In the warmth and color of the room (it is blue, there are green potted plants, a seascape hangs on one wall, a landscape on another), in its smell of wood-smoke and the sound of burning logs, he feels safe, and when she returns with the drinks he treasures the touch of her fingers as she gives him the glass. She puts her drink on the floor and sits at his feet and unlaces his boots. He gives in to this. At first an instinct tells him he is letting her go too far, that by saving him she will possess him, but he wants his boots off, he wants a woman to take them off, and he watches her fingers on the laces, and when she is done and begins to tug at the boot he pulls his foot out. She takes off the other one and he leans back in the chair and sips. Jo remains sitting near his propped feet, her back to the fire. There are long gray streaks in her brown hair and he fondly takes one in his fingers, then smooths it back into place. Her face is awake, her eyes alert, yet about her mouth and eyes is that weariness she will probably always have; tonight he likes it.

'What was it?' she says. 'Do you know?'

'It was a girl named Miranda.'

'Miranda?'

'Miranda Jones. She's twenty-one years old.'

She lights a cigarette and settles her back against the hassock; her ribs touch his calf, her left arm rests on his knee and thigh.

'Tell me about her,' she says.

'I don't have to. I mean, I've been through this before. I don't have to get it all out anymore.'

'I want you to get it all out. For me. I want to look at it.'

He drinks and tells her; once she rises and brings him another hot toddy and sits again resting her arm on his leg and sometimes she takes his hand, fondles his fingers, and when he finishes his story she says: 'You didn't really love her. You only thought you did.'

'I've never understood the difference.'

'She was only a life jacket.'

'A life jacket is enough, if you're out in the ocean.'

Then he yields to her. He takes her hand and squeezes it with intent, he leaves his chair and lies beside her, this sad woman whom tonight he is learning to love; and as his fingers part her robe he says: 'You and I. We're what's left over, after the storm.'

Still he does not sleep. He gets up and puts another log on the fire, then lies on the rug and she returns her head to his shoulder. She lies between him and the fire, he is warm and peaceful, and his hand moves down her side and settles at her waist.

'What did you do today?' he says.

'What did I do?'

'Yes. What did you do.'

'I gave the girls breakfast.'

'What was it?'

'Oatmeal. Oatmeal and French toast.'

'Good. Then what?'

'I washed the dishes, then took the girls to church. Do you think that's silly?'

'No. No, I think it's good.'

'Do you believe in God?'

'Yes.'

'So do I. Do you know anything about Him?'

'Not much. What church was it?'

'The Unitarian.'

'The old white one by the common?'

'Yes. I looked over at your apartment. That's how I told you good morning.'

'What did you do after that?'

'I went to the supermarket. You made me feel guilty last night, about cooking. Something funny happened at the supermarket.'

'What was it?'

'You'll think I'm weird.'

'No I won't.'

'I left my basket and walked out.'

'Why?'

'The basket was full. I had groceries for a week.'

'Why did you walk out?'

'I was sad. I told you you'd think I was weird.'

'I don't. You said you were sad.'

'I was looking at all the women. They looked sad. Some had little children with them. They were barking at their children. Some were smoking. Some had their coats buttoned and they were hot but they didn't take their coats off. One stood at the meat counter. She was looking around. She wanted something. There was no one behind the counter. There's a button on a pipe, and it calls the butchers out of the room where they butcher the meat. She pressed the button. No one came. I looked at her and I looked through the window where the butchers were supposed to be. There was meat on the tables and meat hanging from hooks. But no one was there. She kept pressing the button. That's when I left.'

'Where did you go?'

'I went to a little market on the corner. Right down the street from here. I probably spent ten dollars more. It's a very small place and people nudge each other while they shop. There's a butcher and a man at the cash register. They knew everyone in the store except me. Everyone was talking. The butcher talked to me while he cut the meat. He told me how good the meat was. He told me he was spoiling me. He's old, and the man at the cash register is his son. I figured that out listening to them. The man at the cash register told me it was going to snow three inches. That's what I paid the ten dollars for. I'll go back.'

'I'll go with you.'


Outside the sky is growing light, the night is almost ended, and inside Peter lies awake. Jo sleeps in his arms, his flesh is warm from the fire, and his heart is a piñata: it bursts and streams invisible colors which he can see: they are the colors of fire, the hopeful rose and gold and red of sunrise, and in the colors he sees Jo, her eyes are a laughing pale blue sky, tonight he will bring wine and flowers, this afternoon between records he will say, once and softly: Hello Jo; and he means that hello, his warm heart pounds with it, he will follow the course of it, for love is time too, and lying here before the fire and looking at her sleeping face on his arm he knows he will love her, and with great relief and new strength his blood runs through his body and he kisses her until she warmly wakes and encircles him with her squeezing arms; he ascends; he is Prometheus; and he pauses in his passion to gently kiss her brightened eyes.

# MIRANDA OVER THE VALLEY

ALL THAT DAY she thought of Michaelis: as she packed for
school in Boston and confirmed her reservation and, in
Woodland Hills, did shopping which she knew was foolish: as
though she were going to some primitive land, she bought
deodorant and bath powder and shampoo, and nylons and
leotards for the cold. At one o'clock she was driving the Corvette past cracked tan earth and dry brush, it was a no smoking zone and she put out her cigarette and thought: Now he
has finished his lunch and they have gone back to the roof,
he's not wearing his shirt, he has a handkerchief tied around
his head so sweat won't burn his eyes; he's kneeling down
nailing shingles. She saw them eating dinner, her last good
Mexican food until she flew west again at Thanksgiving, but
she could not see the evening beyond dinner. She saw enchi-
ladas and Margaritas, she saw them talking, she talked with
him now driving to the shopping center, but after that she
saw nothing. And she was afraid. In the evening she brushed
her long dark hair and waited for him and she opened the
front door when he rang; he was tall, he was tanned from his
summer work, and he shook her father's hand and kissed her
mother's cheek. Miranda liked the approval in her parents'
eyes, and she took his arm as they walked out to the driveway,
to his old and dented Plymouth parked behind the Corvette.
They went to dinner and then drove and then stopped on

Mulholland Drive, high above the fog lying over the San Fernando Valley, and out her window she saw stars and a lone cloud slowly passing the moon. She took his thick curly hair in one hand and kissed him and with her tongue she told him yes, told him again and again while she waited for him to know she was saying yes.

The next day her parents and Michaelis took her to the airport.

She met Holly at the terminal and they flew to Boston. She was eighteen years old.

She lived with Holly in a second-floor apartment Holly found on Beacon Street. It was large, and its wide, tall windows overlooked the old, shaded street. They put a red carpet in the living room and red curtains at the windows. Holly's boyfriend, who went to school in Rhode Island, built them a bar in one corner, at the carpet's edge. Holly was a year older than Miranda, this was her second year at Boston University, and the boys who came to the apartment were boys she had known last year. There were also some new ones, and soon Holly was making love with one of them. His name was Brian. When he came to the apartment Miranda watched him and listened to him, but she could neither like him nor dislike him, because she could not understand who he was. He was a student and for him the university was a stalled escalator: he leaned against its handrails, he looked about him and talked and gestured with his hands, his pale face laughed and he stroked his beard, and his hair tossed at his neck. But there was no motion about him.

When he spent the night, Holly unfolded the day bed in the living room and Miranda had the bedroom to herself. She lay on her twin bed at the window and listened to rock music from an all-night FM station; still there were times when, over the music, she could hear Holly moaning in the next room. The sounds and her images always excited her, but sometimes they made her sad too; for on most weekends Tom drove up from Providence and on Friday and Saturday nights Miranda fell asleep after the same sounds had hushed. Brian knew about Tom and seemed as indifferent to his weekend horns as he was to an incomplete in a course or the theft of his bicycle, which he left on the sidewalk outside a Cambridge bar one Sunday afternoon.

Tom knew nothing about Holly's week nights. The lottery had spared him, so he was a graduate student in history and, though he tried not to, at least once each visit he spoke of the diminishing number of teaching jobs. He was robust and shyly candid and Miranda liked him very much. She liked Holly very much too and she did not want to feel disapproval, but there it was in her heart when she heard the week night sounds and then the weekend sounds, and when she looked at Tom's red face and thick brown moustache and thinning hair. One night in late September Miranda and Holly went to a movie and when they came home they sat at the bar in the living room and drank a glass of wine. After a second glass Miranda said Tom had built a nice bar. Then she asked if he was coming this weekend. Holly said he was.

'I'd feel divided,' Miranda said, and she looked at Holly's long blonde hair and at the brown, yellow-tinted eyes that watched her like a wise and preying cat.

Then it was early October and she was afraid. At first it was only for moments which struck her at whim: sometimes in class or as she walked home on cool afternoons she remembered and was afraid. But she did not really believe, so she was only afraid when memory caught her off guard, before she could reassure herself that no one was that unlucky. Another week went by and she told Holly she was late.

'You can't be,' Holly said.

'No. No, it must be something else.'

'What would you do?'

She didn't know. She didn't know anything except that now she was afraid most of the time. Always she was waiting. Whether she was in class or talking to Holly or some other friend, even while she slept and dreamed, she was waiting for that flow of blood that would empty her womb whether it held a child or not. Although she did not think of womb, of child, of miscarriage. She hoped only for blood.

Then October was running out and she knew her luck was too. Late Halloween afternoon she went to the office of a young gynecologist who had the hands of a woman, a plump face and thin, pouting lips. He kept looking at his wrist watch. He asked if she planned to keep the child and when she told him yes he said that if she were still in Boston a month from now to come see him. As she was leaving, the receptionist asked her for twenty dollars. Miranda wrote a check, then went out to the street where dusk had descended and where groups of small witches, skeletons, devils, and ghosts in sheets moved past her as she stopped to light a cigarette; she followed in the wake of their voices. Holly was home. When Miranda told her she said: 'Oh Jesus. Oh Jesus Jesus Jesus.'

'I'm all right,' Miranda said. She noticed that she sounded as if she were reciting something. 'I'm all right. I'm not in trouble, I'm only having a baby. It's too early to call Michaelis. It's only three o'clock in California. He'll still be at school. I'd like to rest a while then eat a nice meal.'

'We only have hamburger. I'll go out and get us some steaks.'

'Here.'

'No. It's my treat.'

While Holly was gone, Miranda put on Simon and Garfunkel and the Beatles and lay on the couch. The doorbell rang and she went downstairs and gave candy to the children. She and Holly had bought the candy yesterday: candy corn, jelly beans, bags of small Tootsie Rolls, orange slices, and chocolate kisses; and now, pouring candy into the children's paper bags, smiling and praising costumes, she remembered how frightened she was yesterday in the store: looking at the cellophane bags of candy, she had felt she did not have the courage to grow a minute older and therefore would not. Now as she passed out the candy she felt numb, stationary, as though she were suspended out of time and could see each second as it passed, and each of them went on without her.

She went upstairs and lay on the couch and the doorbell rang again. The children in this group were costumed too, but older, twelve or thirteen, and one of the girls asked for a cigarette. Miranda told her to take candy or nothing. When she went upstairs she was very tired. She had been to three classes, and she had walked in the cold to the doctor's and back. While the Beatles were singing she went to sleep. The doorbell rang but she didn't answer; she went back into her deep sleep. When Holly came in talking, Miranda woke up, her heart fast with fright. Holly put on the Rolling Stones and broiled the steaks and they drank Burgundy. During dinner Brian called, saying he wanted to come over, but Holly told him to make it tomorrow.

At eight o'clock, when it was five in California, Miranda went to the bedroom and closed the door and sat on her bed. The phone was on the bedside table. She lowered her hand to the receiver but did not lift it. She gazed at her face in the reflecting window. She was still frozen out of time, and she was afraid that if Michaelis wasn't home, if the phone rang and rang against the walls of his empty apartment, something would happen to her, something she could not control, she would go mad in Holly's arms. Then she turned away from her face in the window and looked at the numbers as she dialed; his phone rang only twice and then he answered and time had started again.

'Happy Halloween,' she said.

'Trick or treat.'

'Trick,' she said. 'I'm pregnant.' He was silent. She closed her eyes and squeezed the phone, as though her touch could travel too, as her voice did, and she saw the vast night between their two coasts, saw the telephone lines crossing the dark mountains and plains and mountains between them.

'It's about two months, is that right?'

'It was September second.'

'I know. Do you want to get married?'

'Do you?'

'Of course I do. If that's what you're thinking about.'

'I'm not thinking about anything. I saw the doctor this afternoon and I haven't thought about anything.'

'Look: do you want to do it at Thanksgiving? That'll give me time to arrange things, I have to find out about blood tests and stuff, and your folks'll need some time—you want me to talk to them?'

'No, I will.'

'Okay, and then after Thanksgiving you can go back and finish the semester. At least you'll have that done. I can be looking for another apartment. This is all right for me, *may*be all right for two, but with a—' He stopped.

'Are you sure you want to?'

'Of course I am. It just sounded strange, saying it.'

'You didn't say it.'

'Oh. Anyway, we'll need more room.'


'I didn't think he'd do that,' Holly said. She was sitting on the living room carpet, drinking tea. Miranda could not sit down; she stood at the window over Beacon Street, she went to the bar for a cigarette, she moved back to the window. 'I just didn't think he would,' Holly said.

'You didn't want him to.'

'Are you really going to get *mar*ried?'

'I love him.'

'He's your first one.'

'My first one. You mean the first one I've made love with.'

'Yes.'

'And that's how you mean it.'

'That's how. And you've only done *that* once.'

'That's not what it means to me.'

'How would you know? You've never had anybody else.'

'But you have.'

'What's that mean.'

'I guess it means look at yourself.'

'All right. I'll look at myself. I've never had to get married, and I've never had to get an abortion, and nobody owns me.'

'I want to be owned.'

'You do?'

'Yes. The way you are now, you have to lie.'

'I don't lie to Tom. He doesn't ask.'

'I don't mean just that. I don't know what I mean; it's just all of it. I have to go outside for a minute. I have to walk outside.'

She put on her coat as she went down the gray-carpeted stairs. She walked to the corner and then up the dead-end street and climbed the steps of the walk that crossed Storrow Drive. As she climbed she held the iron railing, but it was cold and she had forgotten her gloves. She put her hands in her pockets. She stood on the walk and watched the cars coming and passing beneath her and listened to their tires on the wet street. To her right was the Charles River, wide and black and cold. On sunny days it was blue and in the fall she had watched sailboats on it. Beyond the river were the lights of Cambridge; she thought of the bars there and the warm students drinking beer and she wanted Michaelis with her now. She knew that: she wanted him. She had wanted him for a long time but she had told him no, had even gone many times to his apartment and still told him no, because all the time she was thinking. On that last night she wasn't thinking, and she had not done any thinking since then: she had moved through September and October in the fearful certainty of love, and she still had that as she stood shivering above the street, looking out at the black river and the lights on the other side.

She phoned her parents at nine-fifteen, during their cocktail hour. Her mother talked on the phone in the break-fast room, and her father went to his den and used the phone there. He would be wearing a cardigan and drinking a martini. Her mother would be wearing a dress; nearly always she put on a dress at the end of the day. She would be sitting on the stool by the phone, facing the blackboard where Miranda and her two older brothers had read messages when they came home from school, and written their own. Once, when she was a little girl, she had come home and read: *Pussycat, I'm playing golf. I'll be home at four, in time to pay Maria.* And she had written: *Maria was not here. I feel sick and I am going to bed.* Beyond her mother's head, the sun would be setting over the bluff behind the house; part of the pool would be in the bluff's shadow, the water close to the house still and sunlit blue.

The sun would be coming through the sliding glass doors that opened to the pool and the lawn, those glass doors that one morning when she was twelve she opened and, looking down, saw a small rattlesnake coiled sleeping in the shade on the flagstone inches from her bare feet. As she shut the doors and cried out for her father it raised its head and started to rattle. Her father came running barechested in pajama pants; then he went to his room and got a small automatic he kept in his drawer and shot the snake as it slithered across the stones. Sunlight would be coming through those doors now and into the breakfast room and shining on her mother in a bright dress.

'Fly home tomorrow,' her mother said.

'Well, I'll be home at Thanksgiving. Michaelis said he'd arrange it for then.'

'We'd like to see you before *that*,' her mother said.

'And don't worry,' her father said. 'You're not the first good kids to get into a little trouble.'

That night she fell asleep listening to her father's deep and soothing voice as it drew her back through October and September, by her long hair (but gently) dragging her into August and the house in Woodland Hills, the pepper trees hanging long over the sidewalks, on summer mornings coffee at the glass table beside the pool and at sixteen (with her father) a cigarette too, though not with her mother until she was seventeen; in the morning she woke to his voice and she heard it on the plane and could not read *Time* or *Holiday* or *Antigone*, and it was his voice she descended through in the night above Los Angeles, although it was Michaelis who waited for her, who embraced her. When they got home and she hugged her father she held him tightly and for a moment she had no volition and wanted none. Just before kissing her mother, Miranda looked at her eyes: they were green and they told her she had been foolish; then Miranda kissed her, held her, and in her own tightening arms she felt again her resolve.

They went to the breakfast room. Before they started talking, Miranda went outside and looked at the pool and lawn in the dark. Fog was settling; tops of trees touched the sky above the bluff. She went in and sat at one end of the table, facing her father and the glass doors behind him. They reflected the room. Her father's neck and bald head were brown from playing golf, his thin moustache clipped, more gray than she had remembered, and there was more gray too (or more than she had seen, thinking of him in Boston) in the short brown hair at the sides of his head. He was drinking brandy. Or he had a snifter of brandy in front of him, but he mostly handled it; he picked it up and put it down; he ran his finger around the rim; he warmed it in his cupped hands but didn't drink; with thumb and fingers he turned it on the table. He was smoking a very thin cigar, and now and then he cheated and inhaled. Her mother sat to his left, at the side of the table; she had pulled her chair close to his end of the table and turned it so she faced Miranda and Michaelis. Her hair had been growing darker for years and she had kept it blonde and long. Her skin was tough and tan, her face lined, weathered, and she wore bracelets that jangled. She was drinking brandy and listening, though she appeared not listening so much as hearing again lines she had played to for a hundred nights, and waiting for her cue. Miranda mostly watched her father, because he was talking, though sometimes she glanced at Michaelis; he was the one she wanted to watch, but she didn't; for she didn't want anyone, not even him, to see how much she was appealing to him. He sat to her left, his chair was pulled toward her so that he faced her parents, and when she looked at him she saw his quiet profile, his dark curly hair, his large hand holding the can of Coors, and his right shoulder, which was turned slightly away from her. She wanted to see his eyes but she did not really need to; for in the way he occupied space, quiet, attentive, nodding, his arms that were so often spread and in motion now close to his chest, she saw and felt what she had seen at the airport: above his jocular mouth the eyes had told her he had not been living well with his fear.

'—so it's not Mother and me that counts. It's *you* two. We've got to think about what's best for you two.'

'And the baby,' Miranda said.

'Come on, sweetheart. That's not a baby. It's just something you're piping blood into.'

'It's alive; that's why you want me to kill it.'

'Sweetheart—'

'Do you *really* want it?' her mother said.

'Yes.'

'I don't believe you. You mean you're happy about it? You're *glad* you're pregnant?'

'I can do it.'

'You can have a baby, sure,' her father said. 'But what about Michaelis? Do you know how much studying there is in law school?'

'I can work,' she said.

'I thought you were having a baby,' her mother said.

'I can work.'

'And hire a Mexican woman to take care of your child.'

'I can work!'

'You're being foolish.'

Her father touched her mother's arm.

'Wait, honey. Listen, sweetheart, I know you can work. That's not the point. The point is, why suffer? Jesus, sweetheart, you're eighteen years old. You've never had to live out there. The hospital and those Goddamn doctors will own you. And you've got to eat once in a while. Michaelis, have another beer.'

Michaelis got up and as he moved behind Miranda's chair she held up her wine glass and he took it. When he came back with his beer and her glass of wine he said: 'I can do it.'

'Maybe you shouldn't,' her mother said. 'Whether you can or not. Maybe it won't be good for Miranda. What are you going to be, pussycat—a dumb little housewife? Your husband will be out in the world, he'll be growing, and all you'll know is diapers and Gerbers. You've got to finish college—' It was so far away now: blackboards, large uncurtained windows looking out at nothing, at other walls, other windows; talking, note-taking; talking, talking, talking … She looked at Michaelis; he was watching her mother, listening. '—You can't make marriage the be-all and end-all. Because if you do it won't work. Listen: from the looks of things we've got one of the few solid marriages around. But it took work, pussycat. Work.' Her eyes gleamed with the victory of that work, the necessity for it. 'And we were older. I was twenty-six, I'd been to school, I'd worked; you see the difference it makes? After all these years with this guy—and believe me some of them have been like standing in the rain—now that I'm getting old and going blind from charcoal smoke at least I know I didn't give anything up to get married. Except my independence. But I was fed up with that. And all right: I'll tell you something else too. I'd had other relationships. With men. That helped too. There—' she lightly smacked the table '—that's my confession for the night.'

But her face was not the face of someone confessing. In her smile, which appeared intentionally hesitant, intentionally vulnerable, and in the crinkling tan flesh at the corners of her eyes, in the wide green eyes themselves, and in the tone of finality in her throaty voice—there: now it's out, I've told you everything, that's how much I care, the voice said; her smacking of the table with a palm said—Miranda sensed a coaxing trick that she did not want to understand. But she did understand and she sat hating her mother, whose eyes and smile were telling her that making love with Michaelis was a natural but subsidiary part of growing up; that finally what she felt that night and since (and before: the long, muddled days and nights when she was not so much trying to decide but to free herself so she could make love without deciding) amounted now to nothing more than anxiety over baby fat and pimples. It meant nothing. Miranda this fall meant nothing. She would outgrow the way she felt. She would look back on those feelings with amused nostalgia as she could now look back on grapefruit and cottage cheese, and the creams she had applied on her face at night, the camouflaging powder during the day.

'You see,' her father said, 'we don't object to you having a lover. Hell, we can't. What scares us, though, is you being unhappy: and the odds are that you *will* be. Now think of it the other way. Try to, sweetheart. I've never forced you to do anything—I've never been *a*ble to—and I'm not forcing you now. I only want you to look at it from a different side for a while. You and Mother fly to New York—' She felt sentenced to death. Her legs were cool and weak, her heart beat faster within images of her cool, tense body under lights, violated. '—the pill, then you're safe. Both of you. You have three years to grow. You can go back to school—'

'To be *what?*' she said. 'To be *what*,' and she wiped her eyes.

'That's exactly it,' her mother said. 'You don't know yet what you want to be but you say you're ready to get married.'

She had not said that. She had said something altogether different, though she couldn't explain it, could not even explain it to herself. When they said married they were not talking about her. That was not what she wanted. Perhaps she wanted nothing. Except to be left alone as she was in Boston to listen to the fearful pulsations of her body; to listen to them; to sleep with them; wake with them. It was not groceries. She saw brown bags, cans. That was not it. She watched Michaelis. He was listening to them, and in his eyes she saw relieved and grateful capitulation. In his eyes that night his passion was like fear. He was listening to them, he was nodding, and now they were offering the gift, wrapped in her father's voice: '—So much better that way, so much more sensible. And this Christmas, say right after Christmas, you could go to Acapulco. Just the two of you. It's nice at that time of year, you know? It could be your Christmas present. The trip could.'

She smiled before she knew she was smiling; slightly she shook her head, feeling the smile like a bandage: they were giving her a honeymoon, her honeymoon lover in the Acapulco hotel after he had been sucked from her womb. She would have cried, but she felt dry inside, she was tired, and she knew the night was ended.

'I was afraid on Mulholland Drive. I was afraid in Boston.

It was the most important thing there was. How I was afraid all the time.' Her parents' faces were troubled with compassion; they loved her; in her father's eyes she saw her own pain. 'I kept wanting not to be afraid, and it was all I thought about. Then I stopped wanting that. I was afraid, and it was me, and it was all right. Now we can go to Acapulco.' She looked at Michaelis. He looked at her, guilty, ashamed; then he looked at her parents as though to draw from them some rational poise; but it didn't work, and he lowered his eyes to his beer can. 'Michaelis? Do you want to go to Acapulco?'

Still he looked down. He had won and lost, and his unhappy face struggled to endure both. He shrugged his shoulders, but only slightly, little more than a twitch, as if in mid-shrug he had realized what a cowardly gesture the night had brought him to. That was how she would most often remember him: even later when she would see him, when she would make love with him (but only one more time), she would not see the nearly healed face he turned to her, but his face as it was now, the eyes downcast; and his broad shoulders in their halted shrug.

It was not remorse she felt. It was dying. In the mornings she woke with it, and as she brushed her hair and ate yogurt or toast and honey and coffee and walked with Holly to school as the November days grew colder, she felt that ropes of her own blood trailed from her back and were knotted in New York, on that morning, and that she could not move forward because she could not go back to free herself. And she could not write to Michaelis. She tried, and she wrote letters like this:—*the lit exam wasn't as hard as I expected. I love reading the Greeks. The first snow has fallen, and it's lovely and I like looking out the window at it and walking in it. I've learned to make a snow angel. You lie on your back in the snow and you spread your arms and legs, like doing jumping jacks, and then you stand up carefully and you've left an angel in the snow, with big, spreading wings. Love, Miranda.* When she wrote *love* she wanted to draw lines through it, to cover it with ink, for she felt she was lying. Or not that. It was the word that lied, and when she shaped it with her pen she felt the false letters, and heard the hollow sound of the word.

She did not like being alone anymore. Before, she had liked coming home in the late afternoon and putting on records and studying or writing to Michaelis or just lying on the couch near the sunset window until Holly came home. But now that time of day (and it was a dark time, winter coming, the days growing short) was like the other time: morning, waking, when there was death in her soul, in her blood, and she thought of the dead thing she wouldn't call by name, and she wished for courage in the past, wished she had gone somewhere alone, New Hampshire or Maine, a small house in the woods, and lived alone with the snow and the fireplace and a general store down the road and read books and walked in the woods while her body grew, and it grew. She would not call it anything even when she imagined February's swollen belly; that would be in June; the second of June. Already she would not think June when she knew she would say: Today is probably the day my baby would have been born. So she could not be alone anymore, not even in this apartment she loved, this city she loved.

She thought of it as a gentle city. And she felt gentle too, and tender. One morning she saw a small yellow dog struck by a car; the dog was not killed; it ran yelping on three legs, holding up the fourth, quivering, and Miranda could feel the pain in that hind leg moving through the cold air. She could not see blood in movies anymore. She read the reviews, took their warnings, stayed away. Sometimes when she saw children on the street she was sad; and there were times when she longed for her own childhood. She remembered what it was like not knowing anything, and she felt sorry for herself because what she knew now was killing her, she felt creeping death in her breast, and bitterly she regretted the bad luck that had brought her this far, this alone; and so she wanted it all to be gone, November and October and September, she wanted to be a virgin again, to go back even past that, to be so young she didn't know virgin from not-virgin. She knew this was dangerous. She knew that nearly everything she was feeling now was dangerous, and so was her not-feeling: her emptiness when she wrote to her parents and Michaelis; in classrooms she felt abstract; when people came to the apartment she talked with them, she got high with them, but she was only a voice. She neither greeted them nor told them goodbye with her body; she touched no one; or, if she did, she wasn't aware of it; if anyone touched her they touched nothing. One night as she was going to bed stoned she said to Holly: 'I'm a piece of chalk.' She thought of seeing a psychiatrist but believed (had to believe) that all this would leave her.

On days when she got home before Holly, she put on music and spent every moment waiting for Holly. Sometimes, waiting, she drank wine or smoked a pipe, and the waiting was not so bad; although sometimes with wine it was worse, the wine seemed to relax her in the wrong way, so that her memory and dread and predictions were even sharper, more cruel. With dope the waiting was always easier. She was worried about drinking alone, smoking alone; but she was finally only vaguely worried. The trouble she was in was too deep for her to worry about its surfaces. When Holly came home, short of breath from climbing the stairs, her fair cheeks reddened from the cold and her blonde hair damp with snow like drops of dew, Miranda talked and talked while they cooked, and she ate heartily, and felt that eating was helping her, as though she were recovering from an illness of the flesh.

Her parents and Michaelis wanted her to fly home at Thanksgiving but she went to Maine with Diane, a friend from school. Holly told her parents she was going too, and she went to Rhode Island with Tom. Diane's parents lived in a large brick house overlooking the sea. They were cheerful and affluent, and they were tall and slender like Diane, who had freckles that were fading as winter came. There was a younger brother who was tall and quiet and did not shave yet, and his cheeks were smooth as a girl's. Around him Miranda felt old.

She had never seen the Atlantic in winter. On Thanksgiving morning she woke before Diane and sat at the window. The sky was gray, a wind was blowing, the lawn sloping down to the sea was snow, and the wind blew gusts of it like powder toward the house. The lawn ended at the beach, at dark rocks; the rocks went out into the sea, into the gray, cold waves. Beyond the rocks she saw a seal swimming. She watched it, sleek and brown and purposeful, going under, coming up. She quickly dressed in corduroy pants and sweater and boots and coat and went downstairs; she heard Diane's parents having coffee in the kitchen, and quietly went outside and down the slippery lawn to the narrow strip of sand and the rocks. But the seal was gone. She stood looking out at the sea. Once she realized she had been daydreaming, though she could not recall what it was she dreamed; but for a minute or longer she had not known where she was, and when she turned from her dreaming to look at the house, to locate herself, there was a moment when she did not know the names of the people inside. Then she began walking back and forth in front of the house, looking into the wind at the sea. Before long a light snow came blowing in on the salt wind. She turned her face to it. I suppose I don't love Diane, she told herself. For a moment I forgot her name.

Then it was December, a long Saturday afternoon that was gray without snow, and Holly was gone for the weekend. In late afternoon Miranda left the lighted apartment and a paper she was writing and walked up Beacon Street. The street and sidewalks were wet and the gutters held gray, dirty snow. She walked to the Public Garden where there were trees and clean snow, and on a bridge over a frozen pond she stopped and watched children skating. Then she walked through the Garden and across the street to the Common; the sidewalks around it were crowded, the Hare Krishna people were out too, with their shaved heads and pigtails and their robes in the cold, chanting their prayer. She did not see any winos. In warm weather they slept on the grass or sat staring from benches, wearing old, dark suits and sometimes a soiled hat. But now they were gone, and where, she wondered, did they go when the sky turns cold? She walked across the Common to the State House; against the gray sky its gold dome looked odd, like something imported from another country. Then she walked home. Already dusk was coming, and she didn't want to be alone. When she got home Brian was ringing the doorbell.

'Holly's not here,' she said.

'I know. Are you here?'

'Sometimes. Come on up.'

He was tall and he wore a fatigue jacket. She looked away from his face, reached in her pocket for the key; she felt him wanting her, it was like a current from his body, and she felt it as she opened the door and as they climbed the stairs. In the apartment she gave him a beer.

'Are you hungry?' she said.

'No.'

'I am. If I cook something, will you eat it?'

'Sure.'

'There's chicken. Is chicken all right? Broiled?'

'Chicken? Why not?'

He followed her to the kitchen. While she cooked they talked and he had another beer and she drank wine. She wasn't hungry anymore. She knew something would happen and she was waiting for it, waiting to see what she would do. She cooked and they ate and then went to the living room and smoked a pipe on the couch. When he took off her sweater she nearly said let's go to bed, but she didn't. She closed her eyes and waited and when he was undressed she kissed his bearded face. Her eyes were closed. She felt wicked and that excited her; he was very thin; her body was quick and wanton; but her heart was a stone; her heart was a clock; her heart was a watching eye. Then he shuddered and his weight rested on her and she said: 'You bastard.'

He left her. He sat at the end of the couch, at her feet; he took a swallow of beer and leaned back and looked at the ceiling.

'I saw it downstairs,' he said. 'You wanted to ball.'

'Don't call it that.'

He looked at her; then he leaned over and picked up his socks.

'No,' she said. 'Call it that.' He put on his socks. 'Say it again.'

'What are you playing?'

'I'm not. I don't play anymore. It's all—What are you doing?'

'I'm putting on my pants.' He was standing, buckling his belt. He picked up his sweater from the floor.

'No,' she said. 'I'm cold.'

'Get dressed.'

'I don't want you to go. Let's get in bed.'

'That'll be the second time tonight I do something you want me to. Will I be a bastard again?'

'No. I'm just screwed up, Brian, that's all.'

'Who isn't?'

In bed he was ribs and hip bone against her side and she liked resting her head on his long hard arm.

'What's the matter?' he said. 'You worried about that guy in California?'

'He's not there anymore.'

'Where'd he go?'

'He's still there. Things happened.'

'Have you had many guys?'

'Just him and you. You won't tell Holly, will you?'

'Why should I?'

'How long have you been in school?'

'Six years, on and off.'

'What will you do?'

'They haven't told me yet.'

'Michaelis is going to be a lawyer.'

'Good for him.'

'I used to love him.'

'Figures.'

'He's going to work with Chicanos. I won't be with him now. For a whole year I thought about that. I was going to marry him and have a baby and carry it like a papoose on the picket lines. We wouldn't have much money. That was it for a whole year and I was feeling all that when I made love with him, it was my first time and I hurt and I bled and I probably wasn't any good, but my God I felt wonderful. I felt like I was going to heaven.'

'You better cheer up, man. There's other guys.'

'Oh yes, I know: there are other guys. Miranda will have other guys.'

Her heart did not change: not that night when they made love again, nor Sunday morning waking to his hands. Late Sunday night Holly came home and Miranda woke up but until Holly was undressed and in bed she pretended she was asleep so Holly wouldn't turn on the lights. Then she pretended to wake up because she wanted to talk to Holly before, in the morning, she saw her face.

'How was your weekend?'

'Fine. What did you do?'

'Stayed in the apartment and studied.'

She lit a cigarette. Holly came over and took one from the pack. Miranda did not look at her: she closed her eyes and smoked and felt the sour cold of the lie. Holly was back in bed, talking into the distance of the lie, and Miranda listened and answered and lay tense in bed, for she was so many different Mirandas: the one with Holly now and the one who made love with Brian (balled; balled; she was sore) and the one who didn't want to make love with Brian (b——); and beneath or among those there were perhaps two other Mirandas, and suddenly she almost cried, remembering September and October when she was afraid but she was one Miranda Jones. She sat up quickly, too quickly, so that Holly stopped talking and then said: 'What's wrong?'

'Nothing. I just want another cigarette.'

'You should get out next weekend.'

'Probably.'

'Come to Providence with me.'

'What would I do?'

'I don't know. Whatever you do here. And we can get you a date.'

'Maybe I will. Probably I won't, though.'


Tuesday after dinner Brian came over. He sat on the couch with Holly, and Miranda faced them from a chair. She tried not to look directly at him but she could not help herself: she drank too much beer and she watched him. He kept talking. Her nakedness was not in his face. She felt it was in hers, though, when Holly's hand dropped to his thigh and rested there. She was not jealous; she did not love Brian; she felt as though something were spilled in the room, something foul and shameful, and no one dared look at it, and no one would clean it up. I'm supposed to be cool, she told herself as she went to the refrigerator and opened three cans of beer. She opened Brian's last. It was his because it was on the left and she would carry it in her left hand and she remembered his hands. I am not for this world, she thought. Or it isn't for me. It's not because I'm eighteen either. Michaelis is twenty-two; he will get brown in the sun talking to Chicanos, he will smell of beer and onions, but his spirit won't rise; Michaelis is of the world, he will be a lawyer.

She brought Holly and Brian their beer. I'm supposed to be cool, she told herself as she watched Holly's hand on his leg, watched his talking face where she didn't live. And where did she live? Whose eyes will hold me, whose eyes will know me when my own eyes look back at me in the morning and I am not in them? I'm supposed to be cool, she told herself as she went to her room and felt the room move as she settled heavily under the blankets; she was bloated with beer, she knew in the morning her mouth would be dry, her stomach heavy and liquid. From the living room the sounds came. It's not me. She was drunk and for a moment she thought she had said it aloud. It's not me they're doing it to. I don't love him. She remembered his hard, thin legs between hers and she saw him with Holly and wary as a thief her hand slid down and she moved against it. It's not me they're doing it to. She listened to the sounds from the other room and moved within them against her hand.


In his bed in his apartment Michaelis held her and his large, dark eyes were wet, and she spoke to him and kissed and dried his tears, though she felt nothing for them; she gave them her lips as she might have given coins to a beggar. She could feel nothing except that it was strange for him to cry; she did not believe she would ever cry again; not for love. It was her first night home, they had left her house three hours earlier, left her mother's voice whose gaiety could not veil her fear and its warning: 'Don't be late,' she said, meaning don't spend the night, don't drive our own nails through our hands; already her mother's eyes (and, yes, her father's too) were hesitant, vulpine. How can we get our daughter back? the eyes said. We have saved her. But now how do we get her back? Her parents' hands and arms were loving; they held her tightly; they drew her to their hearts. The arms and eyes told her not to go to Acapulco after Christmas; not to want to go. No matter. She did not want to go. Michaelis's arms were tight and loving too, he lay on his side, his body spent from loving her, and now she was spending his soul too, watching it drip on his cheeks: '—It didn't mean anything. Don't cry. We won't go to Acapulco. I don't think I'll sleep with Brian again, but we won't go to Acapulco. I want to do other things. I don't know what they'll be yet. You'll have a good life, Michaelis. Don't worry: you will. It'll be a fine life. Don't be sad. Things end, that's all. But you'll be fine. Do you want to take me home now? Or do you want me to stay a while. I'll stay the night if you want—'

She propped on an elbow and looked at him. He had

stopped crying, his cheeks glistened still, and he lay on his back now, staring at the ceiling. She could see in his face that he would not make love with her again or, for some time, with anyone else. She watched him until she didn't need to anymore. Then she called a taxi and put on her clothes. When she heard the taxi's horn she left Michaelis lying naked in the dark.

# SEPARATE FLIGHTS

*The whales, whose periodic suicide instinct has never been explained by scientists, started grounding themselves yesterday afternoon on the Florida Bay side of Grassy Key, about seven miles north of Marathon, in the Florida Keys.*

THE NEW YORK TIMES

*for Lynn*

## 1

ON THE SHORT AFTERNOONS of winter Beth Harrison turned on the lights early and started a fire in the living room; when her daughter Peggy came home from high school they sat in chairs facing the fire, Peggy drinking hot chocolate, Beth drinking a bourbon-and-water which she always thought of as her second, though sometimes it was her third. She was forty-nine years old. She did not know—or did not try to know, since there was no reason to—exactly when her before dinner drinking had slipped into an earlier part of the afternoon. In winter she drank when she turned on the lights and started a fire. But now in May she drank gin and tonic while the sun angled through the kitchen windows, and Mrs. Lester on the

corner played golf, and the Crenshaw boys across the street
yelled and smacked a whiffle ball. She was usually alone, for
Peggy and Bucky ate ice cream cones after school and went
driving and Peggy came home in time for dinner, her cheeks
warm, her eyes bright as though with images of trees turning
green and sunlit farmers plowing their fields.

Today when Lee came home Beth was peeling potatoes
at the kitchen table, drinking her third gin and tonic since
taking the cleaning woman home at three-thirty. When he
saw the drink in her hand his eyes changed, darkened for an
instant as in scolding or scorn; then he said hello and moving
around the table briefly kissed her lips.

'I picked up the tickets,' he said.

'Who's going first?'

'Mine's at three-thirty and yours is four-forty.'

While he was upstairs changing clothes she made two
drinks, and when he came down in sport shirt and loafers he
took his and started toward the living room.

'Will I see you in Chicago?' she said.

He turned at the door.

'My connection's right away, so I'll see you in San
Francisco.'

'Will I have to wait long?'

'Course not. I'll meet your plane.'

'I mean in Chicago.'

'About thirty minutes. You're on 427 from Chicago, I'm on
502.' He was turning toward the living room when she said:
'So if 427 goes down—or 502—we've made a mistake.'

'Well, that's true, but it's better to gamble with losing one
of us than both.'

'Do you know what you're gambling with?'

'It's for Peggy, you know that.'

'No, she's the stakes. I mean what's holding the other hand?'

He looked at her for a moment; then he half-turned to
the living room, standing profiled in the kitchen doorway.

'All I know is it's sound, it's practical. Our company does
it, other companies do it—' Then he stopped. 'Anyhow—' he

said, and shrugged and went into the living room; she heard him sliding the hassock, then snapping straight the front page of the *Des Moines Register*. She finished peeling the potatoes and went outside to light the charcoal. She watched it until Bucky brought Peggy home, then Lee came outside and the three of them sat in lawn chairs around the grill. Peggy held a small red water pistol and shot at steak drippings that flamed on the charcoal.

'Peggy,' Lee said. 'You know the last thing I did before I came home today? I made a call on a woman who buried her husband last week. He was well covered, so she's better fixed for money than she was before, but the point is she's a widow now. And you know how old she is? Fifty-five. Even if that seems old to you, it's mighty young to be a widow in 1967. She'll probably live another twenty years. And her husband: her husband was fifty-eight—'

Beth sipped her drink and watched two young squirrels darting about in the elm tree whose branches nearly touched the roof, and she wondered if she would ever see seventy-five, or if she even wanted to. Then she looked to her right, at Peggy, her blue eyes made brighter by contact lenses, her cheek concave as she drew on a cigarette, faint downy hair on her face catching the sunlight, and Beth could not imagine this child, her second and last—no: she could not imagine her living through the next sixty years. When Beth was a child the years seemed straight and simple as a road. Yet now they were wide and deep, unbounded as corn fields covered by snow, or in early spring when the fields lay bare as far as you could see and wind blew from the southwest and the sky turned black and yellow; you looked out over the blowing dust and scattered, bending trees and waited for the tornado funnel. Now she heard Lee's voice but not what he said, and the squirrels had left the elm or entered its trunk, and she was thinking of long ago when she lived in the country and spring was like that. Her hand had risen to Peggy's shoulder and was resting there.

'What would I do with a thousand dollars?' Peggy said.

'Two, then. I'll give you two.'

'Oh Daddy, I appreciate it. I *really* do. I mean that you care how I die. But I don't want to quit and you know yourself if you don't really want to, you can't.'

'I did.'

'But you were scared enough.'

'And you ought to be. Haven't you heard your mother, the way she breathes when she carries in groceries or climbs the stairs? The way she coughs in the morning?'

'He's right,' Beth said, and she stood and turned over the steaks. 'How's Marsha?'

'Better,' Peggy said. 'Vic comes home on leave around June.'

'Then he goes over?'

'He thinks so.'

'He will,' Lee said.

'You poor children,' Beth said, and jabbed a steak with the fork, and Peggy shot water into the flames.

That night Beth went to bed while Lee was watching the late news. With her eyes closed she lay in the dark for thirty minutes; then Lee came upstairs and when he turned on his bedside lamp she pretended she was asleep. She tried not to be angry, tried to hold onto the little calm she had gained in half an hour of lying still while he emptied his pockets, coins clicking and ringing on the chest of drawers: if she had been asleep, that light and sound would have waked her. He got into bed, turned out the light, and she listened to his breathing as it slowed and deepened (and yes: oh yes, he was right of course about her: she breathed badly), and she wondered what he thought about in those last conscious minutes. They passed quickly: he shifted a leg, and was asleep. She lit a cigarette, knowing that if she were asleep the scrape of flint, the clicking shut of the Zippo, perhaps even the small flame would intrude as jarringly as an alarm clock or the frightful after-midnight ringing of a phone. She believed any sound would do that: a light rain, a gentle wind rustling the elm leaves, Lee or even Peggy down the hall stirring in bed. Sometimes she woke at night and there was no sound at all; she would lie there in the silence, afraid, as though she had been wakened by the presence of fog outside her window.

She had tried everything she knew of except drugs. She had talked to Polly Fairchild, who couldn't sleep either: Polly had told her that a snack before bed would take blood from her brain and help her relax. If she woke in the night she should get up and read, drink some milk, and she shouldn't smoke. Sometimes you could talk yourself to sleep: *my feet are going to sleep, my feet are going to sleep, my ankles are—* And she mustn't worry: if at nine o'clock or so she started worrying about whether or not she could sleep, she'd only make herself more tense. But none of this worked for Polly: she took a pill every night and slept soundly. She told Beth they were mild, they weren't habit-forming, and though it took her longer to feel really awake in the morning, that was an easy price for a good night's sleep.

Beth said no. When Lee suggested drugs, she said no again; she would not, she said, take a drug so she could sleep. If she couldn't do something as natural and inevitable as sleeping, she wanted to know why. So night after night she went to bed and lay awake or, after sleeping for a while, she woke again and lay smoking in the dark for an hour and sometimes more. Yet after all this time alone she still didn't know why she couldn't sleep. She knew this much, though: she was not equipped to solve a problem of this sort. Until now she had always dealt with problems that had alternatives and you weighed them and made a choice, like buying one dishwasher instead of another. But now the buyer's instinct was useless: what was needed was a probing insight into herself, and this was a bitter and unprofitable task. For when she did try to explore herself she found—oh God: she found nothing.

Now she got out of bed, went downstairs to the kitchen, and made a gin and tonic. She sat on the couch in the dark living room, lit a cigarette and exhaled quickly before a cough jerked upward from her chest. She knew it was long after midnight, but being awake down here wasn't altogether bad as long as she didn't think of getting up in the morning, and how tired she would be; she never slept in the afternoon, for she was afraid a nap robbed that much more sleep from the coming night. But if she could give up the idea of sleeping, devote herself to the moment at hand, there was an appealing secretive quality about sitting alone in a quiet and darkened house. She knew why too: because upstairs Lee slept like a child, with his clean lungs, his exercised body, and his mind that worked with the precision of numbers.

After another drink she felt sleepy. She was afraid that climbing the stairs would quicken her blood and breath and wake her again; so stretching out on the couch, she slept. She woke to the pounding of Lee's in-place running in their bedroom directly above her. Peggy came downstairs first and sat at the kitchen table with a cup of coffee. When Lee came down, smelling of after-shave lotion, Beth was pouring buckwheat mix into a bowl.

'What did you do, sleep on the couch?'

'I was down here when I got sleepy, so I stayed.'

'You were asleep when I went up.'

'It didn't last.'

He poured a cup of coffee and sat down.

'You don't have to stay awake,' he said.

'I know.'

'There's nothing wrong with taking something to help you sleep.'

'I used to sleep,' she said.

That afternoon she drove Lee to the Cedar Rapids airport, then went back to Iowa City, picked up Peggy at school, and got to the airport in time for a quick drink in the cocktail lounge, a martini for her and a Coke for Peggy. She was not excited about going to a convention of insurance men in San Francisco, but she pretended to Peggy that she was. She told Peggy what food was in the refrigerator, reminded her to leave the back door unlocked while she was at school so the dry cleaners could deliver the clothes, and told her again the name of the hotel in San Francisco. Then she said: 'Look, I probably

don't have to tell you this, but I ought to anyway: don't have
Bucky over while we're gone.'

'I didn't plan to.'

'Well, I trust you, and if it weren't for the neighbors I
wouldn't care. But you don't want gossip.'

'No.'

'So tell him goodnight on the front porch, okay?'

Peggy did. For the next three nights, after making love in
her bed (and they had never had a bed) she told Bucky goodnight on the dark front porch, the living room behind them
darkened too, so he could slip out and across the lawn to his
car parked down the street.


## 2


'No,' Beth said, on the plane from San Francisco to Chicago,
'I'm really not afraid.'

Her seat was next to the window, and now she looked out,
testing what she had just said. They were flying through
clouds so thick that she couldn't see the wing behind her. She
thought of the pilot flying by instruments, she thought of
human error, she imagined a midair collision. Then she
turned back to Robert Carini, the silversmith from New York,
who a moment ago had lifted his glass in salute and said he
was afraid of flying so he was glad he had someone to talk to.

'My husband would get twenty thousand dollars, though.
I don't like that.'

'That's not so much. I took out sixty-five.'

'Oh, I don't mean those slot machines. He told me to get
some of that, but I didn't. No, he has a policy on me for ten
thousand, with double indemnity.'

'That's an expensive funeral.'

'It's not to bury me. He says women are worth more these
days, and it'd cost that to hire someone to do what I do.'

Then they were smiling at each other.

'Cooking,' Beth said.

'Where is he now?'

'Flying to Chicago. We took separate flights.'

'Oh, I see. So—'

'Yes. So we won't die together.'

Two hours ago she had been drinking coffee with Lee in a lunchroom at the San Francisco airport. At a table to their left a young soldier and his wife were finishing lunch, talking quietly, their eyes shifting and lowering with that distraction of transitional conversations. In the lobby there were soldiers without girls: at the magazine rack, the tobacco counter, sleeping in chairs; as Beth and Lee walked through she said: 'If I were young and single I'd be a soldier's girl.' Relighting his pipe, he glanced at her. He walked too fast, and she was short of breath when they reached the gate. She went through the lobby with him, to the door. He looked up at the sky, said, 'Still cloudy,' then kissed her and said, 'I'll see you in Cedar Rapids.' She stood in the doorway until he boarded the plane, then she found a bar. There were two men sitting apart from each other at the bar, and a young naval officer with a girl at a small table. Beth sat at the end of the bar and ordered a Bloody Mary.

Waiting for a separate flight made her feel she was involved in a childish ruse. But with her second drink she thought of her plane crashing, a death so much quicker than her actual dying would be. A violent death like that would be an awful shock for Peggy, and now she felt sorry for Peggy and Helen and Helen's two children, Wendy and Billy, who would wonder if it hurt Granma when the plane crashed; and she even felt sorry for Lee, who was sentimental and would therefore believe he was burying something, and next year when Peggy went to college he would be lonely in the house at night. And all this time, sipping her drink and thinking of her own death, there was something else in the back of her mind, something desperately mean, and now with a guilty catch of her breath she let it out: what if *his* plane crashed? She finished her drink in a swallow and left the bar.

She boarded her plane; tall Mr. Carini with his thick white

hair and lined dark face was already there, in the aisle seat. The stewardess brought champagne cocktails, and before take off Beth knew his name and that he was a silversmith.

'Are you really?' she had said. 'I thought only Mexicans and Indians did that.'

He had smiled and said oh no, he did it too, although he mostly just ran things now, and once in a while made something for his wife and daughter. She asked if he had anything with him, anything he had made, and he said no but he'd send her a bracelet, and he wrote her address in a notebook. It had been a long time since she had met anyone whose work was either new or interesting. He ordered martinis and she asked questions about his work, real questions that she wanted answers to, and when he lit her cigarettes she took his hand and guided the flame.

'Your husband's a very practical man,' he said now.

'He sells life insurance.'

'Oh. And what do you do?'

'I don't do anything.'

'Of course you do.'

'A lot of this,' she said, and lifted her glass.

'Really?'

'Yes.'

'Why?'

'I don't know.'

'Do you have children?'

'Two girls. One married, one seventeen.'

'So you're alone most of the time.'

'I have friends: you know, wives of my husband's friends. And Helen—she's my married daughter—she lives in Iowa City, so sometimes after shopping I go see her and we drink beer in her kitchen.'

'It's good you're close like that.'

'We're really not, though. I mean we are but she doesn't really talk to me. You know. But at least she's there and she seems to like it when I go over and I try not to go over too often. Most afternoons I do other things.'

'Bridge?'

'That, and other things.'

'Is it so bad?'

'I hate it,' she said.

She was surprised she had said that; then she was glad.

'Not really,' he said.

'Yes. Really.' Then she turned her eyes from his and looked out the window where still there was nothing but air like wet smoke.

'So many people are like that,' he said.

She looked at him.

'But you're not?'

'No,' he said. 'No: maybe I'm fooling myself, but I don't think so.'

'At least you know about other people. My husband doesn't. He lives on routine like a soldier and that's all he sees.'

'But that can be desperation too, living like that. It's like deep water pressure: take some fish out of it and they turn belly-up and die.'

'I'll have to pull him up some time, and see what happens.'

They had second martinis, then the stewardess brought their lunch, chateaubriand, and poured their first glasses of Burgundy, then asked Robert if they wanted to keep the bottle. He said yes. She spoke to them as a couple rather than fellow passengers, and Beth was amused and also felt pleasingly wicked. She was watching Robert's face; he suddenly squinted and she turned to the window: they had broken through the clouds into a glaring sky that was blue and clear as far ahead as she could see. She looked down at green and yellow and brown squares of earth.

'I wonder what state that is.'

Robert leaned toward the window, his face near her shoulder.

'One of those flat ones.'

'Do you feel safer when it's clear?'

'Better, anyway. Clouds are gloomy.'

'And there I was, having such fun drinking with you in a cloud.'

'It'll be more fun in the blue,' he said, and poured wine in her glass.

'I wasn't put on this plane to have fun. I was put on it so I'd die alone.'

'Are you nice to your husband?'

'I think so. I try to be.'

'That's what I thought. But you're pretty tough on him now.'

'I guess I am. And I guess I shouldn't feel sorry for myself just because what happens to most people has happened to me.'

Then in a low, collusive voice, in their odd privacy that was also public so she again felt illicit, she talked about love. She did not know when she had stopped loving her husband, she said. In a way she was grateful it had happened so late because by that time she had stopped believing in love anyway. No, Robert said, it must have been the other way. She thought about that, lighting a cigarette from the one she was smoking (drinking always seemed to clear her bronchial tubes so she could smoke more) then she said yes, he was probably right. She must have stopped loving him long before she admitted it, then still deceiving herself about Lee she stopped believing in love altogether, thus arming herself to come back full circle and admit she did not love him. That way it was easier to take: you suspected something had died in your house, so you looked around and saw that it was long dead in everyone else's house too; then you were able to return and look under your own bed and find, sure enough, a corpse.

She accepted that death. It was as natural and predictable as a wrinkled face. She would not look under that bed again or anyone else's, for oh she had looked too often, too often.... She told Robert of her mother, who was probably content and certainly stupid, for she firmly ignored all failures of the human heart. In her mother's mind everyone lived a life that could be recorded on the obituary page of a newspaper: you were born here, went to school there, were married to a man with such-and-such a job, and you had children. If you asked her about someone she would say: Oh she's doing wonderfully; she has a fine husband and two lovely children.

'She told me that once, about a niece of mine. And I said: I know all that, Mother; what I asked is how *is* she?'

And how could anyone be oblivious to all those signs you could see whether you were looking or not? Give me an hour in a room full of married couples, she said, and I can see their hostilities as plainly as the clothes they wear. Not that she wanted to either. But it was true, all too true, and at least once you understood this, accepted it as commonplace, it wasn't difficult at all to admit that your own life—which long ago you believed was marked for love—had followed the general pattern of humanity. The difficult part was concealing this from your children. At Helen's wedding she had of course cried a little, and for some of the accepted reasons: a daughter had grown, a daughter was leaving, a phase of her own life had ended. But her tears were bitter too, for she knew the rest of Helen's life would never live up to the emotional promise of that day. Like graduation ceremonies where you heard all those words about what lay ahead, then you went out and nothing happened. Helen and Larry would end up, in a friendly way, boring each other, disliking each other. She kept thinking of that during the wedding; in the reception line, when she had to listen to those lecherous old men and tender, hopeful old women, she had to clamp her teeth on ironic replies. And now her seventeen-year-old, Peggy, was in love and she liked to talk about her plans, with this grown-up tone in her voice, and there was nothing to do but listen to her, not as you listen to a child who wants to be a movie star, but to a child whose hope for friends or happiness is so strong yet futile that you know it will break her heart.

'You expected too much,' Robert said. 'Why don't you tell her not to expect too much? Not to stake her whole life on marriage. It's part of her life, but not all.'

'What does your wife do?'

'She's a teacher. Fourth grade.'

'*That* makes a difference.'

They were finishing the wine when the pilot announced their approach to Chicago.

'I've had fun,' Beth said.

'Do you have a layover?'

'An hour.'

'I have two and a half. We can have a drink.'

'We'll be drunk.'

'Well, you like to be and for the flight home I need to be.'

'We'll have a drink.'

'Takeoffs and landings are the worst,' he said. The plane had begun its descent; he took her hand.

In the airport they drank standing at a crowded bar. A clock looked at them from above the rows of bottles. Twenty-five minutes before her flight Robert ordered second drinks; she was about to say there wasn't time, but then she didn't. She turned and watched two Air Force lieutenants come through the door and go to the bar. She was looking at their silver wings when her plane was announced. She turned back to her drink. It was half-finished; she picked it up, then instead of drinking she stirred it with a finger.

'Two pilots just came in,' she said. 'All that time with you on the plane I had forgotten the war.'

He turned and looked at them.

'It's not their fault,' he said. 'They're just kids.'

'I guess so, but *pi*lots—' Sipping her drink she glanced up at the clock. 'We voted for peace in sixty-four, for Johnson.'

'So did we.'

'For peace?'

'Yes. And my son graduates from college this month.'

She touched his wrist.

'Oh, you poor man. Will they get him?'

'Sure they will, sooner or later.'

'I'm glad I don't have a son.'

'I'd like to keep mine. He's—' Then he frowned and shook his head, his eyes somewhere else now, in New York, on his son's face, in Vietnam. 'Wasn't that your plane?'

'I don't know. What did they say?'

'Two twenty-three to Cedar Rapids.'

'My God, yes.'

She looked at the clock, drained her glass, and they walked quickly down the corridor to her gate.

'Could've missed it,' he said.

'Another couple of minutes.'

They found her gate number and walked faster against a crowd of passengers who had just got off a plane.

'Maybe I did,' she said. 'No one's going this way.'

He looked at his watch.

'Three minutes,' he said. 'I enjoyed it.'

'So did I.'

At the gate the clerk grabbed her ticket and shook his head.

'You almost missed it, lady.'

'She's here,' Robert said. 'Just do what you're paid for.'

Hurrying beside her across the small lobby he took her elbow and said: 'I'll send you a bracelet.'

'Good.'

He pressed her hand and she slowed for a moment.

'If you ever get to New York—'

'Right,' she said, then turned and walked as fast as she could out into the warm sunlight. The uniformed man at the foot of the ladder motioned for her to hurry; at the hatch the stewardess, who was annoyed, smiled and said something, and Beth lowered her face so the girl wouldn't smell gin. She sat in an empty seat at the rear. The plane was small, with propellers; the air conditioning wasn't working and the air was stale. Beth was tight. As the plane took off she wondered if Robert was standing at the door, watching. Then she unbuckled her seat belt and lit a cigarette and looked out the window at the flat earth.

Lee and Peggy were waiting at the airport. She kissed them and asked Peggy if everything was all right. Then Lee said: 'Well, it worked.'

'What worked?'

'The planes.' He was grinning. 'Neither one of them crashed.'

# 3

On the way home they stopped at a restaurant for dinner. In a high, delighted voice Beth told Peggy about the fun they had had in San Francisco (she had not had fun in San Francisco), about the Top o' the Mark and Fisherman's Wharf, while all the time, eating her steak, she sat huddled around her warm secret. That night she took it to bed with her and after Lee was sleeping she lit a cigarette and thought of Robert Carini and a hotel in Chicago; she pulled her nightgown above her hips; she moved slowly so Lee wouldn't wake, and the threat of his waking excited her, and thinking of Robert Carini excited her; she felt wicked, and her fingers holding the cigarette trembled. Then she slept.

It became one of her rituals: at first she told herself she was doing it because her heart was unfaithful and in this way she was having her night with Robert (he did not send a bracelet; after ten days she gave up, with more disappointment than she had expected), but after a few nights she didn't really think of Robert, or of anyone else. Later she told herself she was doing it to help her sleep, though usually she slept just as badly. Then she saw the truth: lying beside Lee, moving and breathing in secret passion, she made her loneliness and dislike for him active: she thought of him beside her, knowing nothing of his own wife, of how little he mattered. Afterward she felt guilty, and she treasured that guilt because it was new. But soon enough guilt faded; next the act itself grew boring; yet she clung to it, forced herself into the only emotions that remained: her heart, beating rapidly toward orgasm, felt mean and vengeful.

Which was not enough. Guilt had been the proper ending for those minutes at night: it had made her feel she was returning home after committing a sin. Now, with the loss of guilt, her nights were changed: her passion took her nowhere, returned her from nowhere. It was merely an extension of the bitterness of her days. She did it less frequently.

What she wanted was not so much to sin but to be able to

sin. She started thinking of Robert Carini again. She didn't imagine making love with him. She thought of the guilt: phoning Lee from Chicago to say she had missed connections and would fly to Cedar Rapids tomorrow, then tingling with lies she would have gone to dinner with Robert; after that, in the hotel lobby and elevator and corridor, surely her conscience would have gone to work on her, making her think of Peggy and Helen and Wendy and Billy; and even Lee. And perhaps in the morning she would have opened her eyes to fear and remorse. She might even have returned tender and compassionate to her ordered, disciplined, cuckolded Lee.

But maybe she would have felt nothing except a natural apprehension when she first looked at Lee's face, and when he asked where she had spent the night, was there any trouble finding a room, did she have enough money. Because in order to sin you had to depart from something you believed in, and she had no assurance that being a mother, a grandmother, and a wife would flavor that one night with wickedness. And if that were so, if a night with Robert would have been no more sinful than her private minutes beside Lee, it was better that he had not let her miss the plane.

Yet where had it gone? She had been reared a Catholic, then at some time between starting college and marrying Lee she had stopped being one. She had stopped as unconsciously as your face tans in summer and pales in winter. There had been no iconoclastic teacher, no agnostic roommate: it had been largely a matter of sleeping late on Sunday mornings. Remembering now, she thought there must have been something else, some question on a point of dogma, some dispute with a priest, some book or philosophy course. But there was not, and she was ashamed: not because she had no religion but because she had changed her life without thinking about it. And she had not thought of it since then, except when a friend or relative died (and Kennedy and Marilyn Monroe and Hemingway and Gary Cooper), and for a while she wondered if they were immortal.

But that was all. She assumed there was a God, but maybe

there wasn't; worse still, it didn't seem to matter. She didn't know whether Lee believed or not. She could not remember ever talking about God. You didn't do that, sit around talking about God. You talked with frustration about things outside your life, like Johnson and the war; or you talked about the surfaces of your life: the children and grandchildren and school for Peggy and things you had done and things you had to do:—*had all the groceries there and then I looked in my purse and no wallet, I had left it in the other purse, and no checkbook either, so she had to wait while I went to the courtesy counter and used one of their checks; what should we get Peggy for grad-uation? a watch? you take the VW to work then, and they can pack the wheel bearings on the Lincoln while I'm shopping; a watch, do you think?* You scheduled these things, got them done between the hands of the clock, and at night they gave you conversation. Maybe late some night when Peggy was asleep she ought to make Lee sit down with her and a bottle of gin and she would tell him what she did at night and why, tell him of Robert and how she had waited for a bracelet in the mail, and tell him that on those nights when he made love to her she was eager and hot, but only for herself, and a hand covered her heart and would not yield it to him.

As the summer grew hotter, the idea of such a conversa-tion enticed her. If her belief in God had changed passively, her marriage could change in one violently quick night. The frightening and appealing thing was she could not predict what would happen. Separation, divorce, a marriage coun-selor—even something new and good, both of them with painful and productive honesty voicing all their dislikes, their secrets (she recalled the moment in San Francisco when she had thought of his plane crashing), and after that maybe they could stand among the fallen roof and exploded walls of what they had called their marriage, and wounded and trembling and alone they could hold hands and start from there. But such a dream was nonsense, and she knew it, and the days of summer went on.

Then one night in mid-July she woke and lay smoking

and listened to the hum of the air conditioner in the window. She didn't know what time it was, nor did she want to: she knew she would be awake for at least an hour, probably more. Her hand moved down, then stopped; she didn't want that, it was boring and it took too long and didn't even help her sleep. She got up and put on a summer robe; she would drink gin and tonic in the living room and talk to herself until she was sleepy. Tomorrow was Saturday, so she had no reason to get up; going downstairs she thought of living a nocturnal life when Peggy went to college. She could stay up most of the night until she was truly sleepy, wake up long enough to fix breakfast for Lee, then go back to bed and sleep into the afternoon. Insomnia was only bad if you had to go to sleep and wake at certain times. A bizarre solution, simply to throw away schedules, but you couldn't deny it was a solution; and crossing the kitchen floor in the dark she was pleased, thinking how Lee would despise a life of that sort. He would find several reasons against it but he would never admit his real objection: that people were supposed to be awake in daylight and asleep at night.

She switched on a light and blinked at the clock on the kitchen wall: ten minutes to three. She could hear the air conditioner in the living room; she thought either she had forgotten to turn it off or Peggy and Bucky had come in after their date and turned it on, then Peggy had forgotten it, which was just as well, for already the kitchen was hot and she would go sit in the cool living room and drink gin and perhaps watch the sunrise. She opened the refrigerator and saw there was beer and decided to drink that, because it was simpler and enough of it made her sleepy. She popped open a can and turned off the kitchen light, for she wanted everything dark; she pushed through the swinging door into the living room then stopped, her eyes snapping toward the other sounds which she understood even before she saw the two standing and quick-moving silhouettes at the couch across the room. Her hand darted to the table lamp beside her, but for an instant she squeezed the switch between thumb and finger;

her mouth opened to speak but she didn't do that either; then she turned on the switch and stepped back from the sudden light and what she saw in it: Peggy's face hidden inside the dress she was pulling down and shrugging into, and Bucky with his naked back turned, snapping his trousers at the waist. Beth turned out the light before Peggy's face came out of the dress. She backed through the kitchen door and leaned against the sink and took a long swallow of beer.

They would be whispering now. She couldn't hear them, but she moved farther from the door anyway. She finished the beer before she heard the front door closing, then she waited again. She lit a cigarette and was going to the refrigerator for another beer when Peggy came in, standing with lowered head while the door swung shut behind her. Beth hugged her and stroked her long hair.

'Do you want a beer while we talk?'

Peggy nodded against her shoulder. They went into the living room and, avoiding the couch, Beth chose the easy chairs where she and Lee sat at night to watch television or read. The chairs were side by side, with a table and lamp between; when Beth and Peggy sat down, the lampshade hid their faces.

'Has it been—going on?'

'Yes.'

'I won't tell Daddy.'

'Please don't. Ever.'

'No. No, he won't know. He sees things—I don't know how he sees things, but it's different. And now—'

And now what? Instead of turning on that lamp she could have backed out of the room, gone upstairs to bed, and never mentioned it again: she could have pretended to Peggy and gradually to herself that she thought they were only kissing. Which was still another lie: everyone knew that young people did everything short of making love, yet you called it kissing. And she could have done that tonight, but she hadn't, and by turning on the lamp she had committed herself to something more, to the awful risk of forming words and throwing them out into the dark like so many sparks in a dry season. And now that it was time she had nothing to say, and she nearly said, Let's have a good night's sleep and talk about it tomorrow while Daddy's playing golf. But she would not do that, she would *not*. So she decided to talk about those things she did know, to at least deal with and probably eliminate them.

'If I were still a Catholic then you'd be one too and all I'd have to do is send you to the priest tomorrow. I'd tell you it was a sin and he'd tell you it was a sin and you'd believe it. Then he'd tell you to break up with Bucky. But we're not Catholics or anything else, so that leaves us with clichés, and what's wrong with that is a cliché is an out, it just sort of hangs around and waits for someone to use it and when you do use one it saves you from having to think. So now I could say that nice girls make love for the first time on their wedding nights and they never make love with anyone else unless they're divorced first—' The word divorce made her think of Lee sleeping above them, and that she was forty-nine, and that Peggy was leaving for college in two months and during the next four years her need for parents and a home would gradually diminish. 'But you see there's no sense in my telling you all that because you know it's just not so. I mean, do you *feel* bad? Evil?'

'I do right now, but not—' She took one of Beth's cigarettes.

'Not with him?'

'No.'

'Good. I want you to be happy, and I'm not going to ask you to stop seeing him—'

'You're not?'

'Did you think I would?'

'I thought you'd have to.'

'That would be a lie too. Because I don't really have any reason to. Not any good ones, anyway. And you have to believe this: I don't think you're bad, and I love you very much, and you must never feel ashamed. You can tell Bucky I didn't see anything or you can tell him the truth.'

'The truth.'

'All right.'

'He'll be afraid. When he has to see you.'

'Tell him not to be. Is there anything you need to talk about?'

'No.'

'I mean, I've told you what's not the truth about sex, or at least what I think isn't the truth. I suppose now I ought to tell you—I don't know, something else.'

'You don't have to.'

'You're all right?'

'Yes. I love him.'

'Suppose you get pregnant?'

'He's careful.'

'Those things don't always work.'

'Well, they *have* to.'

'No, they don't, I can at least tell you that. I want you to take the pill.'

The sky was dark still; in another two hours dawn would come; two hours after that, Lee would wake to a house that had changed.

'I'll make the appointment and I'll go with you.'

She rose and stood in front of Peggy, who sat with lowered head, her knees pressed together.

'We'll tell him you're getting married.'

'Well, I can, but—' Then she stopped.

'It's all I ask. Will you do that for me?'

After a moment, Peggy nodded.

'I'd do anything in the world for you,' she said.

With arms around each other they climbed the stairs, then kissed. Beth went to her room and shut the door and looked at Lee's face in the dark: an open-mouthed, weary frown. She thought tenderly of how his face had changed. Then she got into bed and slept. She woke up while Lee was doing pushups on the bedroom floor. She told him she had been awake most of the night and asked if he could fix his breakfast so she could go back to sleep. He said all right, he'd just have some cereal. When she woke after one o'clock she dressed and went downstairs; Peggy was drinking coffee in the kitchen.

'Has Daddy left?'

'Yes.' Peggy blushed. 'Bucky loves you.'

'Oh, you called him?'

'As soon as Daddy left.'

'Good. I'll have a cup of coffee, then take you to lunch. Unless you're doing something else.'

'No, he's still afraid to come over till he picks me up tonight.'

They went in the Volkswagen to a restaurant across the street from the university, then walked in the hot afternoon to several stores and bought Peggy a blouse. They spent the rest of the afternoon talking and laughing about trivial things, and at dinner Lee smiled at them with curiosity and pride. During the next four days Beth was sometimes frightened but always happy: she thought it was a wonderful paradox that Peggy's having an affair made them even closer than they had been before. On the fifth day they drove to a gynecologist in Cedar Rapids. Going there, Peggy was nervous and talked about yesterday's swimming party; coming home she was distant and hardly talked at all.

'He probably didn't believe us,' she said. 'He knows I'm not old enough to get married.'

'It doesn't matter.'

'I guess not.'

'You're safe now. That's what matters.'

That night after dinner, Peggy scraped the dishes, put them in the dishwasher, then went upstairs. After a while Beth went up. Peggy was reading in bed.

'Aren't you going out?'

'No.'

'You aren't having a fight, are you?'

'No.'

'It's so early. Do you feel all right?'

'I'm fine. I just don't feel like going out, that's all.'

'Oh. Well—'

'Don't worry. I'm all right.'

Beth stood in the doorway for a moment, watching her read; then she went downstairs. The next night Peggy went to a movie with Marsha. On the third night Bucky took her to dinner. He was able to look into Beth's eyes again and as she walked with them out on the porch and told them goodbye she felt her collusion was with Bucky, not Peggy. It was almost eight o'clock, but daylight savings time, and the sky was still light. She watched them get into the car. Bucky was talking and Peggy, looking straight ahead, shrugged her shoulders. When they drove off, Beth turned to the door then stopped; she did not want to go in. The dishes were washed, the kitchen cleaned, there was nothing on television, and she did not want to read. She sat on the wooden steps of the porch and watched the night come. When she went back inside, Lee was still sitting in his chair, reading *Time*.

'What were you doing?'

'Just sitting. It's cool, but the mosquitoes got bad.'

She lit a cigarette and sat on the couch, facing him. For a while she watched him read.

'Lee?'

'What,' not raising his eyes.

'Do you believe in God?'

'Sure.'

His eyes lingered, probably finishing a paragraph: then he lowered the magazine.

'Why? Don't you?'

'I don't know.'

'You never told me.'

'No. Will you take me to a movie?'

'Now?'

'If you want to.'

'Can we make it?'

'I'll call and find out.'

The last feature would start in twenty minutes, so they went.

When they got home Lee finished whatever he had been reading in *Time*, and Beth had a drink. She was going to the kitchen for another when Lee started upstairs, so she closed the liquor cabinet and followed him up and they made love.

'You didn't want to talk about God, did you?' he said. His voice was sleepy.

'No.'

'Good thing. I don't know any more than you do.'

'Then you don't know a thing.'

'What made you ask me that anyway?'

'Because I question the way we live.'

'How do you mean?'

'Why we do things.'

'What things.'

'I don't know. I wonder about the girls, how we've done with them.'

'We've done all right.'

'It's not that simple, though.'

'What isn't?'

'Everything. Everything isn't that simple.'

She lay awake for another half hour or so, then slept. She woke up when Peggy closed the front door. The next sound was the refrigerator. After a while Peggy came upstairs and went to her room. Beth wanted to go talk to her, but she could not think of an excuse. She lit a cigarette and got up and stood at the window, looking at the streetlight on the corner. Once in a while she looked back at Lee sleeping on his side, and she wished she were like him: believing she knew those things she had to know, and not caring to know anything else. If she were that way she would not be standing here at the window; she might be sleeping or even talking to Peggy now, maybe they would go down to the kitchen for a snack and sit there eating and talking; because above all, if she were that way, she would not have turned on that lamp.

# 4

Next day after lunch, when Lee had gone to play golf, Beth asked Peggy if she wanted the car. 'No.'

'I need some things in town,' Beth said.

She was going to see Helen, and lying about it to Peggy made her feel more lonely. On the way she bought popsicles for Wendy and Billy. Helen lived in the country; for the last two miles Beth left the highway and drove on a dusty road through fields of tall corn. When she turned into the drive-way Wendy and Billy saw her from the gym set in the back-yard and ran to the car. They wore bathing suits. She hugged and kissed them and unwrapped the melting popsicles, and they walked back toward the gym set. Helen was in the kitchen doorway, holding the screen open.

'Beer?'

'All right.'

'Larry went back to bed. There was a party last night, and we got about three hours sleep.'

'Aren't you going to sleep?'

'Tonight. I could put the kids down for a nap, but I don't like to. Wendy doesn't sleep.'

'She could sit in bed with books or something. She'd be all right.'

'I know, but it makes me feel degenerate. Let's go in the living room.'

'They sat in front of a large fan and Beth looked out the picture window at the willow tree in the front yard, its branches touching the ground. Across the dirt road there was heat shimmer above the corn that grew as far as she could see. As Helen lit a cigarette her hands trembled.

'You're hung over too.'

'Just tired. I don't get drunk at those parties.'

'That's smart.'

'Next time I'll be smart about leaving too. How's Peggy?'

'Fine.'

'Excited about New England?'

'I guess.'

'Still going steady?'

'Oh sure.'

'Then it's good she's leaving. She's too young for that.'

'You weren't much older.'

'No, I guess I wasn't. Shall we have another?'

'It'll just make you sleepier.'

'As long as I'm suffering I might as well drink.'

'Okay.'

Helen took the empty cans to the kitchen. Beth knew she ought to leave and let Helen rest somehow, at least spare her the effort of talking. But she thought of going home to Peggy and she could not. Helen came back eating a sandwich.

'Peanut butter. You want some?'

'No thanks. Listen: you go up and take a nap and I'll stay with the children.'

'I've made it this far, I can make it till tonight.'

'Don't be silly. Finish your beer then go up and sleep.'

'You're being silly. What kind of visit is that?'

'Well, it's not like I drove a hundred miles. Come on: let me. Don't you know I love to be with them?'

Helen took a long swallow and sank in her chair.

'You're tempting me.'

'Do it, then. Think how nice it'll be to just go upstairs and lie down and sleep.'

'I'll do it.'

'Good.'

'But first I'll put Billy to bed.'

'I'll do that. Just finish your beer and go to bed.'

'Oh, my.' She drank. 'Oh my, you're good to me.'

Now that her favor was accepted, Beth wanted something in return. She wanted very much to talk about Peggy, but she recognized her need for what it was. She didn't want advice: if she did, she wouldn't ask it from her twenty-five-year-old daughter. Nor did she want Helen to speak to Peggy. She merely wanted to talk about it, to share with someone else the burden of her decision. But she couldn't do that: it was cowardly, and it wasn't fair to Peggy. So they made small talk, then Helen said, 'That beer's there to be drunk,' and went upstairs. Beth went outside and carried Billy upstairs; his eyes were closing as she covered him with a sheet and turned on the fan. Going downstairs she wanted another beer but she went past the refrigerator and out into the yard. She could not drink beer all afternoon; the day was too hot and she would drink too fast and go home tight. For a while under the hot sun she pushed Wendy in the swing.

'Aren't you hot?' she said.

'No.'

She pushed her again, then held the chains and Wendy swayed, then stopped.

'I am. What do you do with that willow tree?'

'What tree.'

'In the front yard.'

'Nothing.'

'Come on. We'll have a tea party.'

In the kitchen she made grape Kool-Aid. 'Are there some cookies?'

'Mama hides 'em.'

She looked high in the pantry, found chocolate Oreos, and put some on a plate. Wendy carried it out to the willow tree. Beth brought a beer, the pitcher of Kool-Aid, and a glass for Wendy. Under the willow tree there was shade; across the road the cornstalks were moving with a gentle breeze, and after Beth and Wendy had sat still for a while they could feel it.

'This is a good place,' Wendy said.

'It is.'

'I bet nobody can see us.'

'Not unless they look real hard.'

When the cookies were gone Wendy got restless. She walked head first through the hanging branches and stood looking into the dust-covered weeds in the ditch beside the road. Sitting on the grass, Beth said: 'Don't you want to stay here?'

'No.'

'Wait. I'll be right back.'

She went into the house. Upstairs in Wendy's room she found a checkerboard and box of checkers: they were all there. She got a beer and went outside.

'Do you know how to play checkers?'

'I forgot.'

Beth parted the branches and went through and sat in the shade.

'Come here and I'll show you.'

For the next two hours, until Helen and Larry came outside with their faces washed and sleepy-looking, she drank beer and played checkers with Wendy. Driving home she opened all the car windows so air blew on her face, but when she parked in the garage she still felt tight. She had also smoked too much: crossing the lawn she wheezed and when she coughed to clear her chest she brought up something. She swallowed and went inside.

She could hear the record player in Peggy's room, and she was about to call upstairs that she was home but she didn't. She ought to eat something. She sliced cheese and ham and ate standing up. As she cut a piece of lime and filled a glass with ice she told herself to get sober before Lee came home; she poured the gin and tonic, her mind detached as though still deciding whether or not to drink it, then she went upstairs. Peggy's door was open, and she lay across her bed, reading a magazine. Beth turned down the volume on the record player and sat on the bed.

'Where've you been?'

'Helen's.'

'You better eat an onion before Daddy comes home.'

She said it in a friendly way, smiling, and Beth winked. It was their first moment like that since going to the gynecologist.

'I guess I better. Is this what you've been doing?'

'Marsha and I played tennis.'

'In this heat?'

'It gave me a headache.'

'Did you take something?'

'Two aspirins. Marsha has a date, and we're doubling tonight.'

'Does she?'

'I finally talked her into it. Vic'll be in Vietnam for a year and I told her, you know, it's just friendly dating to distract her. She needs it.'

'Course she does.'

Peggy closed the magazine and rolled on her back. Beth went to the window and looked past the elm down at the brick street.

'Peggy?' She did not turn from the window. 'Was I wrong?'

'No.'

Now she looked at Peggy on the bed.

'Is that true?'

'Yes.'

'But you're not happy.'

'That's not your fault.'

'Then you're really not?'

'Not what.'

'Happy.'

'No. No, I'm not.'

'Then I was wrong.'

'No, it wasn't that. That was great. Anybody else's mother would have—I don't know, gone crazy or something. No, it's Bucky. I think I'm getting tired of him.'

'Well, that's normal.'

'It doesn't have to be.'

'But it is, honey. You're barely eighteen.'

The record player shut itself off; Peggy got up and turned the records over and started it again.

'I'll be glad when school starts,' she said.

'Because of Bucky?'

'Yes.'

'Then I'll be glad too. But you could just tell him, you know. You don't have to wait till September.'

'No, I'll wait.'

'But be happy. Don't waste time.'

Peggy shrugged and lay on the bed, one arm across her eyes.

'I'll wait till school. Maybe when I get out there I'll change my mind. You know: maybe I've just been with him too much this summer.'

'Well, I'm glad you told me. I thought it was that other business.'

'No. That was right.'

'Do they make you sick?'

'Not so far.'

'Good. I'm going to shower now. Will you—No: never mind.'

Peggy moved her arm and looked at her.

'Will I what?'

'I was going to ask you to start the charcoal, but forget it. You rest and get over that headache.'

'It's about gone.'

She got up.

'No, I'll do it,' Beth said.

'It's done,' Peggy said, and left the room and went downstairs.

Beth left her drink on the lavatory while she showered. She was under the warm spray for a long time, finishing with a few seconds of cold; when she got out she felt better but still tight. She dried and powdered, then finished her drink while she dressed and perfumed in the bedroom. She wore a yellow dress, the color of lemon sherbet, soft and cool and pretty. She stood at the full-length mirror: her face and arms were tan and cool-looking and she smelled good. Robert had thought she was pretty, she knew that. Then why had he let her catch that plane? Not that it would have made any difference. She went downstairs and mixed a drink and went outside where Peggy sat in a lawn chair, watching the charcoal.

'Beautiful,' Peggy said.

Beth went down the steps like a model, and in front of Peggy did a slow pirouette, then forced a short laugh that almost came out as a sob.

'And so are you,' she said. 'And I want you to be *ever* so happy!'

They sat with their legs in the sun, their bodies in the shade; when the shadows of the elm and house had enclosed their legs, Lee came home. By that time Beth was drunk.

Lee knew it, and she saw in his eyes that he knew it, but he didn't say anything. They ate barbecued chicken and baked beans and potato salad; Beth thought the food would make her sober, and she ate second helpings, and wiped the chicken platter with Italian bread. All this only cleared her head, but she still wasn't sober; faced with a waning drunk, she had to prolong it, so while she cleaned the kitchen she had another drink, knowing that behind his newspaper in the living room Lee was scowling at the sounds of ice cubes and stirring. When the kitchen was clean she took her drink outside and sat on a lawn chair. The sun was very low. Across the street beside the house Mrs. Crenshaw was bent over giving scraps to her dog; she straightened and waved. Then Mrs. Crenshaw went inside, and she was alone. It seemed a long time ago she had played checkers with Wendy under the willow tree. She looked over her shoulder at the house: Peggy's room was lighted, the shades drawn while she dressed for her date. The kitchen was lighted. So was the living room where Lee was reading. Beth looked away: everything was shadowed now, and there was a ribbon of deep bright pink over the rooftops to the west. With her back to the house she felt somehow threatened. But nothing was wrong: the kitchen was clean; Peggy's trouble was with Bucky, not her; Lee was sulking, but that was normal.

The sky was nearly dark when Bucky drove up the street. When he opened the door the interior light went on and Beth saw Marsha and a boy in the back seat. Bucky started across the lawn toward the front door, then he saw her and came over and said hello.

'Just go through the kitchen,' she said. She looked up at Peggy's bedroom. 'I think she's downstairs now.'

She watched him go into the kitchen; then she heard him

knocking on the wall and calling hello. She went to the car; Marsha rolled down the back window and Beth stuck her head in. She stayed there, talking about the heat and tennis with Marsha and the boy whose name she didn't hear, until Peggy and Bucky got into the car. She stepped back, and as they drove away she called: 'Have fun!'

She went to the back door and into the kitchen. She was dropping ice in her glass when Lee came from the living room.

'No,' he said.

She hesitated. Then, not looking at him, she squeezed lime into the glass.

'Jesus. Did you have to go out to the car too? Couldn't you have just stayed wherever the hell you were?'

'I wanted to tell Marsha hello. What's wrong with that?'

'What's *wrong*. You're so Goddamned drunk you don't even know. How do you think Peggy liked it? Her mother out there bellowing her Goddamned drunk talk all over the neighborhood—'

'I wasn't bellowing.'

She poured the gin halfway up, then the tonic.

'You were. It's what you do when you're drunk, but you don't hear it.'

'Oh. Well, it's a good thing I'm not sober like you because you're bellowing a little yourself, and it's a good thing we're all closed up and air-conditioned or the whole neighborhood would hear *you*.'

'That's your last drink tonight.'

'Ha.'

'I've tried to stay out of this, but not tonight.'

'Ha. *They* can't hear you—' she waved an arm toward the windows '—but I can, and being closed up in a house with you *makes* me drink.'

'Forget about me. I know how you feel about me. I'm talking—'

'Well, I'm glad you know *some*thing.'

'I'm talking about Peggy. You don't care about me and you

don't care about yourself either. You're killing yourself with booze and cigarettes—'

'You're Goddamned right I am.'

'—You don't sleep enough but won't go to a doctor. All right: that's *your* business. But it looks like you could at least stay sober while Peggy's home.'

'Peggy. Oh, you *really* don't know anything, you don't know anything at *all*. You don't know—'

She turned and walked fast to the back door, yet when she reached it the anger and speed of her motion were fake; she didn't want to leave, but when she looked back at him he was standing there shaking his head, his lips tight. So she went outside, where now the sky was dark. She stopped in the backyard and drank, went on to the garage and got into the Lincoln. The key was in the ignition. Holding the glass between her legs, she backed out, looking at the house as she passed it: she did not see Lee at the back door or the kitchen window or living room window. She stopped at the corner, looked both ways, then squealed through the intersection.

Her cigarettes were back there on the kitchen table or on the grass beside the lawn chair. She drove toward a super-market that was open until nine; in the dark privacy and quiet hum of the car she felt all right; but walking into the fluorescent lights of the store she felt drunk again. The store was nearly empty, and boys were sweeping. She walked fast so she could follow a straight line, took two packs of Pall Malls from the rack and smacked them on the counter; while the girl rang up the sale Beth looked at the clock on the wall, then at her reflection in the glass front of the store. The girl could surely smell her breath but that was all right if you were dressed up and pretty and had a place to go. She picked up the change, told the girl goodnight, and walked out.

Her drink was on the floor near the accelerator, and now she held it down in her lap until she got out of the parking lot. The streets were lighted at every corner, and in the headlights of the spaced yet steady traffic you could see into cars. Just the sort of thing a cop would enjoy: stopping a lone woman on Saturday night. Hiding the cool glass between the steering wheel and her lap, she drove out of town, onto the highway going west to Helen's.

She finished the drink, tossed the ice and lime out the window, and laid the glass on the seat. On the next curve the glass rolled away from her; she lunged for it and the car veered into the opposite lane but it was clear and when she jerked the wheel she almost went onto the shoulder. She slowed to forty. At the white barn before Helen's road she slowed for a turn; she did not plan to stop at Helen's; she would simply drive past and follow the dirt road and see where it went. But she had left her lighter at home, she could go in and ask Helen if it was there and they'd look in the kitchen and living room and with a flashlight under the willow tree, then she could stay and talk. A half mile from Helen's she went up a gentle rise and saw the lighted house. She slowed to twenty, and going by the house she bent over and looked through the picture window: Helen stood in the living room, talking probably to Larry someplace off to the right. She drove on. She picked up a little speed, followed the beige road past dark fields of corn separating lighted farmhouses. She kept turning right, back toward the highway, and finally she came to it and headed for town. The drinks were wearing off and if she went to a movie now she'd get tired and her mouth and throat would dry. It was too late for a movie anyway.

Then, almost furtively, her right foot pressed the pedal while her left hand slipped down to her seat belt, unbuckled it, and returned to the wheel. She did not look at the speedometer: leaning forward, she watched the curves and gentle slopes ahead for the lights of another car. Coming out of a curve she floorboarded; the highway now was straight but narrow and she fixed her eyes on the center line. She must not hit anyone. She felt the dark, flat country zipping past but she was afraid to look; once in a while there was the white blur of a house. A big truck came toward her and she held her breath and stared at the road as the truck crashed by. Now her legs were weak and the muscles in her right one were tight and quivering. Still she kept the pedal to the floor for another half minute, until she saw the close lights of houses. She lifted her foot and placed it on the floor near the brake pedal; when she reached the houses she was driving thirty miles an hour and thinking how pretty she looked in her bright yellow dress and weeping aloud. She drove home.

The lights were on in the living room; she sat in the car, in the garage, and smoked. She remembered the glass and lay on the seat and picked it up from the floor. She was down there when Lee spoke her name.

'Beth?' he said again.

She sat up and looked around at him framed by the garage door. She got out and started to walk past him; when he didn't move aside, she stopped.

'Are you all right?' he said.

She nodded.

'I went for a ride.'

'Oh.'

They walked back toward the house.

'I was worried,' Lee said.

'I just went for a ride.'

In the kitchen he watched her mix a drink, then he followed her into the living room. A movie was on television.

'What is it?' she said.

'*Pal Joey.*'

'Oh, good.'

She sat in her chair; he sat in his and now the lampshade was between them so all he could watch was her hands while she drank. For about five minutes she watched the movie.

'What is it, honey?' he said.

'I don't know.'

'Do you think maybe the change is coming?'

'No. Besides, the pills postpone it.'

'Maybe it's coming, though.'

'No it's not. I'll die of lung cancer, wearing a Tampax.'

He was quiet for a while.

'About the drinking,' he said.

'What about it?'

'Could you cut down if you wanted to?'

Sinatra was singing 'I Could Write a Book.'

'Wait,' Beth said. 'Let's hear this.'

Then there was a commercial for laundry soap.

'Did you ever notice the commercials for Saturday night movies are mostly for women?' Beth said. 'What do they think men are doing on Saturday night?'

'I don't know. Anyhow, what would happen if you told yourself you just won't have a drink till five o'clock? Would it be easy, or would you start climbing the walls, or what?'

'I don't know. I've never had a reason to try it. But since I'm a lousy mother—'

'No, now wait.' His hand gestured under the lampshade, stopping her. 'I'm not talking about that. Forget all that. I just mean that if you can take it or leave it, well, no problem. But if you can't, then you *are* in trouble and we should do something.'

'Why?'

'Because you might be an alcoholic, that's why.'

'Oh, all right. Tomorrow I won't have a drink till five o'clock.'

'Really?'

'Sure.'

'And Monday too? And after that?'

'Yes: Monday too and after that.'

'That's fine. That's the best thing I've heard in a long time.'

She could feel him watching the movie again.

'Is it? Well, you're mighty easy to please. I guess if I quit smoking you'd be so happy you couldn't stand yourself.'

'Why are you talking like that? The fight's over.'

'Okay.' She stood up. 'I guess since I'm going to be so good tomorrow I can have another one.'

'I'll have one too.'

She brought him one. When the movie was over he stood up and cleaned his pipe.

'Coming up?' he said.

'I think I'll read a while.'

He stood there for a moment, then said goodnight and went upstairs. She turned off the television and the lights and sat down again. It took her about fifteen minutes to admit she was hoping Peggy would come home while she was sitting here. Then she stalled for another five minutes, thinking of what she wanted to tell Peggy: that it was all right about Bucky, she was free of him and anyone else, she didn't have to marry until she was twenty-five or thirty, or maybe not at all. Then she went upstairs. When she entered the dark bedroom Lee rolled toward her, awake. She sat on the edge of the bed and touched him, then let him take off the yellow dress and drop it on the floor, and she let him believe the fight was over and everything was fine.

Next day Peggy and Bucky and Marsha and her date went on a picnic; Lee played golf. At three o'clock Beth started waiting and at exactly five o'clock she mixed a martini. When Lee got home she was sober.

# 5

This lasted until late August. It was neither difficult nor easy: it was a bother, like being hungry. Sometimes she broke her rule: when she drove out to Helen's or when a friend came over and bored her. Most of them did. She knew some interesting men but she only saw them at occasional parties when usually she was trapped by their wives. Polly Fairchild was good company only when she was troubled or confiding. So on afternoons when Polly came over Beth mixed them a drink and got Polly started on the war or Johnson. Or Beth would remark generally about marriage or changing morality, and Polly usually responded with gossip. She was an intelligent woman who paused to find the right word, the right simile, the psychological term, and she had a way of making gossip feel like an objective discussion of marriage and morality. But after these conversations, when Polly had gone, Beth always felt ashamed.

Most days, though, people did not visit, and she did not go to Helen's, and she did not drink until five o'clock. She spent much time with Peggy, planning what she would need at college, and shopping in town for clothes. They had lunches in town, or Cokes, or ice cream; once, their shopping done, they walked past a movie, looked at the pictures outside, agreed it was the best thing to do on a hot afternoon like this, and went in. Still, since telling Beth she was tiring of Bucky, Peggy had been different. She was friendly again, that was true; but she was like Helen after her marriage. Helen had come home from the honeymoon with a secret, married self that she would not expose to Beth. And now too often Peggy's eyes and smile hid a secret. She never talked about Bucky.

One cloudy morning in late August Peggy and Bucky left for a picnic. They went alone. Lee would not have approved, but he was at work. Beth had slept very little the night before, so when Peggy left around ten she went back to bed. When she woke at noon her room was dark and rain was falling hard. She dressed and went downstairs to the kitchen; while she was getting Spam and a Coke from the refrigerator Peggy called hello and came in from the living room. She was wearing her glasses.

'Oh, you came home. Is Bucky with you?'

'Nope.'

'When did it start raining?'

'About an hour ago.'

Beth poured the Coke over ice, sipped it, then handed it to Peggy. 'Here. You want this?'

Peggy took it.

'Why should I drink one of those things when what I really like after a nap is beer?'

'Drink a beer, then.'

'I will. Now that I've proved I don't absolutely have to.'

She opened a beer and started making a sandwich.

'Did you eat lunch?'

'Sitting in the car.'

'Well, I like rain, but it's too bad.' She went to the window and looked out at the dark sky and dark green blowing trees and hard rain washing down the brick street. 'You could have brought him here, I guess.'

'I can think of better people to be indoors with on a rainy day.'

Beth went to the table and finished making the sandwich.

'Oh, he was full of plans for a rainy afternoon. What he really wanted—'

'Wait: let's go to the living room. We can open the windows.'

They turned off the air conditioner, opened the windows facing the front yard, and sat smelling the rain and cool air. Beth was in her chair and Peggy faced her from the couch.

'A motel,' Peggy said. 'That's where he wanted to go. Can you imagine anyone letting him into a motel? He hardly even shaves yet.'

Beth waited.

'What a little rooster he is,' Peggy said. 'His girl takes the pill—wow.'

'Why don't you stop?'

'And have a little Bucky? I'd rather die.'

'No, I mean stop seeing him.'

'Because—oh because I just can't. I wish—' She stretched out on the couch and turned her face away from Beth, toward the open window.

'You wish what?'

'Nothing.'

'No, tell me.'

Peggy was still looking out the window.

'I wish you *had* taken me away. Even if it would've been phony. I wish you had.'

Rain smacked loudly from the gutter near the porch. The windows were under the porch roof, so only the breeze came in; the curtains stirred and Peggy's exhaled smoke drifted back into the room.

'But then you wouldn't have learned anything,' Beth said.

'Learned. What have I learned?'

'That you don't love him. That it wasn't real. If I had taken you away for one of those trips you'd have thought you were heartbroken.'

'I *did* love him.'

'I don't think so.'

'Course I did.' She looked at Beth. 'For God's sake, I slept with him.'

'That doesn't mean anything.'

'Then what *does?*'

'I don't know.'

'You don't.'

'No.'

'That's fine.'

'Did you want me to lie to you? Tell you a love story?'

Peggy shook her head. Beth brought her plate and empty beer can to the kitchen.

'Do you want a beer?' she called.

'No.'

She opened one for herself. For a couple of minutes in the living room she sat quietly drinking, looking past Peggy's lowered head at the rain and dark outside. A car passed slowly up the street.

'Why don't you just break up with him. Right now, baby.'

Peggy shook her head.

'Really, baby. Him and his motels. You're right, he's a child. He's not good enough for you.'

'He was good enough to get pills for.'

'They weren't for him. They were for you.'

'So I could *sleep* with him. So now I just can't stop, because—because then—'

She looked up at the high ceiling.

'You've got it all wrong,' Beth said. 'I wanted to make sure you *wouldn't* be stuck with him, that's why, so you'd be free. So you wouldn't have to take sex seriously.'

'*Jee*sus.' She sat up, glaring at Beth. 'It's the most important thing in my *life* right now, don't you see!' Now she stood,
leaning forward, waving a hand. 'Don't you see that? Because
as soon as I break up with Bucky I'm a girl who *screws*. Don't
you see!'

Beth was pushing herself upward to go hold Peggy, but
then she stopped, for she knew Peggy would be stiff and captive in her arms, so she sank back into the chair and with one
hand over her eyes softly cried.

'Don't,' Peggy said. She was there now, crouched over
Beth, squeezing one shoulder. 'It's not your fault.'

'It *is*.' Her hand still covered her eyes. 'But I didn't mean it
to be *this* way. I just didn't want you to end up like *me*.'

'Like you?'

Peggy stepped back. Beth flicked tears from her eyes,
wiped her cheeks, and looked up.

'Wasted like me. Unhappy like me. *Mar*ried like me.'

'Oh—'

'Don't you *know*?'

'No.' Shaking her head. 'I don't. I didn't.' Shaking it again.

'Well, now you do. I wish it weren't true, but it is. Not just
me, everyone. If you don't believe me, ask Helen. Drive out
there and talk to her, she'll talk. Not now, the roads are muddy,
but before you go to school. Or just look at her. Look at her
face that used to be so *happy*, Peggy. Remember? Remember
how happy she always was?'

Peggy was nodding, backing toward the couch; when her
legs bumped it she sat down.

'Look at her eyes now. It's not just tired, that's not just
housework in her eyes. Oh my baby, save yourself—' She
crossed the room and sat beside Peggy, hugging and rocking
her with both arms. 'You should hear Polly Fairchild, the stories, all these nice people. It's a farce, love, marriage, fidelity—'
Peggy jerked tight in her arms. '—No. No, baby, I've never
done that. But it doesn't *matter*. None of it *matters*.'

'But Daddy—'

'Oh, he's all right, baby. He's a good man. It's just natural, that's all. It just happens, and there's nothing anyone can do about it.'

Peggy's face turned away and her body turned with it, pulling against Beth's arms. Beth let go.

'Are you getting divorced?'

'*No*, baby.' Beth held her again but still Peggy was turned stiffly away, so Beth went to the chair and picked up the beer and swallowed with her back turned. 'No, we're not getting divorced. We can live together like anyone else. We don't hate each other. It's just that nothing's there, and this was supposed to be my life. Every woman's life. But it's not. You and Helen are, and now Wendy and Billy too. But you and Helen have to grow up and have your own lives and that's how it should be. But it shouldn't be this way for me. There should have been something else.'

'For *instance*!'

Looking at the wall ahead of her, Beth shrugged; there were tears in her eyes.

'I don't know, and it's too late for it to matter even if I found out. But it's not too late for you. You're young. It's all ahead of you.'

Then Peggy was moving fast, to the kitchen door, stopping there, turning to Beth.

'Oh *why* did you come in that night! Why! Why! Why didn't you just stay upstairs and mind your own ugly *bus*iness!'

Then crying, her head lifted, her clenched fists at her sides, she strode out of the room and pounded up the stairs.


# 6


On the trip from Iowa to Massachusetts Peggy sat in the back seat with her transistor radio. The college had sent her a summer reading list; she was not going to be tested; it was simply a list of books they wanted her to read. She started the first one, *The Great Gatsby*, as soon as they left Iowa City. During most of the trip Lee spoke very little; he did not even object when Beth put an ice chest of beer on the floor behind the front seat, or when three or four times a day she drank one as they drove. He had been sulking since coming home that rainy day nearly three weeks ago. He had come into the living room where Beth was watching Merv Griffin (before that she had watched a movie; Peggy stayed upstairs and did not come down until dinner); Lee had said hello, looked quickly but closely at her face, then her gin and tonic, then the filled ashtray.

'What happened to five o'clock?'

'Just be quiet. I'm not in the mood for that.'

'Mood hell—'

'I mean it.' Watching the screen she motioned at him to be quiet. 'Besides, Peggy's upstairs.'

He started to speak, then shook his head and went upstairs to change clothes. At dinner there was little talk. Peggy and Lee commented on the rain, and Vic's having been in Vietnam for nearly a month now, and Lee said Bucky had better work for grades and stay in school. They knew she was drunk, and she knew they did, but she acted sober anyway. She ate quietly and slowly and carefully. After dinner Peggy went out with Bucky. Then Lee wanted to talk.

'Was it because you had to? You couldn't stop?'

'No.'

'You just wanted to.'

'That's right. I just wanted to.'

That was all she ever told him. Several times he tried to talk again, but she would not. Finally he gave up. It was a problem he could forget most of the time, because she was not drunk again. She simply drank as she had before. Usually she had one before taking the cleaning woman home; by the time Lee got home she was having her third or fourth. But she was all right: her mind and tongue functioned, she cooked, she cleaned the kitchen after dinner, she paid the bills, she kept track of their engagements, and once a week she drove the Volkswagen to a service station and had it washed. Most nights she drank through dinner and on until she went to bed, but she sipped and spaced them and always appeared sober.

Luckily the shopping for Peggy was done, so they had no reason to be together. Peggy spent most of her time out of the house; during the day she swam or played tennis or rode at the stables or just drove about town with the girls she would leave in September. At night she went out with Bucky. When Beth walked them to the door or told them goodnight from her chair, Peggy looked at her with eyes that were at times coldly curious, at others bitterly defiant, at others mirthful and proud. Each day there were times when they had to talk, and they did this in the hollow courteous tones of lovers after a rending quarrel. Beth waited.

Then in early September, Peggy began to mellow. She spent more time with Beth. She did not truly talk to her; instead they did things together. After dinner Peggy helped in the kitchen. One night they went to a movie. On several after-noons they played badminton or croquet. These periods were obviously planned, some of them even timed: if Marsha were picking up Peggy for tennis, she would be ready an hour early and set up the wickets and stakes and ask Beth to play. At first Beth was hopeful. When she realized Peggy was acting from pity she knew she had lost her.

The college was north of Boston. It was a school for girls, it was a hundred and fifty-eight years old, and so was the four-storied red brick building where, on the front steps among suitcases and trunks, daughters and parents, and maintenance men serving as porters, they kissed and hugged Peggy, spoke of Thanksgiving, and told her goodbye. She stood watching as they drove out of the U-shaped driveway; when they stopped at the street for a final look, she waved. Then Lee drove into the street, toward the low autumn sun. With one finger he wiped his eyes, reached across the seat, and took Beth's hand.

'Our baby,' he said.

'I lost her long before now,' she said, and withdrew her hand.

'What's that supposed to mean?'

'She hates me.'

'Beth!'

'It's true.'

'Beth look—that's crazy. Look—'

'Sure.'

He was not angry. He was chewing his lip, and the car was slowing.

'How can you say that about Peggy? What's *wrong*, Beth—'

'Oh, you don't know anything. You know that? You don't know anything.'

She kneeled on the seat to get a beer, pausing first to watch his face. 'Have you ever been unfaithful?'

'My God.'

She leaned over the seat and reached into the ice chest.

'I have,' she said.

'That's a lie.'

She sat down and popped open the beer. They were on the highway now. She looked out the rear window, then took a long swallow.

'Ah, that's good.'

She pushed in the lighter on the dashboard.

'Drink as many as you want,' he said. 'I mean it.'

'I know you do.'

'You need it. Something's happening to you, and we've got to—'

'His name is Robert Carini.'

'Stop it.'

She lit her cigarette.

'He's a silversmith and he lives in New York. He promised to send me a bracelet but he didn't. What's the name of yours? Or is it more than one. It probably is.'

'Beth, stop.'

'You don't believe me, do you?'

'Course not.'

'That's so funny. Because you had everything worked out so we wouldn't die on the same plane. You see? There's all sorts of things out there—' She waved her beer can in front of her, toward the horizon—'*im*pulses, chances, surprises, things nobody understands. But you don't see them, Lee.'

They were driving through rolling wooded hills; the trees were gold and red and yellow, and looking at them with one hand raised to shield her eyes from the sun she felt a sadness like nostalgia.

'Are you telling me that something happened in San Francisco?'

'No. On the plane back.'

'That's silly.'

'Well, you're right about that, I didn't sleep with him. But I would have, so it's the same.'

'Since when is it the same?'

'Since always. And I talked about you.'

'Oh, you did.'

'I couldn't have been more unfaithful. Think about that, Lee: one afternoon last summer your wife was unfaithful.'

'I wouldn't call it that.'

'Call it what you want, but that's what it was.'

She leaned over the seat again, put the empty can in the chest, and brought a full one up through the ice.

'So what about you,' she said.

He didn't answer; with one hand he was filling a pipe from his tobacco pouch.

'All right,' she said. 'We can talk about scenery and traffic.'

He drove quietly. She finished the beer and started another.

There were nine left. Tomorrow she would buy more and she would drink from Massachusetts to Iowa. That amused her: how many people had drunk beer from the Atlantic—or ten miles from it anyway—right into the heart of the country? Now off the highway there were stores and shopping centers and the traffic was heavier. When they got into the country again, Beth looked out her window at colored leaves and green pines and spruce; the sun was setting, and the sky was rose and orange above the trees; she saw stone fences and sometimes a large house built far back from the road; twice she saw a single white boulder in meadows that were light green in the sun and dark green in the reaching shadows of the woods. When the sun went down she said: 'Can you keep driving? Or are you tired?'

'I'm not tired.'

'Good. Cars are nice at night.'

It was dusk now, so she could not see colors anymore, and she wanted dusk to change quickly to night so she could ride in the dark car with only the faint green light of the dashboard and red tail lights far ahead and pale headlights well on the other side of the divided highway.

'Are you hungry?' he said.

'No. Are you?'

'Not yet.'

'We can eat later, then drive some more.'

'All right,' he said.

'I'm going to do it differently now, since Peggy's gone. I'm not going to bed anymore until I'm really sleepy. Then I'll get up and give you breakfast and then I'll go back to bed and sleep till noon or so. I can do that now.'

'I guess you can.'

'It's what I'll do. I'll read a lot.'

'Yes.'

'You were right not to tell me, though. About other women. Because it doesn't matter. That's what no one admits, that it doesn't matter. Course when you didn't answer, that means you have, doesn't it?'

'Yes.'

'Really? I thought so.'

Her voice sounded strange in her throat. Then she was looking out the window at trees that were darker than the sky and she was crying and she could not stop.

'—under*stand*,' he was saying. 'You *wanted* me to say it, so what is it now?'

She was shaking her head, her hands covering her face.

'Because it does matter and it doesn't matter and it does matter. Because I hate you and I hate me. And that's not true

either, there's nothing true—' She lowered herself onto the
seat, on her side, her head close to Lee. 'Oh Lee,' she said into
the leather upholstery, 'when I die—'

'Hush now.' He patted her arm. 'Hush now, don't say that.'

'You take that ten thousand dollars and you and Peggy go
on a nice long trip, to Europe or someplace.'

Then, to save them both from having to talk, she opened
her mouth and breathed softly and pretended she was asleep.
After a few minutes he took the beer can from her loose fingers, drank what was left, and lowered the can to the floor.

# ADULTERY & OTHER CHOICES

*to my mother*
*& in memory of my father*

*Unless a man has something stronger, something superior to all outside influences, he only needs to catch a bad cold to lose his balance entirely, to take every bird for a fowl of ill omen, and to hear the baying of the hounds in every noise, while his pessimism or his optimism, together with all his thoughts, great and small, significant solely as symptoms and in no other way.*

ANTON CHEKHOV
"A Dull Story"

PART ONE

# AN AFTERNOON
# WITH THE OLD MAN

Now Sunday was over, and Paul Clement lay in bed in his room and wished for Marshall, his one wish in all the world right now (and he was a boy with many wishes; 'If wishes were horses beggars would ride,' his mother said when people wished). But Marshall was in Baton Rouge; he had not seen her since the Clements moved from there to Lafayette after the second grade. Maybe he would never see her again. But he would. When he was old enough to drive a car, he would go to Baton Rouge and surprise her. She would squeal and hug him. He saw her, sixteen years old, running down her front steps and sidewalk to meet him; she had breasts and used lipstick and she wore a white dress. Paul knew that now, at ten, he was good-looking—his face was his only pride, it was why Marshall had been his girl—and when he was sixteen he would be even more handsome and bigger and stronger, too, because he had been praying every night and at mass for God to make him an athlete.

He met Marshall in the second grade, a brown-eyed tomboy; she hated dresses, she got dirty when she played, and she brought two cap pistols and a dump truck to the scrap-iron pile at school. ('We sold the Japs our scrap iron, and now they're using it against us,' his father said.) Once at recess she drove away with rocks fat Warren, who was kicking dust at

Paul. There was a girl named Penny, with long black hair; she sat behind him in class and handed him pictures she drew (he remembered one of her father lying in bed with a broken leg, the leg suspended and weights hanging from it). Penny was prettier than Marshall, but she sometimes irritated him because she always wanted to hold his hand while they waited in line to go into school, and when there was a movie at school she held him captive, pulling him down the auditorium aisle and into a seat beside her, and during the movie her head was warm on his shoulder, her long hair tickling his throat and damp where it pressed his cheek. So he loved Marshall more. His sisters, Amy and Barbara, and his mother knew about Marshall, but his father did not. When Paul told his mother, she said 'Aren't you going to tell Daddy you have a girl friend?'

'No.'

'You should talk more with Daddy. He loves y'all very much, but he doesn't know how to talk to children.'

His mother said she would keep his secret. One warm afternoon after school he was to go to a birthday party at a girl's house. His mother asked if Marshall would be there, and he said yes. She smiled and combed his hair with her fingers. 'Now don't you kiss her,' she said, in her tease voice.

At the party, they played hide-and-seek, and he and Marshall sat on a running board in the garage; the boy who was It passed by without looking in. The lawn and garage were quiet now; the game had passed them, and Marshall said, 'Kiss me.'

'No.'

'Please.' She had olive skin, her brown eyes were large, and a front tooth was missing.

'If you close your eyes,' he said. She did, and he kissed her lips and tasted the line of sweat above her mouth.

After hide-and-seek, Marshall and Paul got on the swing hanging from an oak. Marshall wanted him to sit; she stood facing him, her feet squeezed between his hips and the ropes, her skirt moving against his face as she pumped them higher and higher till they swung up level with the branch where the ropes were tied, and she said, 'I'd like to go all around, over the branch.' Paul hoped she wouldn't try.

When he got home his mother asked if he kissed Marshall and he said yes. She smiled and hugged him.

Here in Lafayette he did not have a girl. He did not even know a girl his age, because he didn't go to a public school now; he went to Cathedral, a boys' school taught by Christian Brothers. At the school in Baton Rouge there had been recess, but no one told you what to play and usually he had been with Penny or Marshall, mostly Marshall. But at Cathedral there was physical education for an hour every day, and it was like being in Baton Rouge when his father still played with them, throwing a tennis ball in the back yard. If Barbara or Amy threw to Paul he sometimes caught it and sometimes did not, but when his father threw it or even if his father was just watching, his muscles stiffened and his belly fluttered and he always missed. At Cathedral it was like that, like being watched by his father.

His father had not played golf in Baton Rouge, or for the first two years in Lafayette; then a priest named Father O'Gorman started coming over and eating supper with them. In summer before supper the men drank beer on the screen porch and listened to the six o'clock news. Father O'Gorman was a bulky man who always smelled like cigars; he liked to tousle Paul's hair. He told Paul's mother not to worry that her husband was an Episcopalian and didn't go to church. 'Any man who kneels down and says his prayers every night the way your husband does is a good man.' That is what Father O'Gorman told her; she told it to Paul, who had not worried about his father going to hell until the day his mother said the priest said he would not.

Father O'Gorman got Paul's father interested in golf. Soon he had clubs and a bag and shoes, and was taking lessons, playing every Saturday and Sunday, and practicing two or three times a week after work and sometimes on Saturday mornings. One night at supper Paul's mother said to Father O'Gorman,

'If I run off with another man it'll be your fault, Father.' She was smiling the way she did when she didn't see anything funny. 'My husband and I used to be together every weekend, now I'm all by myself.'

Paul had not liked those weekends very much. On many Sundays they had gone to New Iberia to visit his mother's family, the Kelleys, who had once had money and lived in a big brick house with Negro women working inside and Negro men working in a yard as big as a school ground, but later all the money was gone and the house, too, and the married aunts and uncles lived like the Clements in small white houses on quiet streets. Those drives to New Iberia were quiet; once there, though, his parents had drinks, and on the way home there was talking.

'I'm home every night,' his father said. 'She knows that.'

'Well, sure you're home, when it's too dark to see the ball, and all your cronies and Betsy Robichaux have gone home, so there's nobody to drink your old beer with.' She was smiling at Paul's father, and winking at Father O'Gorman.

Paul's father practiced on a school ground near their house, and he wanted Paul to shag balls for him. The pay was fifty cents, and it was an easy job to stand daydreaming with a canvas bag in his hand and watch his father's small faceless figure, the quick pencil-small flash of swinging golf club, and then spot the ball in the air and stay clear of it till it struck the ground. Easy enough, and he liked earning the money. But he did not like to shag balls, for it wasn't simply a job like raking leaves. He was supposed to like picking up balls that his father hit; afterward, in the car, he was supposed to be interested while his father explained the different irons and woods, and told why sometimes he sliced and sometimes hooked. And he was supposed to want to caddie, to spend all Sunday afternoon following his father around the golf course. 'Maybe you'll want to caddie one of these Sundays,' his father said as they drove home from the school ground. 'I know you can't miss the Saturday picture show, but maybe Sundays—keeps the money in the family that way.' Paul sat stiffly, looking through the windshield, smelling the leather golf bag and his father's sweat. 'Maybe so,' he said.

Now tonight if Marshall were here with him, and if for some reason his parents and Amy and Barbara left the house and went someplace, like visiting in New Iberia, he and Marshall would go to the kitchen and he would make peanut-butter and blackberry-preserve sandwiches. They would take them with glasses of cold milk to the living room, where the large lazy-sounding oscillating floor fan moved the curtain at one end of its arc, then rustled the Sunday paper on the couch as it swept back. He would sit beside her on the couch, and when they finished the sandwiches he would rest his head in her lap and look up at her bright eyes and tell her about today, how at Sunday dinner his father had said, 'Want to come out today?' and he had chewed a large bite of chocolate cake, trying to think of a reason not to, and then swallowed and said, 'Sure.'

After dinner, his father got an extra pack of Luckies from the bedroom, and then it was time to go. His mother walked out on the screen porch with them; the wisteria climbing the screen was blooming lavender. 'Keep an eye on him in this heat,' she said to his father.

'I will.'

She kissed them. As they walked to the car, she called, 'Look at my two handsome men. Paul, be a good influence on your father, bring him home early.'

In the car, they did not talk for six blocks or so. Then his father told him he ought to have a cap to keep the sun off his head, and Paul said he'd be O.K.

'That mama of yours, if I bring you home with a headache she'll say the golf course is the only place the sun shines.'

Paul smiled. The rest of the way to the golf course, they did not talk. Walking to the clubhouse, Paul trailed a step or two behind his father. Caddies stood near the sidewalk—tall boys with dirty bare feet or ragged sneakers and hard brown biceps. Several of them were smoking. ('It stunts the growth,' his mother said.) They were the kind of boys Paul always yielded the sidewalk to when he walked to the cowboy show and serial in town on Saturdays. Paul looked out at the golf course, shielding his eyes with one hand, and studied the distant greens and fairways as he and his father passed the boys and their smell of cigarette smoke and sweat and sweet hair oil.

'Mr. Clement, you need a caddie?'

'No thanks, Tujack. I got my boy.'

From under his shielding hand, Paul stared over the flat fairway at a tiny red flag, hanging limply over the heat shimmer. As he followed his father into the clubhouse, he felt their eyes on him; then, turning a corner around the showcase of clubs, he was out of their vision, and he followed his father's broad shoulders and brown hairy arms into the locker room. His father sat on a bench and put on his golf shoes.

'That Tujack's going to be a hell of a golfer.'

'He plays?'

'They all play, these caddies.'

Outside, in the hot dust behind the clubhouse, his father strapped the golf bag onto a cart, and Paul pulled it behind him to the first tee. Tujack was there, a tall wiry boy of about sixteen, a golf bag slung over his shoulder. Paul shook hands with Mr. Blanchet, Mr. Voorhies, Mr. Peck. Each of them, as he shook hands, looked Paul up and down, as though to judge what sort of boy their friend had. Paul gave his father the driver and then pulled the cart away from the tee, stopping short of the three caddies, who stood under a sycamore. He was the only one using a cart, and he wished his father hadn't done that. I can carry it, he wanted to say.

The first hole had a long dogleg going to the left around a field of short brown weeds. His father shot first, driving two-thirds of the way down the first leg; he came over and gave Paul the driver and stood between him and the caddies, closing the distance. 'You'll be on in two, Mr. Clement,' Tujack said.

'You could, Tujack. Not me.'

They were quiet while the others shot, and then Paul walked beside his father, pulling the cart behind him. It seemed badly balanced, and he watched the ground ahead of him for those small rises that might tip the cart over on its side with a shamefaced clanking of clubs. After the first nine, they stopped at the clubhouse for a drink, and his father asked him how he was holding up. 'Fine,' Paul said. He was. He didn't tire on the second nine, either. It was a hot afternoon, but he liked to sweat, and there was not much need for talking. ('Good shot.' 'Well, let's see what I can do with the brassie.') Usually, between shots, he walked a little to the rear, and his father talked to one of the men.

When they finished playing, his father gave him a dollar and a quarter and told him he was a good caddie, then asked if he was tired or too hot and what did he want to drink, and took him into the clubhouse and up to the counter. 'Give this boy a Grapette and some cheese crackers,' his father said, his hand coming down on Paul's shoulder, staying there.

'That your boy?' the man behind the counter said.

'That's him,' the hand on Paul's shoulder squeezing now, rocking him back and forth. Paul lowered his eyes and smiled and blushed, just as he did each time his father said, 'I'd like you to meet my boy,' his father smiling, mussing his hair, Paul shaking the large extended hand, squeezing it ('Always squeeze,' his mother told him. 'Don't give someone a dead fish'). 'He's got a good grip,' one man had said, and for a moment Paul had been proud.

Now his father was drinking beer with his friends—what Paul's mother called the nineteenth hole. Paul liked watching him have fun, pouring the good summer-smelling beer in his glass, laughing, talking about the game they just played and other games they had played. They talked about baseball, too; a team called the Dodgers was going to have a colored boy playing this year. Betsy Robichaux and another woman came to their table, and the four men and Paul stood up; Mr. Peck got two chairs from the next table. Paul squeezed the women's hands, too, but not quite as hard.

'He's got his daddy's looks,' Betsy Robichaux said.

His father grinned and his blue eyes twinkled. She was

not really pretty but she was nice-looking, Paul thought. She sat opposite him with her back to the window that ran the length of the clubhouse, so he watched her, caught himself staring at her now and then, but most of the time he remembered to pretend he was looking past her at the eighteenth green, where long-shadowed men leaned on putters. She was deeply tanned and slender. Her voice was husky, she laughed a lot, she said hell and damn, and she was always smoking a Pall Mall, gesturing with it in her ringless left hand. Paul knew she was not a lady like his mother, but he liked watching women smoke, for a cigarette made them somehow different, like women in movies instead of mothers. She sat there talking golf with the men, and Paul knew his father liked talking golf with her better than with his mother, who only pretended she was interested (Paul could tell by her voice). But thinking about his mother made him feel guilty, as though he were betraying his father, as though he were his mother's spy, recording every time his father said 'Betsy.' He decided to count the beers his father drank, so if his mother said something Paul could defend him.

His father drank five beers (Paul had two Grapettes and two packages of cheese crackers with peanut butter), and then it was dusk and they drove home, his father talking all the way in his drinking voice, relaxed, its tone without edges now, rounded by some quality that was almost tenderness, almost affection. He talked golf. Sometimes, when he paused, Paul said yes. As they approached the corner of their street, his father reached over and lightly slapped Paul's leg, then gave it a squeeze.

'Well,' he said. 'It's not so bad to spend an afternoon with the old man, is it?'

'Nope,' Paul said, and knew at once how that sounded, how his father must have heard only their failure in that one little word, because how could his father possibly know, ever forever know, that even that one word had released so much that tears came to his eyes, and it was as if his soul wanted to talk and hug his father but his body could not, and all he could do was in silence love his father as though he were a memory, as the afternoon already was a memory.

His mother met them on the screen porch. 'Did my two men have fun together?'

'Sure we did. He's a good caddie.'

'Did you have fun?' she asked Paul.

He took a quick deep breath, closed his mouth tightly, pressed a finger under his nose, and pretended to hold back a sneeze as he walked past her.


Now in his bed he grew sleepy to the sound of the fan. He wondered if they would have a new car when he was a big boy. He saw the car as a blue one, and it smelled new inside. Now Marshall came out in her white dress and kissed him in the evening sun right there on her front steps; she had the line of sweat over her lips and smelled of perfume. Holding hands, they walked to the car. Her head came to about his shoulder; just before he opened the car door, she put her hand on his bicep and squeezed it. Her face was lovely and sad for him. 'I'm glad you're taking me,' she said.

In the car, she slid close to him. Her arms were dark against the lap of her dress. He offered his pack of Luckies, and they lit them from the dashboard lighter. They drove out of town, then on a long road through woods. The road started climbing and they came out above the woods at trimmed bright grass and spreading live oaks, and in their shade old tombstones and crosses. They left the car and very quietly, holding hands, they walked in the oak shade to his father's grave. He made the sign of the cross, bowed his head, and prayed for his father's soul. When Marshall saw the tears in his eyes, she put her arm around his waist and hugged him tightly while he prayed.

# CONTRITION

AFTER SCHOOL Paul and Eddie walked fast; it was a cold January day, the sky had been growing darker all afternoon, and they could feel rain coming on the wind. They crossed themselves as they passed the Cathedral; then they were walking by the Bishop's huge house, with its iron fence; on his lawn pines and live oaks thrashed in the wind.

'I'm going to learn an instrument,' Eddie said.

Paul looked up at him, and then at the cars driving with their lights on. The whole town seemed to be hurrying home before the winter rain. He thought of Eddie going to a woman's house and taking piano lessons and at the end of the year playing in a recital, taking his turn among girls in velveteen dresses with barrettes in their hair.

'I talked to Brother Eugene yesterday.'

'You didn't tell me.'

'I thought about it during vacation, and I talked to my folks about it.'

'You'd take lessons at school? And be in the band?'

'I couldn't be in the band for a while. It's mostly just high school boys. But maybe by the eighth grade.'

Eddie was walking faster, looking up at the sky and the trees blowing above the rooftops. In the third grade, when they had both entered Cathedral, Paul had chosen Eddie as his friend. Paul was short and thin and often pressed a handkerchief to his sniffling hayfevered nose. Eddie was taller, but like Paul he moved with caution among the other boys, his voice seemed bent on silencing itself, and his gestures were close to his body as though apologizing for the space he occupied. At recess he and Eddie drank Cokes together, and on the athletic field they watched each other's failures. Paul believed they could endure grammar school together and by the time they reached high school they would change or the world would change. He did not know precisely how. At Cathedral the boys started in the third grade and went through the twelfth and sometimes when he thought of that he saw himself and Eddie unchanged and outcast until finally they crossed the stage wearing caps and gowns. But most of the time he believed when they reached high school the days would no longer cost so much of fear and patience and hope.

'We better hurry,' Eddie said, and started to run. They were a block from his house when the rain fell hard and cold, and their faces dripped and they shivered as they stomped into the kitchen where Mrs. Kirkpatrick was moving toward the door, wearing an overcoat and scarf.

'I was just going to get you,' she said, and kissed Eddie. Susan was sitting at the table, and she was smoking. 'Paul, you'd better call your mother and tell her I'll take you home. We'll have hot chocolate.' She hugged Eddie. Paul hung his jacket on a hook by the door and, rubbing his hair with his handkerchief, he secretly watched Susan who was sixteen and pretty, with hair that was light brown, almost blonde, the color of Eddie's, and bright red lips and fingernails. He watched her inhaling, and he tingled with guilt and delightful fascination for the secret and forbidden. One Saturday afternoon as Paul and Eddie were walking home after a Red Ryder movie Eddie said he had gone upstairs yesterday and found Susan and his mother smoking in Susan's room and they had told him not to tell his father because he would be hurt. Eddie told this with the worried, conspiratorial tone of someone confiding a sin. Now here was Susan, and he looked at her brown Philip Morris pack on the table and the cigarette in her hands, then he moved through the kitchen, into the hall, toward the phone.

In the Kirkpatrick house there seemed to be only the one secret, and it was kept from Eddie's father in a lovingly collusive way, like a gift. Eddie had said he told his father about everything that bothered him: how unhappy he was at school when they had to play football and then basketball and then softball. In Paul's house everyone was a secret. One Saturday evening last summer his parents had gone out; it was twilight when they left and Paul was in the back yard; he was lying under the fig tree, pretending he was the last Marine alive on Wake Island, when he heard the car doors slam and the engine start. He crawled out from under the tree and ran around to the front yard, to the driveway, but they were gone, they were at the end of the block, and he watched the tail lights as his father braked and then drove on. His sisters were inside the house but he did not go in. He went back to the fig tree and lay under it, in the darkness and sadness under the wide leaves. Always before his parents went out they kissed him and his sisters. Now he lay unkissed, and thinking of the back of the car as it drove away he began to cry. In the sweet luxury of tears he pressed his face into the grass until he heard the back door close. He lay quietly. In the pale dying light Barbara came across the lawn; she approached him and walked past the tree and stood with her back to him. She was looking up at the sky. Then he saw that she was crying. At first she cried quietly, but then she began to moan and sob. Finally she wiped her face with her hands and went sniffing past him and into the house. He waited a while then left his tree, his tears, his foxhole; from the top of the tree a mockingbird screamed at him.

The memory of Barbara that summer night was pleasurably mysterious, and often when he thought of her he saw her weeping at the sky. There were other memories he kept in his heart like old photographs. His father rarely talked at home, but when friends came for drinks Paul lay on his bed and listened to the drone of the women at one end of the room and the loud talk of the men at the other and, above it all, his father. He heard his father tell stories about when he was first married and he was a surveyor for the utilities company he still worked for; now he was a district manager. His father had worn a holstered .22 Colt Woodsman and shot cottonmouths in the rice fields. Once one of the crew caught a king snake and carried it in a paper bag until they found a cottonmouth; he threw the king snake on it and the crew watched the fight; listening to his father's voice through the wall he could see the twining snakes and the cottonmouth's slow death. A man who owned the land they were surveying told his father to get off and said his company was nothing but a bunch of crooked sons of bitches anyway and his father knocked him down. Once they had to deal with a Negro and when the talking was done the Negro offered his hand and his father took it. In the car one of the crew said: You shook his hand. His father said: And if I hadn't, *then* who would have been the gentleman?

His father often said children should be seen and not heard and at times it seemed that Paul's silence made him invisible too and he could listen like a spy. On an afternoon last summer he sat petting his yellow dog Mike. He sat on the bottom step of the back porch and his father and mother sat on the top step. His father had finished mowing the lawn and Paul smelled his sweat and the beer he was drinking and the smell of clean dog and freshly cut grass; Mike turned on his back and grinned while Paul scratched his belly. Above Paul his parents were murmuring, and with his fingers on Mike's ribs he concentrated all of himself into one ear, and the muted sound of their voices became words.

'I'm afraid to,' his mother said.

'We can use rubbers.'

'Don't talk that way.'

He heard his father's Zippo, then smelled the smoke. It was all he smelled in the air now. His father and mother sat quietly behind him.

When he returned to the kitchen from calling his mother, Mrs. Kirkpatrick was stirring chocolate on the stove. They were drinking it when the front door opened; Susan put her cigarettes in her purse and Mr. Kirkpatrick came in; he was a slender, gentle man whose posture was slightly stooped. He greeted them all and spoke of the rain and tousled Eddie's hair, then made himself a drink and joined them at the table.

'I told Paul I'm going to take an instrument.'

'What do you think of that, Paul?'

*Mine's better*, he thought, looking at Mr. Kirkpatrick's kind brown eyes with crinkled corners and seeing his father's ruddy face and blue eyes and thin wavy hair, nearly black now though his mother said when she met him it was blond curls; seeing his father's broad shoulders and deep hairy chest and hairy arms and hearing the gruff voice; he was shy with all fathers, he went each year in dread to the Rotary father and son luncheon where, in turn, he had to stand on a chair and speak his name to the upturned faces; yet he wasn't shy with Mr. Kirkpatrick, he felt with him now the stirrings of relief, felt drawn to him as though by trust and love, and he wanted to say: *Music is for sissies*; he wanted to say: Susan smokes; he wanted to say: *I could beat up Eddie*; and he wanted to show them he could.

'I guess it's all right,' he said.

'You should do it too,' Susan said. 'Y'all could learn together.'

'Maybe I will,' he said.

Next day the sun and a cold wind dried the earth and after school Paul and Eddie talked to Brother Eugene. He was tall and kept pushing his glasses up on his nose, and his black robe smelled of chalk dust where he had wiped his hands. They told him they wanted to learn the trumpet but he said they should take the French horn. He took them up the wooden stairs to the second floor and unlocked the bandroom and showed them a French horn. He said if they learned to play it they could easily play the trumpet and cornet as well; but they should learn the French horn because the band had all the trumpet players it needed for years to come but soon there would be a shortage of French horns. If they worked hard they could start playing in the regular band in two years when they were only in the seventh grade; they would wear uniforms and go on band trips to play at football games and they would march in the homecoming parade and Mardi Gras parade and many colleges gave band scholarships. He raised the horn to his lips and blew a series of notes.

When Paul got home he told his mother and sisters. Amy said Maybe he'd be a famous trumpet player like Harry James, Barbara said It might be nice and his mother said It was very exciting but they would have to wait and see what Daddy said. She made cinnamon toast and a pot of tea and they all sat at the kitchen table. When his father came home Paul listened through the closed kitchen door to him and Mike. From windows he had watched Mike greeting his father as he emerged from his car, his father's near-scowling face suddenly laughing as the dog ran to him and leaped up at him, his father crouching and pushing Mike back with gentle slaps, Mike growling and wagging his tail and barking, jumping again and again to his father's hands and loving voice. Now in the living room they were laughing and growling, and they came into the kitchen, Mike following through the swinging door, and his father's sweeping glance quizzical in the silence which he then broke with hello, kissed Paul's mother, poured bourbon and water, and went to the living room to read the evening paper.

Usually at supper his mother and sisters talked about school and the nuns or a dress his mother was making for one of them or about other things that Paul paid no attention to while he ate. But that night they were quiet and he knew they were waiting for him. Mike came to watch them and his father said: 'Mike, you know better than that. Go back to the living room. Go on.'

Mike went back and lay on the rug, watching them.

'Paul?' his mother said. 'Did anything new happen at school today?'

Paul looked at her urging brown eyes. Then his father said: 'Why should anything new happen?'

Watching his mother he saw that the question was to her.

'I don't know,' his mother said. 'It can't be the same *every* day.'

Barbara was watching him. He looked at her and said: 'It's pretty much the same every day.'

When they finished eating, his father took a piece of ham to the living room and dropped it between Mike's paws.


That night Paul lay in the dark in his room adjacent to the living room and listened to them through the wall. He knew it was eleven o'clock because his father had finished reading. Every week he read *The Saturday Evening Post, Time, Collier's, The Reader's Digest, Life*, and a mystery or a book by a golf pro. While he read Mike slept beside his chair and now and then his father's hand lowered, with stroking fingers, to Mike's head. At eleven o'clock he slept.

'Paul wants to take the French horn.'

'Where's he going to take it? To the picture show?'

'He's serious about it.'

'Who, him? Who talked him into it?'

'Nobody did. Eddie's going to start, and they've talked it over, but I'm sure Eddie didn't—'

'Ah: Eddie. When was all this?'

'Today.'

'Today. All of a sudden he's a musician. Did you ever hear that boy say he wanted to be a musician till now?'

'Well there has to be a first day for everything.'

'Why didn't he tell me himself? Is that what all that monkey business was about at supper?'

'He was afraid to.'

'Afraid to? Did he tell you that?'

'No, he—'

'Did he ask you to ask me?'

'No, I just—'

'Why is my son afraid of me? Can you tell me that? I've spanked that boy three times in ten years. What's he afraid of?'

'He's very sensitive.'

'Sensitive. If he's so sensitive why doesn't he know— Never mind: do they have the horns at school?'

'You have to buy one.'

'Buy one.'

'Or maybe rent one.'

'Or maybe rent one. Goddamn.'

'It means a lot to him. He'll be in the high school band. Maybe he can get a college scholarship.'

'Goddamn,' his father said.


At breakfast his father was reading the paper. Paul waited. He had finished his oatmeal and milk and toast, the girls had gone to brush their teeth, his mother was putting the dishes in the sink, and finally he rose to leave too when his father lowered the paper and looked at him.

'What's this your mother tells me about a French horn?'

The blue eyes were gazing into his and he could see in them the silence when he and his father were trapped together in a car, and the relief he felt at all his father's departures and the fear at his arrivals.

'I decided not to,' Paul said. 'It costs too much.'

'Wait a minute: that's not what I asked. Do you want to play the horn?'

'I guess so.'

'Son, I can buy a horn; I can borrow for that. Do you or don't you want to learn to play it.'

'Yesterday you wanted to,' his mother said, and he looked at her. She quickly nodded her head, then gestured with it toward his father, then nodded again. In one of his frequent daydreams he was captured by a band of amazons and taken to a tropical island where they lived; they were tall and lovely and they fed him and cared for him and he could not leave. There was some threatening yet attractive mystery about them too, as if they all shared a secret and it had to do with him; perhaps one morning they would tie him to an altar and sacrifice him to the sun; his heart plucked out, his soul would rise above the beautiful women. He wished he were with them now.

'Yes, I'd like to,' he said.

'All right,' his father said, the paper rising into place again; then from behind it he muttered: 'Why didn't you say so.'

Paul stood there until he was sure his father was reading again and was not waiting for an answer.


Twice a week Paul and Eddie arrived at school carrying their cased horns bumping against their legs and in the afternoon, after an hour's lesson, walked home with them. Paul was a victim of newspaper and magazine cartoons. Why hadn't he thought of the *size* of the horn? In cartoons only the inept carried large instruments, usually tubas, and their practicing made cats and dogs howl, neighbors shout, close windows, throw old shoes. Now when he walked home carrying the horn, he was no longer anonymous: anyone driving by could see what he was. After supper he went to his room and closed the door and tried to play the notes. The horn was silver with a shiny brass bell and holding it and depressing its valves smelling of oil he wished he could give it the love it deserved. His father had brought it home and opened the case on the dining room table and displayed for Paul and his sisters and mother the horn nestled in red felt. A hundred dollars, he said; I hope it's worth it. Oh let's don't talk about money, Paul's mother said; I hate the dirty old stuff. Two days later Eddie's father bought a used horn, a gold one with two dents on the bell, and Paul felt deceived.

Sitting in his room he looked at the notes on the page; they made no sense to him. He began to hate the notes themselves, the way they sat inscrutable and arrogant on the stern bars which he didn't understand either. At times he thought he was simply stupid; he would have preferred that to the truth which sometimes surfaced in his mind: that while he and Eddie sat before Brother Eugene tapping the music sheets with his baton, tapping their horns with his baton, sometimes tapping their knuckles and hands with his baton, Paul was not there: he watched himself looking at the notes; he listened to himself trying to blow them; and all the time he was in suspension, waiting. He was waiting for something to happen. One afternoon he would all at once love the horn, he would know and love the notes, and his lips would blow sweet silver. Or one day someone would steal his horn. Or the school would burn to the ground or Brother Eugene would drop dead.

On the first night he practiced at home his father said it sounded like a bullfrog. Paul said it was hard to get the lips right. He played every night for the first two weeks, making sounds that had nothing to do with the notes he glared at on the sheet, wanting to cross them out with a pencil, to gouge them with its point. For the first time in his life he was living a public lie. With his father he had lived a lie for as long as he could remember: he believed his father wanted him to be popular and athletic at school, so Paul never told him about his days. But now the lie had spread: it touched his mother and Amy and Barbara and Brother Eugene and even Eddie. He hated the lie, not for its sin but for its isolation; and every Tuesday and Thursday he carried the horn to school as though it were a dead bird; and in the afternoons he climbed the stairs with Eddie to the band room and to Brother Eugene's growing impatience; then entering his house he put the horn on the closet floor, wanting to kick it, and at supper he answered questions about his music lessons. After two weeks of practicing at home his father asked him, the gruff voice trying to be gentle and bantering, if he'd practice when he came home from school, not at night. As lovely as the French horn is, his father said, it wasn't meant to accompany reading.

Nor was anything else. When his father came home in the evenings Amy took her records off the record player. After supper, except during the Sunday night radio shows, the living room was quiet. If friends of Amy or Barbara came over they went to the girls' bedroom and closed the door. The phone was in the hall and when Paul talked to Eddie at night he turned his back to the living room and spoke in a low, furtive voice. Lying in bed he could hear Mike scratching a flea, his father returning one magazine to the rack and getting another, his mother yawning in the chair where she read. But he was grateful for that silence resting on his horn too. He started practicing before his father came home; but if his mother was shopping or playing bridge he put the horn away and when she came home and asked if he had practiced he said yes. He saw the end coming.

He did not know how it would come, and when it did he felt betrayed again: Eddie phoned Paul on a Wednesday night and said he wasn't going to the lesson tomorrow, he was quitting.

'I haven't enjoyed it very much,' Eddie said. 'Have you?'

'I don't know. It hasn't been so bad.'

'I've hated it. I don't like the French horn. It's big and clumsy and I don't like the sound. I wish now I had taken the clarinet. Daddy says Brother Eugene used us, he talked us into the French horn so he'd have some for the band. He says if I want to take the clarinet after a while I can get lessons from somebody in town.'

'What about the horn? What are you going to do with the horn?'

'He'll sell it back to the store.'

The phone was outside his sisters' room. Barbara had been reading on the bed she shared with Amy; now she was watching him. When he hung up she said: 'Eddie quit, didn't he.'

'Yes.'

'What are you going to do now?'

'I don't know.'

'Why don't you quit?'

He shrugged.

'Just tell Daddy you've tried it and you don't like it. He

can sell the horn. Paul: what are you going to do—take those silly lessons till you're twenty-one years old?'

Next day he went to his lesson. Without Eddie, his clumsy hypocrisy filled the room: as Brother Eugene called for a note Paul assumed a look of memory and concentration while his fingers pressed any valves they touched and he blew into the horn. Brother Eugene paced back and forth, turned his back to Paul, then spun to face him.

'Paul, you're not practicing. You've learned nothing in a month. At least when Eddie was with us you could watch his fingers. Why aren't you practicing? Don't you know you owe it to your father? He had to sacrifice to buy that horn. It's a beautiful horn. If you have no pride in yourself, can't you at least do that much for your father?'

'He won't let me.'

'What do you mean, he won't let you?'

'He won't let me practice. He likes quiet in the house.'

Brother Eugene tapped the music stand once with his baton then pushed his glasses higher on his nose.

'Maybe I better talk to him,' he said.

'You better not,' Paul said. 'He's Episcopalian, and he doesn't like Brothers. He—'

'He what, Paul?'

'I heard him talking once—he wants to—'

'He wants to what, Paul?'

'He wants to use those things. With my mother.'

He looked down at the horn in his lap. Then he stroked it with his fingers and looked at Brother Eugene's robe and shoes.

'We can stop for today,' Brother Eugene said. 'If you'd like to talk about the other—'

Paul shook his head.

'It's all right,' he said. 'And I can practice in the afternoons. Just there's not much time.'

He took the mouthpiece from the horn and put the horn in its case.

In the kitchen his mother said: 'I never did think that was the right instrument for you. But Daddy will be disappointed.'

'Why should he be?' Barbara said. 'Nobody has to play the French horn.'

'Well, he spent a lot of money on that horn.' She looked at Paul. 'Are you going to tell him? I want you to stand up like a man and tell him yourself.'

'Okay,' he said.

He went out to the back yard. The day was blue and warm and he stood waiting in the sunlight, clinging to the vision of tomorrow when it would all be over, until in the shadows of twilight he heard the slamming of his father's car door and then Mike growling happily. When those sounds stopped he went into the kitchen as his father pushed through its door. His mother was at the stove and Barbara was gone. He looked quickly at his father and said: 'I want to quit the horn.'

'What?' His father still wore his hat, and his overcoat was over his arm. 'You want to *what?*'

'Now don't shout at him,' his mother said.

His father looked at them both, then sighed and shook his head.

'Goddamn,' he said, and went back through the door; he went through it fast and it swung twice behind him before it closed.

'You should have waited till he had his drink. You know I always wait till he's had his drink.'

When his father came back he had taken off his coat and tie and rolled up the cuffs of his white shirt. He was midway across the kitchen toward the liquor cabinet when he stopped and looked at Paul: 'What do you mean, you want to quit? You've only been at it a month! You haven't even *started* the Goddamn thing! Why do you want to *quit?*'

Paul shrugged and looked down, then raised his eyes to his father; his father's face was blurred. He blinked and it was clear again and he was too ashamed of the tears on his cheeks to wipe them.

'Goddamnit what are you *crying* for. What's he *crying* for.' His father stood between them, his fierce clenched jaws now turned to her. '*Why* is he crying! Okay, he wants to quit the Goddamn horn. *Okay*. I can't *make* him play it. He stands there crying. *I'm* the one who borrowed the Goddamn hundred dollars. What'll I do with that horn now, huh?' He looked at Paul. 'Huh? Can you tell me that?'

'We can sell it,' his mother said.

'We can sell it.' His father looked at her. 'That's not even the point. Why in the hell did he ever think he wanted to play the Goddamn thing to begin with? He didn't *ever* want to. It's just something he and the other one, Eddie, dreamed up. When did Eddie quit?'

'I don't know,' his mother said. 'Yesterday. Brother Eugene shouldn't have—'

'The hell with Brother Eugene. What's *he* got to do with it? I pity the poor bastard for wasting his time. With *what?*' Looking at her, he pointed a finger at Paul. 'What's he good for? Not a Goddamn thing. He doesn't do one Goddamn thing but mope around the house, he's not good for one Goddamn thing but to go to cowboy shows and shoot Japs and Indians in the back yard. What the hell else does he do? Huh? What else?—' Paul would not remember the rest. In the explosion of his father's voice he stood with the tears he would not wipe. Once he felt he was kneeling with his head bowed. Finally the sound ended and he left the room and his father's face. He went to his room and lay face-down on his bed and wiped his eyes. Then he lay on his back and looked at the ceiling. Barbara came in and sat on the bed and held his hand. She looked as though she might cry.

'He's terrible,' she said.

In her pink cheeks and blue eyes he saw himself, saw the narrow breadth of his soul which in ten years had learned nothing of courage and so much of lies; to her face and the

clasp of her hand he silently asked his father's question—
*What's he good for?*—and he could not accept the answer of
her gaze and touch, that he was a little brother she loved.
Closing his eyes he found no answer there either, in the dark
of his mind where memories of himself swam: he saw the day
of snow when he was five, the only time in his life he had seen
snow and that night it melted; in the afternoon his father came
home and threw snowballs at them and one hit Paul in the eye
and he cried and his mother said: *You're too rough with him*,
he's only a little boy; and he saw the night when he was two
and after supper his father picked him up and held him laughing and tossed him in the air and caught him, then again, both
of them laughing as his father tossed and tossed while his
mother's voice cut through the blur of ceiling and walls and
his father's arms and laughing upturned face: *You'll make him
sick*, and then he was, in the air, and on the rug as his father
lowered him to the floor and her voice started again. Opening
his eyes to look at Barbara he murmured: 'No he isn't.'

# THE BULLY

He did not tell even Eddie about the cat. It was in summer, in August. The Clements were renting a strange house then. It had been built by the owner and a Negro; it was two stories and its brick and cement walls were a foot thick. It was shaped like a box. For some reason no one had ever explained, the owner had dug a basement under the house after it was built; perhaps he could not stop building. A mule had dragged the dirt away, climbing up the steep ramp which later became the driveway. After that the mule died. It was the only basement in town, it was always wet, and there was a sump pump they could hear inside the house when it rained.

It was raining the day Paul found the cat down there, crouched between the car and the wall at the driest side of the basement. It was white with a large brown spot on its left side, and the right forepaw was brown. Paul picked it up and stared into its eyes. When the cat tried to look away Paul held its head. He could feel the cat's heart above his hand; it was beating as fast as his was. Then he walked with it to the pump, walking barefooted in the cool rainwater that ran down the ramp and across the floor. He squatted over the round hole of the pump. Then he thrust the cat's head under water. The cat's legs kicked and reached but Paul's hands were behind its head. Then he was afraid of what he was doing and he put the cat on the floor. It ran under the car and lay watching him.

Paul quickly left the basement, walked up the ramp, into the rain. He looked up into the rain at God.

The cat was young, little more than a kitten. An older cat would have been smarter; Paul knew that. But this one stayed. Next morning it gripped the screen door with its front paws and watched the family in the kitchen eating fresh figs on cereal. Amy was eighteen and she had hated all five dogs Paul had lost to cars, age, and sudden disappearance; but she loved cats and when she heard it then saw it she left the table and went outside and picked it up. She stood with the early sunlight on her black hair and held the cat and stroked it and talked to it and it stretched against her breasts.

'I'll give him some milk,' she said through the door.

'Oh no,' his mother said. 'Don't feed strays.'

Barbara went on eating and reading the paper. She was fifteen and smart and plump and she wanted a boy friend and Paul knew she was seldom happy. Paul's father was reading the sports section.

'Come eat before your cereal gets mushy,' his mother said, and Amy came in.

The cat was mewing at the screen again. Paul looked at it and knew if he was alone this morning he would do it, he knew he had to and he wanted to but he faintly hoped someone would stay home and he would be saved. But after his father went to work some girls came in a car and took Amy swimming, his mother went shopping, and Barbara rode her bicycle to a friend's house. In the house alone he felt wicked and he could feel the cat down there in the yard. He went downstairs and into the kitchen. It was on the back porch, a small square of concrete with an iron railing. When the cat heard him it stood on its hind legs and clung to the screen and mewed, and Paul looked at its pink mouth and small pointed teeth.

'Hello, cat,' he said softly.

Then he opened the screen, fast and hard and wide, and slammed the cat against the railing. He stepped out and let the screen shut behind him. The cat was crouched in the corner made by the railing and the brick wall; it watched him;

then it looked away and licked its paws. An older cat would have arched its back and prepared to fight or, with a wise and determined face, darted past him. But this one was afraid and uncertain and was now pretending that nothing had happened. When Paul leaned forward and stroked its back it quivered and looked at him. He wished the cat would fight him, would spring at him howling and hissing and clawing. He imagined him and the cat rolling off the concrete steps and onto the ground, fighting. He picked it up and carried it down the back stairs into the basement; all the time he was stroking it. He went to the dark corner where the old clothes-line lay on the floor; he picked it up and climbed the stairs again, into the bright sun. He crossed the back yard and went behind the neighbor's garage, where the sycamore tree was. While he slipped the noose over the cat's head the cat was very still. Paul's breath and heart were quick.


Larry Guidry was a short wiry boy with biceps like baseballs, thin curly hair, a small head, and a face the color of housedust. Paul thought his head looked like a cottonmouth's. Larry had no friends but sometimes at recess he joined a group that was joking about girls or parts of girls and when he laughed his eyes were bright. They were bright too when he hurt Paul. In the fifth grade the Brothers had stopped failing him. That was the first year Paul was his classmate. It was, he thought, as if Larry had been waiting for him to catch up. For two years Larry punched his arms, twisted his ears, yanked his hair, and stomped his cold instep as the class waited in line outside of school on winter mornings. Once at supper his mother saw the bruise on his arm and asked him what had happened. He told her a boy hit him. She said he must tell the boy not to do it again, a bruise like that could cause cancer. Did you hit him back? his father said. We were playing, Paul said. Walking home from school in the afternoons and in bed at night Paul fought with Larry, blackened and closed his eyes, broke his nose and jaw, covered his small crinkled face with cuts and blood, and hearing Larry's helpless and defeated pleas, his breast filled as with the brass and bass drum of a passing parade.

Larry came from a poor family. Paul knew this because he came on the school bus from the north end of town and because everything he wore was old: the clean starched and ironed khakis in the fall and spring, the corduroys and sweat shirts and mackinaw in winter, and the black tennis shoes with their soles worn nearly smooth. Paul also believed he had many brothers and sisters. He looked like he came from one of those families. In the summer Larry sold snowballs. He had a roofed, glass-windowed cart attached to the front of his bicycle and he rode about town. Usually he worked the north end where the swimming pool and golf course were and where poor white families lived on the borders of the Negro section. But sometimes on summer afternoons when Paul and Eddie walked to a movie they saw him on the main street and bought a snowball from him. The three of them spoke nervously and politely, like old schoolmates who hadn't been close. Paul knew Larry wouldn't do anything to them, though he didn't know how he knew it or why it was true: whether because working and bullying didn't go together or because it was summer and bullying was left back there with books and desks and blackboards and ringing bells. I saw Brother Daniel driving somewhere. I saw Louis at the pool. Larry bent over the block of ice, his head and arms inside the cart as he scraped with the hand-scraper; then he packed ice into paper cups and poured over it the flavored syrup. I'll take grape this time. The small hand gave him the cup. He placed a nickel in the palm, his thumb and finger touching the hand.

When Paul went back to school for the seventh grade Larry was sixteen years old, his voice was deeper, but he had not grown; the khakis he wore could have been the same he had worn the autumn before. On the first day of school, about twenty minutes late, Roland Comeaux joined the class. He missed the first bell which summoned the boys to line up in two files facing their teacher, and the second bell which rang usually as the principal, a large, jovial and irascible Frenchman, emerged from the building and stood on the back steps and, with his hands resting on his round belly, looked down at the entire school: the third graders to his left, the high school seniors to his right, and the black-robed Christian Brothers standing with roll books at the head of each column. Brother Gauthier, the seventh-grade teacher, was also from France and he used snuff. In other years Paul had smelled oiled wooden floors, washed blackboards, chalk dust, and the glossy pages of new books. The seventh grade would be the year that smelled of snuff.

Roland Comeaux missed more than the morning line: he missed the morning prayers recited in the classroom, Brother Gauthier leading, each boy standing at his desk, fingering the black rosaries they all carried. Roland came in after they had recited the first decade of the joyful mysteries. They were seated and Larry, sitting behind Paul, had just given his tricep a long hard pinch, and Paul had turned to him a smiling face. When he looked to the front of the class again Roland was coming through the door. He wore khakis and a T-shirt whose sleeves were taut around his veined biceps; in tennis shoes he strode poised and graceful to the desk where he smiled at Brother Gauthier and then, turning, smiled at the class. The smile did not ask for anything. Then he turned back to Brother Gauthier.

At recess that morning the class crowded around the Coke machine, five or six hands at once waiting with a coin at the slot. Paul was toward the rear, holding his nickel in his fist and pocket too, so he didn't see Roland and Wayne until the crowd moved back from the machine with that sudden and quiet shifting that always meant a fight. He could feel the anticipation in their bodies as he squeezed between them and got toward the front. Roland was perhaps an inch taller than Wayne but much lighter; Wayne Landry was short, chubby, and strong, one of the boys the high school football coach waited for.

'Pick it up,' Wayne said.

Then he pushed Roland's chest. In the fights Paul had seen, this pushing was a ritual: boys pushed each other until fear left their eyes, then they fought. Roland did not return Wayne's push. He hit him in the jaw with a left hook (Paul noticed that: not a round-house right but a left, and a hook at that); the second blow was a right to the stomach that would have folded Wayne if it weren't for the left and right which struck almost the same point on his chin. He went to the pavement as though he had slipped on ice. Leaning forward, Paul saw that one outstretched hand lay next to the nickel. Wayne was looking up at Roland, whose fists were unclenched, one hand going into his pocket as he turned to the machine and said: 'I didn't hit your nickel. You dropped it.'

He bought a Coke, opened it, then he bought another. He opened that one and held it down toward Wayne. Wayne sat up and looking at some point past Roland's knees, took it. Roland walked slowly through the crowd of boys. Paul wanted to touch him as he passed. Instead he murmured: 'You looked like Bob Steele.'

The smile Roland turned on him was friendly; Roland's brown eyes looked into his, as though asking his name.

'Who's Bob Steele?' Roland said.

Then he walked on.


Sometimes on winter afternoons when yesterday's mud was hard footprinted earth, Paul lingered after school and watched the boxers in the gym. He sat with his books in the bleachers and watched Roland in a grey suit skipping rope and then handing the rope to an older boy and crossing the gym where, waiting at the large bag, he talked with a high school boy who fought at a hundred and forty-five pounds. Then Paul watched him working on the bag. The older boy watched too and sometimes spoke to Roland. When the boxers finished in the gym the coach took them for a six-mile run in the cold twilight. Mounting his bicycle Paul watched them leaving. They ran in a formation of two files and Roland, ninety-five pounds and shorter than everyone, ran in front. As Paul pumped past them on the opposite side of the road he could see Roland turning his head, talking to the boy beside him; he was laughing. Paul turned on his light and rode home.

'I don't want to go,' Eddie said. 'I've never been to one.'

'Neither have I,' Paul said.

It was recess, and they stood with hands in their jacket pockets. Paul was looking up at Eddie's face. He liked Eddie's face but sometimes he did not like to be seen with it and now he was thinking of that face at a boxing match. The face showed Eddie's life: good grades, the state of grace, uncertainty about his body in a world of running, pushing, yelling boys, and an imagination that lifted him to other places, other deeds. Looking at Eddie he saw everything he had learned about him in their three years together and he knew that their faces were too much alike and he wished they or at least he had a sneer, a glare, a tightened jaw to show to the world.

'We ought to see Roland anyway,' he said. 'He's fighting first. If we don't like the rest we can leave.'

'Your hero.'

'He's not my *hero*,' thinking of Bob Steele, the quickest fist fighter of all the Saturday cowboys, fading, almost gone, for in the nights now it was Roland he thought of, Roland's quick fists on Larry's face, and lying in bed it was him merging with the image of Roland, him hitting Larry, only the arms were Roland's or his arms were like Roland's, hard and bulging and fast, and then sometimes his face became Roland's or Roland's his so he didn't know in his daydream whether he was watching Roland or Roland was watching him or whether he had become a stronger Paul or had become instead someone else.

'You talk about him a lot.'

'I don't think so.'

'Sometimes he's all you talk about.'

'Well, I like him. Come on; let's go to the fights.'

That night the gym was filled. Clusters of Paul's classmates were scattered through the crowd of men and women and students; Paul and Eddie sat in front of some girls they did not know. They were from the public high school and smelled of perfume and chewing gum. The lights went off except for the light over the ring and then Roland was climbing into it, stepping through the ropes held apart by the coach; Paul's gaze fixed on that. Paul was not close enough to see Roland's eyes but he knew from his profiled jaw and lips and his arms stretched to the ropes as he worked his feet in the rosin box that he was not afraid. Then the bell rang and Paul knew it was true: Roland glided into the ring and in purple trunks and gold sleeveless jersey he danced and jabbed and hooked and crossed, and within a minute the other boy was bewildered, lunging, swinging wildly, and backing up. The sounds of Roland's large stinging gloves filled the gym, grabbed yells from the throats of men and soft cries from the girls behind Paul. In the third round the other boy's nose suddenly bled; the red spurt covered his mouth and flowed onto his shirt while Roland closed in with a flurry and the referee pranced between them and stopped the fight. Roland put his arm around the boy's back, rested a glove on his shoulder, and walked him to the corner, toward his coach who was bringing a white towel.

Every Friday night he won and when the fights were at home Paul and Eddie watched. Eddie liked it too and walking home from the Saturday serial and cowboy movies he talked about Roland last night with the speed of a striking snake. Since his fight with Wayne, Roland had moved among those boys who from the third grade had been the athletes and class officers and good students as well and who were growing into half-backs and quarterbacks and fullbacks and ends. Larry Guidry did not go into that world. He did not seem to even look at it. Nor did they look at him. At the end of the season Roland went to Baton Rouge and won the state championship. When he came back to school, Paul waited for his chance, got it between classes, and shook his hand.

On most days when the final bell rang and they had recited the last decade of the rosary Paul got quickly out of the door and was down the corridor and outside before Larry could hurt him. Sometimes as he fled Larry kicked his rump or punched his back. But usually he escaped and rode home on his bicycle while Larry waited in front of school for the bus. One April afternoon he and Eddie walked across the front lawn of the school, Paul glancing at the boys waiting for school buses; he did not see Larry; they walked past the group and into town, to Borden's. When they got back to school licking their ice-cream cones the buses had come and the boys were gone and Larry was on the sidewalk, crouched beside his bicycle, twisting a broken spoke around one that was intact. Paul quickened his pace but Larry saw their legs and looked up. Then he stood. Paul kept looking at the bicycle. It was green and had been thickly repainted, by hand, and Paul thought of Larry with his intent face and a paint brush, painting. The rear fender was dented.

'Broken spoke?' Paul said.

Larry watched him.

'What's it doing, hitting the chain guard?'

Larry reached out and took the ice-cream cone from Paul's hand. It was chocolate, and Paul smiled and watched him taking a large bite. Larry's tongue darted over the ice cream, licked it till it was a smooth mound; he took another large bite and sucked it. Then he licked again. He was getting close to the cone. When the ice cream was level with the cone he bit into its rim, turning it and biting, and then with one large bite he ate the small end. He had not looked at Paul. He was turning to his bicycle when Eddie said: 'Well, I hope you enjoyed your ice-cream cone.'

Larry had both hands on the handlebars and one foot poised at the kickstand; he spun quickly and with his right hand slapped the cone from Eddie's fist and then with the same hand a fist now he hit Eddie in the stomach and Eddie doubled over holding his stomach and gasping, but from his hurt and panicked face there was no sound. Paul knew where

Larry had hit him; he had read about the body and its vulnerable spots and how he could use them, and he knew that Eddie now was not only in pain but he could not breathe. He watched Larry watching Eddie, watched the burning eyes. Eddie was shuffling in a semicircle. Still he did not make a sound. Then bent over he walked past Larry and onto the front lawn, toward the school, toward the back of it where his bicycle was. For a moment Paul watched him. Then smiling at Larry he went after Eddie and, from behind him, placed a hand on his shoulder.

'Eddie? Are you all right?'

Eddie shook his head. Looking down from Eddie's rear Paul saw the left cheek turning red. Then with a hoarse wheeze Eddie breathed. He breathed deeply and let it out fast and still bent forward he breathed again. He kept walking and Paul's hand dropped behind him. He stopped and breathed again and stood straight; Paul moved beside him and looked at his face and the tears on his cheeks.

'Are you okay?'

'I'm going home,' Eddie said; his shoulders jerking, he crossed the lawn toward the school. Paul watched him go. His back was to Larry. Then he shifted so he was profiled to Larry. When Eddie had gone around the corner of the school Paul looked at Larry, who leaned on his bicycle, watching.

'You sure got him,' Paul said. 'Right in the solar plexus.'

Larry moved his hands to the handlebars and kicked up the kickstand.

'You could probably beat Roland. Do you think you could beat Roland?'

There was neither fear nor challenge in Larry's eyes, only the dark watching, so quiet and removed that looking into Larry's eyes Paul seemed to be watching himself. They stood perhaps forty feet apart but Paul felt Larry's closeness, as though they were seated in school, with Larry at his back through the years, and he seemed to smell the starched khakis, the hair oil, the sweat, and the mustard and milk after lunch. Then Larry rode away.

That summer on a July afternoon Larry Guidry drowned in Black Bayou. The police found his bicycle and snowball cart on the bank, and beside them were his clothes and sneakers. That was the day after his parents told the police he had not come home. In the evening paper there were front-page photographs of policemen on the bank of the bayou, and men in outboards, dragging the muddy bottom. There was also a school picture of Larry; Paul remembered the day last fall when they had combed their hair and lined up to sit on the stool. He remembered he had hay fever that day and while the photographer took his picture he held his breath so he wouldn't sneeze. They found Larry at the bottom of the bayou. It was a hot afternoon and he had gone swimming alone.

'He was in your *class?*' Amy said at supper.

'He should never have gone in the bayou,' his mother said. 'It's treacherous.'

'Did you know him well?' Barbara said.

'I sat right in front of him for three years.'

That night he calmly prepared for sleep: kissed his father and mother and sisters and kneeled in prayer while inside the vast cavern of his body he shivered and tingled in anticipation of what waited for him in bed. He did not think Larry had committed any real mortal sins, with all the conditions they required, so he would not be in hell but in the fire of purgatory where souls thrashed in pain but their faces gazed with the serenity of hope; caressing his heart with a prayer he asked God to take Larry out of purgatory soon, and he saw him in khakis in the flames, his small hard hands clasped beneath his upturned housedust face. Then in bed Paul saw in the dark between him and the pale ceiling Larry getting off his bicycle and looking at the muddy bayou. For a while Larry stood looking at it; in the middle a stick swirled and went downstream. Then he undressed and walked down the bank and into the water. The bottom was soft and slippery and he threw himself forward in the shallow water and began to swim. Near the middle of the bayou the current hit him. He turned and stroked toward shallow water but the current pushed and twisted him, a thousand hands on his body, and in moaning panic he swallowed water and his arms weakened, his legs dragged heavily behind him, then he was under, somersaulting down and down, an acrobat slowly sinking in thick muddy water that rushed into his throat as he sank until he lay at the bottom, in the deep soft mud. He lay on his back, his arms angling out from his body, his mouth open and eyes closed, as in sleep. He lay in the dark cold all afternoon and all night and when the sun rose he was down there and he lay all morning until a grappling hook came slowly toward him in a cloud of mud like brown smoke.

# GRADUATION

SOMETIMES OUT IN CALIFORNIA, she wanted to tell her husband. That was after they had been married for more than two years (by then she was twenty-one) and she had settled into the familiarity so close to friendship but not exactly that either: she knew his sounds while he slept, brought some recognition to the very weight of his body next to her in bed, knew without looking the expressions on his face when he spoke. As their habits merged into common ritual, she began to feel she had never had another friend. Geography had something to do with this too. Waiting for him at the pier after the destroyer had been to sea for five days, or emerging from a San Diego movie theater, holding his hand, it seemed to her that the first eighteen years of her life in Port Arthur, Texas had no meaning at all. So, at times like that, she wanted to tell him.

She would look at the photograph which she had kept hidden for four years now, and think, as though she were speaking to him: *I was seventeen years old, a senior in high school, and I got up that day just like any other day and ate Puffed Wheat or something with my parents and went to school and there it was, on the bulletin board—*But she didn't tell him, for she knew that something was wrong: the photograph and her years in Port Arthur were true, and now her marriage in San Diego was true. But it seemed that for both of them to remain true they had to exist separately, one as history, one as now, and that if she disclosed the history, then those two truths added together would somehow produce a lie which in turn would call for more analysis than she cared to give. Or than she cared for her husband to give. So she would simply look at the picture of herself at sixteen, then put it away, in an old compact at the bottom of her jewelry box.

The picture had been cut out of the high school yearbook. Her blonde hair had been short then, an Italian boy; her face was tilted down and to one side, she was smiling at the camera, and beneath her face, across her sweater, was written: *Good piece.*

It had been thumbtacked to the bulletin board approximately two years after she had lost her virginity, parked someplace with a boy she loved. When they broke up she was still fifteen, a long way from marriage, and she wanted her virginity back. But this was impossible, for he had told all his friends. So she gave herself to the next boy whose pledge was a class ring or football sweater, and the one after that (before graduation night there were three of them, all with loose tongues) and everyone knew about Bobbie Huxford and she knew they did.

She never found out who put the picture on the bulletin board. When she got to school that day, a group of students were standing in the hall; they parted to let her through. Then she met the eyes of a girl, and saw neither mischief nor curiosity but fascination. A boy glanced at the bulletin board and quickly to the floor, and Bobbie saw the picture. She walked through them, pulled out the thumbtacks, forcing herself to go slowly, taking out each one and pressing it back into the board. She dropped the picture into her purse and went down the hall to her locker.

So at graduation she was not leaving the camaraderie, the perfunctory education, the ball games and dances and drives on a Sunday afternoon; she was leaving a place where she had always felt watched, except when Sherri King had been seduced by an uncle and somehow that word had got out. But the Kings had moved within a month, and Bobbie's classmates went back to watching her again. Still there was nostalgia: sitting on the stage, looking at the audience in the dark, she was remembering songs. Each of her loves had had a song, one she had danced to, pressed sweating and tight-gripped and swaying in dance halls where they served beer to anyone and the juke box never stopped: Nat 'King' Cole singing 'Somewhere Along the Way,' 'Trying' by the Hilltoppers, 'Your Cheatin' Heart' by Joni James, all of them plaintive songs: you drank two or three beers and clenched and dipped and weaved on the dance floor, and you squeezed him, your breasts against his firm narrow chest feeling like your brassiere and wrinkled blouse and his damp shirt weren't even there; you kept one hand on the back of his neck, sweat dripped between your fused cheeks, and you sang in nearly a whisper with Joni or Nat and you gave him a hard squeeze and said in his ear: *I love you, I'll love you forever.*

She had not loved any of them forever. With each one something had gone sour, but she was able to look past that, farther back to the good times. So there was that: sitting on the stage she remembered the songs, the love on waxed dance floors. But nostalgia wasn't the best part. She was happy, as she had been dancing to those songs that articulated her feelings and sent them flowing back into her blood, her heart. This time she didn't want to hold anyone, not even love anyone. She wanted to fly: soar away from everything, go higher than rain. She wanted to leave home, where bright and flowered drapes hung and sunlight moved through the day from one end of the maroon sofa to the other and formed motes in the air but found dustless the coffee table and the Bible that set on it.

She was their last child, an older brother with eight years in the Army and going for twenty, and an older sister married to a pharmacist in Beaumont, never having gone farther than Galveston in her whole life and bearing kids now like that was the only thing to do.

In the quiet summer afternoons when her mother was taking a nap and her father was at work, she felt both them and the immaculate house stifling her. One night returning from a date she had walked quietly into the kitchen. From there she could hear them snoring. Standing in the dark kitchen she smoked a cigarette, flicking the ashes in her hand (there was only one ashtray in the house and it was used by guests). Then looking at their bedroom door she suddenly wanted to holler: *I drank too much beer tonight and got sick in the john and Bud gave me 7-Up and creme de menthe to settle my stomach and clean my breath so I could still screw and that's what we did:* WE SCREWED. *That's what we always do.*

Now, looking out into the dark, Bobbie wondered if her parents were watching her. Then she knew they were, and they were proud. She was their last child, she was grown now, they had done their duty (college remained but they did not consider it essential) and now in the clean brightly-colored house they could wait with calm satisfaction for their souls to be wafted to heaven. Then she was sad. Because from the anxiety and pain of her birth until their own deaths, they had loved her and would love her without ever knowing who she was.

After the ceremony there was an all-night party at Rhonda Miller's camp. Bobbie's date was a tall shy boy named Calvin Tatman, who was popular with the boys but rarely dated; three days before graduation he had called Bobbie and asked her to be his date for Rhonda's party. The Millers' camp was on a lake front, surrounded by woods; behind the small house there was a large outdoor kitchen, screened on all sides. In the kitchen was a keg of beer, paper cups, and Rhonda's record player; that was how the party began. Several parents were there, drinking bourbon from the grown-ups' bar at one side of the kitchen; they got tight, beamed at the young people jitterbugging, and teased them about their sudden liking for cigarettes and beer. After a while Mr. Miller went outside to the barbecue pit and put on some hamburgers.

At first Bobbie felt kindly toward Calvin and thought since it was a big night, she would let him neck with her. But after Calvin had a few tall cups of beer she changed her mind.

He stopped jitterbugging with her, dancing only the slow dances, holding her very close; then, a dance ended, he would join the boys at the keg. He didn't exactly leave her on the dance floor; she could follow him to the keg if she wanted to, and she did that a couple of times, then stopped. Once she watched him talking to the boys and she knew exactly what was going on: he had brought her because he couldn't get another date (she had already known that, absorbed it, spent a long time preparing her face and hair anyway), but now he was saving face by telling people he had brought her because he wanted to get laid.

Then other things happened. She was busy dancing, so she didn't notice for a while that she hadn't really had a conversation with anyone. She realized this when she left Calvin at the beer keg and joined the line outside at the barbecue pit, where Mr. Miller was serving hamburgers. She was last in line. She told Mr. Miller it was a wonderful party, then she went to the table beside the barbecue pit and made her hamburger. When she turned to go back to the kitchen, no one was waiting: two couples were just going in the door, and Bobbie was alone with Mr. Miller. She hesitated, telling herself that it meant nothing, that no one waited for people at barbecue pits. Still, if she went in alone, who would she sit with? She sat on the grass by the barbecue pit and talked to Mr. Miller. He ate a hamburger with her and gave her bourbon and water from the one-man bar he had set up to get him through the cooking. He was a stout, pleasant man, and he told her she was the best-looking girl at the party.

As soon as she entered the kitchen she knew people had been waiting for her. The music and talk were loud, but she also felt the silence of waiting; looking around, she caught a few girls watching her. Then, at her side, Rhonda said: 'Where you been, Bobbie?'

She glanced down at Rhonda, who sat with her boy friend, a class ring dangling from a chain around her neck, one possessive hand on Charlie Wright's knee. She doubted that Rhonda was a virgin but she had heard very little gossip because she had no girl friends. Now she went to the keg, pushed through the boys, and filled a cup.

Some time later, when the second keg had been tapped and both she and Calvin were drunk, he took her outside. She knew by now that everyone at the party was waiting to see if Calvin would make out. She went with him as far as the woods, kissed him standing up, worked her tongue in his mouth until he trembled and gasped; when he touched her breast she spun away and went back to the kitchen, jerking out of his grasp each time he clutched her arm. He was cursing her but she wasn't afraid. If he got rough, they were close enough to the kitchen so she could shout for Mr. Miller. Then Calvin was quiet anyway, realizing that if anyone heard they would know what had happened. When they stepped into the kitchen people were grinning at them. Bobbie went to the beer keg and Calvin danced with the first girl he saw.

When Charlie Wright got drunk he came over and danced with her. They swayed to 'Blue Velvet,' moved toward the door, and stumbled outside. They lay on the ground just inside the woods; because of the beer he took a long time and Bobbie thought of Rhonda waiting, faking a smile, dancing, waiting... Charlie told her she did it better than Rhonda. When they returned to the kitchen, Rhonda's face was pale; she did not dance with Charlie for the rest of the night.

At breakfast, near dawn, she sat on the bar and ate bacon and eggs with Mr. Miller, hoping Rhonda would worry about that too. Calvin tried to leave without her, but she had taken his car key, so he had to drive her home. It was just after sunrise, he was drunk, and he almost missed two curves.

'Hell, Calvin,' she said, 'just 'cause you can't make out doesn't mean you got to kill us.'

He swung at her, the back of his open hand striking her cheekbone, and all the way home she cried. Next day there was not even a bruise.

The lawnmower woke her that afternoon. She listened to it, knowing she had been hearing it for some time, had been fighting it in her sleep. Then she got up, took two aspirins which nearly gagged her, and made coffee and drank it in the kitchen, wanting a cigarette but still unable to tell her parents that she smoked. So she went outside and helped her father rake the grass. The day was hot; bent over the rake she sweated and fought with her stomach and shut her eyes to the pain pulsing in her head and she wished she had at least douched with a Coke, something she had heard about but had never done. Then she wished she had a Coke right now, with ice, and some more aspirin and a cool place in the house to sit very still. She did not want to marry Charlie Wright. Then she had to smile at herself, looking down at the grass piling under her rake. Charlie would not marry her. By this time everyone in school knew she had done it with him last night, and they probably thought she had done it with Calvin too. If she were pregnant, it would be a joke.

That night she told her parents she wanted to finish college as soon as possible so she could earn her own money. They agreed to send her to summer school at L.S.U., and two weeks later they drove her to Baton Rouge. During those two weeks she had seen no one; Charlie had called twice for dates, but she had politely turned him down, with excuses; she had menstruated, felt the missed life flowing as a new life for herself. Then she went away. Sitting in the back of the car, driving out of Port Arthur, she felt incomplete: she had not told anyone she was going to summer school, had not told anyone goodbye.

She went home after the summer term, then again at Thanksgiving, each time feeling more disengaged from her house and the town. When she went home for Christmas vacation, her father met her at the bus station. It was early evening. She saw him as the bus turned in: wiry, a little slumped, wearing the hat that wasn't a Stetson but looked like one. He spoke of the Christmas lights being ready and she tried to sound pleased. She even tried to feel pleased. She thought of him going to all that trouble every Christmas and maybe part of it was for her; maybe it had all started for her delight, long ago when she was a child. But when they reached the house she was again appalled by the lights strung on its front and the lighted manger her father had built years before and every Christmas placed on the lawn: a Nativity absurdly without animals or shepherds or wise men or even parents for the Child Jesus (a doll: Bobbie's) who lay utterly alone, wrapped in blankets on the straw floor of the manger. Holding her father's arm she went into the kitchen and hugged her mother, whose plumpness seemed emblematic of a woman who was kind and good and clean. Bobbie marvelled at the decorated house, then sat down to supper and talk of food and family news. After supper she told them, with even more nervousness than she had anticipated, that she had started smoking and she hoped they didn't mind. They both frowned, then her mother sighed and said:

'Well, I guess you're a big girl now.'

She was. For at L.S.U. she had learned this: you could become a virgin again. She finally understood that it was a man's word. They didn't mean you had done it once; they meant you did it, the lost hymen testimony not of the past but the present, and you carried with you a flavor of accessibility. She thought how much she would have been spared if she had known it at fifteen when she had felt changed forever, having focused on the word *loss* as though an arm or leg had been amputated, so she had given herself again, trying to be happy with her new self, rather than backing up and starting over, which would have been so easy because Willie Sorrells— her first lover—was not what you would call irresistible. Especially in retrospect.

But at L.S.U. she was a virgin; she had dated often in summer and fall, and no one had touched her. Not even Frank Mixon, whom she planned to marry, though he hadn't asked her yet. He was an economics major at Tulane, and a football player. He was also a senior. In June he was going into the Navy as an ensign and this was one of her reasons for wanting to marry him. And she had him fooled.

One night, though, she had scared herself. It was after

the Tulane–L.S.U. game, the traditional game which Tulane traditionally lost. It was played in Baton Rouge. After the game Bobbie and Frank double-dated with the quarterback, Roy Lockhart, and his fiancée, Annie Broussard. Some time during the evening of bar-hopping, when they were all high, Roy identified a girl on the dance floor by calling her Jack Shelton's roommate of last year.

'What?' Bobbie said. 'What did you say?'

'Never mind,' Roy said.

'No: listen. Wait a minute.'

Then she started. All those things she had thought about and learned in silence came out, controlled, lucid, as though she had been saying them for years. At one point she realized Frank was watching her, quiet and rather awed, but a little suspiciously too. She kept talking, though.

'You fumbled against Vanderbilt,' she said to Roy. 'Should we call you fumbler for the rest of your life?'

Annie, the drunkest of the four, kept saying: That's *right*, that's *right*. Finally Bobbie said:

'Anyway, that's what *I* think.'

Frank put his arm around her.

'That takes care of gossip for tonight,' he said. 'Anybody want to talk about the game?'

'We tied 'em till the half,' Roy said. 'Then we should have gone home.'

'It wasn't your fault, fumbler,' Annie said, and she was still laughing when the others had stopped and ordered more drinks.

When Frank took Bobbie to the dormitory, they sat in the car, kissing. Then he said:

'You were sort of worked up tonight.'

'It happened to a friend of mine in high school. They ruined her. It's hard to believe, that you can ruin somebody with just talking, but they did it.'

He nodded, and moved to kiss her, but she pulled away.

'But that's not the only reason,' she said.

She shifted on the car seat and looked at his face, a good

ruddy face, hair neither long nor short and combed dry, the college cut that would do for business as well; he was a tall strong young man, and because of his size and strength she felt that his gentleness was a protective quality reserved for her alone; but this wasn't true either, for she had never known him to be unkind to anyone and, even tonight, as he drank too much in post-game defeat, he only got quieter and sweeter.

'I don't have one either,' she said.

At first he did not understand. Then his face drew back and he looked out the windshield.

'It's not what you think. It's awful, and I'll never forget it but I've never told anyone, no one knows, they all think—'

Then she was crying into his coat, not at all surprised that her tears were real, and he was holding her.

'I was twelve years old,' she said.

She sat up, dried her cheeks, and looked away from him.

'It was an uncle, one of those uncles you never see. He was leaving someplace and going someplace else and he stopped off to see us for a couple of days. On the second night he came to my room and when I woke up he was doing it—'

'Hush,' he said. 'Hush, baby.'

She did not look at him.

'I was so scared, so awfully *scared*. So I didn't tell. Next morning I stayed in bed till he was gone. And I felt so rotten. Sometimes I still do, but not the way I did then. He's never come back to see us, but once in a while they mention him and I feel sick all over again, and I think about telling them but it's too late now, even if they did something to him it's too late, I can never get it back—'

For a long time that night Frank Mixon held his soiled girl in his arms, and, to Bobbie, those arms seemed quite strong, quite capable. She knew that she would marry him.

Less than a month later she was home for Christmas, untouched, changed. She spent New Year's at Frank's house in New Orleans. In the cold dusk after the Sugar Bowl game they walked back to his house to get the car and go to a party.

Holding his arm, she watched a trolley go by, looked through car windows at attractive people leaving the stadium, breathed the smell of exhaust which was somehow pleasing, and the damp winter air, and another smell as of something old, as though from the old lives of the houses they passed. She knew that if she lived in New Orleans only a few months, Port Arthur would slide away into the Gulf. Climbing a gentle slope to his house, she was very tired, out of breath. The house was dark. Frank turned on a light and asked if she wanted a drink.

'God, no,' she said. 'I'd like to lie down for a few minutes.'

'Why don't you? I'll make some coffee.'

She climbed the stairs, turned on the hall light, and went to the guest room. She took off her shoes, lay clothed on the bed, and was asleep. His voice woke her: he stood at the bed, blocking the light from the hall. She propped on an elbow to drink the coffee, and asked him how long she had been asleep.

'About an hour.'

'What did you do?'

'Watched some of the Rose Bowl.'

'That was sweet. I'll hurry and get freshened up so we won't be too late.'

But when she set the empty cup on the bedside table he kissed her; then he was lying on top of her.

'Your folks—'

'They're at a party.'

She was yielding very slowly, holding him off tenderly then murmuring when his hand slipped into her blouse, stayed there, then withdrew to work on the buttons. She delayed, gave in, then stalled so that it took a long while for him to take off the blouse and brassiere. Finally they were naked, under the covers, and her hands on his body were shy. Then she spoke his name. With his first penetration she stiffened and he said It's all right, sweet darling Bobbie, it's all right now— and she eased forward, wanting to enfold him with her legs but she kept them outstretched, knees bent, and gave only tentative motion to her hips. When he was finished she held him there, his lips at her ear; she moved slowly as he whispered; then whimpering, shuddering, and concealing, she came.

'Will you?' he said. 'Will you marry me this June?'

'Oh *yes*,' she said, and squeezed his ribs. 'Yes I will. This is my first time and that other never happened, not ever, it's all over now—Oh I'm so *happy*, Frank, I'm so *happy*—'

# THE FAT GIRL

HER NAME WAS LOUISE. Once when she was sixteen a boy kissed her at a barbecue; he was drunk and he jammed his tongue into her mouth and ran his hands up and down her hips. Her father kissed her often. He was thin and kind and she could see in his eyes when he looked at her the lights of love and pity.

It started when Louise was nine. You must start watching what you eat, her mother would say. I can see you have my metabolism. Louise also had her mother's pale blonde hair. Her mother was slim and pretty, carried herself erectly, and ate very little. The two of them would eat bare lunches, while her older brother ate sandwiches and potato chips, and then her mother would sit smoking while Louise eyed the bread box, the pantry, the refrigerator. Wasn't that good, her mother would say. In five years you'll be in high school and if you're fat the boys won't like you; they won't ask you out. Boys were as far away as five years, and she would go to her room and wait for nearly an hour until she knew her mother was no longer thinking of her, then she would creep into the kitchen and, listening to her mother talking on the phone, or her footsteps upstairs, she would open the bread box, the pantry, the jar of peanut butter. She would put the sandwich under her shirt and go outside or to the bathroom to eat it.

Her father was a lawyer and made a lot of money and

came home looking pale and happy. Martinis put color back in his face, and at dinner he talked to his wife and two children. Oh give her a potato, he would say to Louise's mother. She's a growing girl. Her mother's voice then became tense: If she has a potato she shouldn't have dessert. She should have both, her father would say, and he would reach over and touch Louise's cheek or hand or arm.

In high school she had two girl friends and at night and on weekends they rode in a car or went to movies. In movies she was fascinated by fat actresses. She wondered why they were fat. She knew why she was fat: she was fat because she was Louise. Because God had made her that way. Because she wasn't like her friends Joan and Marjorie, who drank milk shakes after school and were all bones and tight skin. But what about those actresses, with their talents, with their broad and profound faces? Did they eat as heedlessly as Bishop Humphries and his wife who sometimes came to dinner and, as Louise's mother said, gorged between amenities? Or did they try to lose weight, did they go about hungry and angry and thinking of food? She thought of them eating lean meats and salads with friends, and then going home and building strange large sandwiches with French bread. But mostly she believed they did not go through these failures; they were fat because they chose to be. And she was certain of something else too: she could see it in their faces: they did not eat secretly. Which she did: her creeping to the kitchen when she was nine became, in high school, a ritual of deceit and pleasure. She was a furtive eater of sweets. Even her two friends did not know her secret.

Joan was thin, gangling, and flat-chested; she was attractive enough and all she needed was someone to take a second look at her face, but the school was large and there were pretty girls in every classroom and walking all the corridors, so no one ever needed to take a second look at Joan. Marjorie was thin too, an intense, heavy-smoking girl with brittle laughter. She was very intelligent, and with boys she was shy because she knew she made them uncomfortable, and because she was smarter than they were and so could not understand or could not believe the levels they lived on. She was to have a nervous breakdown before earning her PhD. in philosophy at the University of Califorlnia, where she met and married a physicist and discovered within herself an untrammelled passion: she made love with her husband on the couch, the carpet, in the bathtub, and on the washing machine. By that time much had happened to her and she never thought of Louise. Joan would finally stop growing and begin moving with grace and confidence. In college she would have two lovers and then several more during the six years she spent in Boston before marrying a middle-aged editor who had two sons in their early teens, who drank too much, who was tenderly, boyishly grateful for her love, and whose wife had been killed while rock-climbing in New Hampshire with her lover. She would not think of Louise either, except in an earlier time, when lovers were still new to her and she was ecstatically surprised each time one of them loved her and, sometimes at night, lying in a man's arms, she would tell how in high school no one dated her, she had been thin and plain (she would still believe that: that she had been plain; it had never been true) and so had been forced into the week-end and night-time company of a neurotic smart girl and a shy fat girl. She would say this with self-pity exaggerated by Scotch and her need to be more deeply loved by the man who held her.

She never eats, Joan and Marjorie said of Louise. They ate lunch with her at school, watched her refusing potatoes, ravioli, fried fish. Sometimes she got through the cafeteria line with only a salad. That is how they would remember her: a girl whose hapless body was destined to be fat. No one saw the sandwiches she made and took to her room when she came home from school. No one saw the store of Milky Ways, Butterfingers, Almond Joys, and Hersheys far back on her closet shelf, behind the stuffed animals of her childhood. She was not a hypocrite. When she was out of the house she truly believed she was dieting; she forgot about the candy, as a man speaking into his office dictaphone may forget the lewd photographs hidden in an old shoe in his closet. At other times, away from home, she thought of the waiting candy with near lust. One night driving home from a movie, Marjorie said: 'You're lucky you don't smoke; it's incredible what I go through to hide it from my parents.' Louise turned to her a smile which was elusive and mysterious; she yearned to be home in bed, eating chocolate in the dark. She did not need to smoke; she already had a vice that was insular and destructive.

She brought it with her to college. She thought she would leave it behind. A move from one place to another, a new room without the haunted closet shelf, would do for her what she could not do for herself. She packed her large dresses and went. For two weeks she was busy with registration, with shyness, with classes; then she began to feel at home. Her room was no longer like a motel. Its walls had stopped watching her, she felt they were her friends, and she gave them her secret. Away from her mother, she did not have to be as elaborate; she kept the candy in her drawer now.

The school was in Massachusetts, a girls' school. When she chose it, when she and her father and mother talked about it in the evenings, everyone so carefully avoided the word boys that sometimes the conversations seemed to be about nothing but boys. There are no boys there, the neuter words said; you will not have to contend with that. In her father's eyes were pity and encouragement; in her mother's was disappointment, and her voice was crisp. They spoke of courses, of small classes where Louise would get more attention. She imagined herself in those small classes; she saw herself as a teacher would see her, as the other girls would; she would get no attention.

The girls at the school were from wealthy families, but most of them wore the uniform of another class: blue jeans and work shirts, and many wore overalls. Louise bought some overalls, washed them until the dark blue faded, and wore them to classes. In the cafeteria she ate as she had in high school, not to lose weight nor even to sustain her lie, but because eating lightly in public had become as habitual as good manners. Everyone had to take gym, and in the locker room with the other girls, and wearing shorts on the volleyball and badminton courts, she hated her body. She liked her body most when she was unaware of it: in bed at night, as sleep gently took her out of her day, out of herself. And she liked parts of her body. She liked her brown eyes and sometimes looked at them in the mirror: they were not shallow eyes, she thought; they were indeed windows of a tender soul, a good heart. She liked her lips and nose, and her chin, finely shaped between her wide and sagging cheeks. Most of all she liked her long pale blonde hair, she liked washing and drying it and lying naked on her bed, smelling of shampoo, and feeling the soft hair at her neck and shoulders and back.

Her friend at college was Carrie, who was thin and wore thick glasses and often at night she cried in Louise's room. She did not know why she was crying. She was crying, she said, because she was unhappy. She could say no more. Louise said she was unhappy too, and Carrie moved in with her. One night Carrie talked for hours, sadly and bitterly, about her parents and what they did to each other. When she finished she hugged Louise and they went to bed. Then in the dark Carrie spoke across the room: 'Louise? I just wanted to tell you. One night last week I woke up and smelled chocolate. You were eating chocolate, in your bed. I wish you'd eat it in front of me, Louise, whenever you feel like it.'

Stiffened in her bed, Louise could think of nothing to say. In the silence she was afraid Carrie would think she was asleep and would tell her again in the morning or tomorrow night. Finally she said Okay. Then after a moment she told Carrie if she ever wanted any she could feel free to help herself; the candy was in the top drawer. Then she said thank you.

They were roommates for four years and in the summers they exchanged letters. Each fall they greeted with embraces, laughter, tears, and moved into their old room, which had been stripped and cleansed of them for the summer. Neither girl enjoyed summer. Carrie did not like being at home because her parents did not love each other. Louise lived in a small city in Louisiana. She did not like summer because she had lost touch with Joan and Marjorie; they saw each other, but it was not the same. She liked being with her father but with no one else. The flicker of disappointment in her mother's eyes at the airport was a vanguard of the army of relatives and acquaintances who awaited her: they would see her on the streets, in stores, at the country club, in her home, and in theirs; in the first moments of greeting, their eyes would tell her she was still fat Louise, who had been fat as long as they could remember, who had gone to college and returned as fat as ever. Then their eyes dismissed her, and she longed for school and Carrie, and she wrote letters to her friend. But that saddened her too. It wasn't simply that Carrie was her only friend, and when they finished college they might never see each other again. It was that her existence in the world was so divided; it had begun when she was a child creeping to the kitchen; now that division was much sharper, and her friendship with Carrie seemed disproportionate and perilous. The world she was destined to live in had nothing to do with the intimate nights in their room at school.

In the summer before their senior year, Carrie fell in love. She wrote to Louise about him, but she did not write much, and this hurt Louise more than if Carrie had shown the joy her writing tried to conceal. That fall they returned to their room; they were still close and warm, Carrie still needed Louise's ears and heart at night as she spoke of her parents and her recurring malaise whose source the two friends never discovered. But on most week-ends Carrie left, and caught a bus to Boston where her boy friend studied music. During the week she often spoke hesitantly of sex; she was not sure if she liked it. But Louise, eating candy and listening, did not know whether Carrie was telling the truth or whether, as in her letters of the past summer, Carrie was keeping from her those delights she may never experience.

Then one Sunday night when Carrie had just returned from Boston and was unpacking her overnight bag, she looked at Louise and said: 'I was thinking about you. On the bus coming home tonight.' Looking at Carrie's concerned, determined face, Louise prepared herself for humiliation. 'I was thinking about when we graduate. What you're going to do. What's to become of you. I want you to be loved the way I love you. Louise, if I help you, *really* help you, will you go on a diet?'

Louise entered a period of her life she would remember always, the way some people remember having endured poverty. Her diet did not begin the next day. Carrie told her to eat on Monday as though it were the last day of her life. So for the first time since grammar school Louise went into a school cafeteria and ate everything she wanted. At breakfast and lunch and dinner she glanced around the table to see if the other girls noticed the food on her tray. They did not. She felt there was a lesson in this, but it lay beyond her grasp. That night in their room she ate the four remaining candy bars. During the day Carrie rented a small refrigerator, bought an electric skillet, an electric broiler, and bathroom scales.

On Tuesday morning Louise stood on the scales, and Carrie wrote in her notebook: *October 14: 184 lbs*. Then she made Louise a cup of black coffee and scrambled one egg and sat with her while she ate. When Carrie went to the dining room for breakfast, Louise walked about the campus for thirty minutes. That was part of the plan. The campus was pretty, on its lawns grew at least one of every tree native to New England, and in the warm morning sun Louise felt a new hope. At noon they met in their room, and Carrie broiled her a piece of hamburger and served it with lettuce. Then while Carrie ate in the dining room Louise walked again. She was weak with hunger and she felt queasy. During her afternoon classes she was nervous and tense, and she chewed her pencil and tapped her heels on the floor and tightened her calves. When she returned to her room late that afternoon, she was so glad to see Carrie that she embraced her; she had felt she could not bear another minute of hunger, but now with Carrie she knew she could make it at least through tonight. Then she would sleep and face tomorrow when it came. Carrie broiled her a steak and served it with lettuce. Louise studied while Carrie ate dinner, then they went for a walk.

That was her ritual and her diet for the rest of the year, Carrie alternating fish and chicken breasts with the steaks for dinner, and every day was nearly as bad as the first. In the evenings she was irritable. In all her life she had never been afflicted by ill temper and she looked upon it now as a demon which, along with hunger, was taking possession of her soul. Often she spoke sharply to Carrie. One night during their after-dinner walk Carrie talked sadly of night, of how darkness made her more aware of herself, and at night she did not know why she was in college, why she studied, why she was walking the earth with other people. They were standing on a wooden foot bridge, looking down at a dark pond. Carrie kept talking; perhaps soon she would cry. Suddenly Louise said: 'I'm sick of lettuce. I never want to see a piece of lettuce for the rest of my life. I hate it. We shouldn't even buy it, it's immoral.'

Carrie was quiet. Louise glanced at her, and the pain and irritation in Carrie's face soothed her. Then she was ashamed. Before she could say she was sorry, Carrie turned to her and said gently: 'I know. I know how terrible it is.'

Carrie did all the shopping, telling Louise she knew how hard it was to go into a supermarket when you were hungry. And Louise was always hungry. She drank diet soft drinks and started smoking Carrie's cigarettes, learned to enjoy inhaling, thought of cancer and emphysema but they were as far away as those boys her mother had talked about when she was nine. By Thanksgiving she was smoking over a pack a day and her weight in Carrie's notebook was one hundred and sixty-two pounds. Carrie was afraid if Louise went home at Thanksgiving she would lapse from the diet, so Louise spent the vacation with Carrie, in Philadelphia. Carrie wrote her family about the diet, and told Louise that she had. On the plane to Philadelphia, Louise said: 'I feel like a bed wetter. When I was a little girl I had a friend who used to come spend the night and Mother would put a rubber sheet on the bed and we all pretended there wasn't a rubber sheet and that she hadn't wet the bed. Even me, and I slept with her.' At Thanksgiving dinner she lowered her eyes as Carrie's father put two slices of white meat on her plate and passed it to her over the bowls of steaming food.

When she went home at Christmas she weighed a hundred and fifty-five pounds; at the airport her mother marvelled. Her father laughed and hugged her and said: 'But now there's less of you to love.' He was troubled by her smoking but only mentioned it once; he told her she was beautiful and, as always, his eyes bathed her with love. During the long vacation her mother cooked for her as Carrie had, and Louise returned to school weighing a hundred and forty-six pounds.

Flying north on the plane she warmly recalled the surprised and congratulatory eyes of her relatives and acquaintances. She had not seen Joan or Marjorie. She thought of returning home in May, weighing the hundred and fifteen pounds which Carrie had in October set as their goal. Looking toward the stoic days ahead, she felt strong. She thought of those hungry days of fall and early winter (and now: she was hungry now: with almost a frown, almost a brusque shake of the head, she refused peanuts from the stewardess): those first weeks of the diet when she was the pawn of an irascibility which still, conditioned to her ritual as she was, could at any moment take command of her. She thought of the nights of trying to sleep while her stomach growled. She thought of her addiction to cigarettes. She thought of the people at school: not one teacher, not one girl, had spoken to her about her loss of weight, not even about her absence from meals. And without warning her spirit collapsed. She did not feel strong, she did not feel she was committed to and within reach of achieving a valuable goal. She felt that somehow she had lost more than pounds of fat; that some time during her dieting she had lost herself too. She tried to remember what it had felt like to be Louise before she had started living on meat and fish, as an unhappy adult may look sadly in the memory of childhood for lost virtues and hopes. She looked down at the earth far below, and it seemed to her that her soul, like her body aboard the plane, was in some rootless flight. She neither knew its destination nor where it had departed from; it was on some passage she could not even define.

During the next few weeks she lost weight more slowly and once for eight days Carrie's daily recording stayed at a hundred and thirty-six. Louise woke in the morning thinking of one hundred and thirty-six and then she stood on the scales and they echoed her. She became obsessed with that number, and there wasn't a day when she didn't say it aloud, and through the days and nights the number stayed in her mind, and if a teacher had spoken those digits in a classroom she would have opened her mouth to speak. What if that's me, she said to Carrie. I mean what if a hundred and thirty-six is my real weight and I just can't lose anymore. Walking hand-in-hand with her despair was a longing for this to be true, and that longing angered her and wearied her, and every day she was gloomy. On the ninth day she weighed a hundred and thirty-five and a half pounds. She was not relieved; she thought bitterly of the months ahead, the shedding of the last twenty and a half pounds.

On Easter Sunday, which she spent at Carrie's, she weighed one hundred and twenty pounds, and she ate one slice of glazed pineapple with her ham and lettuce. She did not enjoy it: she felt she was being friendly with a recalcitrant enemy who had once tried to destroy her. Carrie's parents were laudative. She liked them and she wished they would touch sometimes, and look at each other when they spoke. She guessed they would divorce when Carrie left home, and she vowed that her own marriage would be one of affection and tenderness. She could think about that now: marriage. At school she had read in a Boston paper that this summer the cicadas would come out of their seventeen year hibernation on Cape Cod, for a month they would mate and then die, leaving their young to burrow into the ground where they would stay for seventeen years. That's me, she had said to Carrie. Only my hibernation lasted twenty-one years.

Often her mother asked in letters and on the phone about the diet, but Louise answered vaguely. When she flew home in late May she weighed a hundred and thirteen pounds, and at the airport her mother cried and hugged her and said again and again: You're so *beautiful*. Her father blushed and bought her a martini. For days her relatives and acquaintances congratulated her, and the applause in their eyes lasted the entire summer, and she loved their eyes, and swam in the country club pool, the first time she had done this since she was a child.


She lived at home and ate the way her mother did and every morning she weighed herself on the scales in her bathroom. Her mother liked to take her shopping and buy her dresses and they put her old ones in the Goodwill box at the shopping center; Louise thought of them existing on the body of a poor woman whose cheap meals kept her fat. Louise's mother had a photographer come to the house, and Louise posed on the couch and standing beneath a live oak and sitting in a wicker lawn chair next to an azalea bush. The new clothes and the photographer made her feel she was going to another country or becoming a citizen of a new one. In the fall she took a job of no consequence, to give herself something to do.

Also in the fall a young lawyer joined her father's firm, he came one night to dinner, and they started seeing each other. He was the first man outside her family to kiss her since the barbecue when she was sixteen. Louise celebrated Thanksgiving not with rice dressing and candied sweet potatoes and mince meat and pumpkin pies, but by giving Richard her virginity which she realized, at the very last moment of its existence, she had embarked on giving him over thirteen months ago, on that Tuesday in October when Carrie had made her a cup of black coffee and scrambled one egg. She wrote this to Carrie, who replied happily by return mail. She also, through glance and smile and innuendo, tried to tell her mother too. But finally she controlled that impulse, because Richard felt guilty about making love with the daughter of his partner and friend. In the spring they married. The wedding was a large one, in the Episcopal church, and Carrie flew from Boston to be maid of honor. Her parents had recently separated and she was living with the musician and was still victim of her unpredictable malaise. It overcame her on the night before the wedding, so Louise was up with her until past three and woke next morning from a sleep so heavy that she did not want to leave it.

Richard was a lean, tall, energetic man with the metabolism of a pencil sharpener. Louise fed him everything he wanted. He liked Italian food and she got recipes from her mother and watched him eating spaghetti with the sauce she had only tasted, and ravioli and lasagna, while she ate antipasto with her chianti. He made a lot of money and borrowed more and they bought a house whose lawn sloped down to the shore of a lake; they had a wharf and a boathouse, and Richard bought a boat and they took friends waterskiing. Richard bought her a car and they spent his vacations in Mexico, Canada, the Bahamas, and in the fifth year of their marriage they went to Europe and, according to their plan, she conceived a child in Paris. On the plane back, as she looked out the window and beyond the sparkling sea and saw her country, she felt that it was waiting for her, as her home by the lake was, and her parents, and her good friends who rode in the boat and waterskied; she thought of the accumulated warmth and pelf of her marriage, and how by slimming her body she had bought into the pleasures of the nation. She felt cunning, and she smiled to herself, and took Richard's hand.

But these moments of triumph were sparse. On most days she went about her routine of leisure with a sense of certainty about herself that came merely from not thinking. But there were times, with her friends, or with Richard, or alone in the house, when she was suddenly assaulted by the feeling that she had taken the wrong train and arrived at a place where no one knew her, and where she ought not to be. Often, in bed with Richard, she talked of being fat: 'I was the one who started the friendship with Carrie, I chose her, I started the conversations. When I understood that she was my friend I understood something else: I had chosen her for the same reason I'd chosen Joan and Marjorie. They were all thin. I was always thinking about what people saw when they looked at me and I didn't want them to see two fat girls. When I was alone I didn't mind being fat but then I'd have to leave the house again and then I didn't want to look like me. But at home I didn't mind except when I was getting dressed to go out of the house and when Mother looked at me. But I stopped looking at her when she looked at me. And in college I felt good with Carrie; there weren't any boys and I didn't have any other friends and so when I wasn't with Carrie I thought about her and I tried to ignore the other people around me, I tried to make them not exist. A lot of the time I could do that. It was strange, and I felt like a spy.'

If Richard was bored by her repetition he pretended not to be. But she knew the story meant very little to him. She could have been telling him of a childhood illness, or wearing braces, or a broken heart at sixteen. He could not see her as she was when she was fat. She felt as though she were trying to tell a foreign lover about her life in the United States, and if only she could command the language he would know and love all of her and she would feel complete. Some of the acquaintances of her childhood were her friends now, and even they did not seem to remember her when she was fat.

Now her body was growing again, and when she put on a maternity dress for the first time she shivered with fear. Richard did not smoke and he asked her, in a voice just short of demand, to stop during her pregnancy. She did. She ate carrots and celery instead of smoking, and at cocktail parties she tried to eat nothing, but after her first drink she ate nuts and cheese and crackers and dips. Always at these parties Richard had talked with his friends and she had rarely spoken to him until they drove home. But now when he noticed her at the hors d'œuvres table he crossed the room and, smiling, led her back to his group. His smile and his hand on her arm told her he was doing his clumsy, husbandly best to help her through a time of female mystery.

She was gaining weight but she told herself it was only the baby, and would leave with its birth. But at other times she knew quite clearly that she was losing the discipline she had fought so hard to gain during her last year with Carrie. She was hungry now as she had been in college, and she ate between meals and after dinner and tried to eat only carrots and celery, but she grew to hate them, and her desire for sweets was as vicious as it had been long ago. At home she ate bread and jam and when she shopped for groceries she bought a candy bar and ate it driving home and put the wrapper in her purse and then in the garbage can under the sink. Her cheeks had filled out, there was loose flesh under her chin, her arms and legs were plump, and her mother was concerned. So was Richard. One night when she brought pie and milk to the living room where they were watching television, he said: 'You already had a piece. At dinner.'

She did not look at him.

'You're gaining weight. It's not all water, either. It's fat. It'll be summertime. You'll want to get into your bathing suit.'

The pie was cherry. She looked at it as her fork cut through it; she speared the piece and rubbed it in the red juice on the plate before lifting it to her mouth.

'You never used to eat pie,' he said. 'I just think you ought to watch it a bit. It's going to be tough on you this summer.'

In her seventh month, with a delight reminiscent of climbing the stairs to Richard's apartment before they were married, she returned to her world of secret gratification. She began hiding candy in her underwear drawer. She ate it during the day and at night while Richard slept, and at breakfast she was distracted, waiting for him to leave.

She gave birth to a son, brought him home, and nursed both him and her appetites. During this time of celibacy she enjoyed her body through her son's mouth; while he suckled she stroked his small head and back. She was hiding candy but she did not conceal her other indulgences: she was smoking again but still she ate between meals, and at dinner she ate what Richard did, and coldly he watched her, he grew petulant, and when the date marking the end of their celibacy came they let it pass. Often in the afternoons her mother visited and scolded her and Louise sat looking at the baby and said nothing until finally, to end it, she promised to diet. When her mother and father came for dinners, her father kissed her and held the baby and her mother said nothing about Louise's body, and her voice was tense. Returning from work in the evenings Richard looked at a soiled plate and glass on the table beside her chair as if detecting traces of infidelity, and at every dinner they fought.

'Look at you,' he said. 'Lasagna, for God's sake. When are you going to start? It's not simply that you haven't lost any weight. You're gaining. I can see it. I can feel it when you get in bed. Pretty soon you'll weigh more than I do and I'll be sleeping on a trampoline.'

'You never touch me anymore.'

'I don't want to touch you. Why should I? Have you *looked* at yourself?'

'You're cruel,' she said. 'I never knew how cruel you were.'

She ate, watching him. He did not look at her. Glaring at his plate, he worked with fork and knife like a hurried man at a lunch counter.

'I bet you didn't either,' she said.

That night when he was asleep she took a Milky Way to the bathroom. For a while she stood eating in the dark, then she turned on the light. Chewing, she looked at herself in the mirror; she looked at her eyes and hair. Then she stood on the scales and looking at the numbers between her feet, one hundred and sixty-two, she remembered when she had weighed a hundred and thirty-six pounds for eight days. Her memory of those eight days was fond and amusing, as though she were recalling an Easter egg hunt when she was six. She stepped off the scales and pushed them under the lavatory and did not stand on them again.

It was summer and she bought loose dresses and when Richard took friends out on the boat she did not wear a bathing suit or shorts; her friends gave her mischievous glances, and Richard did not look at her. She stopped riding on the boat. She told them she wanted to stay with the baby, and she sat inside holding him until she heard the boat leave the wharf. Then she took him to the front lawn and walked with him in the shade of the trees and talked to him about the blue jays and mockingbirds and cardinals she saw on their branches. Sometimes she stopped and watched the boat out on the lake and the friend skiing behind it.

Every day Richard quarrelled, and because his rage went no further than her weight and shape, she felt excluded from it, and she remained calm within layers of flesh and spirit, and watched his frustration, his impotence. He truly believed they were arguing about her weight. She knew better: she knew that beneath the argument lay the question of who Richard was. She thought of him smiling at the wheel of his boat, and long ago courting his slender girl, the daughter of his partner and friend. She thought of Carrie telling her of smelling chocolate in the dark and, after that, watching her eat it night after night. She smiled at Richard, teasing his anger.


He is angry now. He stands in the center of the living room, raging at her, and he wakes the baby. Beneath Richard's voice she hears the soft crying, feels it in her heart, and quietly she rises from her chair and goes upstairs to the child's room and takes him from the crib. She brings him to the living room and sits holding him in her lap, pressing him gently against the folds of fat at her waist. Now Richard is pleading with her. Louise thinks tenderly of Carrie broiling meat and fish in their room, and walking with her in the evenings. She wonders if Carrie still has the malaise. Perhaps she will come for a visit. In Louise's arms now the boy sleeps.

'I'll help you,' Richard says. 'I'll eat the same things you eat.'

But his face does not approach the compassion and determination and love she had seen in Carrie's during what she now recognizes as the worst year of her life. She can remember nothing about that year except hunger, and the meals in her room. She is hungry now. When she puts the boy to bed she will get a candy bar from her room. She will eat it here, in front of Richard. This room will be hers soon. She considers the possibilities: all these rooms and the lawn where she can do whatever she wishes. She knows he will leave soon. It has been in his eyes all summer. She stands, using one hand to pull herself out of the chair. She carries the boy to his crib, feels him against her large breasts, feels that his sleeping body touches her soul. With a surge of vindication and relief she holds him. Then she kisses his forehead and places him in the crib. She goes to the bedroom and in the dark takes a bar of candy from her drawer. Slowly she descends the stairs. She knows Richard is waiting but she feels his departure so happily that, when she enters the living room, unwrapping the candy, she is surprised to see him standing there.

# PART TWO

# CADENCE

*to Tommie*

He stood in the summer Virginia twilight, an officer candidate, nineteen years old, wearing Marine utilities and helmet, an MI rifle in one hand, its butt resting on the earth, a pack high on his back, the straps buckled too tightly around his shoulders; because he was short he was the last man in the rank. He stood in the front rank and watched Gunnery Sergeant Hathaway and Lieutenant Swenson in front of the platoon, talking quietly to each other, the lieutenant tall and confident, the sergeant short, squat, with a beer gut; at night, he had told them, he went home and drank beer with his old lady. He could walk the entire platoon into the ground. Or so he made them believe. He had small, brown, murderous eyes; he scowled when he was quiet or thinking; and, at rest, his narrow lips tended downward at the corners. Now he turned from the lieutenant and faced the platoon. They stood on the crest of a low hill; beyond Hathaway the earth sloped down to a darkened meadow and then rose again, a wooded hill whose black trees touched the grey sky.

'We're going back over the Hill Trail,' he said, and someone groaned and at first Paul fixed on that sound as a source of strength: someone else dreaded the hills as much as he did.

Around him he could sense a fearful gathering of resolve, and now the groan he had first clung to became something else: a harbinger of his own failure. He knew that, except for Hugh Munson standing beside him, he was the least durable of all; and since these men, a good half of them varsity athletes, were afraid, his own fear became nearly unbearable. It became physical: it took a penetrating fall into his legs and weakened his knees so he felt he was not supported by muscle and bone but by faint nerves alone.

'We'll put the little men up front,' Hathaway said, 'so you long-legged pacesetters'll know what it's like to bring up the rear.'

They moved in two files, down a sloping trail flanked by black trees. Hugh was directly behind him. To his left, leading the other file, was Whalen; he was also short, five-eight or five-seven; but he was wide as a door. He was a wrestler from Purdue. They moved down past trees and thick underbrush into the dark of the woods, and behind him he heard the sounds of blindness: a thumping body and clattering rifle as someone tripped and fell; there were curses, and voices warned those coming behind them, told of a branch reaching across the trail; from the rear Hathaway called: 'Close it up close it up, don't lose sight of the man in front of you.' Paul walked step for step beside Whalen and watched tall Lieutenant Swenson setting the pace, watched his pack and helmet as he started to climb and, looking up and past the lieutenant, up the wide corridor between the trees, he saw against the sky the crest of the first hill.

Then he was climbing, his legs and lungs already screaming at him that they could not, and he saw himself at home in his room last winter and spring, getting ready for this: push-ups and sit-ups, leg lifts and squat jumps and deep kneebends, exercises which made his body feel good but did little for it, and as he climbed and the muscles of his thighs bulged and tightened and his lungs demanded more and more of the humid air, he despised that memory of himself, despised himself for being so far removed from the world of men that he had believed in calisthenics, had not even considered running, though he had six months to get in condition after signing the contract with the Marine captain who had come one day like salvation into the student union, wearing the blue uniform and the manly beauty that would fulfill Paul's dreams. Now those dreams were an illusion: he was close to the top of the first hill, his calf and thigh muscles burning, his lungs gasping, and his face, near sobbing, was fixed in pain. His one desire that he felt with each breath, each step up the hard face of the hill, was not endurance: it was deliverance. He wanted to go home, and to have this done for him in some magical or lucky way that would give him honor in his father's eyes. So as he moved over the top of the hill, Whalen panting beside him, and followed Lieutenant Swenson steeply down, he wished and then prayed that he would break his leg.

He descended: away from the moonlight, down into the shadows and toward the black at the foot of the hill. His strides were short now and quick, his body leaned backward so he wouldn't fall, and once again his instincts and his wishes were at odds: wanting a broken leg, he did not want to fall and break it; wanting to go home, he did not want to quit and pack his seabag and suitcase, and go. For there was that too: they would let him quit. That was the provision which had seemed harmless enough, even congenial, as he lifted his pen in the student union. He could stop and sit or lean against a tree and wait for the platoon to pass and Sergeant Hathaway's bulk to appear like an apparition of fortitude and conscience out of the dark, strong and harsh and hoarse, and he could then say: 'Sir, I want to go home.' It would be over then, he would drift onto the train tomorrow and then to the airport and fly home in a nimbus of shame to face his father's blue and humiliated eyes, which he had last seen beaming at him before the embrace that, four and a half weeks ago, sent him crossing the asphalt to the plane.

It was a Sunday. Sergeants met the planes in Washington and put the men on buses that were green and waxed, and drove them through the last of the warm setting sun to Quantico. The conversations aboard the bus were apprehensive and friendly. They all wore civilian clothes except Paul. At home he had joined the reserve and his captain had told him to wear his uniform and he had: starched cotton khaki, and it was wrinkled from his flight. The sergeants did not look at the uniform or at him either; or, if they did, they had a way of looking that was not looking at him. By the time he reached the barracks he felt that he existed solely in his own interior voice. Then he started up the stairs, carrying seabag and suitcase, guided up by the press of his companions, and as he went down a corridor toward the squad bay he passed an open office and Sergeant Hathaway entered his life: not a voice but a roar, and he turned and stood at attention, seabag and suitcase heavy in each hand, seeing now with vision narrowed and dimmed by fear the raging face, the pointing finger; and he tried for the voice to say Me, sir? but already Hathaway was coming toward him and with both fists struck his chest one short hard blow, the fists then opening to grip his shirt and jerk him forward into the office; he heard the shirt tear; somewhere outside the door he dropped his luggage; perhaps they hit the door-jamb as he was going through, and he stood at attention in the office; other men were there, his eyes were aware of them but he was not, for in the cascade of curses from that red and raging face he could feel and know only his fear: his body was trembling, he knew as though he could see it that his face was drained white, and now he had to form answers because the curses were changing to questions, Hathaway's voice still at a roar, his dark loathing eyes close to Paul's and at the same height; Paul told him his name.

'Where did it happen?'

'Sir?'

'Where did she do it. Where the fuck were you *born*.'

'Lake Charles, Louisiana, sir.'

'Well no shit Lake Charles Louisiana sir, you college idiot, you think I know where that is? Where is it?'

'South of New Orleans sir.'

'South of New Orleans. How *far* south.'

'About two hundred miles sir.'

'Well no shit. Are you a fucking fish? Answer me, candidate shitbird. Are you a fucking fish?'

'No sir.'

'No sir. Why aren't you a fish?'

'I don't know sir.'

'You don't know. Well you better be a Goddamn fish because two hundred miles south of New Orleans is in the Gulf of fucking *Mexico*.'

'West sir.'

'You said south. Are you calling me a liar, fartbreath? I'll break your jaw. You know that? Do you *know* that?'

'Sir?'

'Do you know I can break your Goddamn jaw?'

'Yes sir.'

'Do you want me to?'

'No sir.'

'Why not? You can't use it. You can't Goddamn talk. If I had a piece of gear that wasn't worth a shit and I didn't know how to use it anyway I wouldn't give a good rat's ass if somebody broke it. Stop shaking. Who told you to wear that uniform? I said stop shaking.'

'My captain sir.'

'My *cap*tain. Who the fuck is your captain.'

'My reserve captain sir.'

'Is he a ragpicker?'

'Sir?'

'Is he a *rag*picker. How does he *eat*.'

'He has a hardware store, sir.'

'He's a ragpicker. Say it.'

'He's a ragpicker, sir.'

'I told you to stop shaking. Say my reserve captain is a ragpicker.'

'My reserve captain is a ragpicker, sir.'

Then the two fists came up again and struck his chest and gripped the shirt, shaking him back and forth, and stiff and quivering and with legs like weeds he had no balance, and when Hathaway shoved and released him he fell backward and crashed against a steel wall locker; then Hathaway had him pressed against it, holding the shirt again, banging him against the locker, yelling: 'You can't wear that uniform you shit you don't even know how to wear that uniform you wore it on the Goddamn plane playing Marine Goddamnit—Well you're not a Marine and you'll never be a Marine, you won't make it here one week, you will not be here for chow next Sunday, because you are a shit and I will break your ass in five days, I will break it so hard that for the rest of your miserable fucking life every time you see a man you'll crawl under a table and piss in your skivvies. Give me those emblems. Give them to me! Take them off, take them off, take them off—' Paul's hands rising first to the left collar, the hands trembling so that he could not hold the emblem and collar still, his right hand trying to remove the emblem while Hathaway's fists squeezed the shirt tight across his chest and slowly rocked him back and forth, the hands trembling; he was watching them and they couldn't do it, the fingers would not stop, they would not hold; then with a jerk and a shove Hathaway flung him against the locker, screaming at him; and he felt tears in his eyes, seemed to be watching the tears in his eyes, pleading with them to at least stay there and not stain his cheeks; somewhere behind Hathaway the other men were still watching but they were a blur of khaki and flesh: he was enveloped and penetrated by Hathaway's screaming and he could see nothing in the world except his fingers working at the emblems.

Then it was over. The emblems were off, they were in Hathaway's hand, and he was out in the corridor, propelled to the door and thrown to the opposite wall with such speed that he did not even feel the movement: he only knew Hathaway's two hands, one at the back of his collar, one at the seat of his pants. He picked up his suitcase and seabag, and feeling bodiless as a cloud, he moved down the hall and into the lighted squad bay where the others were making bunks and hanging clothes in wall lockers and folding them into foot lockers, and he stood violated and stunned in the light. Then someone was helping him. Someone short and muscular and calm (it was Whalen), a quiet mid-western voice whose hand took the seabag and suitcase, whose head nodded for him to follow the quick athletic strides that led him to his bunk. Later that night he lay in the bunk and prayed dear please God please dear God may I have sugar in my blood. The next day the doctors would look at them and he must fail, he must go home; in his life he had been humiliated, but never never had anyone made his own flesh so uninhabitable. He must go home.

But his body failed him. It was healthy enough for them to keep it and torment it, but not strong enough, and each day he woke tired and rushed to the head where men crowded two or three deep at the mirrors to shave and others, already shaved, waited outside toilet stalls; then back to the squad bay to make his bunk, the blanket taut and without wrinkle, then running down the stairs and into the cool first light of day and, in formation with the others, he marched to chow where he ate huge meals because on the second day of training Hatha-way had said: 'Little man, I want you to eat everything but the table cloth'; so on those mornings, not yet hungry, his stomach in fact near-queasy at the early morning smell of hot grease that reached him a block from the chow hall, he ate cereal and eggs and pancakes and toast and potatoes and milk, and the day began. Calisthenics and running in formation around the drill field, long runs whose distances and pace were at the whim of Lieutenant Swenson, or the obstacle course, or assaulting hills or climbing the Hill Trail, and each day there came a point when his body gave out, became a witch's curse of one hundred and forty-five pounds of pain that he had to bear, and he would look over at Hugh Munson trying to do a push-up, his back arching, his belly drawn to the earth as though gravity had chosen him for an extra, jesting pull; at Hugh hanging from the chinning bar, his face contorted, his legs jerking, a man on a gibbet; at Hugh climbing the Hill Trail, his face pale and open-mouthed and dripping, the eyes showing pain and nothing more, his body swaying like a

fighter senseless on his feet; at Hugh's arms taking him halfway up the rope and no more so he hung suspended like an
exclamation point at the end of Hathaway's bellowing scorn.

In the squad bay they helped each other. Every Saturday
morning there was a battalion inspection and on Friday
nights, sometimes until three or four in the morning, Paul and
Hugh worked together, rolling and unrolling and rolling again
their shelter halves until, folded in a U, they fit perfectly on
the haversacks which they had packed so neatly and squarely
they resembled canvas boxes. They took apart their rifles and
cleaned each part; in the head they scrubbed their cartridge
belts with stiff brushes, then put them in the dryer in the
laundry room downstairs; and they worked on shoes and
boots, spit-shining the shoes and one pair of boots, and saddle-
soaping a second pair of boots which they wore to the field;
they washed their utility caps and sprayed them with starch
and fitted them over tin cans so they would shape as they
dried. And, while they worked, they drilled each other on the
sort of questions they expected the battalion commander to
ask. What *is* enfilade fire, candidate Hugh? Why that, colonel,
is when the axis of fire coincides with the axis of the enemy.
And can you name the chain of command as well? I can, my
colonel, and, sorry to say, it begins with Ike. At night during
the week and on Saturday afternoons they studied for exams.
Hugh learned quickly to read maps and use the compass, and
he helped Paul with these, spreading the map on his foot locker,
talking, pointing, as Paul chewed his lip and frowned at the
brown contour lines which were supposed to become, in his
mind, hills and draws and ridges and cliffs. On Sunday afternoons they walked to the town of Quantico and, dressed in
civilian clothes, drank beer incognito in bars filled with sergeants. Once they took the train to Washington and saw the
Lincoln Memorial and pretended not to weep; then, proud of
their legs and wind, they climbed the Washington Monument.
One Saturday night they got happily and absolutely drunk in
Quantico and walked home singing love songs.

Hugh slept in the bunk above Paul's. His father was dead,

he lived with his mother and a younger sister, and at night in the squad bay he liked talking about his girl in Bronxville; on summer afternoons he and Molly took the train into New York.

'What do you do?' Paul said. He stood next to their bunk; Hugh sat on his, looking down at Paul; he wore a T-shirt, his bare arms were thin, and high on his cheekbones were sparse freckles.

'She takes me to museums a lot.'

'What kind of museums?'

'Art.'

'I've never been to one.'

'That's because you're from the south. I can see her now, standing in front of a painting. Oh Hugh, she'll say, and she'll grab my arm. Jesus.'

'Are you going to marry her?'

'In two years. She's a snapper like you, but hell I don't care. Sometimes I go to mass with her. She says I'll have to sign an agreement; I mean it's not *her* making me, and she's not bitchy about it; there's nothing she can do about it, that's all. You know, agree to raise the kids Catholics. That Nazi crap your Pope cooked up.'

'You don't mind?'

'Naw, it's *Molly* I want. *Her*, man—'

Now in his mind Paul was miles and months away from the squad bay and the smells of men and canvas and leather polish and gun oil, he was back in those nights last fall and winter and spring, showing her the stories he wrote, buying for her Hemingway's books, one at a time, chronologically, in hardcover; the books were for their library, his and Tommie's, after they were married; he did not tell her that. Because for a long time he did not know if she loved him. Her eyes said it, the glow in her cheeks said it, her voice said it. But she never did; not with her controlled embraces and kisses, and not with words. It was the words he wanted. It became an obsession: they drank and danced in night clubs, they saw movies, they spent hours parked in front of her house, and he told her his dreams and believed he was the only young man who had ever had such dreams and had ever told them to such a tender girl; but all this seemed incomplete because she didn't give him the words. Then one night in early summer she told him she loved him. She was a practical and headstrong girl; the next week she went to see a priest. He was young, supercilious, and sometimes snide. She spent an hour with him, most of it in anger, and that night she told Paul she must not see him again. She must not love him. She would not sign contracts. She spoke bitterly of incense and hocus-pocus and graven images. Standing at Hugh's bunk, remembering that long year of nights with Tommie, yearning again for the sound of his own voice, gently received, and the swelling of his heart as he told Tommie what he had to and wanted to be, he felt divided and perplexed; he looked at Hugh's face and thought of Molly's hand reaching out for that arm, holding it, drawing Hugh close to her as she gazed at a painting. He blinked his eyes, scratched his crew-cut head, returned to the squad bay with an exorcising wrench and a weary sigh.

'—Sometimes she lets me touch her, just the breasts you see, and that's fine, I don't push it. When she lets me I'm God-damn grateful. Jesus, you got to get a girl again. There's nothing like it. You know that? *Nothing*. It's another world, man.'

On a hot grey afternoon he faced Hugh on the athletic field, both of them wearing gold football helmets, holding pugil sticks at the ready, as if they were rifles with fixed bayonets. Paul's fists gripped and encircled the smooth round wood; on either end of it was a large stuffed canvas cylinder; he looked into Hugh's eyes, felt the eyes of the circled platoon around him, and waited for Hathaway's signal to begin. When it came he slashed at Hugh's shoulder and neck but Hugh parried with the stick, then he jabbed twice at Hugh's face, backing him up, and swung the lower end of the stick around in a butt stroke that landed hard on Hugh's ribs; then with speed he didn't know he had he was jabbing Hugh's chest, Hathaway shouting now: 'That's it, little man: keep him going, keep him going; Munson get your balance, use your feet, Goddamnit—' driving Hugh back in a circle, smacking him hard on the helmeted ear; Hugh's face was flushed, his eyes betrayed, angry; Paul jabbing at those eyes, slashing at the head and neck, butt stroking hip and ribs, charging, keeping Hugh off balance so he could not hit back, could only hold his stick diagonally across his body, Paul feinting and working over and under and around the stick, his hands tingling with the blows he landed until Hathaway stopped him: 'All right, little man, that's enough; Carmichael and Vought, put on the headgear.'

Paul took off the helmet and handed it and the pugil stick to Carmichael. He picked up his cap from the grass; it lay next to Hugh's, and as he rose with it Hugh was beside him, stooping for his cap, murmuring: 'Jesus, you really like this shit, don't you.'

Paul watched Carmichael and Vought fighting, and pretended he hadn't heard. He felt Hugh standing beside him. Then he glanced at Hathaway, across the circle. Hathaway was watching him.

In the dark he was climbing the sixth and final hill, even the moon was gone, either hidden by trees or clouds or out of his vision because he was in such pain that he could see only that: his pain; the air was grey and heavy and humid, and he could not get enough of it; even as he inhaled his lungs demanded more and he exhaled with a rush and again drew in air, his mouth open, his throat and tongue dry, haunting his mind with images he could not escape: cold oranges, iced tea, lemonade, his canteen of water—He was falling back. He wasn't abreast of Whalen anymore, he was next to the man behind Whalen and then back to the third man, and he moaned and strove and achieved a semblance of a jog, a tottering climb away from the third man and past the second and up with Whalen again, then from behind people were yelling at him, or trying to, their voices diminished, choked off by their own demanding lungs: they were cursing him for lagging and then running to catch up, causing a gap which they had to close with their burning legs. Behind him Hugh was silent and Paul wondered if that silence was because of empathy or because Hugh was too tired to curse him aloud; he decided it was empathy and wished it were not.

And now Lieutenant Swenson reached the top, a tall helmeted silhouette halted and waiting against the oppressive and mindless sky, and Paul's heart leaped in victory and resilience, he crested the hill, went happily past Swenson's panting and sweating face, plunged downward, leaning back, hard thighs and calves bouncing on the earth, then Swenson jogged past him, into the lead again and, walking now, brought them slowly down the hill and out of the trees, onto the wide quiet gravel road and again stepped aside and watched them go past, telling them quietly to close it up, close it up, you people, and Paul's stride was long and light and drunk with fatigue; he tried to punch Whalen's arm but couldn't reach him and didn't have the strength to veer from his course and do it— Then Swenson's voice high and clear: 'tawn: ten*huhn?*' and he straightened his back and with shoulders so tired and aching that he barely felt the cutting packstraps, he marched to Swenson's tenor cadence, loving now the triumphant rhythm of boots in loose gravel, cooling in his drying sweat, able now to think of water as a promise the night would keep. Then Swenson called out: 'Are you ready, Gunny?' and, from the rear, Hathaway's answering growl: 'Aye, Lieutenant—' and Paul's heart chilled, he had heard the mischievous threat in Swenson's voice and now it came: 'Dou-ble time—' a pause: crunching boots: groans, and then '—*huhn.*'

Swenson ran past him on long legs, swerved to the front of the two files, and slowed to a pace that already Paul knew he couldn't keep. For perhaps a quarter of a mile he ran step for step with Whalen, and then he was finished. His stride shortened and slowed. Whalen was ahead of him and he tried once to catch up, but as he lifted his legs they refused him, they came down slower, shorter, and falling back now he moved to his left so the men behind him could go on. For a moment he ran beside Hugh. Hugh jerked his pale face to the left, looked at him, tried to say something; then he was gone. Paul was running alone between the two files, they were moving past him, some spoke encouragement as they went—hang in there, man—then he was among the tall ones at the rear and still he was dropping back, then a strong hand extended from a gasping shadowed face and took his rifle and went on.

He did not look behind him but he knew: he could feel at his back the empty road, and he was dropping back into it when the last two men, flanking him, each took an arm and held him up. 'You can do it,' they said. 'Keep going,' they said. He ran with them. Vaguely above the sounds of his breathing he could hear the pain of others: the desperate breathing and always the sound of boots, not rhythmic now, for each man ran in step with his own struggle, but anyway steady, and that is what finally did him in: the endlessness of that sound. Hands were still holding his arms; he was held up and pulled forward, his head lolled, he felt his legs giving way, his arms, his shoulders, he was sinking, they were pulling him forward but he was sinking, his eyes closed, he saw red-laced black and then it was over, he was falling forward to the gravel, and then he struck it but not with his face: with his knees and arms and hands. Then his face settled forward onto the gravel. He was not unconscious, and he lay in a shameful moment of knowledge that he would remember for the rest of his life: he had quit before his body failed; the legs which now lay in the gravel still had strength which he could feel; and already, within this short respite, his lungs were ready again. They hurt, they labored, but they were ready.

'He passed out, sir.'

They were standing above him. The platoon was running up the road.

'Who is it?' Hathaway said.

'It's Clement, sir.'

'Leave his rifle here and you men catch up with the platoon.'

'Aye-aye, sir.'

There were two of them. They went up the road, running hard to catch up, and he wanted to tell them he was sorry he had lied, but he knew he never would. Then he heard or felt Hathaway squat beside him, the small strong hands took his shoulders and turned him over on his back and unbuckled his chin strap. He blinked up at Hathaway's eyes: they were concerned, interested yet distant, as though he were disassembling a weapon whose parts were new to him; and they were knowing too, as if he were not appraising the condition of Paul's body alone but the lack of will that had allowed it to fall behind, to give up a rifle, to crap out.

'What happened, Clement?'

'I don't know, sir. I blacked out.'

Hathaway's hands reached under Paul's hip, lifted him enough to twist the canteen around, open the flaps, pull it from the cover. The crunching of the platoon receded and was gone up the road in the dark. Hathaway handed him the canteen.

'Take two swallows.'

Paul lifted his head and drank.

'Now stand up.'

He stood, replaced the canteen on his hip, and buckled his chin strap. His shirt was soaked; under it the T-shirt clung to his back and chest.

'Here's your weapon.'

He took the MI and slung it on his shoulder.

'Let's go,' Hathaway said, and started jogging up the road, Paul moving beside him, the fear starting again, touching his heart like a feather and draining his legs of their strength. But it didn't last. Within the first hundred yards it was gone, replaced by the quick-lunged leg-aching knowledge that there was no use being afraid because he knew, as he had known the instant his knees and hands and arms hit the gravel, that he was strong enough to make it; that Hathaway would not let him do anything but make it; and so his fear was impotent, it offered no chance of escape, and he ran now with Hathaway, mesmerized by his own despair. He tried to remember the road, how many bends there were, so he could look forward to that last curve which would disclose the lighted streets of what now felt like home. He could not remember how many curves there were. Then they rounded one and Hathaway said, 'Hold it,' and walked toward the edge of the road. Paul wiped sweat from his eyes, blinked them, and peered beyond Hathaway's back and shoulders at the black trees. He followed Hathaway and then he saw, at the side of the road, a man on his hands and knees. As he got closer he breathed the smell.

'Who is it?' Hathaway said.

'Munson.' His voice rose weakly from the smell. Paul moved closer and stood beside Hathaway, looking down at Hugh.

'Are you finished?' Hathaway said.

'I think so.'

'Then stand up.' His voice was low, near coaxing in its demand.

Hugh pushed himself up, stood, then retched again and leaned over the ditch and dry-heaved. When he was done he remained bent over the ditch, waiting. Then he picked up his rifle and stood straight, but he did not turn to face them. He took off his helmet and held it in front of him, down at his waist, took something from it, then one hand rose to his face. He was wiping it with a piece of toilet paper. He dropped the paper into the ditch, then turned and looked at Hathaway. Then he saw Paul, who was looking at Hugh's drained face and feeling it as if it were his own: the cool sweat, the raw sour throat.

'Man—' Hugh said, looking at Paul, his voice and eyes petulant; then he closed his eyes and shook his head.

'We'll run it in now,' Hathaway said.

Hugh opened his eyes.

'I threw up,' he said.

'And you're done.' Hathaway pointed up the road. 'And the barracks is that way.'

'I'll walk.'

'When you get back to New York you can do that, Munson. You can diddle your girl and puke on a six-pack and walk back to the frat house all you want. But here you run. Put on your helmet.'

Hugh slung his rifle on his shoulder and put his helmet on his head.

'Buckle it.'

He buckled it under his chin, then looked at Hathaway.

'I can't run. I threw up.' He gave Paul a weary glance, and looked up the road. 'It's not that I won't. I just can't, that's all.'

He stood looking at them. Then he reached back for his canteen, it rose pale in the moonlight, and he drank.

'All right, Munson: two swallows, then start walking; Clement, let's go.'

He looked at Hugh lowering the canteen, his head back gargling, then his eyes were on the road directly in front of him as he ran up a long stretch then rounded a curve and looked ahead and saw more of the road, the trees, and the black sky at the horizon; he was too tired to lift his head and see the moon and stars and this made him feel trapped on a road that would never end. Before the next curve he reached the point of fatigue he had surrendered to when he fell, and he moved through it into a new plane of struggle where he was certain that now his body would truly fail him, would fold and topple in spite of the volition Hathaway gave him. And then something else happened, something he had never experienced. Suddenly his legs told him they could go as far as he wanted them to. They did not care for his heat-aching head, for his thirst; they did not care for his pain. They told him this so strongly that he was frightened, as though his legs would force him to hang on as they spent the night jogging over Virginia hills; then he regained possession of them. They were his, they were running beside a man who had walked out of the Chosin Reservoir, and they were going to make it. When Paul turned the last bend and saw the street lights and brick buildings and the platoon, which had reached the black-top road by the athletic field and was marching now, he felt both triumphant and disappointed: he wanted to show Hathaway he could keep going.

They left the gravel and now his feet pounded on the gift of smooth blacktop. They approached the platoon, then ran alongside it, and as they came abreast of Lieutenant Swenson, Hathaway said: 'Lieutenant, you better send a jeep back for Munson. Me and Clement's going to hit the grinder; we had a long rest up the road.' The lieutenant nodded. Paul and Hathaway passed the platoon and turned onto the blacktop parade field and started to circle it. It was a half-mile run. For a while Paul could hear Swenson's fading cadence, then it stopped and he knew Swenson was dismissing the platoon. In the silence of the night he ran alongside Hathaway, listened to Hathaway's breath and pounding feet, glanced at him, and looked up at the full moon over the woods. They left the parade field and jogged up the road between brick barracks until they reached Bravo Company and Hathaway stopped. Paul faced him and stood at attention. His legs felt like they were still running. He was breathing hard; he looked through burning sweat at Hathaway, also breathing fast and deep, his face dripping and red. Hathaway's eyes were not glaring, not even studying Paul; they seemed fixed instead on his own weariness.

'You get in the barracks, you get some salt tablets and you take 'em. I don't care if you've been drinking Goddamn Gulf water all your life. Dismissed.'

The rest of the platoon were in the showers. As he climbed the stairs he heard the spraying water, the tired, exultant, and ironic voices. In the corridor at the top of the stairs he stopped and looked at the full-length mirror, looked at his short lean body standing straight, the helmet on his head, the pack with a protruding bayonet handle, the rifle slung on his shoulder. His shirt and patches on his thighs were dark green with sweat. Then he moved on to the water fountain and took four salt tablets from the dispenser and swallowed them one at a time, tilting his head back to swallow, remembering the salt tablets on the construction job when he was sixteen and his father got him the job and drove him to work on the first day and introduced him to the foreman and said: 'Work him, Jesse; make a man of him.' Jesse was a quiet wiry Cajun; he nodded, told Paul to stow his lunch in the toolshed and get a pick and a spade. All morning he worked bare-headed under the hot June sun; he worked with the Negroes, digging a trench for the foundation, and at noon he was weak and nauseated and could not eat. He went behind the shed and lay in the shade. The Negroes watched him and asked him wasn't he going to eat. He told them he didn't feel like it. At one o'clock he was back in the trench, and thirty minutes later he looked up and saw his father in seersucker and straw hat standing with Jesse at the trench's edge. 'Come on up, son,' his father said. 'I'm all right,' and he lifted the pick and dropped more than drove it into the clay at his feet. 'You just need a hat, that's all,' his father said. 'Come on up, I'll buy you one and bring you back to work.' He laid the pick beside the trench, turned to the Negro working behind him, and said, 'I'll be right back.' 'Sure,' the Negro said. 'You get that hat.' He climbed out of the trench and walked quietly beside his father to the car. 'Jesse called me,' his father said in the car. 'He said the nigras told him you didn't eat lunch. It's just the sun, that's all. We'll get you a hat. Did you take salt tablets?' Paul said yes, he had. His father bought him a pith helmet and, at the soda fountain, a Seven-Up and a sandwich. 'Jesse said you didn't tell anybody you felt bad.' 'No,' Paul said. 'I didn't.' His father stirred his coffee, looked away. Paul could feel his father's shy pride and he loved it, but he was ashamed too, for when he had looked up and seen his father on the job, he had had a moment of hope when he thought his father had come to tenderly take him home.

By the time he got out of his gear and hung his wet uniform by the window and wiped his rifle clean and lightly oiled it, the rest of the platoon were out of the showers, most were in their bunks, and the lights would go out in five minutes. Paul went to the shower and stayed long under the hot spray, feeling the sweat and dirt leave him, and sleep rising through his aching legs, to his arms and shoulders, to all save his quick heart. He was drying himself when Whalen came in, wearing shorts, and stood at the urinal and looked over his shoulder at Paul.

'You and Hathaway run all the way in?'

'Yeah.'

'Then the grinder?'

Paul nodded.

'Good,' Whalen said, and turned back to the urinal. Paul looked at his strong, muscled wrestler's back and shoulders. When Whalen passed him going out, Paul swung lightly and punched his arm.

'See you in the morning,' he said.

The squad bay was dark when Paul entered with a towel around his waist. Already most of them were asleep, their breath shallow and slow. There was enough light from the corridor so he could see the rifle rack in the middle of the room, and the double bunks on either side, and the wall lockers against the walls. He went to his bunk. Hugh was sitting on the edge of it, his elbows on his knees, his forehead resting on his palms. His helmet and rifle and pack and cartridge belt were on the floor in front of his feet. He looked up, and Paul moved closer to him in the dark.

'How's it going,' he said softly.

'I threw *up*, man. You see what I mean? That's stupid, Goddamnit. For *what*. What's the point of doing something that makes you puke. I was going to keep running till the Goddamn stuff came up all over me. Is that smart, man?' Hugh stood; someone farther down stirred on his bunk; Hugh took Paul's arm and squeezed it; he smelled of sweat, his breath was sour, and he leaned close, lowering his voice. 'Then you crapped out and I thought good. *Good*, Goddamnit. And man I peeled off and went to the side of the road and waited for it to come up. Then I was going to find you and walk in and drink Goddamn water and piss in the road and piss on all of them.' He released Paul's arm. 'But that Goddamn Doberman pinscher made you run in. Jesus Christ what am I *do*ing here. What am I *do*ing here,' and he turned and struck his mattress, stood looking at his fist on the bed, then raised it and struck again. Paul's hand went up to touch Hugh's shoulder, but stopped in the space between them and fell back to his side. He did not speak either. He looked at Hugh's profiled staring face, then turned away and bent over his foot locker at the head of the bunk and took out a T-shirt and a pair of shorts, neatly folded. He put them on and sat on his locker while Hugh dropped his clothes to the floor and walked out of the squad bay, to the showers.

He got into the lower bunk and lay on his back, waiting for his muscles to relax and sleep to come. But he was still awake when Hugh came back and stepped over the gear on the floor and climbed into his bunk. He wanted to ask Hugh if he'd like him to clean his rifle, but he could not. He lay with aching legs and shoulders and back and arms, and gazed up at Hugh's bunk and listened to his shifting weight. Soon Hugh settled and breathed softly, in sleep. Paul lay awake, among silhouettes of bunks and wall lockers and rifle racks. They and the walls and the pale windows all seemed to breathe, and to exude the smells of men. Farther down the squad bay someone snored. Hugh murmured in his sleep, then was quiet again.

When the lights went on he exploded frightened out of sleep, swung his legs to the floor, and his foot landed on the stock of Hugh's rifle. He stepped over it and trotted to the head, shaved at a lavatory with Whalen, waited outside a toilet stall but the line was too long and with tightening bowels he returned to the squad bay. Hugh was lying on his bunk. Going past it to the wall locker he said: 'Hey Hugh. Hugh, reveille.' He opened his locker and then looked back; Hugh was awake, blinking, looking at the ceiling.

'Hugh—' Hugh did not look at him. 'Your *gear*, Hugh; what about your *gear*.'

He didn't move. Paul put on utilities and spit-shined boots and ran past him. At the door he stopped and looked back. The others were coming, tucking in shirts, putting on caps. Hugh was sitting on the edge of his bunk, watching them move toward the door. Outside the morning was still cool and Hathaway waited, his boots shining in the sunlight. The platoon formed in front of him and his head snapped toward the space beside Paul.

'Clement, did Munson Goddamn puke and die on the road last night?'

'He's coming, sir.'

'He's coming. Well no shit he's coming. What do you people think this is—Goddamn civilian life where everybody crosses the streets on his own time? A platoon is not out of the barracks until every member of that platoon is out of the barracks, and you people are not out of the barracks yet. You are still *in* there with—o-ho—' He was looking beyond them, at the barracks to their rear. 'Well now here he is. You people are here now. Munson, you asshole, come up here.' Paul heard Munson to his left, coming around the platoon; he walked slowly. He entered Paul's vision and Paul watched him going up to Hathaway and standing at attention.

'Well no shit Munson.' His voice was low. 'Well no shit now. Mr. Munson has joined us for chow. He slept a little late this morning. I understand, Munson. It tires a man out, riding home in a jeep. It gets a man tired, when he knows he's the only one who can't hack it. It sometimes gets him so tired he *doesn't even fucking shave!* Who do you think you are that you don't shave! I'll tell you who you are: you are *noth*ing you are *noth*ing you are *noth*ing. The best part of you dripped down your old man's *leg!* Paul watched Hugh's flushed open-mouthed face; Hathaway's voice was lower now: 'Munson, do you know about the Goddamn elephants. Answer me Munson or I'll have you puking every piece of chow the Marine Corps feeds your ugly face. Elephants, Munson. Those big grey fuckers that live in the boondocks. They are like Marines, Munson. They stick with the herd. And if one of that herd fucks up in such a way as to piss off the rest of the herd, you know what they do to him? They exile that son of a bitch. They kick his ass out. You know what he does then? Son of a bitch gets lonesome. So everywhere the herd goes he is sure to follow. But they won't let him back in, Munson. So pretty soon he gets so lonesome he goes crazy and he starts running around the boondocks pulling up trees and stepping on troops and you have to go in and shoot him. Munson, you have fucked up my herd and I don't want your scrawny ass in it, so you are going to march thirty paces to the rear of this platoon. Now move out.'

'I'm going home.'

He left Hathaway and walked past the platoon.

'Munson!'

He stopped and turned around.

'I'm going home. I'm going to chow and then I'm going to see thechaplain and I'm going home.'

He turned and walked down the road, toward the chow hall.

'Mun*son!*'

He did not look back. His hands were in his pockets, his head down; then he lifted it. He seemed to be sniffing the morning air. Hathaway's mouth was open, as though to yell again; then he turned to the platoon. He called them to attention and marched them down the road. Paul could see Hugh ahead of them, until he turned a corner around a building and was gone. Then Hathaway, in the rhythm of cadence, called again and again: 'You won't *talk* to Mun-son talk talk *talk* to Mun-son you won't *look* at Mun-son look look *look* at Mun-son—'

And, in the chow hall, no one did. Paul sat with the platoon, listened to them talking in low voices about Hugh and, because he couldn't see him, Hugh seemed to be everywhere, filling the chow hall.


Later that morning, at close order drill, the platoon was not balanced. Hugh had left a hole in the file, and Paul moved up to fill it, leaving the file one man short in the rear. Marching in fresh starched utilities, his cartridge belt brushed clean, his oiled rifle on his shoulder, and his boot heels jarring on the blacktop, he dissolved into unity with the rest of the platoon. Under the sun they sweated and drilled. The other three platoons of Bravo Company were drilling too, sergeants' voices lilted in the humid air, and Paul strode and pivoted and ignored the tickling sweat on his nose. Hathaway's cadence enveloped him within the clomping boots. His body flowed with the sounds. 'March from the waist down, people. Dig in your heels. That's it, people. Lean back. Swing your arms. That's it, people—' With squared shoulders and sucked-in gut, his right elbow and bicep pressed tight against his ribs, his sweaty right palm gripping the rifle butt, Paul leaned back and marched, his eyes on the clipped hair and cap in front of him; certainty descended on him; warmly, like the morning sun.

# CORPORAL OF ARTILLERY

AFTER THREE YEARS, eleven months, and two days service, Corporal Fitzgerald re-enlisted for six years, collected a re-enlistment bonus and, that same afternoon, went to the bank in Oceanside and paid the balance of the note on his 1959 Chevrolet which was four years old. He had thought that would make him feel good, but it didn't. The balding man who took his money also took the pleasure, as though it hovered between them and the banker inhaled it and grinned before Fitzgerald had a chance. So he went home and paid the rest of the bills by mail: the hospital in San Diego, because the government would pay for your wife to have babies but not a nervous breakdown; the set of encyclopedias, and the revolving charge account which he had told Carol was supposed to revolve, not rocket. That had been for clothes and he realized when he wrote the check that he was paying ten per cent service charges. He walked to the corner and dropped the envelopes in the mail box, then stood there for a moment looking at the red and blue container of at least six years of his life (already knowing, though, that it was actually fifteen and a half, for if a man did ten years—halfway to retirement—he was a fool to get out). For a while he did not turn away from the mailbox. Even after being deprived at the bank, he had expected this final settling of accounts to yield a satisfaction which would carry him through at least the next two weeks in the desert. But he felt nothing. Or he would not acknowledge what he was beginning to feel. He read the times for mail pick-up and walked home to Carol, who seemed happy, free of burden.

For re-enlisting he rated thirty days leave, all at one shot, and the First Sergeant had even told him he could miss the two week firing exercise at 29 Palms. That was how happy the First Sergeant was; been trying to fill the Battery's re-enlistment quota and he had worked on Fitzgerald for a long time: a series of what began as a rather formal interview in the First Sergeant's office, changed to friendly conversations on the drill field or atop some hill at Camp Pendleton, and evolved into fervid sermons, these occurring again behind the closed door of the office where First Sergeant Reichert—a slender man with a thick soft black moustache and a red dissipated face—asked him questions he could not answer and gave him answers he did not want and which he tried to resist. Fitzgerald had a whimsical variety of answers, but most frequently *I don't know,* to the recurring question: *What are you getting out* FOR? *What are you going to* DO?

Almost four years ago he had spurted into marriage: on leave in Bakersfield, after Boot Camp and infantry training, he had become convinced that he could not return to the Marines without Carol. So he had brought her along, finding himself after bare transition the head of a household, and easily and amazingly enough able to feed his wife and himself as well as the three children who came as steadily as the combination of Carol and diaphragm failed to work. He had counted on his breadwinning lasting forever, though he was uncertain about what form it would take. As the expiration of his enlistment drew near, First Sergeant Reichert stepped in with the disrupting ability to convince him—for hours and sometimes days at a time—that his life was comfortably made for him. That it could never get better than it was now. Reichert finally won by writing the sum of Fitzgerald's debts on one scrap of paper and his re-enlistment bonus—fourteen hundred and forty dollars—on another, then dangling them over his desk, crumpling them together with a clap of his hands, throwing the ball of paper into the wastebasket, and saying: *You see? Redemption, lad, redemption.*

Besides that, he could go to Bakersfield next day and forget about 29 Palms. But Fitzgerald had been smart about taking leave: he told the First Sergeant he would wait until payday, the week after the firing exercise. He did not tell the First Sergeant, or Carol either, that if he went home right after shipping over he wouldn't want to come back. And with Feeney there maybe he just by God wouldn't.

There were a lot of things he didn't tell Carol because she was finally a good girl and it wasn't her fault. Even during her bad time, she had chosen as her targets the children and the people who wanted the bills paid, leaving him fairly unscathed. Or most of the time. Still he was a little tough on her the morning after his re-enlistment, when he woke knowing he had to get aboard a truck and ride out to 29 Palms for two weeks of Mickey Mouse. She got up before he did and put on make-up. While he was eating buckwheat cakes, she woke the children and they all got in the car to drive him to the barracks. It touched him that Carol was looking pretty just to feed him and drive him in and he wondered if she'd still do that six years from now, in 1969, when—if he was very lucky—he might be a staff sergeant. He decided she wouldn't, so now her face and hair and smell only annoyed him. As she turned into the Battery parking lot, he said: 'Look: it's just two weeks. Anybody comes around selling encyclopedias for kids that can't read, you lock the door.'

'That's not fair.'

'It's expensive and it's paid for.'

'Well he *did* make me feel like a bad mother.'

'Yeah: well you're not, so let's learn from experience. I learn, and I'm just twenty-two years old. That's what everybody keeps forgetting around here.'

She was hurt instead of angry and, once in the truck, he was sorry. In that evening's sunset he squatted outside his tent and wrote her a letter. She answered by return mail and they were all right again.

He was a scout-observer for a forward observation team, so he spent the entire two weeks in the desert sitting on steep hills of loose rock, his lips chapping, his face burning, though it would not change color for it was densely freckled. He and the lieutenant took turns calling in fire missions, adjusting the 105 Howitzers on imaginary targets: convoys of trucks, tanks, gun emplacements, and columns of advancing troops. He got through the two weeks without making any mistakes, and on the final evening he sat on a small rock at the base camp, his metal tray of food resting across his knees. The camp was in a horseshoe of low cliffs which were beginning to turn purple in the sunset. At one end, the officers' large pyramidal tents were in line on a rise of sand overlooking the rest of the camp. The lower walls of these tents were uniformly rolled up and, when he looked up there once, he could see the cots inside. Below the officers' area were the Staff NCOs' pyramidals and the troops' tents.

He ate everything on his tray. It was too much and he did not particularly enjoy its taste, but the meal was something he deserved at the end of the firing exercise. When he finished he smoked a Camel, thinking that was one commercial that didn't lie, then he field-stripped it, rose lethargically, and joined the line of troops waiting to clean their trays. Then he walked slowly over deep yielding sand, back to his tent. The cliffs were dark purple now and the camp was in their shadow.

His tent was waist-high. On hands and knees he crawled through the opening, squeezing past the tent pole, then squatted to brush off his trousers before lying on his outstretched sleeping bag, which was zipped against sand and dust. Thorton was lying opposite him, almost as near as Carol in the double bed at home.

'Duty on the moon,' Thorton said. 'Nothing growing, nothing moving.'

He had said that about a dozen times in the last two weeks.

'Nothing but Marines,' Fitzgerald said.

'Like I said: nothing. Got a cigarette?'

'Not for a short-timer.'

He tossed his pack onto Thorton's chest.

'Why don't I just keep 'em?'

'Go ahead. I got two more packs.'

'Call me when your hitch is up, and I'll put you on the payroll.'

'What payroll?'

'I don't know.'

'You better find out fast, before the First Sergeant gets you.'

Thorton sat up and folded his arms on his knees.

'When my hitch is up,' Fitzgerald said, 'I'll ship for six more.'

'Okay, John Wayne.'

'I'd be throwing ten years away.'

'If you can take twenty years of this, lots o' luck.'

'Nineteen and a half.'

Then it was dark outside. Breathing the smells of dust and canvas, Fitzgerald made desultory conversation with Thorton: cursing by rote sand and chapped lips, conjuring a shower hot at first then cold; and they talked about Gunny Palenski whom they at once liked and hated, and beer from the very bottom of a chest of ice, and girls in the back seats of cars. They had said all this nearly every night, and they realized it together and stopped. Fitzgerald sat up, took off his boots and shirt and trousers, and squirmed into his sleeping bag; he left it unzipped, lying on his back, looking up at the tent wall sloping across his face.

Reveille—Gunny Palenski's hoarse raging voice—was at five o'clock Friday morning; he woke and stared at the forward tent pole outlined against pre-dawn light at the tent's opening. Some time during the night he had zipped his sleeping bag and now he did not want to get up into the gelid morning and shave with cold water and stand in line for chow; he smelled hot grease from the field galley and tried not to think of those fried eggs turning cool on his tray quicker than he could eat them. He knew one thing: for a month or even two after he retired he would sleep late, getting up about ten or whenever his body refused to stay in bed any longer, putting on a T-shirt and khakis, drinking coffee for a while, maybe shaving, maybe not. Then he would get a job, having had that space of slow mornings when there was no ringing clock to force him out of bed and into uniform while Carol was sleep-walking in the kitchen, pushing himself to the table and eating because he had to, just as he made himself go to the barracks for another day of sometimes doing nothing, not one damned thing, and on other days people ran around and hollered at you until you wanted to kick over all the bunks and wall lockers and set the place on fire. He looked over at Thorton who had closed his eyes again and said:

'Let's hit it.'

They got up, dressed quickly, rolled up their sleeping bags, took the tent down and helped each other fold the shelter halves into U-shaped blanket rolls which they strapped to their field marching packs. Fitzgerald laid the packs side by side and placed their helmets on top of them; then he and Thorton walked to chow, passing troops who cursed and panted as they broke their tents; to the east, a smear of rose-colored light showed over the hills.

'First ones finished,' Thorton said.

'Goddamn right.'


When they reached Camp Pendleton in late afternoon, Carol was waiting in the parking lot. The red Chevrolet was shining, its grill and hood seeming to show off for him as he approached. From the back seat Mike and Susan were calling him. He got in, leaned over Jerry in the car seat, and kissed Carol; all of it happened so fast and awkwardly that he didn't really see her, so he pulled away. She was wearing a pink dress, her blonde hair was shorter, and its dark streaks had disappeared.

'I washed the car,' she said. 'And I got my hair done.'

'It looks great.'

'The car or my hair?'

'Both. I meant the hair.'

She smiled at him and backed out of the parking lot. Mike, who was three and the oldest child, said:

'You buy me gum?'

'Daddy didn't go to the store,' Fitzgerald said. With his left hand he was touching Mike and Susan: rubbing their shoulders, stroking their heads; but he was looking at Carol.

'You've been sunbathing,' he said.

'Every day.'

'All over?'

'Just what you see.'

'I want to see the rest.'

'It won't be long,' she said. 'I didn't give them naps, except Jerry.'

Mike and Jerry were blond, but Susan had red hair like his and, so far, she had been spared his freckles. He sank a little in the seat and smiled at that splash of color in one family.

'How was it?' Carol said.

'All right. They brought beer out last Sunday and we played volleyball.'

'Did you have enough money?'

'I had two bucks and I got one off Thorton. I wasn't going to shave that day, but the Gunny caught me and reamed me out.'

'He *did*?'

'I told him to shove it up his ass.'

She grinned suddenly. She always got tickled when he talked that way, and once in a while after a beer or two she'd try to say something nasty-funny. She had told him it was nice, knowing that nobody could tell you how to talk, and he thought that was funny and sort of sad too, as though she were playing grown-up when here she was with three kids and not even old enough to vote yet. Not that he had ever voted, or ever would either. He never got the word on what those politicians were talking about and he didn't believe them anyway.

'You see that doctor again?'

'Just once. He said I won't have to see him much longer, 'cause the birth control pills will help me relax.'

'Good.'

'You don't mind about my hair, do you?'

'Long as you had the money. It looks good.'

'I got groceries and cigarettes till payday and filled the car and opened a charge account at the drug store so I can get tranquilizers and the pills. Did I leave anything out?'

He was going to say something about the charge account, but he remembered how she was before and now it looked like she'd be all right, so he let it pass.

'Beer,' he said. 'Did you get beer?'

'A whole case.' She sounded so pleased that he felt sorry for her. 'And I put a six-pack in the refrigerator.'

'Three apiece.'

'What?'

'It's four days till payday, so we get three apiece a day.'

'Oh.'

They lived in a government housing area in Oceanside: two-storied red brick buildings, with grey roads curving in from the highway then out again, paved oxbows which existed to get Marines to and from the Base. Fitzgerald took a long shower, just the way he and Thorton had talked about it; when he finished, Jerry was in the playpen and Mike and Susan were watching cartoons. Carol opened two beers and they went outside, sitting on a slab of concrete they called the porch. They sat close to each other, their bare feet on a patch of dirt where the grass had died. Just over the roofs across the street, the sun was falling toward the ocean they could not see.

'We'll get to Bakersfield Tuesday evening,' Fitzgerald said. 'Wednesday we'll have everybody out to my place, starting at noon.'

'*Can* we?'

'Sure. The old man'll like that.'

'I wonder what they're all doing now.'

'Same old things.'

He smiled, thinking of big crazy Feeney with a beer in his fist and a long narrow cigar between his teeth.

'Except Feeney,' he said. 'He's probably thought up something different.'

'You think he's still there?'

'Feeney? Sure he's there.'

'I love that silly man.'

'Yeah, well don't tell *him* that.'

'I didn't mean that way.'

'I know.'

She lit a cigarette and he watched her fingers: they were deliberate and steady.

'You take a tranquilizer today?'

'Not a one.'

He patted her knee.

'You won't tell anybody at home, will you?' she said.

'Nobody's business.'

'I'll be so glad to see Vicki, I'll probably tell her myself.'

He went inside and got two more beers, then listened quietly as she talked about her visit to the doctor, and going to the beach with Cathy Thorton, and how the kids had behaved without him. Then he said: 'About that charge account. Let's close it.'

From the corner of his eye he watched her jaws tighten on whatever it was she had to hold back.

'Okay,' she said. 'I don't need tranquilizers much more anyway and I can stock up on the pills on paydays.'

'Sure. It'll work out.'

'I don't know how you close one. Do you just walk in and say I want to close my account?'

'I don't know either, but I'll find out tomorrow. You remember Feeney shoplifting? The time he got brassieres 'cause he said everything else was guarded?'

She was laughing now.

'I bet he just wanted them,' she said.

'Not Feeney: he didn't have to steal 'em. Suppose I don't shave all week-end.'

'I don't care.'

'It's not enough to scratch anyway.'

'Yes it is, but I never feel it.'

She pressed her leg against his.

'Is that right?' he said.

'That's right. I missed you.'

'I got kinda tired of Thorton too. Okay: I won't shave till Monday. I'll get in shape for Bakersfield. Maybe I won't stick to it, but I'm planning on not shaving for thirty days.'

'Don't. Grow a red beard.'

'It'd take me three months, but I'll get some itchy fuzz. And we'll tell the folks we want my old room so the sun won't come in and every morning we'll by God sleep till we can't sleep anymore. And they better not bust in on us either, 'cause they might get embarrassed.'

'It'll be safe too.'

'Damn right. Do they make you sick?'

'No. I'm not gaining weight either.'

She stood up.

'I have to start dinner.'

'Hell with it. Let's sit here till dark then we'll pick up some hamburgers and go to the drive-in.'

'What's on?'

'Who cares? How 'bout a beer while you're up.'

'Your last one?'

'Nope. We'll drink as much as we want then buy some more.'

At dark they reached the movie—a musical—and Fitzgerald said: Anyway, it's not *The Sands of Iwo Goddamn Jima* and Carol laughed and unwrapped his hamburger for him. Soon the children were sleeping on the back seat. The movie was all right but Fitzgerald didn't care much for Debbie Reynolds and he grew restless, looking into the cars around him until he could see nothing but silhouettes. He slid down in the seat, watching Debbie through the steering wheel, and remembered he and Carol going to the drive-in at Bakersfield, sometimes with Feeney and that wild black-haired girl, whatever her name was, but most of the time alone.

'We never saw the movies,' he said.

'What movies?'

'At home.'

'Not many,' she said, and he could hear the grin in her voice.

'Remember—what was the name of it? When it rained?'

'*Marjorie Morningstar*,' she said.

She slid close to him and he put his arm around her.

'Vicki told me it was so good, and I wanted to see it,' she said.

'It was the rain. Everybody was staying in their cars and you couldn't see much through the windows.'

'It wasn't the rain. It was you.'

'I wanted my clothes off.'

'So did I,' she said.

'We could've got caught anyway, naked during the whole movie, and I bet we did it more times than Natalie Wood.'

'Because we really did it. You want to go home now?'

'Don't you want to see the rest?' he said. 'I thought you liked it.'

'Not anymore. Let's go.'

He lifted the speaker off his window and hung it up outside.

'We'll have to be careful when we carry the kids in,' she said.

'They won't wake up. You sure you don't want to see the rest?'

'If you don't hurry and take us home, it'll be just like Bakersfield.'

He drove home and carried each child to bed; none of them stirred. He tiptoed out of their bedroom and into his own, where Carol waited in the dark. She lifted her arms to him as, undressing, he stared at the stretch of white between her tan shoulders and legs. But it was over in a rush, before he had even got started. After that he slept badly. At half past two by the bedside clock he woke, his palms pressing against the mattress as though to push him upright. For a moment he thought he was back in the desert. Then he turned to Carol and, silently, with quick hands, he pulled her out of sleep.

This time it took longer and he was able to marvel and antici-
pate and remember all at once, recalling the first time parked
right in front of her house, the porch light watching them but
they were safe down in the darkness of the seat and anyway it
was late, her parents were asleep, and anyway it happened so
fast they hadn't worried about anything except letting it happen, then she had sighed, peaceful, relieved, and said *We
finally did it* and squeezed him till he grunted; after that it was
all the time and they even had a bed when she was babysitting,
and once the Heatheringtons had come home early so he had
to escape through the bedroom window, unbuckled, shoes in
hand, leaving her to smooth the bed, her skirt, and her face
before fleeing to a lighted part of the house; best of all was
home on that first leave, pulsating with four months' absence,
and they had spent entire afternoons on a blanket in the woods—

Now he fell away from her, sprawled and grateful and
silent, his body sinking into the mattress, into a heavy sleep
that lasted until almost noon. He woke to the sound of Carol's
voice in the living room. She was talking on the phone, telling someone—probably Cathy Thorton—about going to
Bakersfield.

'It'll be like a honeymoon,' she said. 'What? Oh they're
*great*. You ought to take 'em—they don't make you sick or anything, you just have to remember to take 'em. Uh-uh, not a
pound. Really, they're great—'

She sounded very happy and he was not ready for that—
not right now—so when she hung up and came toward the
bedroom he closed his eyes and pretended he was asleep.

# THE SHOOTING

THE GUN FIGHT between the sailor and the Marine riot squad was in a Navy housing area on the base, so the civilian police were not involved, and during much of the fight Sergeant Chuck Everett was in sole command. Moments after the fight ended, a Navy photographer took a picture of Sergeant Everett; two days later the picture was on the front page of the local newspaper, a weekly which reported the news of Oak Harbor for its thirty-five hundred citizens. Except for occasional accidents (a curving road, treacherous to drunks, led north from the town to Deception Pass, where a high bridge crossed the water from Whidbey Island to the mainland), the newspaper's tragedies were drawn from the Naval Air Station: a year ago a bomber had crashed on Olympic Peninsula; three months ago another had gone into the cold sea off Puget Sound. The story of the gun fight was the first of its kind.

Chuck Everett was twenty-five years old, in his seventh year of peacetime service; he was a large man with a wide face that always looked sunburned, though at Whidbey Island there was more rain than sun, more grey than blue. Every Thursday he went to the Post Exchange and got a crewcut. At the Marine Barracks he worked as a Sergeant of the Guard, rotating the duty with two other sergeants. It was a good job, and he didn't mind when his duty came every third day. On those nights he inspected posts between midnight and dawn.

There were twelve posts, some on the west side of the island, some on the east side. Crossing the island, he drove through Oak Harbor; at that time of night the town was silent, and he could hear only the engine of his pick-up, and the sound of its tires on the pavement, which was usually wet from fog. He liked driving through town, liked to wonder if all those civilians were asleep or if maybe some of them were up to a little hanky-pank. It took him over an hour to inspect all the sentries, and as he drove he often daydreamed about things whose details he could not recall the next day. He could only remember having a pleasant drive in the wet sea-smelling air.

There were other nights, though, when he felt a vague restlessness, and he thought about girls. One April night a month before the gunfight, he went to see Toni. Her husband was with a bomber squadron on a carrier in the Pacific. She lived in a fourplex, in Navy housing just off the base, up the road from the main gate. The Navy Shore Patrol would be out in their truck, and if they saw his pick-up at Toni's, he'd get busted to corporal at the very least. He was both scared and excited, and as he turned off the headlights and drove slowly down her street, he wondered if he'd be able to get one up, and he remembered one of his favorite pieces ever, when he was a senior in high school and he and Loretta Cain had one school day afternoon sneaked into a storage compartment for athletic equipment. It was under the bleachers in the gym, there was a lot of floor space, and you could walk in it if you bent nearly double. Its only door opened onto the gym floor. Chuck and Loretta lay on a wrestling mat among basketballs, volley balls, tackling dummies and the smell of old sweat. They were just getting started when a P.E. class came in to play basketball. Chuck paused and listened to the dribbling, the shouts, the whistle. Then he went ahead and did it.

Now he parked down the street from Toni's, realizing as he walked back to her house that the truck's exact location didn't matter, that if the Shore Patrol saw it anywhere in Navy housing he would have to make up one hell of a story. Then he wondered how loud he'd have to knock to wake her up. He was in luck. There was a light on at the back of the house, in the kitchen; he went to the back door and watched her putting dishes away, a sixteen-ounce Hamm's on the kitchen table and a burning cigarette in the ashtray. He waited to see if another Hamm's would come in from the living room, with a man holding it. When he thought she was alone he tapped the glass and her shoulders jerked, then she saw him and was frightened and surprised and pleased all at once. She didn't look caught, though, so he knew it was all right. He didn't think she was playing around, but you had to figure if a married woman would go with you, she'd go with another. She had a chain lock on the door and as she worked it she started to giggle, a fine-looking dark little girl, not twenty yet, alone at one-thirty in the morning but still her hair combed and some lipstick left, and he thought what a good idea this was. She spoke in a laughing whisper: 'What are you *doing*?'

'Patrolling,' he said, and grinned and shut the door. 'How come you're awake?'

'Johnny Carson.' She stepped back and cocked her head, hands on her hips, playing wife with him. 'You crazy man. Want a beer?'

'Nope,' he said. 'I'm on duty.'

Then he was laughing and she was too, but she stopped when he took off his cap, careful not to touch its spit-shined visor, and laid it on the table; then he unbuckled his white web pistol belt and lowered it to a chair. By the time he got to the buttons of his battle jacket she was pulling her blouse out of her Levis and walking away from him, past the room where the child was sleeping, to the bedroom. When he finished he drove to the Shore Patrol office and had a cup of coffee with the sailors.

The sailor, they said afterward, had always been funny. Someone remembered that he never laughed much. Someone else remembered that he never talked much either. The Senior Medical Officer gave the final opinion. He was a bear-shaped captain, perhaps the only officer in the Navy who had taken advantage of an old regulation allowing beards: his was red and bushy. He had considerable wit, a large and colorful vocabulary, and he loved to talk, to lead a conversation to some strange point which existed largely for his own amusement, then to end it with a deep laugh, a slap on the shoulder, the ordering of another round. His fellow officers liked to listen to him, to quote him, to retell his stories; but his beard, his diction, his playfulness, kept them instinctively on guard. This captain read a copy of the investigation, pulled at his beard, and said Philip Korsmeyer had probably had a passive-aggressive reaction to service life in general and to his new role as a husband and nascent father. Everyone else, or at least everyone who by that time was still interested, readily agreed that this was so.

The written report of the investigation—original and five copies—had the appearance or at least the heft of finality. There were statements by an ensign and chief petty officer who commanded Korsmeyer's division. They said he was quiet, did his job, never caused any trouble; yet there had been, they felt, something different about him. From the six members of the Marine riot squad came six statements which all, in their repetition, presented a rock-like segment of truth: when the Corporal of the Guard sounded the buzzer they reported to his desk; he told them this was the real thing, issued them ammunition for the four riot guns and two MI's, and sent them by truck to the housing area, where Corporal Visconti deployed them for a fire fight with someone whom they couldn't see and didn't shoot at anyway, the fire fight being led by Sergeant Everett and, later, Captain Melko.

There were also statements by a sailor and his wife, who lived next door to the Korsmeyers; Mary Korsmeyer had used their phone to call the Marine Barracks. The longest statements were by Mary Korsmeyer, Captain Melko, and Sergeant Everett. The Commanding Officer of the Marine Barracks, a major, was mostly concerned with the statements of Captain Melko and Sergeant Everett; for there was the question of a cease fire order having gone unheard. The Major was not entirely satisfied with the opinion of the investigating officer, a lieutenant-commander, who concluded that 'in the heat of battle, Sergeant Everett did not hear Captain Melko's order to cease fire.' Except for an interest in the story itself, the Senior Medical Officer found that Mary Korsmeyer's statement was the only one useful to him. It was from this statement that he decided what had been wrong with Philip Korsmeyer.

Phil Korsmeyer himself did not know what was wrong, though for a month or so he knew something terribly strange was happening to him, and he also knew that it was terribly unique: that his friends in the squadron and his plump sweet Mary were not the sort of people who were visited by such nightmares, which were fearfully repetitious so that some mornings after a free night he woke relieved, but brave and curious enough to lie there for a while and try to remember if perhaps he had had the dream after all and had forgotten it. While Mary made breakfast he lay with his eyes closed, trying to force his mind back into the mysteries of night and sleep; then, satisfied that he had been spared for a night, he would get up and dress with the hope that whatever it was had left him forever.

After two months his hope became desperate, he started smoking before breakfast, and he was doing a couple of things that Mary called a nervous habit and which she said made her nervous too. He pinched his cheek while they talked over soiled plates at the dinner table, and he did a lot of pacing in the living room, his hands in his pockets, his shoulders slumped. They were six months married and she was three months pregnant and she thought he was nervous about being a father and maybe a husband as well. He was twenty years old, tall and slender, and she had believed that marriage would fill him out (it was what her mother told her), but instead he seemed to be getting thinner. Or maybe she only thought so because, with her baby, she was gaining weight.

About two weeks before the gunfight he became very quiet, distracted; when she asked if he wanted to try another channel or what he wanted to eat, he wouldn't answer. At first she simply asked him again in a louder voice. But after a few days she was certain that he regretted her pregnancy and therefore their life together. So one night when she asked him to throw her the cigarettes and he kept staring at the television, she said 'Hey!' and loudly clapped her hands. His face jerked at her, his eyes returning in a startled instant from that fearful distance. She left the room and he followed her. She stood at the kitchen sink, gulping milky water from a glass unwashed since dinner, looking out the window at the dark, while he asked her what was wrong.

'You don't love me,' she said.

He tried to soothe her, but his hands on her shoulders and arms were no more intimate than the brushing touch of a stranger on a bus.

Phil's dream was this: six people (he finally got their number straight) came for him and carried him alive to his grave. They took him from a bed and a room of eclectic familiarity: he could not recall these in detail, but in his daylight memory he felt that the bed was from some other house and time in his life, the enclosing walls and ceiling from another. He thought some of the people were women, but their bodies were vague or robed—he didn't know which—and their faces were merely shapes without features. They lifted him from the bed and all at once he was in a dark cemetery, and above the staring faces were black crowns of trees. They always brought him to the edge of a grave whose waiting depth he sensed yet never saw, for he was looking up at them, pleading with them and sometimes asking who they were and why were they doing this to him, but he never knew whether all his questions and pleas were only in his mind and for some reason not being voiced, or if he was indeed talking aloud and they were simply ignoring him. In any case, they never seemed to hear. They spoke to him, though, but he wasn't sure what they said. Remembering—next morning, afternoon, evening, night—he thought they only said one or two words at odd and meaningless intervals.

Then on a foggy Monday morning in May, two days before he went (as the Navy doctor and the newspaper said) berserk, he learned what they were saying at night. He had just stepped out of the shower, dried himself, put on his shorts, and stood at the steamed mirror; he was wiping it so he could shave when he heard the voice behind him, at the toilet. It said *Yes*. He spun around, already knowing his eyes were useless for something like this.

For the next two days he heard the voices, fought them, tried to get back to the far-off land he had left behind, so that sometimes he knew quite clearly that he loved his wife, he was looking forward with curiosity to the birth of a child, he had only one more year to do in the Navy, and he had a job waiting in his uncle's auto body shop in Eugene, Oregon. He saw all this, knew it to be true, knew that if he could rid himself of the voices of night he could return to those modest yet pleasurable expectancies of his days. But this knowledge came to him only in moments which were more and more separated until, watching television Wednesday night, he suddenly rose, upsetting an ashtray from the arm of his chair, and went quickly to the kitchen: not running only because there wasn't enough room, for he wanted to run—fear at first, then a sense of victorious flight, of ultimate purpose, having left the voices in the room with the television, though as he jerked open the kitchen drawer and fumbled for a handle, any handle of any knife, they were after him again, at his back in the kitchen: *Yes—Well: you, surely—Yes*; and he got the paring knife and slashed then sawed at his wrist, the knife had always been dull, then Mary was there, moving at him, reaching for him, and he slashed at her too, missing the breasts, and she turned screaming and ran from the house.

The knife had done little: three cuts, like the footprint of a bird, were scratched near bloodlessly into the pale underside of his left wrist. He laid the knife on the stove and stood holding his wrist, though still there was only enough blood to cover the scratches. He wished he hadn't struck at Mary, he wished she hadn't run out, and he wished with all his heart she would come back; yet at the core of his despair, of his knowledge that she was never coming back, there opened for him a despair so ultimate that it gave him hope: abandoned forever, beset by the shades who quietly watched him now from some point which was in his mind yet in the kitchen too—by the refrigerator or stove—so his mind was the kitchen and the kitchen his mind, he now saw that he was about to escape forever. He would move out of this network of betrayal and attack, he would ascend crashing through the night. It was motion he wanted now, and though he was weeping and actually moaning (he hadn't known that for a minute or two), there was an affirmative briskness in his steps through the living room, three paces down the hall, left into the bedroom where he switched on the overhead light, glancing at the bed covered by a green spread, and at the bedside table which held Mary's *Redbook* and package of Rolaids. He took the .22 rifle from the closet and sat on the bed to load the tubular magazine. After inserting four rounds he realized that was three more than he needed, but he liked the joke, liked sitting there in the middle of this joke that was in the middle of the swirl of devils and Mary's reaching hands and the silence that felt like chaotic voices, as though he sat dying and unnoticed at a party of strange drunks. So he kept loading until the magazine was filled. He was considering trying for the heart or sticking the barrel in his mouth when he heard the siren, then an abrupt squeal of tires outside his house.

He rose and turned out the light; when he again faced the room there was a dull flashing red light breaking the shadows, reflected from the walls. Going to the open window he saw the truck, the blinking light atop its cab, and now entering the lawn a Marine wearing a white belt. Phil shot twice from the hip and the Marine scuttled away into the dark of the lawn or the road. Watching the window as if not a bullet but a man might come through, Phil moved backwards around the bed and pushed it against the wall beneath the windows. Then the bullets came: twice the blaze and report of a .45, shattering a raised window, cracking into the wall behind him. He fired several shots at the truck, then kneeling at the bed as in prayer, his chin on the mattress, the rifle resting across it, he waited.

Crouched behind the fender, Chuck wished he had his deer rifle, his Winchester .30-.30 that he kept in the Barracks armory. With the first two shots from the house he had crawled into the truck and, with the brake and clutch pedals jamming his ribs, he had radioed the Corporal of the Guard, then switched off the blinking red light. Now there was nothing to do but wait for the riot squad.

They got there quickly, just as in drills, and he watched proudly as the panel truck halted a block away, the riot squad running low from the rear of the truck, spreading out as they crossed the road to the lawns and went down on their bellies, weapons thumping and rattling as they struck the earth. Chuck yelled for Visconti, and after a few moments saw him crawling in the shadow of a darkened house, and for the first time he realized that in all these dark houses people were watching, their faces exposed just enough so they could see out the windows. When Visconti reached a point where the truck was between him and the sailor's house, he sprinted across the road, bent low, his rifle at port, then squatted beside Chuck who saw the scene as a blending of his infantry training and movies of World War II.

'Gimmee the rifle,' he said.

Visconti gave it to him.

'The belt too. Okay. Here's what you do—' As he spoke he took clips from the pouches and, reaching up, placed them on the fender. He told Visconti to send two men to the rear of the house, that they would take cover and wait, and if the sailor ran out, they would shoot him. Then he gave Visconti the .45 and told him to bring the other three troops back to the truck, where they would set up a base of fire on the house while he and Visconti assaulted it.

'Jesus Christ,' Visconti said.

'You got it?'

Visconti nodded and told it back to him while Chuck, on one knee, pulled back the MI's bolt a couple of inches, glanced down in the dark at the dull yellow of the chambered brass cartridge, and eased the bolt forward again. Then he fired eight quick rounds over the hood; as he ducked again, one sweeping hand brought a new clip from the fender. Visconti was gone. Chuck waited for return fire from the window, but there was none. He watched the troops crawl into a cluster around Visconti three lawns away; after what seemed a long time for such simple orders, two men broke the cluster, rose and sprinted across the road. Chuck gave them two minutes to get behind the house, then he emptied three clips at the windows, remembering this time to sweep from left to right, aiming low. Still the sailor did not fire. He looked around, spotted his cap beside the truck, put it on the rifle's muzzle, steadied it so the visor pointed forward, then slowly raised it. Two slugs plunked into the hood and he jerked the rifle so the cap fell; then turning to pick it up he looked into the face of Captain Melko, bareheaded, his face tense but competent, the pale silver bars on his collar and epaulets already speaking for the silent man who wore them, relieving Chuck of command.

'Did they bring tear gas?' Melko said.

'No sir.'

Melko shut his lips impatiently; he opened the truck door and crawled in. While he was talking on the radio, Visconti shouted 'Cover us!' and Chuck fired while they crossed the road and kneeled behind the truck and watched him. As he crouched to insert a new clip, Melko gripped his arm, not in anger or even haste, and said: 'Don't fire again till the gas comes.'

For a moment their eyes met, then Chuck looked away, to his left, at the end of the road where, above a tall black mass of pines, a glowing cloud hid the moon.

It took five silent minutes for the truck to come, then Visconti had the tear gas, squatting beside Chuck who stood isolated within the percussion and flash of each round, aware of nothing save the kick of the rifle against his shoulder and cheek bone, the smell of powder, the dark rectangles of the windows and what he sensed behind them. When the clip pinged out and clattered against the fender he reloaded, half-crouched yet exposed over the hood, his eyes on the windows where Phil, surprised by the gas, had filled his lungs with a hot burning solid which he immediately recognized; he expelled it, then dropping the rifle he held his nose and mouth. His lungs were empty. He stood up, his flesh and tightly closed eyes burning; he waved an arm toward the window and the men behind the truck, and was about to flee out of the room and into the air when Chuck, standing erectly now, fired his last clip, hearing at some time Melko yelling 'Cease fire! Cease fire!' He did not know how many rounds he fired after that: perhaps four, perhaps three. Then Melko grabbed his shoulder and rifle and spun him around, both of them exposed to the acrid-smelling windows, as if already they knew the firing was over.

'Goddammit, Sergeant! We had him! We had him!'

Next morning after chow he offered to clean Visconti's rifle; but Visconti, with the awe of a bat boy, said he would clean it himself. Late the following afternoon the Corporal of the Guard showed him the Oak Harbor paper; he glanced at his picture, grunted, and went outside to the blacktop parade field, where a corporal was drilling troops. The day was hazy, with a faint glare from the covered sun. For nearly an hour he stood smoking, field-stripping the butts, and watching the troops in pressed green utilities marching back and forth and in squared turns, their rifles slanted upward in perfect angles, their boot heels clomping in unison. Then he went back inside. By Taps that night he had picked up six newspapers: one on the deck in the head, four on bunks in squad bays, and one under the pool table in the rec room. The ones in the head and rec room were easiest, for each room was empty. He stalked the other four, waiting until a squad bay was either empty (this happened twice) or until no one was around the bunk that held it, and he could stand with his back to the scattered troops and slip the paper under his shirt.

The other two sergeants were married, so he shared his room with no one. That night, while outside his closed door the barracks grew quiet, he lay on his bunk and read the story and studied his picture: a full length profile, his right side to the camera, his cap restored to his head, his right arm down at his side, holding the rifle. On the second page were small pictures of the Korsmeyers, only their faces. The picture of Korsmeyer distorted Chuck's memory of the other face: drained white, turned in frozen anguish to one side, averting its open eyes from the holes in its chest and throat. To recall clearly the man who had tried to stab his wife and who had shot at him with a .22, Chuck turned back to the first page, to his own picture, where he stood forever poised in peaceful silence.

But that night's silence stayed with him and changed to something else, as if he had taken restful leave of a woman's bed, only to fall unwillingly into months of continence. It stayed with him through the long summer, broken by nights with Toni; it stayed with him through the fall when, on the eve of her husband's return, Toni told him goodbye with ceremonial lust and sorrow, Chuck feigning both and leaving her house long before dawn. In the dull rains of winter he returned often to the newspapers; they were faded yellow as in sickness, dry and delicate in his fingers, and he handled them like butterfly wings, fearing for their lives.

# ANDROMACHE

Pete WENT HOME and Becky slept with her. But Ellen woke three hours later when the couple next door returned from the New Year's Eve party at the Officers' Club. She heard car doors slamming and women's high laughter—there seemed to be two couples—then a man singing. She reached out, and her hand touched Becky's breast; she withdrew it and lay awake for the rest of the night. She thought of Posy, nine years old now, and perhaps in twenty years or even less she would go through this too. She thought of Ronnie, fatherless at five, and already so much like his father; but Ronnie wouldn't have to bear this: he was a man, so he would merely die. And she thought of Joe trying to reach the escape hatch as the plane dived faster toward earth.

They found Joe's body, but she never saw it, and the funeral was with closed caskets. Ellen sat erectly between Posy and Ronnie. She did not cry, though her mother and Joe's mother did: subdued but continual sobbing, while the two older men sat quietly, their faces transfixed in bewildered grief. Posy didn't cry, either. Ronnie sniffled once but Ellen whispered in his ear: *Be a strong Marine*; and he bit his lip and stared at Joe's casket, flanked by the caskets of the pilot and the crewman.

At the funeral Ellen learned that the enlist crewman, a petty officer, had been only twenty-four years old; so next day she called a friend at Navy Relief, asking her to check on his widow. He probably didn't have much insurance, Ellen said, and she may need money to get home. Then Ellen drove south with her parents, to Sacramento.

She found an apartment near a school for Posy, and started taking courses in shorthand and typing. She didn't try to make friends. Some nights she had a drink with a couple across the hall. They were in their late twenties, and they bored her. Gradually she realized that she was boring them too: her talk was of the Marine Corps—the Fleet Marine Force bases and travel and funny anecdotes—a world as alien to this odd flabby couple as theirs was to her.

On most nights she stayed in the apartment and watched television or read magazines. Or, when Posy and Ronnie were asleep, she looked at the photographs in her album or projected home movies on a portable screen. The pictures were painful, but she was glad she had taken them. For sometimes she could not remember Joe's face. His image often appeared in her mind but when she concentrated on it, tried to keep it there, it began to fade. Then she would look at a picture. If she were out of the apartment, she turned to one in her billfold. In that one he was wearing his green uniform and major's oak leaves. At home, she would hurry to the bedroom where an eight-by-ten colored photograph was on the dressing table: he wore blues and captain's bars. She had no pictures of Joe in civilian clothes, except in the movies.

It took her four months to look at the movie she had taken on Christmas Day: Ronnie and Posy with their presents and Joe sipping coffee and smiling and lighting a pipe; then he was running beside Ronnie, holding the bicycle seat, and three times she reversed the film and watched the moment when he released the bicycle and she had focused on his face as he called softly: *keep steering, Son, keep steering*—She began to cry, but she watched the rest: the sandwiches and cookies and punch bowl, the living room and Joe in his blues, and her clean kitchen.

She remembered an uncle's funeral when she was fifteen.

His widow had spent almost an entire day at the funeral home, where his dead face was there to look at; it wasn't his real face, it was younger than Ellen had ever seen it, but it was dead. A woman could look at it, speak to it, touch it. But *she* couldn't. Her memories of Joe were alive: he was talking, he was smiling at her, he was stern, he was walking on the cold beach at Whidbey Island, or kissing her and going to the plane.

She went to the kitchen and made an Old Fashioned, then sat in the living room again, staring at the white movie screen. She wanted to talk, but not to the couple across the hall, or to the young girls in the business school, or to her mother. For she was thinking about Camp Pendleton and Marine wives: *Remember during Korea how we'd read two papers every day, the morning and evening ones, and we'd be waiting for the mail as soon as we woke up in the morning, that was almost the first thing you thought about—except sometimes you woke up, mostly on Sundays when there's no mail, and you'd lie there thinking it'll always be like this: alone in the morning—but most days it was mail you thought about and you'd try to forget it because the postman wouldn't come until ten and about nine-fifteen or so you could see women opening their front doors and looking in the mailbox, sometimes even sticking a hand in it, then they'd look up and down the street. They'd have brooms or mops in their hands. They knew the mail hadn't come yet but they couldn't help looking—Oh, I was the same. Remember how it was? How terrible? But we made it, didn't we. We by God made it—*

The next day she wrote to Colonel James Harkness at Camp Pendleton, California. He answered within a week: he had taken action on her request, he wrote, and he could assure her that a position with Navy Relief would always be open for her. If she would notify him several weeks prior to her arrival, he would find quarters in Oceanside. He and Marcia looked forward to seeing her again, and the Corps had lost one of its finest officers.

She replied that she would be there in June, then she

took the children to her mother's and told them she wanted to see Pete and Becky again before moving to Oceanside. As she told them this, she looked at Posy and wanted to say: *I'll send you to college in the mid-west, far away from the Corps, and you can marry a man like that one across the hall, a man who—who what? A man you can live with.* But she said: 'We'll do a lot of swimming there.'

Then she flew to Seattle. Pete and Becky met her at the airport; she sat between them in the car, and from Seattle to Deception Pass they talked about Whidbey Island friends and the weather. The sky was grey and the air damp and chilling. But when they approached Deception Pass, Ellen was silent. They rounded a curve and she looked at the grey roiling water and, across it, at the evergreens of Whidbey Island, and her heart quickened. She saw the rapids under the bridge, then they were on it: high above the Pass, and ahead of them were dark tall trees, and a winding blacktop road and, trembling, she lit a cigarette. Becky took her hand. As they left the bridge and entered the trees, Ellen said: 'Pete, would you take me to the salvage area tomorrow?'

'Sure.'

'I want to see the plane. I never saw Joe, or the plane either. Did they bring it here?'

Pete said yes, they had; and Becky squeezed her hand.


Two days before Christmas, nine days before his death, Joe Forrest had come home in the evening while Ellen was in the kitchen, making pastries. He looked at them for a while, pausing over each tray as if he were inspecting the enlisted mess, tasted a couple of them, then said gently: 'Make big cookies. The troops like big cookies.'

'Oh, Joe,' she said, 'do you really think I have to? What'll we do with these?'

'We'll eat them,' he said, and mixed her a martini.

He went to the bedroom to take off his uniform, and she

thought of him going through the ritual, carefully hanging the trousers and shirt on a wooden hangar, the blouse on another. Then he would spitshine the shoes, cordovans so heavily coated with polish now that his daily shining took hardly any time at all. He would finish by polishing the brass buckle and tip of his web belt, putting on a sport shirt and slacks, and then he would mix their second drinks. But she didn't wait for it. While he was still in the bedroom she called that she was going to Becky's for a minute and a roast was in the oven, but she'd be back before it was done.

Walking to Becky's, she looked through the windows of the officers' houses, all of them alike: picture windows and fireplaces and car ports, and cords of wood stacked outside. Though it wasn't six o'clock yet, the sky had been black for an hour. The wind was cold and damp, and she shivered. She always told Joe that she loved Whidbey Island and she told the officers' wives too; but she was from California and she hated the island and Puget Sound which enclosed it. She was certain that Joe felt the same, but he had been a Marine for too long and was cheerfully resigned to discomfort. She turned up the Crawfords' sidewalk, hurrying, her overcoat useless against the wind. Becky answered the door with a drink in her hand; they went to the living room, and Pete stood up.

'Where's the old man?' he said.

'Shining his shoes and drinking. What else do Marines do before dinner?'

Pete had been an ace in the Second World War and he was now a squadron commander. Ellen looked condescendingly at his uniform: he was wearing two-thirds of his Navy blues, having taken off his coat and tie and rolled up the sleeves of his white shirt.

'Those pastries I spent all afternoon on,' she said to Becky. 'The Major has just disapproved them.'

'He *did*?'

Becky smiled, and her face wrinkled. She was a tall woman with bleached hair and a face that was lined and tan. She played golf nearly every day, even at Whidbey Island; she had said only snow could keep her away from golf, and if it ever snowed she might even paint the balls red and play in that.

'Make big cookies,' Ellen said. 'The troops like big cookies.'

Pete brought Ellen a Scotch and water, then put another log on the fire.

'He'll probably tell me to make hot dogs too,' she said.

Pete was smiling at her.

'What are they drinking?' he said.

'Joe's making that rum punch.'

'Drunk Marines in Officers' Country. You stay in the house, Becky.'

'Maybe I won't. Who was that snappy one at the main gate today? About five o'clock.'

'Langley,' Ellen said.

She knew them all. Joe had their photographs on the bulkhead in his office and each time a new man reported in, he brought the photograph home and showed it to her. When he had brought Langley's picture home she had studied it for a long while, speaking his name aloud, and thinking of *lanky*, because Joe said he was. A week later he was a gate sentry and as Ellen stopped the car she had rolled her window down; when he saluted she had smiled and said: *Good afternoon, Langley.* He had never seen her before, but he knew the Major's car, and for a moment after his salute they had grinned at each other, proudly.

'He's darling,' Becky said.

The fresh log was burning now and its warmth reached Ellen's face.

'He didn't salute when I drove through,' Pete said.

'He didn't?' Ellen said. 'Did you tell Joe?'

'Oh, he's teasing. It was the sharpest salute he's had in weeks.'

'They're *all* sharp,' Pete said. 'I wish the Navy was like that.'

Becky brought an ashtray to Ellen. As she leaned over to place it on the arm of the chair, Ellen looked closely at her face. Then she glanced at Pete, who was talking about the old Navy when sailors had discipline. She was thinking that pilots'

wives were a little better off—in the matter of aging anyway.
Becky looked a year or two older than Pete, but at least they
both appeared near middle-age. Perhaps because of jet-flying,
pilots aged nearly as quickly as their wives.

But not infantry officers: during peacetime Joe's work was
almost relaxing, or Ellen thought so. He was outdoors more
often than not—hiking, climbing hills, running—and his trou-
ser size had increased only one inch since their wedding,
while she had gone from size ten to twelve. Even at Whidbey
Island, where he commanded a security barracks and his
troops did little more than stand guard, Joe exercised daily:
handball or running at noon. During his tours of infantry duty
he went to the field for days or weeks and came back looking
relaxed and sunburned, to tell her funny stories: a lieutenant
who got lost, a king snake in the chaplain's sleeping bag...

To occupy herself during their separations, and also
because it was expected of her, she was active in wives' clubs.
At Whidbey Island she was their president, a good one and
proud of it; she felt that she was like Joe: the senior Marine at
a Naval air station, and she had impressed the rival service. At
the Armed Forces Day cocktail party, she had invited the
Admiral's wife to go riding with her. *But it won't be much of a
ride,* she had said, *because all the horses are nags.* Then she
had talked about that for ten minutes. Three weeks later there
was a new petty officer in charge of the stables and the Admiral had appointed a full commander to buy horses. Through
the Special Services Officer, Ellen had arranged for a ladies'
night at the hobby shop on Tuesdays and the indoor swimming pool, which had been used solely for water survival
training, on Thursdays, so that wives of deployed pilots could
make pottery, and swim. She felt a special pity for pilots'
wives. Their husbands were gone for seven months each year,
flying from carriers in the Western Pacific. They flew A3D's
and it was rare when a year passed without at least one wife
attending a corpseless memorial service.

Flames from the big log were reaching the chimney now,
and Ellen leaned back in her chair, moving her face from the

heat. Her legs were comfortably hot. Pete rose to mix another drink, but Ellen told him she had to leave.

'I've had a break,' she said. 'Now I can go back and be a Marine again.'

By the time she reached the sidewalk in front of the Crawfords' house, she was cold. The wind was stronger and she blinked and wiped her eyes. Across the island, on the west side, she could hear A3D's taking off and climbing into the wet black sky.

The next day, Christmas Eve, Ellen baked large cookies. She also stuffed and roasted their turkey, for she was having Christmas dinner that night, so it wouldn't interfere with the open house. Pete and Becky were coming to dinner.

She didn't mind the work. Having the open house was her idea, because they had never had one for Joe's troops, at any duty station, and she told him this was their last chance. He would be a lieutenant-colonel soon, his next command a battalion. Then, except for a few Staff NCOs and clerks at battalion headquarters, she wouldn't know the names and faces of his troops anymore. So she had planned the Christmas open house, and Joe had placed a handwritten invitation on the bulletin board at the barracks. He had told his Staff NCOs and two officers that no Marine would be forced to attend.

Christmas Eve morning, Ellen was up at five. Hers was the only lighted house among the officers' quarters; from her living room window she could see the red light of the radar tower at the Seaplane Base; out her kitchen window, which faced the water, there was only darkness. She was outside in the cold fog getting kindling and two logs when she heard six-thirty reveille being sounded for the sailors in the squadrons' barracks a mile away. By the time her neighbors' lights went on, she was giddy from coffee and cigarettes on an empty stomach, the kitchen and living room smelled of freshly-baked cookies and wood smoke, and one countertop was filled with platters of cookies. Shortly after eight o'clock, she looked out the kitchen window at the grey choppy water and a crash boat moving slowly through the fog, clearing the seaplane lanes of driftwood; by then she had baked three hundred and fifty cookies.

She was only beginning. Posy helped her and they were in the kitchen all day, making sandwiches and stuffing the turkey. The fog never lifted and Posy kept adding wood to the fire. At four o'clock there were three hundred sandwiches and a thousand cookies; then Ellen put the turkey in the oven and Posy delivered platters of sandwiches to twelve neighbors who would store them in refrigerators. Just before Joe came home, Ellen made up her face and combed her hair; when he entered the house, unbuttoning his green raincoat, she said:

'You'd better get some more rum.'

'There's plenty.'

'You know these Marines, Joe.'

He started to object, but then he smiled and said all right, and went out into the fog again.

The Crawfords arrived for dinner at eight, and they drank with Joe in the living room, the three of them gathered at the fireplace, while Ellen had her drink in the kitchen. Becky offered to help but Ellen said no, it was all done and there wasn't room for two in the kitchen anyway. She put her drink down among the dishes on the countertop and then forgot it; when she noticed it again, Joe was mixing second drinks for the Crawfords and himself and she gave him her glass and told him to stiffen it. Once she had two cigarettes burning in different ashtrays.

She lighted two candles on the table and said: Let's eat the bird. They filed past the counter separating kitchen from dinette and served themselves turkey and dressing, peas and creamed cauliflower, rolls and jello salad. Joe went around the table, pouring the first glasses of wine; he gave wine to Posy and Ronnie too. Ellen served herself last and sat down. Then she found that she wasn't hungry. All day she had nibbled, eating cookies and small sandwiches as unconsciously as she had lighted thirty or more cigarettes. For the past hour she had tasted the dinner. So she took only a few bites of every-thing and drank a lot of wine and before dessert she was tight:

not cheerfully, though, but tired and foggy. She drank three cups of coffee while Joe and the Crawfords started on the second bottle of wine and their voices grew louder. Then Joe was telling her that he would fly to southern California next week, to buy uniforms from the tailor shop at Camp Pendleton.

'Who's flying you?' she said.

'Larry Sievers. In an A3D.'

'Why one of *those?* They won't let you aboard anyway, will they?'

'We'll run him through the pressure chamber,' Pete said.

'Oh. Why don't you just go down on a prop plane?'

'I've never been in one of the big birds before.'

There was no argument to that. It had been his reason too often: for going to a three week Army Jungle Warfare school, returning to tell her of eating monkeys; going to a mountain leadership course in the Sierras, where he learned to rapelle from cliffs; and, also in the Sierras, a survival school where he was interrogated and thrown into a cold mountain stream and kept for hours in a wooden box and finally was left in the field for three days with only a knife and no food.

'Well, if you're going down where all the sunshine is, you'd better bring me a nice present. I rate it—' she looked at Becky '—since you're making me a pilot's wife. Pilots always bring back nice things from their deployments.'

The lines deepened and spread in Becky's face as she smiled at Ellen. But Ellen looked down, into her coffee cup, then she drained it and poured herself a glass of wine. She was remembering an afternoon last winter when Pete had been deployed on a carrier; there was a light, cold rain, blown almost horizontally from the sea. Driving past the golf course, Ellen had seen a solitary player, clothed in what appeared to be a wool jacket and ski pants and, over them, a hooded plastic suit. Then she recognized Becky and sounded the horn and Becky turned: the golf bag hanging from one shoulder— the earth was too soaked for carts—an iron in her left hand, and the right arm lifted in a cheerful wave.

'Joe, don't we have some brandy?'

'Sure. Becky? Pete?'

The men took their brandy to the living room. Posy and Becky cleared the table and scraped plates, while Ellen put Ronnie to bed.

'I want to put up the tree,' he said when she had him covered.

'You had three glasses of wine, corporal. You'd be drunk on duty.'

When she got back to the kitchen, Posy had filled the dishwasher and turned it on.

'The pots wouldn't go in,' she said.

Ellen kissed her.

'Thank you, baby. We can do them while Daddy puts up the tree.'

She took her brandy to the living room, where Pete was standing with his back to the fire and saying: 'We had a good summer last year, but I missed it: I had the duty that day.'

Ellen chuckled. It was an old island joke, but like all good jokes it was true and you either had to laugh or curse. She was feeling better now that her work was nearly done, and she was going to tease Joe again about his three day deployment to California; but with her mouth open to speak, she looked at Becky and said:

'It's good brandy.'

You could never tell. Navy wives often talked of deployments, but Becky rarely did. Ellen recalled a wives' bridge party at the Officers' Club at Camp Pendleton during the Korean War: at one table a major's wife was talking loudly about the Chosin Reservoir. *They're cut off and outnumbered*, she had said, *but by God you wait and see. They'll make it to the beach.* Until finally a young girl, probably a lieutenant's wife, threw down her cards and rose suddenly, her chair overturning, and cried: *Shut up! Shut up, you hard-nosed bitch!* She had left the Club then, walking quickly past the quiet staring tables of foursomes. Ellen had tried to catch up with her in the parking lot, but she hurried away: an unknown girl whom Ellen never saw again and never forgot.

Deployments weren't that bad, no one was being shot at, but you couldn't really tell what was bad. When Joe returned from Korea, Ellen had thought if he could finish his career without ever going to war again, she could bear anything. But three years ago he had gone to Okinawa with an infantry battalion for thirteen months and, after a while, that separation was no better than the first. Again, though her mother invited her to Sacramento, she had stayed at Camp Pendleton with the other battalion wives. They did Navy Relief work, interviewing Marines who needed money, recommending loans or grants. At bridge tables their conversations finally came to sex; sometimes they jokingly alluded to their husbands' probable infidelities, but they grinned with only their lips. Once at a luncheon a captain's wife finished her second martini then looked around the table and said *God*DAMN, *I'm horny*, and they all laughed, their raised glasses tilting and dripping.

Maybe it didn't really matter whether your husband was being shot at, or was flying jet bombers in peacetime, or was merely being tempted by Okinawan whores. Maybe, at the heart of it, it was simply that he was gone; and when a man is gone he might not come back. Even when he does, nothing can replenish the four hundred days you spent without him. So, glancing at Becky, she did not mention planes or separations.

When the Crawfords left they all stood under the mistletoe and kissed. Joe put his arm around her waist, and she drew in her stomach muscles, and they stood in the open doorway until the Crawfords had walked out of sight. Ellen shivered. Joe closed the door, then put a log on the fire and went to the kitchen to mix Old Fashioneds. Ellen went to the bedroom for her diaphragm. The children were asleep; she went to the couch in the living room, and waited for Joe.

By Christmas morning the fog was gone. They were awake at six, bringing Posy and Ronnie to the living room where the gifts were laid out. Posy no longer believed in Santa Claus but, for Ronnie, she pretended; while he was trying to play with all his toys at once, she quietly kissed Joe and Ellen. At precisely seven o'clock, as she had planned, Ellen served breakfast.

All morning the sky was grey. The water was grey too, and choppy, and the visible portion of beach was covered with grey and brown driftwood. At mid-morning Posy went to the neighbors' and brought back the sandwiches. Joe was outside with Ronnie, teaching him to ride his new bicycle. Ellen had thought he was too young, but Joe said there were five-year-old kids riding bikes all over the neighborhood. When Posy came back with the twelfth and last platter of sandwiches, Ellen took the movie camera outside. She told Posy to come get in the pictures but Posy, whose face was red and eyes watering, wanted to stay by the fire.

From a distance of perhaps a hundred feet, Ellen focused on Joe and Ronnie: they were approaching her, Joe running alongside the bicycle, holding the seat. Then he let go. Ellen got that in the picture too: held the camera on him as he called softly: Keep steering, Son, keep steering—

She turned quickly to Ronnie. The front wheel was veering from left to right, his pedalling was slowing, and finally the bicycle leaned to one side and he went with it: falling on his shoulder, lying for only an instant on the hard earth, the dead grass, then rising again. Ellen moved in for a close-up of his face: hurt and determined, he looked at the camera as if he were about to curse, then he turned away and, grabbing the handlebars, jerked the bicycle upright. Ellen went back into the house. By noon, Ronnie was beginning to ride.

The open house was to begin at two o'clock. At one-thirty Joe put on his blues and she fastened the high collar for him and, with masking tape, removed lint from his blouse. She changed clothes, then took moving pictures of the table: silver punch bowl and silver platters of sandwiches and cookies. She swung the camera toward the living room, pausing on the fireplace, the hors d'oeuvres on the coffee table, and Joe, who was sitting in his easy chair. She went to the kitchen and, smiling at herself, focused the camera on the clean stove, bare of pots; the empty sink; the countertops which she had cleared and sponged; and the deck. Then she went to the living room and waited.

She didn't wait long. At exactly two o'clock Captain Jack Flaherty arrived, wearing a suit and tie. He was a bachelor. Then Lieutenant Ed Williams came, with his wife Katie. He was slim and boyish and wore civilian clothes; he looked afraid when he saw Joe in blues. Then he came into the living room and saw Jack in the dark suit and tie, and his relief was so apparent that Ellen almost laughed aloud. Katie was a pretty brunette with rather dark skin and faintly rouged cheeks; she began talking as soon as she entered the front door, but by the time she was settled on the couch with a glass of punch, she was quiet. Ed had done more preparation: he didn't run out of conversation until at least five minutes had gone by. Then he was finished. He looked around the room and said, very quietly to Katie, that it was a nice house. She nodded and asked for a cigarette. They had a friendly low-voiced argument about who was smoking more. Then Katie noticed that the others were listening and she blushed and said: 'He smokes more than I do.'

'He drinks more too,' Ellen said. 'He needs a refill.'

She got up and took his glass to the punch bowl. Then First Sergeant Rosener came, with Paula; they had been in for twenty-one years and they talked. So did Gunnery Sergeant Holmes, who got there shortly before three; his wife had divorced him two years ago, when he was ordered to Whidbey Island, because she refused to go with him. She was tired of moving, she said, and she stayed in San Diego. Or that is the way he told it. Holmes and First Sergeant Rosener were wearing green winter uniforms; Jack and Ed seemed embarrassed by that.

So with the arrival of the Staff NCOs, there was conversation: five men talking shop, and Ellen and Paula joined them whenever they could. Ellen called Rosener and Holmes First Sergeant and Gunny; she addressed the officers by their first names. All the men called her ma'am, and Paula and Katie called her Ellen, but Katie was uncomfortable about it. Then at three o'clock Ellen began waiting again. At three-thirty she and Ed Williams looked simultaneously at their watches. Ed and Gunny Holmes exchanged frowns. Ellen waited another fifteen minutes, listening beneath the conversation for a knock at the front door, then she excused herself and went to the kitchen. She stared through the window. Their back yard sloped down to the beach: dead grass, then dirty sand littered with driftwood. She clasped her hands together as in prayer, squeezing until her fingers reddened. From the living room she could hear Gunny Holmes's voice above the others: 'Does the Major know Colonel 'Cold Steel' Harkness?'

'*Very* well. I was his S-3 on my last tour.'

'I was in his battalion in the Fifth Marines. In fifty-six. I see in the *Gazette* where he's made bird colonel.'

'Now *that's* a Marine officer,' the First Sergeant said—

But Ellen didn't hear the rest. She didn't hear anything distinctly now, only the sound of their voices, for at that moment a dark grey seaplane appeared to her left, descending toward the water. Her first reaction was anger: the plane had probably been on patrol since morning and, now that Christmas was over, the men were coming home. In the enlisted Quonset huts and officers' houses, women had been alone all day; watching the children with their toys, taking pictures, receiving phone calls from home. The plane smoothly struck the water and moved westward, toward the Seaplane base, and now Ed Williams was talking: '—dropped four points all the way, then he got to three hundred rapid and put on the wrong dope, and got seven maggies and three deuces—' then laughter, and First Sergeant Rosener now, starting another story about rifle ranges. Watching the seaplane, she clasped her hands and squeezed until the fingers reddened. Then she looked at the table in the dinette, at the stacked cookies and sandwiches, and thought of the troops: some would be in the barracks, lying on bunks and talking about women or what they would do when they got out of the Corps; others would be in bars, playing bowling machines: losers buy the beer. *They should be bachelors*, she thought. *They should all*—Then she had to raise her hands to her face and quickly wipe her eyes.

She was going to the punch bowl when she heard a knock on the front door. She turned quickly, immediately angered by her speed and the leap of hope in her breast. Before going to the door, she paused to fill her glass and light a cigarette. But when she opened the door, she looked over the shoulders of the lone Marine standing there and scanned the front lawn and the street before the house. Then she looked at him. It was Anderson, and for an instant she thought of slamming the door and leaving him to stand there, cold and puzzled, before returning to the barracks to tell the others.

He was a tall nineteen year old boy with a round, pleading face which was now smiling at her. The width of his belly and hips was more than even an old officer or Staff NCO could bear with any sort of pride. He had his own car, he received money from home, and he was the only private in the barracks. Joe was thinking of giving him an Undesirable Discharge, because of repeated minor offenses. Ellen smiled.

'Merry Christmas, Anderson. I'm glad you could come.'

In spite of herself, she nearly was. For she spent the next hour controlling her face and voice, adding to the conversation, smiling and nodding and passing platters and filling glasses, knowing that no one else was coming.

Captain Flaherty was the first to leave. Anderson left when the First Sergeant and Paula did; Ellen watched him from the door, walking on the First Sergeant's left, nodding his head and laughing. Then Gunny Holmes glanced at Ed, who nodded, and all three of them stood at once. At the door Ellen told Katie to drop by some time. She didn't watch them walk to their cars; she firmly closed the door, and went to the living room, where Joe was looking out the window and biting his pipestem.

'I wish Ed wouldn't do that,' he said.

Ellen went to the window. On the sidewalk Ed and Gunny Holmes were talking angrily.

'Is Holmes arguing?' she said.

'Agreeing. Ed's probably telling him he wants a piece of the Staff NCOs tomorrow. The ones that didn't come.'

'Good for him.'

Joe flushed, but she didn't care.

'And Holmes will probably take the troops to the drill field tomorrow and chew them out,' Joe said. 'Then he'll harass them for a few days.'

'I hope he does.'

He flushed again and started to say something, but instead he knocked the ashes from his pipe.

'Bad for morale,' he said.

'*Morale*. Oh, Joe—Joe, *look* at that food!'

She pointed at the table, where sandwiches and cookies were piled. Only the punch bowl was nearly empty.

'And there's more in the kitchen. They don't even *care* about you. You bring their problems home at night, you get them out of jail and make them write to their mothers and you patch up their marriages. You even work out their *bud*-gets and you don't do that in your own home—'

He interrupted her. He only said her name, very quietly, but his face was stern.

'I know,' she said. 'I'm not complaining, but they don't *care*, Joe. You give them everything and they don't care if you're even alive.'

'They probably don't, during peacetime. But that doesn't matter. It's combat that counts, and when the shooting starts they look for a leader. Even Rosener and Holmes would. I remember—' He paused, staring into the fire place, and when he spoke again his voice was impassioned with memory '—when I took over that company in Korea, it was up on the lines. There weren't any platoon leaders left and the exec was run-ning the show. I don't think he even had a year in the Corps and he was so confused that he got tied down to the CP, look-ing at maps and talking to battalion on the radio. I got there about noon—'

She turned her back and went to the punch bowl, then past it, to the kitchen where the bourbon was. He followed her.

'Are you listening?'

'Yes.'

'Here: I'll make you an Old Fashioned. Anyway, I wanted to get oriented, so I crawled up to the perimeter—' He went to the sink, looking out the window. '—I went to different foxholes, checking out the terrain with binoculars, and pretty soon I could feel the effect I was having, and I stopped crawling. They hadn't seen an officer for a day or so, I guess. I walked up and down the line and stopped at each hole and chatted with the men—' He chuckled, and gave her the drink. '—pretty soon I drew some incoming, but it didn't matter: they knew where we were anyway.'

'I wish they could need you without getting shot at.'

'Oh, there's more to it than that. Most of them didn't come because they'd be uncomfortable or because it would look like brown-nosing.'

'Like Anderson.'

Joe smiled.

'He came for an Honorable Discharge. But he won't get it. The others came because they're professionals.'

'I should have known it would be that way.'

'I should have warned you.'

'No: I should have known.'

She called Posy, who had been watching television in a bedroom. Ronnie was playing at a friend's house.

'Would you like to have some friends over tomorrow?' Ellen said. 'You'll have plenty of refreshments.'

She waved toward the sandwiches and cookies on the table. Posy watched her quietly.

'But there's still enough for eighty hungry Marines, so let's give most of it to the neighbors.'

Joe kissed her cheek and hugged her, then went to the bedroom. Posy covered a platter of sandwiches with waxed paper, and took it outside. When Joe came to the kitchen, wearing a sport shirt and slacks, Ellen asked him to make an Old Fashioned. He touched her shoulder.

'I'm sorry,' he said.

'Don't worry about it. I just to have to figure out what to do.'

'Looks like Posy's taking care of it.'

'That's not what I mean.'

'What *do* you mean?'

'I don't know yet.'

During the short dusk and the beginning of night, Posy delivered all but a hundred cookies and twenty sandwiches. Sometimes Ellen stood at the living room window and watched her: a platter held in both arms, walking straight-backed under the streetlights. When she had finished, she called friends and asked them to come over the next after-noon. Once Ellen heard her say: We have a few left-overs from this big open house Mother had. Ellen brought her a glass of sherry.

'It'll make your feet warm,' she said.

At nine o'clock, when she was kissing Posy goodnight, the phone rang. Joe answered. Ellen went to Ronnie's bedroom and pulled the blankets over his shoulders. Near his face on the pillow was a half-eaten oatmeal cookie. She dropped it in the wastebasket. In the hall, Joe was chuckling into the phone.

'Okay, boy,' he said. 'Then we can get a battalion from Lejeune and occupy.'

He laughed again. Ellen was putting on her coat and scarf when he hung up.

'I'm going to Becky's for a minute. Who was that?'

'Larry Sievers. He says we'll steal that A3D next week and bomb Castro.'

'Where's he drinking tonight?'

'At home.'

'That's nice, for a change.'

She stepped outside. The wind was strong and, walking against it, she turned her face and clenched her hands in her pockets. She hadn't told Joe goodbye, and that bothered her. When she got to Becky's she knocked fast and loud, her back to the wind.

'A flop,' she said, when Becky opened the door.

She had three drinks. With the first one she was still controlling herself, telling them very calmly why no one had come. After the second she was complaining bitterly, and she knew it, but she couldn't stop.

'Goddamnit,' she said to Becky, when she was finally ready to leave, 'we don't have ranks and service numbers. We're *wo*men.'

'Bless you for that,' Pete said, and he put his arm around her waist as they walked to the door. She forgot to draw in her stomach muscles.

'A lot of good it does,' she said, and kissed them both and left. The wind struck her back now, pushing her forward.

Joe was asleep in his chair in the living room, an open book on his lap; the fire was dying. She poked the coals and put another log on the andirons. Then in their bedroom she undressed and put on a silk kimono. Joe had brought it from Japan and once, when she was wearing it over her naked body as she was now, he had reached inside the wide arm and touched her breast. She had wondered how he learned that. At the mirror she combed her hair and freshened her lipstick and dabbed perfume on her wrists and throat. Then she was ready. She did not even look at the drawer where her diaphragm was. She walked past it, and into the living room where she turned off the lamps and arranged throw-pillows on the carpet before the fire. With the cover flap, she marked Joe's place in the book, *Russia and the West Under Lenin and Stalin*, and set it on the coffee table. Then she started waking him up. He was annoyed at first, but soon she was taking care of that.

At the dinner table two days after Christmas, Joe told her about the pressure chamber. They had simulated forty thousand feet and taught him to use an oxygen mask. They also taught him to bail out. There were three seats in an A3D, he told her, two facing forward and one aft. The escape hatch was opposite the seat facing aft; it opened onto a chute in the belly of the plane. A horizontal bar was at the top of the hatch and you had to grab it with your arms crossed and pull yourself into the chute. Ellen watched him across the table as he held up his arms, the forearms crossed and the hands grasping an imaginary bar. Then he stood up to show how his body would turn as he uncrossed his arms, and he would slide out of the plane on his belly.

'There's not much time,' he said. 'Everybody's got to move out fast.'

But no one did. She told him goodbye four days before New Year's and he said he'd be back for the party. On New Year's Eve they flew back from California and, minutes away from Whidbey Island, they went down.

When her doorbell rang in mid-afternoon Ellen was in the bedroom checking her social calendar. She found the date of the wives' club luncheon in December; that was when her last period had begun. Then she counted days on the calendar, until her finger touched Christmas. She counted them again, and decided she had probably not conceived. Now she wasn't sure whether she wanted to or not. *It's up to you,* Joe had said Christmas night and a couple of times since then. But she was thirty-five and she had gained weight and maybe a pregnancy would ruin her figure forever. When the child was five, she would be forty; fifteen, fifty; twenty, fifty-five. That was all right. But her weight. . . And if Joe got orders in June she would be—she counted on her fingers—six months pregnant and travelling perhaps across the country: motels and those weary distorted days of emptying one house and filling another: packing boxes and wardrobes and scratched furniture and confusion.

But she was thirty-five. She'd be forty soon, and she had two children (*a boy and a girl*, people said, *such nice planning*) and she was the president of the wives' club and she was the Major's wife. Gunny Holmes might have marched the troops to the drill field and chewed them out, but it wouldn't have been for her and even if he had mentioned her name, it wouldn't have mattered to them. Ed Williams might have admonished the Staff NCOs about courtesy and loyalty to the Commanding Officer. No one, though, would be told: *You hurt*

*Mrs. Forrest*. There was no recourse, either. She couldn't scowl at the Marines as they saluted her at the gates; they would only smile at her and joke about it in the barracks. There was nothing, nothing at all, and she was again counting the calendar days since the last wives' club luncheon when the doorbell rang.

She waited for Posy to answer it, but heard nothing; then she rose, still trying to decide, wishing it were already decided for her, that she had already conceived, but size twelve, she'd have to diet and exercise.... Going through the living room she saw Posy out the back window, getting two logs from the wood pile, and as her hand went to the doorknob she glimpsed the dying fire: *sweet sweet Posy*. Then she opened the door and Pete was standing there, his white cap in his hand—that was the first thing she noticed—and the collar of his blue topcoat turned up: six feet of somber dark blue and beyond his anguished face and bare head was the grey sky. Her hand tightened on the doorknob and she opened her mouth to speak but couldn't, silenced by a welling urge to be suspended here forever, to be deceived and comforted and never to know anything at all. But he was looking at his cap, then at her, and a hand went up and through his hair, and he said: 'Ellen. Ellen, baby—'

And stopped again. She saw fire, explosions, a parachute failing to open and someone unreal—it wasn't Joe, it *wasn't*—falling down and down without cease, as in a dream. Then she was underwater and a plane was sinking past her, descending slowly and without hope, and she had to get to it and open it somehow but she couldn't breathe—

'Is it Joe?' she said.

He nodded and stepped forward but before he could touch her she said: 'In the water?'

He said: 'No, Olympic Peninsula,' then grabbed her as she fell toward him; she gave all her weight to his locked arms and pressed her face against his coarse Navy topcoat, not breathing; then finally she did: a deep dry audible breath, and she said: 'He didn't get out?'

She felt his head shaking against her own, heard him

whisper: 'Nobody did,' and as if on some strangely distant part of her body she felt his hand patting her back, and she suddenly knew she hadn't conceived, it could never work out that way, nothing ever could, he was gone and she would have a period soon, her womb's dark red weeping. How could he be gone? It was the last day of the year and he was gone, the year was over, and he was over; but he was turning at the plane to wave; then she was crying heavily, but still she heard or felt Posy behind her, and she spun around. Posy was holding two logs across her chest, and her face and ears were red from the cold. Then her lips began to quiver and she dropped the logs. Ellen went to her knees and pressed Posy to her breast, crying: 'Oh, Pete! She knew too! She knew too!'

And she hugged Posy even more tightly, as if for all time.

# PART THREE

# ADULTERY

*... love is a direction and not a state of the soul.*
SIMONE WEIL
*Waiting on God*

to Gina Berriault

WHEN THEY HAVE finished eating Edith tells Sharon to clear the table then brush her teeth and put on her pajamas; she brings Hank his coffee, then decides she can have a cup too, that it won't keep her awake because there is a long evening ahead, and she pours a cup for herself and returns to the table. When Sharon has gone upstairs Edith says: 'I'm going to see Joe.'

Hank nods, sips his coffee, and looks at his watch. They have been silent during most of the meal but after her saying she is going to see Joe the silence is uncomfortable.

'Do you have to work tonight?' she says.

'I have to grade a few papers and read one story. But I'll read to Sharon first.'

Edith looks with muted longing at his handlebar moustache, his wide neck, and thick wrists. She is lighting a cigarette when Sharon comes downstairs in pajamas.

'Daddy quit,' Sharon says, 'Why don't you quit?'

Edith smiles at her, and shrugs.

'I'm going out for awhile,' she says. 'To see a friend.'

Sharon's face straightens with quick disappointment that borders on an angry sense of betrayal.

'What friend?'

'Terry,' Edith says.

'Why can't she come here?'

'Because Daddy has work to do and we want to talk.'

'I'll read to you,' Hank says.

Sharon's face brightens.

'What will you read?'

'Kipling.'

'"Rikki-Tikki-Tavi"?'

'Yes: "Rikki-Tikki-Tavi."'

She is eight and Edith wonders how long it will be before Sharon senses and understands that other presence or absence that Edith feels so often when the family is together. She leaves the table, puts the dishes and pots in the dishwasher, and turns it on. She is small and slender and she is conscious of her size as she puts on her heavy coat. She goes to the living room and kisses Hank and Sharon, but she does not leave through the front door. She goes to the kitchen and takes from the refrigerator the shrimp wrapped in white paper; she goes out the back door, into the dark. A light snow has started to fall.

It is seven-thirty. She has told Joe not to eat until she gets there, because she wants to cook shrimp scampi for him. She likes cooking for Joe, and she does it as often as she can. Wreathed in the smells of cooking she feels again what she once felt as a wife: that her certain hands are preparing a gift. But there were times, in Joe's kitchen, when this sense of giving was anchored in vengeful images of Hank, and then she stood in the uncertainty and loss of meaningless steam and smells. But that doesn't happen anymore. Since Joe started to die, she has been certain about everything she does with him. She has not felt that way about anyone, even Sharon, for a long time.

The snow is not heavy but she drives slowly, cautiously, through town. It is a small town on the Merrimack River, and tonight there are few cars on the road. Leaving town she enters the two-lane country road that will take her to Joe. She tightens her seat belt, turns on the radio, lights a cigarette, and knows that none of these measures will slow the tempo of her heart. The road curves through pale meadows and dark trees and she is alone on it. Then there are houses again, distanced from each other by hills and fields, and at the third one, its front porch lighted, she turns into the driveway. She turns on the interior light, looks at her face in the rearview mirror, then goes up the shovelled walk, her face lowered from the snow, and for a moment she sees herself as Joe will see her coming inside with cheeks flushed and droplets in her long black hair. Seeing herself that way, she feels loved. She is thirty years old.

When Joe opens the door she feels the awkward futility of the shrimp in her hand. She knows he will not be able to eat tonight. He has lost thirty pounds since the night last summer when they got drunk and the next day he was sick and the day after and the day after, so that finally he could not blame it on gin and he went to a doctor and then to the hospital where a week later they removed one kidney with its envelope of cancer that had already spread upward. During the X-ray treatments in the fall, five days a week for five weeks, with the square drawn in purple marker on his chest so the technician would know where to aim, he was always nauseated. But when the treatments were finished there were nights when he could drink and eat as he used to. Other nights he could not. Tonight is one of those: above his black turtleneck the pallor of his face is sharpened; looking from that flesh his pale blue eyes seem brighter than she knows they are. His forehead is moist; he is forty years old, and his hair has been grey since his mid-thirties. He holds her, but even as he squeezes her to him, she feels him pulling his body back from the embrace, so she knows there is pain too. Yet still he holds her tightly so his pulling away causes only a stiffening of his torso while his chest presses against her. She remembers the purple square and is glad it is gone now. She kisses him.

'I'm sorry about the shrimp,' he says. 'I don't think I can eat them.'

'It's all right; they'll keep.'

'Maybe tomorrow.'

'Maybe so.'

The apartment is small, half of the first floor of a small two-story house, and it is the place of a man who since his boyhood has not lived with a woman except housekeepers in rectories. The front room where they are standing, holding each other lightly now like dancers, is functional and, in a masculine disorderly way, orderly; it is also dirty. Fluffs of dust have accumulated on the floor. Edith decides to bring over her vacuum cleaner tomorrow. She puts her coat on a chair and moves through the room and down the short hall toward the kitchen; as she passes his bedroom she glances at the bed to see if he rested before she came; if he did, he has concealed it: the spread is smooth. She wonders how he spent his day, but she is afraid to ask. The college is still paying him, though someone else is teaching his philosophy courses that he started in the fall and had to quit after three days. She puts the shrimp in the refrigerator; always, since they were first lovers, when she looks in his refrigerator she feels a tenderness whose edges touch both amusement and pathos. The refrigerator is clean, it has four ice trays, and it holds only the makings of breakfast and cocktail hour. Behind her he is talking: this afternoon he took a short walk in the woods; he sat on a log and watched a cock pheasant walking across a clearing, its feathers fluffed against the cold. The land is posted and pheasants live there all winter. After the walk he tried to read Unamuno but finally he listened to Rachmaninoff and watched the sun setting behind the trees.

While he gets ice and pours bourbon she looks around the kitchen for signs. In the dish drainer are a bowl, a glass, and a spoon and she hopes they are from lunch, soup and milk, but she thinks they are from breakfast. He gives her the drink and opens a can of beer for himself. When he feels well he drinks gin; once he told her he'd always loved gin and that's why he'd never been a whiskey priest.

'Have you eaten since breakfast?'

'No,' he says, and his eyes look like those of a liar. Yet he and Edith never lie to each other. It is simply that they avoid the words cancer and death and time, and when they speak of his symptoms they are looking at the real words like a ghost between them. At the beginning she saw it only in his eyes: while he joked and smiled his eyes saw the ghost and she did too, and she felt isolated by her health and hope. But gradually, as she forced herself to look at his eyes, the ghost became hers too. It filled his apartment: she looked through it at the food she cooked and they ate; she looked through it at the drinks she took from his hand; it was between them when they made love in the dark of the bedroom and afterward when she lay beside him and her eyes adjusted to the dark and discerned the outlines and shapes of the chest of drawers against the wall at the foot of the bed and, hanging above it, the long black crucifix, long enough to hang in the classroom of a parochial school, making her believe Joe had taken with him from the priesthood a crucifix whose size would assert itself on his nights. When they went to restaurants and bars she looked through the ghost at other couples; it delineated these people, froze their gestures in time. One night, looking in his bathroom mirror, she saw that it was in her own eyes. She wondered what Joe's eyes saw when they were closed, in sleep.

'You should eat,' she says.

'Yes.'

'Do you have something light I could fix?'

'My body.' He pats his waist; he used to have a paunch; when he lost the weight he bought clothes and now all his slacks are new.

'Your head will be light if you take walks and don't eat and then drink beer.'

He drinks and smiles at her.

'Nag.'

'Nagaina. She's the mother cobra. In "Rikki-Tikki-Tavi."
Would you eat some soup?'

'I would. I was wondering first—' (His eyes start to lower
but he raises them again, looks at her) '—if you'd play trainer
for a while. Then maybe I'd take some soup.'

'Sure. Go lie down.'

She gets the heating ointment from the medicine cabinet
in the bathroom; it lies beside the bottle of sleeping pills. On
the shelf beneath these are his shaving cream, razor, after-
shave lotion, and stick deodorant. The juxtaposition disturbs
her, and for a moment she succumbs to the heavy weariness
of depression. She looks at her hand holding the tube of ointment. The hand does not seem to be hers; or, if it is, it has no
function, it is near atrophy, it can touch no one. She lowers
the hand out of her vision, closes the cabinet door, and looks
at herself in the mirror. She is pretty. The past three years
show in her face, but still she is pretty and she sips her drink
and thinks of Joe waiting and her fingers caress the tube.

In the bedroom Joe is lying on his back, with his shirt off.
The bedside lamp is on. He rolls on his belly and turns his
face on the pillow so he can watch her. She lights him a cigarette then swallows the last of her bourbon and feels it. Looking at his back she unscrews the cap from the tube; his flesh is
pale and she wishes it were summer so she could take him to
the beach and lie beside him and watch his skin assume a
semblance of health. She squeezes ointment onto her fingers
and gently rubs it into the flesh where his kidney used to be.
She is overtaken by a romantic impulse which means nothing
in the face of what they are facing: she wishes there were no
cancer but that his other kidney was in danger and he needed
hers and if only he had hers he would live. Her hands move
higher on his back. He lies there and smokes, and they do not
talk. The first time she rubbed his back they were silent
because he had not wanted to ask her to but he had anyway;
and she had not wanted to do it but she had, and her flesh had

winced as she touched him, and he had known it and she had known that he did. After that, on nights when she sensed his pain, or when he told her about it, she rose from the bed and got the ointment and they were silent, absorbing the achieved intimacy of her flesh. Now his eyes are closed and she watches his face on the pillow and feels what she is heating with her anointed hands.

When she is done she warms a can of vegetable soup and toasts a slice of bread. As she stirs the soup she feels him watching from the table behind her. He belches and blames it on the beer and she turns to him and smiles. She brings him the bowl of soup, the toast, and a glass of milk. She puts ice in her glass and pours bourbon, pouring with a quick and angry turning of the wrist that is either defiant or despairing—she doesn't know which. She sits with him. She would like to smoke but she knows it bothers him while he is eating so she waits. But he does not finish the soup. He eats some of the toast and drinks some of the milk and pretends to wait for the soup to cool; under her eyes he eats most of the soup and finishes the toast and is lifting a spoonful to his mouth when his face is suffused with weariness and resignation which change as quickly to anger as he shakes his head and lowers the spoon, his eyes for a moment glaring at her (but she knows it isn't her he sees) before he pushes back from the table and moves fast out of the kitchen and down the hall. She follows and is with him when he reaches the toilet and standing behind him she holds his waist with one arm and his forehead with her hand. They are there for a long time and she doesn't ask but knows he was here after breakfast and perhaps later in the day. She thinks of him alone retching and quivering over the toilet. Still holding his waist she takes a washcloth from the towel rack and reaches to the lavatory and dampens it; she presses it against his forehead. When he is finished she walks with him to the bedroom, her arm around his waist, his around her shoulder, and she pulls back the covers while he undresses. The telephone is on the bedside table. He gets into bed and she covers him then turning her back to him she dials her home. When Hank answers she says: 'I might stay a while.'

'How is he?'

She doesn't answer. She clamps her teeth and shuts her eyes and raising her left hand she pushes her hair back from her face and quickly wipes the tears from beneath her eyes.

'Bad?' Hank says.

'Yes.'

'Stay as long as you want,' he says. His voice is tender and for a moment she responds to that; but she has been married to him for eight years and known him for the past three and the moment passes; she squeezes the phone and wants to hit him with it.

She goes to the kitchen, the bathroom, and the living room, getting her drink and turning out lights. Joe is lying on his belly with his eyes closed. She undresses, hoping he will open his eyes and see her; she is the only woman he has ever made love with and always he has liked watching her undress; but he does not open his eyes. She turns out the lamp and goes around the bed and gets in with her drink. Propped on a pillow she finishes it and lowers the glass to the floor as he holds her hand. He remains quiet and she can feel him talking to her in his mind. She moves closer to him, smelling mouth-wash and ointment, and she thinks of the first time they made love and the next day he bought a second pillow and two satin pillowcases and that night showing them to her he laughed and said he felt like Gatsby with his shirts. She said: Don't make me into that Buchanan bitch; I don't leave bodies in the road. Months later when she went to the hospital to see him after the operation she remembered what she had said. Still, and strangely, there is a sad but definite pleasure remember-ing him buying the pillow and two satin pillowcases.

Suddenly he is asleep. It happens so quickly that she is afraid. She listens to his slow breath and then, outstretched beside him, touching as much of the length of his body as she can, she closes her eyes and prays to the dark above her. She feels that her prayers do not ascend, that they disseminate in the dark beneath the ceiling. She does not use words, for she cannot feel God above the bed. She prays with images: she sees Joe suffering in a hospital bed with tubes in his body and she does not want him to suffer. So finally her prayer is an image of her sitting beside this bed holding his hand while, gazing at her peacefully and without pain, he dies. But this doesn't touch the great well of her need and she wishes she could know the words for all of her need and that her statement would rise through and beyond the ceiling, up beyond the snow and stars, until it reached an ear. Then listening to Joe's breathing she begins to relax, and soon she sleeps. Some time in the night she is waked by his hands. He doesn't speak. His breath is quick and he kisses her and enters with a thrust she receives; she feels him arcing like Icarus, and when he collapses on her and presses his lips to her throat she knows she holds his entire history in her body. It has been a long time since she has felt this with a man. Perhaps she never has.

## 2

All she had ever wanted to be was a nice girl someone would want to marry. When she married Hank Allison she was twenty-two years old and she had not thought of other possibilities. Husbands died, but one didn't think of that. Marriages died too: she had seen enough corpses and heard enough autopsies in Winnetka (the women speaking: sipping their drinks, some of them afraid, some fascinated as though by lust; no other conversation involved them so; Edith could feel flesh in the room, pores, blood, as they spoke of what had destroyed or set free one of their kind); so she knew about the death of love as she knew about breast cancer. And, just as she touched and explored her breasts, she fondled her marriage, stroked that space of light and air that separated her from Hank.

He was her first lover; they married a year earlier than they had planned because she was pregnant. From the time she missed her first period until she went to the gynecologist she was afraid and Hank was too; every night he came to her apartment and the first thing he asked was whether she had started. Then he drank and talked about his work and the worry left his eyes. After she had gone to the doctor she was afraid for another week or so; Hank's eyes pushed her further into herself. But after a while he was able to joke about it. We should have done it right, he said—gone to the senior prom and made it in the car. He was merry and resilient. In her bed he grinned and said the gods had caught up with him for all the times he'd screwed like a stray dog.

When she was certain Hank did not feel trapped she no longer felt trapped, and she became happy about having a child. She phoned her parents. They seemed neither alarmed nor unhappy. They liked Hank and, though Edith had never told them, she knew they had guessed she and Hank were lovers. She drove up to Winnetka to plan the wedding. While her father was at work or gone to bed she had prenatal conversations with her mother. They spoke of breast-feeding, diet, smoking, natural childbirth, saddleblocks. Edith didn't recognize the significance of these conversations until much later, in her ninth month. They meant that her marriage had begun at the moment when she was first happy about carrying a child. She was no longer Hank's lover; she was his wife. What had been clandestine and sweet and dark was now open; the fruit of that intimacy was shared with her mother. She had begun to nest. Before the wedding she drove back to Iowa City, where Hank was a graduate student, and found and rented a small house. There was a room where Hank could write and there was a room for the baby, as it grew older. There was a back yard with an elm tree. She had money from her parents, and spent a few days buying things to put in the house. People delivered them. It was simple and comforting.

In her ninth month, looking back on that time, she began to worry about Hank. Her life had changed, had entered a trajectory of pregnancy and motherhood; his life had merely shifted to the side, to make more room. But she began to wonder if he had merely shifted. Where was he, who was he, while she talked with her mother, bought a washing machine, and felt the baby growing inside her? At first she worried that he had been left out, or anyway felt left out; that his shifting aside had involved enormous steps. Then at last she worried that he had not shifted at all but, for his own survival, had turned away.

She became frightened. She remembered how they had planned marriage: it would come when he finished school, got a job. They used to talk about it. Hank lived in one room of an old brick building which was owned by a cantankerous and colorful old man who walked with the assistance of a stout, gnarled, and threatening cane; like most colorful people, he knew he was and he used that quality, in his dealings with student-tenants, to balance his cantankerousness, which he was also aware of and could have controlled but instead indulged, the way some people indulge their vicious and beloved dogs. In the old brick house there was one communal kitchen, downstairs; it was always dirty and the refrigerator was usually empty because people tended to eat whatever they found there, even if the owner had attached a note to it asking that it be spared.

Edith did not cook for Hank in that kitchen. When she cooked for him, and she liked to do that often, she did it in her own apartment, in a tiny stifling kitchen that was little more than an alcove never meant to hold the refrigerator and stove, which faced each other and could not be opened at the same time. Her apartment itself was narrow, a room on one side of a house belonging to a tense young lawyer and his tenser young wife and their two loud sons who seemed oblivious to that quality which permeated their parents' lives. Neither the lawyer nor his wife had ever told Edith she could not keep a man overnight. But she knew she could not. She knew this because they did not drink or smoke or laugh very much either, and because of the perturbed lust in the lawyer's eyes when he glanced at her. So she and Hank made love on the couch that unfolded and became a narrow bed, and then he went home. He didn't want to spend the night anyway, except on some nights when he was drunk. Since he was a young writer in a graduate school whose only demand was that he write, and write well, he was often drunk, either because he had written well that day or had not. But he was rarely so drunk that he wanted to stay the night at Edith's. And, when he did, it wasn't because liquor had released in him some need he wouldn't ordinarily yield to; it was because he didn't want to drive home. Always, though, she got him out of the house; and always he was glad next morning that she had.

He had little money, only what an assistantship gave him, and he didn't like her to pay for their evenings out, so when they saw each other at night it was most often at her apartment. Usually before he came she would shower and put on a dress or skirt. He teased her about that but she knew he liked it. So did she. She liked being dressed and smelling of perfume and brushing her long black hair before the mirror, and she liked the look in his eyes and the way his voice heightened and belied his teasing. She put on records and they had drinks and told each other what they had done that day. She was pretending to be in her first year of graduate school, in American history, so she could be near Hank; she attended classes, even read the books and wrote the papers, even did rather well; but she was pretending. They drank for a while, then she stood between the hot stove and the refrigerator and cooked while he stood at the entrance of the alcove, and they talked. They ate at a small table against the wall of the living room; the only other room was the bathroom. After dinner she washed the dishes, put away leftovers in foil, and they unfolded the couch and made love and lay talking until they were ready to make love again. It all felt like marriage. Even at twenty-seven, looking back on those nights after five years of marriage, she still saw in them what marriage could often be: talk and dinner and, the child asleep, living-room lovemaking long before the eleven o'clock news which had become their electronic foreplay, the weather report the final signal to climb the stairs together and undress.

On those nights in the apartment they spoke of marriage. And he explained why, even on the nights of Iowa winter when his moustache froze as he walked from her door around the lawyer's house and down the slippery driveway to his car, he did not want to spend the night with her. It was a matter of ritual, he told her. It had to do with his work. He did not want to wake up with someone (he said *someone*, not *you*) and then drive home to his own room where he would start the morning's work. What he liked to do, he said (already she could see he sometimes confused like to with have to) was spend his first wakeful time of the day alone. In his room, each working morning, he first made his bed and cleared his desk of mail and books, then while he made his coffee and cooked bacon and eggs on the hot plate he read the morning paper; he read through the meal and afterward while he drank coffee and smoked. By the time he had finished the paper and washed the dishes in the bathroom he had been awake for an hour and a half. Then, with the reluctance which began as he reached the final pages of the newspaper, he sat at his desk and started to work.

He spoke so seriously, almost reverently, about making a bed, eating some eggs, and reading a newspaper, that at first Edith was amused; but she stifled it and asked him what was happening during that hour and a half of quiet morning. He said, That's it: quiet: silence. While his body woke he absorbed silence. His work was elusive and difficult and had to be stalked; a phone call or an early visitor could flush it. She said, What about after we're married? He smiled and his arm tightened her against him. He told her of a roommate he had, when he was an undergraduate. The roommate was talkative. He woke up talking and went to bed talking. Most of the talk was good, a lot of it purposely funny, and Hank enjoyed it. Except at breakfast. The roommate liked to share the newspaper with Hank and talk about what they were reading. Hank was writing a novel then; he finished it in his senior year, read it at home that summer in Phoenix, and, with little ceremony or despair, burned it. But he was writing it then, living with the roommate, and after a few weeks of spending an hour and a half cooking, reading, and talking and then another hour in silence at his desk before he could put the first word on paper, he started waking at six o'clock so that his roommate woke at eight to an apartment that smelled of bacon and, walking past Hank's closed door, he entered the kitchen where Hank's plate and fork were in the drainer, the clean skillet on the stove, coffee in the pot, and the newspaper waiting on the table.

So in her ninth month she began worrying about Hank. What had first drawn her to him was his body: in high school he had played football; he was both too light and too serious to play in college; he was short, compact, and hard, and she liked his poised, graceful walk; with yielding hands she liked touching his shoulders and arms. When he told her he ran five miles every day she was pleased. Later, not long before they were lovers, she realized that what she loved about him was his vibrance, intensity; it was not that he was a writer; she had read little and indiscriminately and he would have to teach her those things about his work that she must know. She loved him because he had found his center, and it was that center she began worrying about in her ninth month. For how could a man who didn't want to spend a night with his lover be expected to move into a house with a woman, and then a baby? She watched him.

When he finished the novel, Sharon was two and they were buying a house in Bradford, Massachusetts, where he taught and where Edith believed she could live forever. Boston was forty minutes to the south, and she liked it better than Chicago; the New Hampshire beaches were twenty minutes away; she had been land-locked for twenty-four years and nearly every summer day she took Sharon to the beach while Hank wrote; on sunny days when she let herself get trapped into errands or other trifles that posed as commitments, she felt she had wronged herself; but there were not many of those days. She loved autumn—she and Hank and Sharon drove into New Hampshire and Vermont to look at gold and red and yellow leaves—and she loved winter too—it wasn't as cold and windy as the Midwest—and she loved the evergreens and snow on the hills; and all winter she longed for the sea, and some days she bundled up Sharon and drove to it and looked at it from the warmth of the car. Then they got out and walked on the beach until Sharon was cold.

Hank was happy about his novel; he sent it to an agent who was happy about it too; but no one else was and, fourteen months later, with more ceremony this time (a page at a time, in the fireplace, three hundred and forty-eight of them) and much more despair, he burned it. That night he drank a lot but was still sober; or sad enough so that all the bourbon did was make him sadder; in bed he held her but he was not really holding her; he lay on his side, his arms around her; but it was she who was holding him. She wanted to make love with him, wanted that to help him, but she knew it would not and he could not. Since sending his novel to the agent he had written three stories; they existed in the mail and on the desks of editors of literary magazines and then in the mail again. And he had been thinking of a novel. He was twenty-six years old. He had been writing for eight years. And that night, lying against her, he told her the eight years were gone forever and had come to nothing. His wide hard body was rigid in her arms; she thought if he could not make love he ought to cry, break that tautness in his body, his soul. But she knew he could not. All those years meant to him, he said, was the thousands of pages, surely over three, maybe over four, he had written: all those drafts, each one draining him only to be stacked in a box or filing cabinet as another draft took its place: all those pages to get the two final drafts of the two novels that had gone into ashes, into the air. He lived now in a total of fifty-eight typed pages, the three stories that lived in trains and on the desks of men he didn't know.

'Start tomorrow,' she said. 'On the new novel.'

For a few moments he was quiet. Then he said: 'I can't. It's three in the morning. I've been drinking for eight hours.'

'Just a page. Or else tomorrow will be terrible. And the day after tomorrow will be worse. You can sleep late, sleep off the booze. I'll take Sharon to the beach, and when I come home you tell me you've written and run with Jack and you feel strong again.'

At the beach next day she knew he was writing and she felt good about that; she knew that last night he had known it was what he had to do; she also knew he needed her to tell him to do it. But she felt defeated too. Last night, although she had fought it, her knowledge of defeat had begun as she held him and felt that tautness which would yield to neither passion nor grief, and she had known it was his insular will that would get him going again, and would deny her a child.

When he finished the novel fourteen months ago she had started waiting for that time—she knew it would be a moment, an hour, a day, no more: perhaps only a moment of his happy assent—when she could conceive. For by this time, though he had never said it, she knew he didn't want another child. And she knew it was not because of anything as practical and as easily solved as money. It was because of the very force in him which had first attracted her, so that after two years of marriage she could think wryly: one thing has to be said about men who've found their center: they're sometimes selfish bastards. She knew he didn't want another child because he believed a baby would interfere with his work. And his believing it would probably make it true.

She knew he was being shortsighted, foolish, and selfish; she knew that, except for the day of birth itself and perhaps a day after, until her mother arrived to care for Sharon, a baby would not prevent, damage, or even interrupt one sentence of all those pages he had to write and she was happy that he wrote and glad to listen to on those nights when he had to read them too; those pages she also resented at times, when after burning three hundred and forty-eight of them he lay in despair and the beginnings of resilience against her body she had given him more than three hundred and forty-eight times, maybe given him a thousand times, and told her all the eight years meant to him were those pages. And she resented them when she knew they would keep her from having a second child; she wanted a son; and it would do no good, she knew, to assure him that he would not lose sleep, that she would get up with the baby in the night.

Because that really wasn't why he didn't want a baby; he probably thought it was; but it wasn't. So if she told him how simple it would be, he still wouldn't want to do it. Because, whether he knew it or not, he was keeping himself in reserve. He had the life he wanted: his teaching schedule gave him free mornings; he had to prepare for classes but he taught novels he knew well and could skim; he had summers off, he had a friend, Jack Linhart, to talk, drink, and run with; he had a woman and a child he loved, and all he wanted now was to write better than he'd ever written before, and it was that he saved himself for. They had never talked about any of this, but she knew it all. She almost felt the same way about her life; but she wanted a son. So she had waited for him to sell his novel, knowing that would be for him a time of exuberance and power, a time out of the fearful drudgery and isolation of his work, and in that spirit he would give her a child. Now she had to wait again.

In the winter and into the spring when snow melted first around the trunks of trees, and the ice on the Merrimack broke into chunks that floated seaward, and the river climbed and rushed, there was a girl. She came uninvited in Christmas season to a party that Edith spent a day preparing; her escort was uninvited too, a law student, a boring one, who came with a married couple who were invited. Later Edith would think of him: if he had to crash the party he should at least have been man enough to keep the girl he crashed with. Her name was Jeanne, she was from France, she was visiting friends in Boston. That was all she was doing: visiting. Edith did not know what part of France she was from nor what she did when she was there. Probably Jeanne told her that night while they stood for perhaps a quarter of an hour in the middle of the room and voices, sipping their drinks, nodding at each other, talking the way two very attractive women will talk at a party: Edith speaking and even answering while her real focus was on Jeanne's short black hair, her sensuous, indolent lips, her brown and mischievous eyes. Edith had talked with the law student long enough—less than a quarter of an hour—to know he wasn't Jeanne's lover and couldn't be; his confidence was still young, wistful, and vulnerable; and there was an impatience, a demand, about the amatory currents she felt flowing from Jeanne. She remarked all of this and recalled nothing they talked about. They parted like two friendly but competing hunters after meeting in the woods. For the rest of the night—while talking, while dancing—Edith watched the law student and the husbands lining up at the trough of Jeanne's accent, and she watched Jeanne's eyes, which appeared vacant until you looked closely at them and saw that they were selfish: Jeanne was watching herself.

And Edith watched Hank, and listened to him. Early in their marriage she had learned to do that. His intimacy with her was private; at their table and in their bed they talked; his intimacy with men was public, and when he was with them he spoke mostly to them, looked mostly at them, and she knew there were times when he was unaware that she or any other woman was in the room. She had long ago stopped resenting this; she had watched the other wives sitting together and talking to one another; she had watched them sit listening while couples were at a dinner table and the women couldn't group so they ate and listened to the men. Usually men who talked to women were trying to make love with them, and she could sense the other men's resentment at this distraction, as if during a hand of poker a man had left the table to phone his mistress. Of course she was able to talk at parties; she wasn't shy and no man had ever intentionally made her feel he was not interested in what she had to say; but willy-nilly they patronized her. As they listened to her she could sense their courtesy, their impatience for her to finish so they could speak again to their comrades. If she had simply given in to that patronizing, stopped talking because she was a woman, she might have become bitter. But she went further: she watched the men, and saw that it wasn't a matter of their not being interested in women. They weren't interested in each other either. At least not in what they said, their ideas; the ideas and witticisms were instead the equipment of friendly, even loving, competition, as for men with different interests were the bowling ball, the putter, the tennis racket. But it went deeper than that too: she finally saw that. Hank needed and loved men, and when he loved them it was because of what they thought and how they lived. He did not measure women that way; he measured them by their sexuality and good sense. He and his friends talked with one another because it was the only way they could show their love; they might reach out and take a woman's hand and stroke it while they leaned forward, talking to men; and their conversations were fields of mutual praise. It no longer bothered her. She knew that some women writhed under these conversations; they were usually women whose husbands rarely spoke to them with the intensity and attention they gave to men.

But that night, listening to Hank, she was frightened and angry. He and Jeanne were watching each other. He talked to the men but he was really talking to her; at first Edith thought he was showing off; but it was worse, more fearful: he was being received and he knew it and that is what gave his voice its exuberant lilt. His eyes met Jeanne's over a shoulder, over the rim of a lifted glass. When Jeanne left with the law student and the invited couple, Edith and Hank told them goodbye at the door. It was only the second time that night Edith and Jeanne had looked at each other and spoken; they smiled and voiced amenities; a drunken husband lurched into the group; his arm groped for Jeanne's waist and his head plunged downward to kiss her. She quickly cocked her head away, caught the kiss lightly on her cheek, almost dodged it completely. For an instant her eyes were impatient. Then that was gone. Tilted away from the husband's muttering face she was looking at Hank. In her eyes Edith saw his passion. She reached out and put an arm about his waist; without looking at him or Jeanne she said goodnight to the law student and the couple. As the four of them went down the walk, shrugging against the cold, she could not look at Jeanne's back and hair; she watched the law student and wished him the disaster of bad grades. Be a bank teller, you bastard.

She did not see Jeanne again. In the flesh, that is. For now she saw her in dreams: not those of sleep which she could forget but her waking dreams. In the mornings Hank went to his office at school to write; at noon he and Jack ran and then ate lunch; he taught all afternoon and then went to the health club for a sauna with Jack and afterward they stopped for a drink; at seven he came home. On Tuesdays and Thursdays he didn't have classes but he spent the afternoon at school in conferences with students; on Saturday mornings he wrote in his office and, because he was free of students that day, he often worked into the middle of the afternoon then called Jack to say he was ready for the run, the sauna, the drinks. For the first time in her marriage Edith thought about how long and how often he was away from home. As she helped Sharon with her boots she saw Jeanne's brown eyes; they were attacking her; they were laughing at her; they sledded down the hill with her and Sharon.

When she became certain that Hank was Jeanne's lover she could not trust her certainty. In the enclosed days of winter she imagined too much. Like a spy, she looked for only one thing, and she could not tell if the wariness in his eyes and voice were truly there; making love with him she felt a distance in his touch, another concern in his heart; passionately she threw herself against that distance and wondered all the time if it existed only in her own quiet and fearful heart. Several times, after drinks at a party, she nearly asked Jack if Hank was always at school when he said he was. At home on Tuesday and Thursday and Saturday afternoons she wanted to call him. One Thursday she did. He didn't answer his office phone; it was a small school and the switchboard operator said if she saw him she'd tell him to call home. Edith was telling Sharon to get her coat, they would go to school to see Daddy, when he phoned. She asked him if he wanted to see a movie that night. He said they had seen everything playing in town and if she wanted to go to Boston he'd rather wait until the weekend. She said that was fine.

In April he and Jack talked about baseball and watched it on television and he started smoking Parliaments. She asked him why. They were milder, he said. He looked directly at her but she sensed he was forcing himself to, testing himself. For months she had imagined his infidelity and fought her imagination with the absence of evidence. Now she had that: she knew it was irrational but it was just rational enough to release the demons: they absorbed her: they gave her certainty. She remembered Jeanne holding a Parliament, waiting for one of the husbands to light it. She lasted three days. On a Thursday afternoon she called the school every hour, feeling the vulnerability of this final prideless crumbling, making her voice as casual as possible to the switchboard operator, even saying once it was nothing important, just something she wanted him to pick up on the way home, and when he got home at seven carrying a damp towel and smelling faintly of gin she knew he had got back in time for the sauna with Jack and had spent the afternoon in Jeanne's bed. She waited until after dinner, when Sharon was in bed. He sat at the kitchen table, talking to her while she cleaned the kitchen. It was a ritual of theirs. She asked him for a drink. Usually she didn't drink after dinner, and he was surprised. Then he said he'd join her. He gave her the bourbon then sat at the table again.

'Are you having an affair with that phony French bitch?'

He sipped his drink, looked at her, and said: 'Yes.'

The talk lasted for days. That night it ended at three in the morning after, straddling him, she made love with him and fell into a sleep whose every moment, next morning, she believed she remembered. She had slept four hours. When she woke to the news on the radio she felt she had not slept at all, that her mind had continued the talk with sleeping Hank. She did not want to get up. In bed she smoked while Hank showered and shaved. At breakfast he did not read the paper. He spoke to Sharon and watched Edith. She did not eat. When he was ready to leave, he leaned down and kissed her and said he loved her and they would talk again that night.

All day she knew what madness was, or she believed she was at least tasting it and at times she yearned for the entire feast. While she did her work and made lunch for Sharon and talked to her and put her to bed with a coloring book and tried to read the newspaper and then a magazine, she could not stop the voices in her mind: some of it repeated from last night, some drawn up from what she believed she had heard and spoken in her sleep, some in anticipation of tonight, living tonight before it was there, so that at two in the afternoon she was already at midnight and time was nothing but how much pain she could feel at once. When Sharon had been in bed for an hour without sleeping Edith took her for a walk and tried to listen to her and said yes and no and I don't know, what do you think? and even heard most of what Sharon said and all the time the voices would not stop. All last night while awake and sleeping and all day she had believed it was because Jeanne was pretty and Hank was a man. Like any cliché, it was easy to live with until she tried to; now she began to realize how little she knew about Hank and how much she suspected and feared, and that night after dinner which she mostly drank she tucked in Sharon and came down to the kitchen and began asking questions. He told her he would stop seeing Jeanne and there was nothing more to talk about; he spoke of privacy. But she had to know everything he felt; she persisted, she harried, and finally he told her she'd better be as tough as her questions were, because she was going to get the answers.

Which were: he did not believe in monogamy. Fidelity, she said. You see? he said. You distort it. He was a faithful husband. He had been discreet, kept his affair secret, had not risked her losing face. He loved her and had taken nothing from her. She accused him of having a double standard and he said no; no, she was as free as she was before she met him. She asked him how long he had felt this way, had he always been like this or was it just some French bullshit he had picked up this winter. He had always felt this way. By now she could not weep. Nor rage either. All she could feel and say was: Why didn't I ever know any of this? You never asked, he said.

It was, she thought, like something bitter from Mother Goose: the woman made the child, the child made the roof, the roof made the woman, and the child went away. Always she had done her housework quickly and easily; by ten-thirty on most mornings she had done what had to be done. She was not one of those women whose domesticity became an obsession; it was work that she neither liked nor disliked and, when other women complained, she was puzzled and amused and secretly believed their frustration had little to do with scraping plates or pushing a vacuum cleaner over a rug. Now in April and May an act of will got her out of bed in the morning. The air in the house was against her: it seemed wet and grey and heavy, heavier than fog, and she pushed through it to the bathroom where she sat staring at the floor or shower curtain long after she was done; then she moved to the kitchen and as she prepared breakfast the air pushed down on her arms and against her body. *I am beating eggs*, she said to herself, and she looked down at the fork in her hand, yolk dripping from the tines into the eggs as their swirling ceased and they lay still in the bowl. *I am beating eggs.* Then she jabbed the fork in again. At breakfast Hank read the paper. Edith talked to Sharon and ate because she had to, because it was morning, it was time to eat, and she glanced at Hank's face over the newspaper, listened to the crunching of his teeth on toast, and told herself: *I am talking to Sharon.* She kept her voice sweet, motherly, attentive.

Then breakfast was over and she was again struck by the seductive waves of paralysis that had washed over her in bed, and she stayed at the table. Hank kissed her (she turned her lips to him, they met his, she did not kiss him) and went to the college. She read the paper and drank coffee and smoked while Sharon played with toast. She felt she would fall asleep at the table; Hank would return in the afternoon to find her sleeping there among the plates and cups and glasses while Sharon played alone in a ditch somewhere down the road. So once again she rose through an act of will, watched Sharon brushing her teeth (*I am watching. . .*), sent her to the cartoons on television, and then slowly, longing for sleep, she washed the skillet and saucepan (*always scramble eggs in a saucepan,* her mother had told her; *they stand deeper than in a skillet and they'll cook softer*) and scraped the plates and put them and the glasses and cups and silverware in the dishwasher.

Then she carried the vacuum cleaner upstairs and made the bed Hank had left after she had, and as she leaned over to tuck in the sheet she wanted to give in to the lean, to collapse in slow motion face down on the half-made bed and lie there until—there had been times in her life when she had wanted to sleep until something ended. Unmarried in Iowa, when she missed her period she wanted to sleep until she knew whether she was or not. Now *until* meant nothing. No matter how often or how long she slept she would wake to the same house, the same heavy air that worked against her every move. She made Sharon's bed and started the vacuum cleaner. Always she had done that quickly, not well enough for her mother's eye, but her mother was a Windex housekeeper: a house was not done unless the windows were so clean you couldn't tell whether they were open or closed; but her mother had a cleaning woman. The vacuum cleaner interfered with the cartoons and Sharon came up to tell her and Edith said she wouldn't be long and told Sharon to put on her bathing suit—it was a nice day and they would go to the beach. But the cleaning took her longer than it had before, when she had moved quickly from room to room, without lethargy or boredom but a sense of anticipation, the way she felt when she did other work which required neither skill nor concentration, like chopping onions and grating cheese for a meal she truly wanted to cook.

Now, while Sharon went downstairs again and made lemonade and poured it in the thermos and came upstairs and went down again and came up and said yes there was a little mess and went downstairs and wiped it up, Edith pushed the vacuum cleaner and herself through the rooms and down the hall, and went downstairs and started in the living room while Sharon's voice tugged at her as strongly as hands gripping her clothes, and she clamped her teeth on the sudden shrieks that rose in her throat and told herself: *Don't: she's not the problem*; and she thought of the women in supermarkets and on the street, dragging and herding and all but cursing their children along (one day she had seen a woman kick her small son's rump as she pulled him into a drugstore), and she thought of the women at parties, at dinners, or on blankets at the beach while they watched their children in the waves, saying: *I'm so damned bored with talking to children all day—no*, she told herself, *she's not the problem*. Finally she finished her work, yet she felt none of the relief she had felt before; the air in the house was like water now as she moved through it up the stairs to the bedroom, where she undressed and put on her bathing suit. Taking Sharon's hand and the windbreakers and thermos and blanket, she left the house and blinked in the late morning sun and wondered near-prayerfully when this would end, this dread disconnection between herself and what she was doing. At night making love with Hank she thought of him with Jeanne, and her heart, which she thought was beyond breaking, broke again, quickly, easily, as if there weren't much to break any more, and fell into mute and dreary anger, the dead end of love's grief.

In the long sunlit evenings and the nights of May the talk was sometimes philosophical, sometimes dark and painful, drawing from him details about him and Jeanne; she believed if she possessed the details she would dispossess Jeanne of Hank's love. But she knew that wasn't her only reason. Obsessed by her pain, she had to plunge more deeply into it, feel all of it again and again. But most of the talk was abstract, and most of it was by Hank. When she spoke of divorce he calmly told her they had a loving, intimate marriage. They were, he said, simply experiencing an honest and healthful breakthrough. She listened to him talk about the unnatural boundaries of lifelong monogamy. He remained always calm. Cold, she thought. She could no longer find his heart.

At times she hated him. Watching him talk she saw his life: with his work he created his own harmony, and then he used the people he loved to relax with. Probably it was not exploitative; probably it was the best he could do. And it was harmony she had lost. Until now her marriage had been a circle, like its gold symbol on her finger. Wherever she went she was still inside it. It had a safe, gentle circumference, and mortality and the other perils lay outside of it. Often now while Hank slept she lay awake and tried to pray. She wanted to fall in love with God. She wanted His fingers to touch her days, to restore meaning to those simple tasks which now drained her spirit. On those nights when she tried to pray she longed to leave the world: her actions would appear secular but they would be her communion with God. Cleaning the house would be an act of forgiveness and patience under His warm eyes. But she knew it was no use: she had belief, but not faith: she could not bring God under her roof and into her life. He awaited her death.

Nightly and fearfully now, as though Hank's adulterous heart had opened a breach and let it in to stalk her, she thought of death. One night they went with Jack and Terry Linhart to Boston to hear Judy Collins. The concert hall was filled and darkened and she sat in the sensate, audible silence of listening people and watched Judy under the spotlight in a long lavender gown, her hair falling over one shoulder as she lowered her face over the guitar. Soon Edith could not hear the words of the songs. Sadly she gazed at Judy's face, and listened to the voice, and thought of the voice going out to the ears of all those people, all those strangers, and she thought how ephemeral was a human voice, and how death not only absorbed the words in the air, but absorbed as well the act of making the words, and the time it took to say them. She saw Judy as a small bird singing on a wire, and above her the hawk circled. She remembered reading once of an old man who had been working for twenty-five years sculpting, out of a granite mountain in South Dakota, a 563-foot-high statue of Chief Crazy Horse. She thought of Hank and the novel he was writing now, and as she sat beside him her soul withered away from him and she hoped he would fail, she hoped he would burn this one too: she saw herself helping him, placing alternate pages in the fire. Staring at the face above the lavender gown she strained to receive the words and notes into her body.

She had never lied to Hank and now everything was a lie. Beneath the cooking of a roast, the still affectionate chatting at dinner, the touch of their flesh, was the fact of her afternoons ten miles away in a New Hampshire woods where, on a blanket among shading pines and hemlocks, she lay in sin-quickened heat with Jack Linhart. Her days were delightfully strange, she thought. Hank's betrayal had removed her from the actions that were her life; she had performed them like a weary and disheartened dancer. Now, glancing at Hank reading, she took clothes from the laundry basket at her feet and folded them on the couch, and the folding of a warm towel was a manifestation of her deceit. And, watching him across the room, she felt her separation from him taking shape, filling the space between them like a stone. Within herself she stroked and treasured her lover. She knew she was doing the same to the self she had lost in April.

There was a price to pay. When there had been nothing to lie about in their marriage and she had not lied, she had always felt nestled with Hank; but with everyone else, even her closest friends, she had been aware of that core of her being that no one knew. Now she felt that with Hank. With Jack she recognized yet leaped into their passionate lie: they were rarely together more than twice a week; apart, she longed for him, talked to him in her mind, and vengefully saw him behind her closed eyes as she moved beneath Hank. When she was with Jack their passion burned and distorted their focus. For two hours on the blanket they made love again and again, they made love too much, pushing their bodies to consume the yearning they had borne and to delay the yearning that was waiting. Sometimes under the trees she felt like tired meat. The quiet air which she had broken in the first hour with moans now absorbed only their heavy breath. At those moments she saw with detached clarity that they were both helpless, perhaps even foolish. Jack wanted to escape his marriage; she wanted to live with hers; they drove north to the woods and made love. Then they dressed and drove back to what had brought them there.

This was the first time in her life she had committed herself to sin, and there were times when she felt her secret was venomous. Lying beside Terry at the beach she felt more adulterous than when she lay with Jack, and she believed her sun-lulled conversation was somehow poisoning her friend. When she held Sharon, salty and cold-skinned from the sea, she felt her sin flowing with the warmth of her body into the small wet breast. But more often she was proud. She was able to sin and love at the same time. She was more attentive to Sharon than she had been in April. She did not have to struggle to listen to her, to talk to her. She felt cleansed. And looking at Terry's long red hair as she bent over a child, she felt both close to her yet distant. She did not believe women truly had friends among themselves; school friendships dissolved into marriages; married women thought they had friends until they got divorced and discovered other women were only wives drawn together by their husbands. As much as she and Terry were together, they were not really intimate; they instinctively watched each other. She was certain that Terry would do what she was doing. A few weeks ago she would not have known that. She was proud that she knew it now.

With Hank she loved her lie. She kept it like a fire: some

evenings after an afternoon with Jack she elaborately fanned it, looking into Hank's eyes and talking of places she had gone while the sitter stayed with Sharon; at other times she let it burn low, was evasive about how she had spent her day, and when the two couples were together she bantered with Jack, teased him. Once Jack left his pack of Luckies in her car and she brought them home and smoked them. Hank noticed but said nothing. When two cigarettes remained in the pack she put it on the coffee table and left it there. One night she purposely made a mistake: after dinner, while Hank watched a ball game on television, she drank gin while she cleaned the kitchen. She had drunk gin and tonic before dinner and wine with the flounder and now she put tonic in the gin, but not much. From the living room came the announcer's voice, and now and then Hank spoke. She hated his voice; she knew she did not hate him; if she did, she would be able to act, to leave him. She hated his voice tonight because he was talking to ballplayers on the, screen and because there was no pain in it while in the kitchen her own voice keened without sound and she worked slowly and finished her drink and mixed another, the gin now doing what she had wanted it to: dissolving all happiness, all peace, all hope for it with Hank and all memory of it with Jack, even the memory of that very afternoon under the trees. Gin-saddened, she felt beyond tears, at the bottom of some abyss where there was no emotion save the quivering knees and fluttering stomach and cold-shrouded heart that told her she was finished. She took the drink into the living room and stood at the door and watched him looking at the screen over his lifted can of beer. He glanced at her, then back at the screen. One hand fingered the pack of Luckies on the table, but he did not take one.

'I wish you hadn't stopped smoking,' she said. 'Sometimes I think you did it so you'd outlive me.'

He looked at her, told her with his eyes that she was drunk, and turned back to the game.

'I've been having an affair with Jack.' He looked at her, his eyes unchanged, perhaps a bit more interested; nothing more. His lips showed nothing, except that she thought they seemed ready to smile. 'We go up to the woods in New Hampshire in the afternoons. Usually twice a week. I like it. I started it. I went after him, at a party. I told him about Jeanne. I kept after him. I knew he was available because he's unhappy with Terry. For a while he was worried about you but I told him you wouldn't mind anyway. He's still your friend, if that worries you. Probably more yours than mine. You don't even look surprised. I suppose you'll tell me you've known it all the time.'

'It wasn't too hard to pick up.'

'So it really wasn't French bullshit. I used to want another child. A son. I wouldn't want to now: have a baby in this.'

'Come here.'

For a few moments, leaning against the doorjamb, she thought of going upstairs and packing her clothes and driving away. The impulse was rooted only in the blur of gin. She knew she would get no farther than the closet where her clothes hung. She walked to the couch and sat beside him. He put his arm around her; for a while she sat rigidly, then she closed her eyes and eased against him and rested her head on his shoulder.

In December after the summer which Hank called the summer of truth, when Edith's affair with Jack Linhart had both started and ended, Hank sold his novel. On a Saturday night they had a celebration party. It was a large party, and some of Hank's students came. His girl friend came with them. Edith had phoned Peter at the radio station Friday and invited him, had assured him it was all right, but he had said he was an old-fashioned guilt-ridden adulterer, and could not handle it. She told him she would see him Sunday afternoon.

The girl friend was nineteen years old and her name was Debbie. She was taller than Edith, she wore suede boots, and she had long blonde hair. She believed she was a secret from everyone but Edith. At the party she drank carefully (only wine), was discreet with Hank, and spent much time talking with Edith, who watched the face that seemed never to have borne pain, and thought: These Goddamn young girls don't care what they do any more. Hank had said she was a good student. Edith assumed that meant the girl agreed with what he said and told it back to him in different words. What else could come out of a face so untouched? Bland and evil at the same time. Debbie was able to believe it when Hank told her Edith was not jealous. Sometimes Debbie stayed with Sharon while Hank and Edith went out. Hank drove her back to the dormitory; on those nights, by some rule of his own, he did not make love with Debbie. A bit drunk, standing in the kitchen with the girl, Edith glanced at her large breasts stretching the burgundy sweater. How ripe she must be, this young piece. Her nipples thrust against the cashmere. They made love in the car. Hank could not afford motels like Peter could. When Edith was in the car she felt she was in their bed. She looked at the breasts.

'I always wanted big ones,' she murmured.

The girl blushed and took a cigarette from her purse.

'Hank hasn't started smoking again,' Edith said. 'It's amazing.'

'I didn't know he ever did.'

'Until last summer. He wants to live a long time. He wants to publish ten books.'

Edith studied the girl's eyes. They were brown, and showed nothing. A student. Couldn't she understand what she was hearing? That she had come without history into not history, that in a year or more or less she would be gone with her little heart broken or, more than likely, her cold little heart intact, her eyes and lips intact, having given nothing and received less: a memory for Hank to smile over in a moment of a spring afternoon. But then Edith looked away from the eyes. None of this mattered to the girl. Not the parentheses of time, not that blank space between them that one had to fill. It was Edith who would lose. Perhaps the next generation of students would be named Betty or Mary Ann. Well into his forties Hank would be attractive to them. Each year he would pluck what he needed. Salaried and tenured adultery. She would watch them come into her home like ghosts of each other. Sharon would like their attention, as she did now. Edith was twenty-seven. She had ten more years, perhaps thirteen; fifteen. Her looks would be gone. The girls would come with their loose breasts under her roof, and brassiered she would watch them, talk with them. It would not matter to Hank where they had come from and where they were going. He would write books.

She could not read it: the one he sold, the one she had urged him that summer night to begin next day, helping him give birth to it while she gave up a son. When he finished it a month ago and sent it to the agent he gave her the carbon and left her alone with it; it was a Saturday and he went to Jack's to watch football. She tried all afternoon. He needed her to like it; she knew that. He only pretended to care about what she thought of other books or movies. But handing her the manuscript he had boyishly lowered his eyes, and then left. He left because he could not be in the house with her while she read it. When she had read the other one, the one he burned, he had paced about the house and lawn and returned often to watch her face, to see what his work was doing to it. This time he knew better. All of that was in his eyes and voice when he said with such vulnerability that for a moment she wanted to hold him with infinite forgiveness: 'I think I'll go to Jack's and watch the game.'

She tried to recall that vulnerability as she read. But she could not. His prose was objective, concrete, precise. The voice of the book was the voice of the man who last spring and summer had spoken of monogamy, absolved and encouraged her adultery, and in the fall announced that he was having an affair with Debbie. Through the early chapters she was angry. She pushed herself on. Mostly she skimmed. Then she grew sad: this was the way she had wanted it when she first loved him: he would bring her his work and he would need her praise and before anyone else read it the work would be consummated between them. Now she could not read it through the glaze of pain that covered the pages. She skimmed, and when he returned in the evening she greeted him with an awed and tender voice, with brightened eyes; she held him tightly and told him it was a wonderful novel and she thought of how far she had come with this man, how frequent and convincing were her performances.

He wanted to talk about it; he was relieved and joyful; he wanted to hear everything she felt. That was easy enough: they talked for two hours while she cooked and they ate; he would believe afterward that she had talked to him about his book; she had not. Recalling what she skimmed she mentioned a scene or passage, let him interrupt her, and then let him talk about it. Now it would be published, and he would write another. Looking at Debbie she wondered if Peter would leave his wife and marry her. She had not thought of that before; and now, with images in her mind of herself and Peter and Sharon driving away, she knew too clearly what she had known from the beginning: that she did not love Peter Jackman. All adultery is a symptom, she thought. She watched Debbie, who was talking about Hank's novel; she had read it after Edith. Hank brought to his adultery the protocol of a professional. Who *was* this girl? What was she *doing*? Did she put herself to sleep in the dormitory with visions of herself and Hank driving away? In her eyes Edith found nothing; she could have been peering through the windows of a darkened cellar.

'I'm going to circulate,' she said.

In the living room she found Jack, and took his hand. Looking at his eyes she saw their summer and his longing and she touched his cheek and beard and recalled the sun over his shoulder and her hot closed eyes. He did not love Terry but he could not hurt her, nor leave his children, and he was faithful now, he drank too much, and often he talked long and with embittered anger about things of no importance.

'I hope there was *some*thing good,' she said. 'In last summer.'

'There was.' He pressed her hand.

'Doesn't Hank's girl look pretty tonight?' she said.

'I hate the little bitch.'

'So do I.'

Once in Iowa, while Edith was washing clothes at a launder-
ette, a dreary place of graduate students reading, Mann juxta-
posed with Tide, and stout wives with curlers in their hair, a
place she gladly abandoned when she married Hank and
moved into the house with her own washer and dryer, she
met a young wife who was from a city in the south. Her husband was a student and he worked nights as a motel clerk.
Because they found one for sixty dollars a month, they lived
in a farmhouse far from town, far from anyone. From her
window at night, across the flat and treeless land, she could
see the lights of her closest neighbor, a mile and a half away.
She had a small child, a daughter. She had never lived in the
country and the farmers liked to tell her frightening stories.
While she was getting mail from the box at the road they
stopped their tractors and talked to her, these large sunburned farmers who she said had grown to resemble the hogs
they raised. They told her of hogs eating drunks and children
who fell into the pens. And they told her a year ago during the
long bad winter a man had hanged himself in the barn of the
house she lived in; he had lived there alone, and he was buried in town.

So at night, while her husband was at the motel desk, the
woman was afraid. When she was ready for bed she forced
herself to turn off all the downstairs lights, though she wanted
to leave every light burning, sleep as if in bright afternoon;
then she climbed the stairs and turned out the hall light too,
for she was trying to train the child to sleep in the dark. Then
she would go to bed and, if she had read long enough, was
sleepy enough, she'd go to sleep soon; but always fear was
there and if she woke in the night—her bladder, a sound from
the child, a lone and rare car on the road in front of the house—
she lay terrified in the dark which spoke to her, touched her.
In those first wakeful moments she thought she was afraid of

the dark itself, that if she dispelled it with light her fear would subside. But she did not turn on the light. And as she lay there she found that within the darkness were spaces of safety. She was not afraid of her room. She lay there a while longer and thought of other rooms. She was not afraid of her child's room. Or the bathroom. Or the hall, the stairs, the living room. It was the kitchen. The shadowed corner between the refrigerator and the cupboard. She did not actually believe someone was crouched there. But it was that corner that she feared. She lay in bed seeing it more clearly than she could see her own darkened room. Then she rose from the bed and, in the dark, went downstairs to the kitchen and stood facing the dark corner, staring at it. She stared at it until she was not afraid; then she went upstairs and slept.

On other nights she was afraid of other places. Sometimes it was the attic, and she climbed the stairs into the stale air, past the dusty window, and stood in the center of the room among boxes and cardboard barrels and knew that a running mouse would send her shouting down the stairs and vowed that it would not. The basement was worse: it was cool and damp, its ceiling was low, and no matter where she stood there was always a space she couldn't see: behind the furnace in the middle of the floor, behind the columns supporting the ceiling. Worst of all was the barn: on some nights she woke and saw its interior, a dread place even in daylight, with its beams. She did not know which one he had used; she knew he had climbed out on one of them, tied the rope, put the noose around his neck, and jumped. On some nights she had to leave her bed and go out there. It was autumn then and she only had to put on her robe and shoes. Crossing the lawn, approaching the wide dark open door, she was not afraid she would see him: she was afraid that as she entered the barn she would look up at the beam he had used and she would know it was the beam he had used.

Driving home Sunday night Edith thought of the woman— she could not remember her name, only her story—caught as an adult in the fears of childhood: for it was not the hanged man's ghost she feared; she did not believe in ghosts. It was the dark. A certain dark place on a certain night. She had gone to the place and looked at what she feared. But there was something incomplete about the story, something Edith had not thought of until now: the woman had looked at the place where that night her fear took shape. But she had not discovered what she was afraid of.

In daylight while Hank and Sharon were sledding Edith had driven to the bar to meet Peter. They had gone to the motel while the December sun that stayed low and skirting was already down. When he drove her back to the bar she did not want to leave him and drive home in the night. She kissed him and held him tightly. She wanted to go in for a drink but she didn't ask, for she knew he was late now; he had to return to his wife. His marriage was falling slowly, like a feather. He thought his wife had a lover (she had had others), but they kept their affairs secret from each other. Or tried to. Or pretended to. Edith knew they were merely getting by with flimsy deception while they avoided the final confrontation. Edith had never met Norma, or seen her. In the motels Peter talked about her. She released him and got out of the car and crossed the parking lot in the dark.

She buckled her seatbelt and turned on the radio and cautiously joined the traffic on the highway. But it was not a wreck she was afraid of. The music was bad: repetitious rock from a station for teenagers. It was the only station she could get and she left it on. She had a thirty-minute drive and she did not know why, for the first time in her adult life, she was afraid of being alone in the dark. She had been afraid from the beginning: the first night she left Peter at a parking lot outside a bar and drove home; and now when Sharon was asleep and Hank was out she was afraid in the house and one night alone she heard the washing machine stop in the basement but she could not go down there and put the clothes in the dryer. Sometimes on grey afternoons she was frightened and she would go to the room where Sharon was and sit with her. Once when Sharon was at a birthday party she fell asleep in late afternoon and woke alone with dusk at the windows and fled through the house turning on lights and Peter's disc-jockey program and fire for the teakettle. Now she was driving on a lovely country road through woods and white hills shimmering under the moon. But she watched only the slick dark road. She thought of the beach and the long blue afternoons and evenings of summer. She thought of grilling three steaks in the back yard. She and Hank and Sharon would be sunburned, their bodies warm and smelling of the sea. They would eat at the picnic table in the seven o'clock sun.

She hoped Hank would be awake when she got home. He would look up from his book, his eyes amused and arrogant as they always were when she returned from her nights. She hoped he was awake. For if he was already asleep she would in silence ascend the stairs and undress in the dark and lie beside him unable to sleep and she would feel the house enclosing and caressing her with some fear she could not name.

## 3

Before Joe Ritchie was dying they lay together in the cool nights of spring and he talked. His virginal, long-stored and (he told her) near-atrophied passion leaped and quivered inside her; during the lulls he talked with the effusion of a man who had lived forty years without being intimate with a woman. Which was, he said, pretty much a case of having never been intimate with anyone at all. It was why he left the priesthood. Edith looked beyond the foot of the bed and above the chest of drawers at the silhouette of the hanging crucifix while he told her of what he called his failures, and the yearnings they caused.

He said he had never doubted. When he consecrated he knew that he held the body, the blood. He did not feel proud or particularly humble either; just awed. It was happening in his two lifted hands (and he lifted them above his large and naked chest in the dark), his two hands, of his body; yet at the same time it was not of his body. He knew some priests who doubted. Their eyes were troubled, sometimes furtive. They kept busy: some were athletic, and did that; some read a lot, and others were active in the parish: organized and supervised fairs, started discussion groups, youth groups, pre-Cana groups, married groups, counselled, made sick calls, jail calls, anything to keep them from themselves. Some entered the service, became chaplains. One of them was reported lost at sea. He had been flying with a navy pilot, from a carrier. The poor bastard, Joe said. You know what I think? He wanted to be with that pilot, so he could be around certainty. Watch the man and the machine. A chaplain in an airplane. When I got the word I thought: That's it: in the destructive element immerse, you poor bastard.

Joe had loved the Eucharist since he was a boy; it was why he became a priest. Some went to the seminary to be pastors and bishops; they didn't know it, but it was why they went, and in the seminary they were like young officers. Some, he said, went to pad and shelter their neuroses—or give direction to them. They had a joke then, the young students with their fresh and hopeful faces: behind every Irish priest there's an Irish mother wringing her hands. But most became priests because they wanted to live their lives with God; they had, as the phrase went, a vocation. There were only two vocations, the church taught: the religious life or marriage. Tell that to Hank, she said; he'd sneer at one and laugh at the other. Which would he sneer at? Joe said. I don't really know, she said.

It was a difficult vocation because it demanded a marriage of sorts with a God who showed himself only through the volition, action, imagination, and the resultant faith of the priest himself; when he failed to create and complete his union with God he was thrust back upon himself and his loneliness. For a long time the Eucharist worked for Joe. It was the high point of his day, when he consecrated and ate and drank. The trouble was it happened early in the morning. He rose and said mass and the day was over, but it was only beginning. That was what he realized or admitted in his mid-thirties: that the morning consecration completed him but it didn't last; there was no other act during the day that gave him that completion, made him feel an action of his performed in time and mortality had transcended both and been received by a God who knew his name.

Of course while performing the tasks of a parish priest he gained the sense of accomplishment which even a conscripted soldier could feel at the end of a chore. Sometimes the reward was simply that the job was over: that he had smiled and chatted through two and a half hours of bingo without displaying his weariness that bordered on panic. But with another duty came a reward that was insidious: he knew that he was a good speaker, that his sermons were better than those of the pastor and the two younger priests. One of the younger priests should have been excused altogether from speaking to gathered people. He lacked intelligence, imagination, and style; with sweaty brow he spoke stiffly of old and superfluous truths he had learned as a student. When he was done, he left the pulpit and with great relief and concentration worked through the ritual, toward the moment when he would raise the host. When he did this, and looked up at the Eucharist in his hands, his face was no longer that of the misfit in the pulpit; his jaw was solemn, his eyes firm. Joe pitied him for his lack of talent, for his anxiety each Sunday, for his awareness of each blank face, each shifting body in the church, and his knowledge that what he said was ineffectual and dull.

Yet he also envied the young priest. In the pulpit Joe loved the sound of his own voice: the graceful flow of his words, his imagery, his timing, and the tenor reaches of his passion; his eyes engaged and swept and recorded for his delight the upturned and attentive faces. At the end of his homily he descended from the pulpit, his head lowered, his face set in the seriousness of a man who has just perceived truth. His pose continued as he faced the congregation for the Credo and the prayers of petition; it continued as he ascended the three steps to the altar and began the offertory and prepared to consecrate. In his struggle to rid himself of the pose, he assumed another: he acted like a priest who was about to hold the body of Christ in his hands, while all the time, even as he raised the host and then the chalice, his heart swelled and beat with love for himself. On the other six days, at the sparsely attended week-day masses without sermons, he broke the silence of the early mornings only with prayers, and unaware of the daily communicants, the same people usually, most of them old women who smelled of sleep and cleanliness and time, he was absorbed by the ritual, the ritual became him, and in the privacy of his soul he ate the body and drank the blood; he ascended; and then his day was over.

The remaining hours were dutiful, and he accepted them with a commitment that nearly always lacked emotion. After a few years he began to yearn; for months, perhaps a year or more, he did not know what he yearned for. Perhaps he was afraid to know. At night he drank more; sometimes the gin curbed his longings that still he wouldn't name; but usually, with drinking, he grew sad. He did not get drunk, so in the morning he woke without hangover or lapse of memory, and recalling last night's gloom he wondered at its source, as though he were trying to understand not himself but a close friend. One night he did drink too much, alone, the pastor and the two younger priests long asleep, Joe going down the hall to the kitchen with less and less caution, the cracking sound of the ice tray in his hands nothing compared to the sound that only he could hear: his monologue with himself; and it was so intense that he felt anyone who passed the kitchen door would hear the voice that resounded in his skull. In the morning he did not recall what he talked about while he drank. He woke dehydrated and remorseful, his mind so dissipated that he had to talk himself through each step of his preparation for the day, for if he didn't focus carefully on buttoning his shirt, tying his shoes, brushing his teeth, he might fall again into the shards of last night. His sleep had been heavy and drunken, his dreams anxious. He was thankful that he could not recall them. He wished he could not recall what he did as he got into bed: lying on his side he had hugged a pillow to his breast, and holding it in both arms had left consciousness saying to himself, to the pillow, to God, and perhaps aloud: I must have a woman. Leaving the rectory, crossing the lawn to the church in the cool morning, where he would say mass not for the old ladies but for himself, he vowed that he would not get drunk again.

It was not his holding the pillow that frightened him; nor was it the words he had spoken either aloud or within his soul: it was the fearful and ascendant freedom he had felt as he listened to and saw the words. There was dew on the grass beneath his feet; he stopped and looked down at the flecks of it on his polished black shoes. He stood for a moment, a slight cool breeze touching his flesh, the early warmth of the sun on his hair and face, and he felt a loving and plaintive union with all those alive and dead who had at one time in their lives, through drink or rage or passion, suddenly made the statement whose result they had both feared and hoped for and had therefore long suppressed. He imagined a multitude of voices and pained and determined faces, leaping into separation and solitude and fear and hope. His hand rose to his hair, grey in his thirties. He walked on to the church. As he put on his vestments he looked down at the sleepy altar boy, a child. He wanted to touch him but was afraid to. He spoke gently to the boy, touched him with words. They filed into the church, and the old women and a young couple who were engaged and one old man rose.

There were ten of them. With his gin-dried mouth he voiced the prayers while his anticipatory heart beat toward that decision he knew he would one day reach, and had been reaching for some time, as though his soul had taken its own direction while his body and voice moved through the work of the parish. When the ten filed up to receive communion and he placed the host on their tongues and smelled their mouths and bodies and clothes, the sterile old ones and the young couple smelling washed as though for a date, the boy of after-shave lotion, the girl of scented soap, he studied each face for a sign. The couple were too young. In the wrinkled faces of the old he could see only an accumulation of time, of experience; he could not tell whether, beneath those faces, there was a vague recollection of a rewarding life or weary and muted self-contempt because of moments denied, choices run from. He could not tell whether any of them had reached and then denied or followed an admission like the one that gin had drawn from him the night before. Their tongues wet his fingers. He watched them with the dread, excitement, and vulnerability of a man who knows his life is about to change.

After that he stayed sober. The gin had done its work. Before dinner he approached the bottle conspiratorially, held it and looked at it as though it contained a benevolent yet demanding genie. He did not even have to drink carefully. He did not have to drink at all. He drank to achieve a warm nimbus for his secret that soon he would bare to the pastor. In the weeks that followed his drunken night he gathered up some of his past, looked at it as he had not when it was his present, and smiling at himself he saw that he had been in trouble, and the deepest trouble had been his not knowing that he was in trouble. He saw that while he was delivering his sermons he had been proud, yes; perhaps that wasn't even sinful; perhaps it was natural, even good; but the pride was no longer significant. The real trap of his sermons was that while he spoke he had acted out, soberly and with no sense of desperation, the same yearning that had made him cling to the pillow while drunk. For he realized now that beneath his sermons, even possibly at the source of them, was an abiding desire to expose his soul with all his strengths and vanities and weaknesses to another human being. And, further, the other human being was a woman.

Studying himself from his new distance he learned that while he had scanned the congregation he had of course noted the men's faces; but as attentive, as impressed, as they might be, he brushed them aside, and his eyes moved on to the faces of women. He spoke to them. It was never one face. He saw in

all those eyes of all those ages the female reception he had to
have: grandmothers and widows and matrons and young wives
and young girls all formed a composite woman who loved him.

She came to the confessional too, where he sat profiled to
the face behind the veiled window, one hand supporting his
forehead and shielding his eyes. He sat and listened to the
woman's voice. He had the reputation of being an understanding confessor; he had been told this by many of those
people who when speaking to a priest were compelled to talk
shop; not theirs: his. Go to Father Ritchie, the women told
him at parish gatherings; that's what they all say, Father. He
sat and listened to the woman's voice. Usually the sins were
not important; and even when they were he began to sense
that the woman and the ritual of confession had nothing to do
with the woman and her sin. Often the sins of men were pragmatic and calculated and had to do with money; their adulteries were restive lapses from their responsibilities as husbands
and fathers, and they confessed them that way, some adding
the assurance that they loved their wives, their children.
Some men confessed not working at their jobs as hard as they
could, and giving too little time to their children. Theirs was a
world of responsible action; their sins were what they considered violations of that responsibility.

But the women lived in a mysterious and amoral region
which both amused and attracted Joe. Their sins were instinc-
tual. They raged at husbands or children; they fornicated or
committed adultery; the closest they came to pragmatic sin
was birth control, and few of them confessed that anymore. It
was not celibate lust that made Joe particularly curious about
their sexual sins: it was the vision these sins gave him of their
natures. Sometimes he wondered if they were capable of sinning at all. Husbands whispered of one-night stands, and in
their voices Joe could hear self-reproach that was rooted in
how they saw themselves as part of the world. But not so with
the women. In passion they had made love. There was no
other context for the act. It had nothing to do with their husbands or their children; Joe never said it in the confessional

but it was clear to him that it had nothing to do with God either. He began to see God and the church and those activities that he thought of as the world—education, business, politics—as male and serious, perhaps comically so; while women were their own temples and walked cryptic, oblivious, and brooding across the earth. Behind the veil their voices whispered without remorse. Their confessions were a distant and dutiful salute to the rules and patterns of men. He sat and listened to the woman's voice.

And his reputation was real: he was indeed understanding and kind, but not for God, not for the sacrament that demanded of him empathy and compassion as God might have; or Christ. For it was not God he loved, it was Christ: God in the flesh that each morning he touched and ate, making his willful and faithful connection with what he could neither touch nor see. But his awareness of his duty to imitate Christ was not the source of his virtues as a confessor.

Now, as he prepared to leave the priesthood, he saw that he had given kindness and compassion and understanding because he had wanted to expose that part of himself, real or false, to a faceless nameless woman who would at least know his name because it hung outside the confessional door. And he understood why on that hungover morning he had wanted to touch the altar boy but had been afraid to, though until then his hands had instinctively gone out to children, to touch, to caress; on that morning he had been afraid he would not stop at a touch; that he would embrace the boy, fiercely, like a father.

He did not lose his faith in the Eucharist. After leaving the priesthood he had daily gone to mass and received what he knew was the body and blood of Christ. He knew it, he told Edith, in the simplest and perhaps most profound way: most profound, he said, because he believed that faith had no more to do with intellect than love did; that touching her he knew he loved her and loving her he touched her; and that his flesh knew God through touch as it had to; that there was no other way it could; that bread and wine becoming body and blood was neither miracle nor mystery, but natural, for it happened within the leap of the heart of man toward the heart of God, a leap caused by the awareness of death. Like us, he had said. Like us what? she said, lying beside him last spring, his seed swimming in her, thinking of her Episcopal childhood, she and her family Christian by skin color and pragmatic in belief. When we make love, he said. We do it in the face of death. (And this was in the spring, before he knew.) Our bodies aren't just meat then; they become statement too; they become spirit. If we can do that with each other then why can't we do it with God, and he with us? I don't know, she said; I've never thought about it. Don't, he said; it's too simple.

After they became lovers he continued going to daily mass but he stopped receiving communion. She offered to stop seeing him, to let him confess and return to his sacrament. He told her no. It was not that he believed he was sinning with her; it was that he didn't know. And if indeed he were living in sin it was too complex for him to enter a confessional and simply murmur the word *adultery*; too complex for him to burden just any priest with, in any confessional. He recognized this as pride: the sinner assuming the anonymous confessor would be unable to understand and unwilling to grapple with the extent and perhaps even the exonerating circumstances of the sin, but would instead have to retreat and cling to the word *adultery* and the divine law forbidding it. So he did not confess. And there were times at daily mass when he nearly joined the others and received communion, because he felt that he could, that it would be all right. But he did not trust what he felt: in his love for Edith he was untroubled and happy but he did not trust himself enough to believe he could only be happy within the grace of God. It could be, he told her, that his long and celibate need for earthly love now satisfied, he had chosen to complete himself outside the corridor leading to God; that he was not really a spiritual man but was capable of, if not turning his back on God, at least glancing off to one side and keeping that glance fixed for as long as he and Edith loved. So he did not receive, even though at times he felt that he could.

If she were not married he was certain he would receive communion daily while remaining her lover because, although he knew it was rarely true, he maintained and was committed to the belief that making love could parallel and even merge with the impetus and completion of the Eucharist. Else why make love at all, he said, except for meat in meat, making ourselves meat, drawing our circle of mortality not around each other but around our own vain and separate hearts. But if she were free to love him, each act between them would become a sacrament, each act a sign of their growing union in the face of God and death, freed of their now-imposed limitations on commitment and risk and hope. Because he believed in love, he said. With all his heart he believed in it, saw it as a microcosm of the Eucharist which in turn was a microcosm of the earth-rooted love he must feel for God in order to live with certainty as a man. And like his love for God, his love for her had little to do with the emotion which at times pulsated and quivered in his breast so fiercely that he had to make love with her in order to bear it; but it had more to do with the acts themselves, and love finally was a series of gestures with escalating and enduring commitments.

So if she were free to love him he could receive communion too, take part without contradiction in that gesture too. And if their adultery were the classic variety involving cuckoldry he would know quite simply it was a sin, because for his own needs he would be inflicting pain on a man who loved his wife. But since her marriage was not in his eyes a marriage at all but an arrangement which allowed Hank to indulge his impulses within the shelter of roof, woman, and child which apparently he also needed, the sin—if it existed— was hard to define. So that finally his reason for not receiving communion was his involvement in a marriage he felt was base, perhaps even sordid; and, in love as he was, he reeked or at least smelled faintly of sin, which again he could neither define nor locate; and indeed it could be Hank's sin he carried about with him and shared. Which is why he asked her to marry him.

'It's obvious you love Hank,' he said.

'Yes,' she said, her head on his bare shoulder; then she touched his face, stroked it.

'If you didn't love him you would divorce him, because you could keep Sharon. But your love for him contradicts its purpose. It empties you without filling you, it dissipates you, you'll grow old in pieces.'

'But if I were divorced you couldn't be married in the church. What about your Eucharist? Would you give that up?'

'I'd receive every day,' he said. 'Who would know? I'd go to mass and receive the Eucharist like any other man.'

'I don't think you're a Catholic at all.'

'If I'm not, then I don't know what I am.'


# 4


She wakes frightened beside Joe and looks in the grey light at the clock on the bedside table—six-forty. Joe is sleeping on his back, his mouth open; his face seems to have paled and shrunk or sagged during the night, and his shallow breath is liquid. She quietly gets out of bed. Her heart still beats with fright. This is the first time she has ever spent the night with Joe, or with any of her lovers; always the unspoken agreement with Hank was that for the last part of the night and the breakfast hour of the morning the family would be together under one roof; sometimes she had come home as late as four in the morning and gotten into bed beside Hank, who slept; always when he came home late she was awake and always she pretended she was asleep.

She dresses quickly, watching Joe's face and thinking of Sharon sleeping and hoping she will sleep for another half-hour; although if she wakes and comes down to the kitchen before Edith gets home, Edith can explain that she has been to the store. Yet she knows that discovery by Sharon is not what she really fears, that it will probably be another seven years before Sharon begins to see what she and Hank are doing. At the thought of seven more years of this her fear is instantly replaced by a rush of despair that tightens her jaws in resignation. Then she shakes her head, shakes away the image of those twenty-eight seasons until Sharon is fifteen, and continues to dress; again she is afraid. She needs a cigarette and goes to the kitchen for one; at the kitchen table she writes a note telling Joe she will be back later in the morning. She plans to clean his apartment but does not tell him in the note, which she leaves propped against the bedside clock so he will see it when he wakes and will not have to call her name or get up to see if she is still with him. She writes only that she will be back later and that she loves him. She assumes it is true that she loves him, but for a long time now it has been difficult to sort out her feelings and understand them.

As now, driving home, and knowing it is neither discovery by Sharon nor rebuke by Hank that makes her grip on the wheel so firm and anxious that the muscles of her arms tire from the tension. For she knows Hank will not be disturbed. He likes Joe and will understand why she had to stay the night; although, on the road now, in the pale blue start of the day, her decision to sleep with Joe seems distant and unnecessary, an impulse born in the hyperbole of bourbon and night. She wishes she had gone home after Joe was asleep. But if she is home in time to cook breakfast, Hank will not be angry. So why, then, driving through the streets of a town that she now thinks of as her true home, does she feel like a fugitive? She doesn't know.

And yet the feeling persists through breakfast, even though she is in luck: when she enters the kitchen she hears the shower upstairs; she brings a glass of orange juice upstairs, stopping in her room long enough to hang up her coat and change her sweater and pants; then she goes to Sharon's room. Sharon sleeps on her back, the long brown hair spread on the pillow, strands of it lying on her upturned cheek; her lips are slightly parted and she seems to be frowning at a dream. The room smells of childhood: the neutral and neuter scents of bedclothes and carpet and wood, and Edith recalls the odors of Joe's apartment, and of Joe. She sits on the side of the bed, pausing to see if her weight will stir Sharon from the dream and sleep. After a while she touches Sharon's cheek; Sharon wakes so quickly, near startled, that Edith is saddened. She likes to watch Sharon wake with the insouciance of a baby, and she regrets her having to get up early and hurry to school. Sharon pushes up on her elbows, half-rising from the bed while her brown eyes are blinking at the morning. Edith kisses her and gives her the juice. Sharon blinks, looks about the room, and asks what time it is.

'There's plenty of time,' Edith says. 'Would you like pancakes?'

Sharon gulps the juice and says yes, then pushes back the covers and is waiting for Edith to get up so she can swing her feet to the floor. Edith kisses her again before leaving the room. In the hall she is drawn to the sound of the shower behind her, needs to say something to Hank, but doesn't know what it is; with both loss and relief she keeps going down the hall and the stairs, into the kitchen.

Hank and Sharon come down together; by this time Edith has made coffee, brought the *Boston Globe* in from the front steps and laid it at Hank's place; the bacon is frying in the iron skillet, the pancake batter is mixed, and the electric skillet is heated. Her eyes meet Hank's. He does not kiss her good-morning before sitting down; that's no longer unusual but this morning the absence of a kiss strikes her like a mild but intended slap. They tell each other good-morning. Since that summer three years ago she has felt with him, after returning from a lover, a variety of emotions which seem unrelated: vengeance, affection, weariness, and sometimes the strange and frightening lust of collusive sin. At times she has also felt shy, and that is how she feels this morning as he props the paper on the milk pitcher, then withdraws it as Sharon lifts the pitcher and pours into her glass. Edith's shyness is no different from what it would be if she and Hank were new lovers, only hours new, and this was the first morning she had waked in his house and as she cooked breakfast her eyes and heart reached out to him to see if this morning he was with her as he was last night. He looks over the paper at her, and his eyes ask about Joe. She shrugs then shakes her head, but she is not thinking of Joe, and the tears that cloud her eyes are not for him either. She pours small discs of batter into the skillet, and turns the bacon. Out of her vision Hank mumbles something to the paper. She breathes the smells of the batter, the bacon, the coffee.

When Hank and Sharon have left, Edith starts her work. There is not much to do, but still she does not take time to read the paper. When she has finished in the kitchen she looks at the guest room, the dining room, and the living room. They are all right; she vacuumed yesterday. She could dust the bookshelves in the living room but she decides they can wait. She goes upstairs; Sharon has made her bed, and Edith smooths it and then makes the other bed where the blankets on her side are still tucked in. The bathroom is clean and smells of Hank's after-shave lotion. He has left hair in the bathtub and whiskers in the lavatory; she picks these up with toilet paper. She would like a shower but she wants to flee from this house. She decides to shower anyway; perhaps the hot water and warm soft lather will calm her. But under the spray she is the same, and she washes quickly and very soon is leaving the house, carrying the vacuum cleaner. On the icy sidewalk she slips and falls hard on her rump. For a moment she sits there, hoping no one has seen her; she feels helpless to do everything she must do; early, the day is demanding more of her than she can give, and she does not believe she can deal with it, or with tomorrow, or the days after that either. She slowly stands up. In the car, with the seatbelt buckled around her heavy coat, she turns clumsily to look behind her as she backs out of the driveway.

At Joe's she moves with short strides up the sidewalk, balancing herself against the weight of the vacuum cleaner. She doesn't knock, because he may be sleeping still. But he is not. As she pushes open the front door she sees him sitting at the kitchen table, wearing the black turtleneck. He smiles and starts to rise, but instead turns his chair to face her and watches her as, leaving the vacuum cleaner, she goes down the hall and kisses him, noting as she lowers her face his weary pallor and the ghost in his eyes. In spite of that and the taste of mouthwash that tells her he has vomited again, she no longer feels like a fugitive. She doesn't understand this, because the feeling began when she woke beside him and therefore it seems that being with him again would not lift it from her. This confuses and frustrates her: when her feelings enter a terrain she neither controls nor understands she thinks they may take her even further, even into madness. She hugs Joe and tells him she has come to clean his apartment; he protests, but he is pleased.

He follows her to the living room and sits on the couch. But after a while, as she works, he lies down, resting his head on a cushion against the arm of the couch. Quietly he watches her. She watches the path of the vacuum cleaner, the clean swath approaching the layers and fluffs of dust. She feels the touch of his eyes, and what is behind them. When she is finished she moves to the bedroom and again he follows her; he lies on the bed, which he has made. For a while she works in a warm patch of sunlight from the window. She looks out at the bright snow and the woods beyond: the spread and reaching branches of elms and birches and maples and tamaracks are bare; there are pines and hemlocks green in the sun. She almost stops working. Her impulse is to throw herself against the window, cover it with her body, and scream in the impotent rage of grief. But she does not break the rhythm of her work; she continues to push the vacuum cleaner over the carpet, while behind her he watches the push and pull of her arms, the bending of her body, the movement of her legs.

When she has vacuumed and dusted the apartment and cleaned the bathtub and lavatory she drinks coffee at the kitchen table while he sits across from her drinking nothing, then with apology in his voice and eyes he says: 'I called the doctor this morning. He said he'd come see me, but I told him I'd go to the office.'

She puts down her coffee cup.

'I'll drive you.'

He nods. Looking at him, her heart is pierced more deeply and painfully than she had predicted: she knows with all her futile and yearning body that they will never make love again, that last night's rushed and silent love was their last, and that except to pack his toilet articles and books for the final watch in the hospital, he will not return to his apartment she has cleaned.

It is night, she is in her bed again, and now Hank turns to her, his hand moving up her leg, sliding her nightgown upward, and she opens her legs, the old easy opening to the hand that has touched her for ten years; but when the nightgown reaches her hips she does not lift them to allow it to slip farther up her body. She is thinking of this afternoon when the priest came to the room and she had to leave. She nodded at the priest, perhaps spoke to him, but did not see him, would not recognize him if she saw him again, and she left and walked down the corridor to the sunporch and stood at the windows that gave back her reflection, for outside the late afternoon of the day she cleaned Joe's apartment was already dark and the streetlights and the houses across the parking lot were lighted. She smoked while on the hospital bed Joe confessed his sins, told the priest about her, about the two of them, all the slow nights and hurried afternoons, and she felt isolated as she had when, months ago, he had begun to die while, healthy, she loved him.

Since breakfast her only contact with Hank and Sharon was calling a sitter to be waiting when Sharon got home, and calling Hank at the college to tell him she was at the hospital and ask him to feed Sharon. Those two phone calls kept her anchored in herself, but the third set her adrift and she felt that way still on the sun-porch: Joe had asked her to, and she had phoned the rectory and told a priest whose name she didn't hear that her friend was dying, that he was an ex-priest, that he wanted to confess and receive communion and the last sacrament. Then she waited on the sun-porch while Joe in confession told her goodbye. She felt neither anger nor bitterness but a vulnerability that made her cross her arms over her breasts and draw her sweater closer about her shoulders, though the room was warm. She felt the need to move, to pace the floor, but she could not. She gazed at her reflection in the window without seeing it and gazed at the streetlights and the lighted windows beyond the parking lot and the cars of those who visited without seeing them either, as inside Joe finally confessed to the priest, any priest from any rectory. It did not take long, the confession and communion and the last anointing, not long at all before the priest emerged and walked briskly down the corridor in his black overcoat. Then she went in and sat on the edge of the bed and thought again that tomorrow she must bring flowers, must give to this room scent and spirit, and he took her hand.

'Did he understand everything?' she said.

He smiled. 'I realized he didn't have to. It's something I'd forgotten with all my thinking: it's what ritual is for: nobody has to understand. The knowledge is in the ritual. Anyone can listen to the words. So I just used the simple words.'

'You called us adultery?'

'That's what I called us,' he said, and drew her face down to his chest.

Now she feels that touch more than she feels Hank's, and she reaches down and takes his wrist, stopping the hand, neither squeezing nor pushing, just a slight pressure of resistance and his hand is gone.

'I should be with him,' she says. 'There's a chair in the room where I could sleep. They'd let me: the nurses. It would be a help for them. He's drugged and he's sleeping on his back. He could vomit and drown. Tomorrow night I'll stay there. I'll come home first and cook dinner and stay till Sharon goes to bed. Then I'll go back to the hospital. I'll do that till he dies.'

'I don't want you to.'

She looks at him, then looks away. His hand moves to her leg again, moves up, and when she touches it resisting, it moves away and settles on her breast.

'Don't,' she says. 'I don't want to make love with you.'

'You're grieving.'

His voice is gentle and seductive, then he shifts and tries to embrace her but she pushes with her hands against his chest and closing her eyes she shakes her head.

'Don't,' she says. 'Just please don't. It doesn't mean anything any more. It's my fault too. But it's over, Hank. It's because he's dying, yes—' She opens her eyes and looks past her pushing hands at his face and she feels and shares his pain and dismay; and loving him she closes her eyes. 'But you're dying too. I can feel it in your chest just like I could feel it when I rubbed him when he hurt. And so am I: that's what we lost sight of.'

His chest still leans against her hands, and he grips her shoulders. Then he moves away and lies on his back.

'We'll talk tomorrow,' he says. 'I don't trust this kind of talk at night.'

'It's the best time for it,' she says, and she wants to touch him just once, gently and quickly, his arm or wrist or hand; but she does not.

In late afternoon while snow clouds gather, the priest who yesterday heard Joe's confession and gave him the last sacrament comes with the Eucharist, and this time Edith can stay. By now Hank is teaching his last class of the day and Sharon is home with the sitter. Tonight at dinner Sharon will ask as she did this morning: Is your friend dead yet? Edith has told her his name is Mr. Ritchie but Sharon has never seen him and so cannot put a name on a space in her mind; calling him *your friend* she can imagine Joe existing in the world through the eyes of her mother. At breakfast Hank watched them talking; when Edith looked at him, his eyes shifted to the newspaper.

When the priest knocks and enters, Edith is sitting in a chair at the foot of the bed, a large leather chair, the one she will sleep in tonight; she nearly lowers her eyes, averts her face; yet she looks at him. He glances at her and nods. If he thinks of her as the woman in yesterday's confession there is no sign in his face, which is young: he is in his early thirties. Yet his face looks younger, and there is about it a boyish vulnerability which his seriousness doesn't hide. She guesses that he is easily set off balance, is prone to concern about trifles: that caught making a clumsy remark he will be anxious for the rest of the evening. He does not remove his overcoat, which is open. He moves to the bed, his back to her now, and places a purple stole around his neck. His hands are concealed from her; then they move toward Joe's face, the left hand cupped beneath the right hand which with thumb and forefinger holds the white disc.

'The body of Christ,' he says.

'Amen,' Joe says.

She watches Joe as he closes his eyes and extends his tongue and takes the disc into his mouth. His eyes remain closed; he chews slowly; then he swallows. The priest stands for a moment, watching him. Then with his right palm he touches Joe's forehead, and leaves the room. Edith goes to the bed, sits on its edge, takes Joe's hand and looks at his closed eyes and lips. She wants to hold him hard, feel his ribs against hers, has the urge to fleshless insert her ribs within his, mesh them. Gently she lowers her face to his chest, and he strokes her hair. Still he has not opened his eyes. His stroke on her hair is lighter and slower, and then it stops; his hands rest on her head, and he sleeps. She does not move. She watches as his mouth opens and she listens to the near gurgling of his breath.

She does not move. In her mind she speaks to him, telling him what she is waiting to tell him when he wakes again, what she has been waiting all day to tell him but has not because once she says it to Joe she knows it will be true, as true as it was last night. There are still two months of the cold and early sunsets of winter left, the long season of waiting, and the edges of grief which began last summer when he started to die are far from over, yet she must act: looking now at the yellow roses on the bedside table she is telling Hank goodbye, feeling that goodbye in her womb and heart, a grief that will last, she knows, longer than her grieving for Joe. When the snow is melted from his grave it will be falling still in her soul as it is now while she recalls images and voices of her ten years with Hank and quietly now she weeps, not for Joe or Sharon or Hank, but for herself; and she wishes with all her splintered heart that she and Hank could be as they once were and she longs to touch him, to cry on his broad chest, and with each wish and each image her womb and heart toll their goodbye, forcing her on into the pain that waits for her, so that now she is weeping not quietly but with shuddering sobs she cannot control, and Joe wakes and opens his eyes and touches her wet cheeks and mouth. For a while she lets him do this. Then she stops crying. She kisses him, then wipes her face on the sheet and sits up and smiles at him. Holding his hand and keeping all nuances of fear and grief from her voice, because she wants him to know he has done this for her, and she wants him to be happy about it, she says: 'I'm divorcing Hank.'

He smiles and touches her cheek and she strokes his cool hand.

# EDITOR'S NOTE

*Joshua Bodwell*

THERE IS PERHAPS no greater double-edged compliment in literature than the phrase "writer's writer." It is at once both high praise and an intimation of authorial obscurity. The phrase inevitably brings to mind writers of undeniable skill and power whose work has not easily or effortlessly found a large readership.

Andre Dubus was a writer's writer. His short stories and novellas have for decades been discussed regularly and reverently among other writers as exemplars of the forms. He was a master of narrative compression, a writer of unyielding compassion, and like his literary mentor Anton Chekhov, an author of far-reaching empathy. And like Chekhov, Dubus deserves to be discovered by generation after generation of new readers.

It was with all this and more in mind that I proposed this project to gather together the vast majority of Andre Dubus's short stories and novellas into three volumes with new introductions by some of those writers who most admire his work.

This volume brings together Andre Dubus's first two critically acclaimed collections of short stories and novellas: *Separate Flights* and *Adultery & Other Choices*.

*THE TITLE OF VOLUME ONE*

We faced a unique challenge when it came to titling the books in this three-volume project: it was awkward and inelegant to merge the titles of two different books, yet Dubus was not alive to offer new alternatives.

My challenge then was to find new titles while staying true to Dubus's voice. The solution arrived when I realized Dubus had, over the years, toyed with naming collections after different stories within a collection before settling on an eventual title. Scanning the table of contents for volume one, we had myriad title options for the book, and they were all Dubus's very own words.

This volume opens with "We Don't Live Here Anymore," making it the first novella in Dubus's first collection. Just as the phrase "We don't live here anymore..." obviously haunted Dubus when he first heard it uttered by a drunken friend, the words resonate today with a kind of lyrical melancholy.

"We Don't Live Here Anymore" is the first story of what would become a trilogy of novellas about the intersecting lives of two young couples: Hank and Edith Allison, and Jack and Terry Linhart. The importance of the novella in the context of Dubus's ongoing body of work can't be understated: it is the foundation—taken together with "Adultery" and "Finding a Girl in America"—of some of his most important fiction.

*THE SHORT STORIES & NOVELLAS OF VOLUME ONE*

Dubus spent a considerable amount of time contemplating the sequence of the stories in his collections. "The arrangement is important to the reading, and I do take the trouble," he told interviewer Thomas Kennedy. "I learned that from Richard Yates and assume that all short story writers take the trouble. Therefore, when I buy a book of stories, I read them in order." With this in mind, we have honored and retained Dubus's story sequencing here.

*Separate Flights* was warmly received in 1975: it won the *Boston Globe*'s inaugural L. L. Winship Award (now the Laurence L. & Thomas Winship/PEN New England Award), which honors a New England author or book with a New England setting or subject. *The Atlantic Monthly* raved, "Dubus is the sort of writer who instructs the heart, and he ought to be discovered by any number of readers."

The publication history of the collection's third story is a perfect example of how long Dubus waited out rejection and the pressure to write a novel before landing at David R. Godine: while publication today in the venerated pages of *The New Yorker* seems a predication of near immediate success, "The Doctor" appeared the magazine in 1969, and it would be six years before the publication of Dubus's debut collection. That same year, "If They Knew Yvonne" appeared in the *North American Review* and went on to be selected for the *Best American Short Stories 1970*—it would be the first of several Dubus stories selected for the celebrated annual anthology.

Just two years after *Separate Flights*, Dubus's *Adultery & Other Choices* appeared in 1977. The collection's opening stories focus on the fragile nature of youth, such as "An Afternoon with the Old Man," which appeared in *The New Yorker* in 1972, and "The Fat Girl," which has become one of Dubus's most revered, often discussed stories; "The Fat Girl" went on to be included in *The Pushcart Prize III: Best of the Small Presses* in 1978, and a decade later was collected in *American Short Story Masterpieces*, edited by Raymond Carver and Tom Jenks.

The middle stories of *Adultery & Other Choices* shift to darker struggles of adulthood, such as in "Cadence"—which appeared in *The Sewanee Review* before being selected for the *Best American Short Stories 1976*—and "Andromache," a breathtaking story that traces the death of a peacetime Marine, and which was actually Dubus's first story to appear in *The New Yorker* (1968).

The collection closes with "Adultery," a novella that revisits the lives of Hank and Edith Allison, Jack and Terry Linhart. Reviewing Dubus's sophomore collection, *The New York Times* opined "The title story alone will make it worth your while to go out and get the book." The novella was one of the most difficult undertakings of Dubus's career: he wrote seven drafts and four hundred manuscript pages before wrangling the piece into a sixty-page final draft.

## EDITOR'S ACKNOWLEDGMENTS

In 2007, Kevin Larimer at *Poets & Writers Magazine* accepted my pitch to write a long piece entitled "The Art of Reading Andre Dubus: We Don't Have to Live Great Lives." Kevin was, as he always is, a patient, shrewd, and thoughtful editor of that piece. The joys of writing that article became the seed of this three-volume project, and for that I will be eternally grateful to the encouragement of Kevin and *Poets & Writers Magazine*.

At David R. Godine, Publisher, the talented team of Sue Ramin and Chelsea Bingham was endlessly helpful, as was the calm, steadying advice of George Gibson, for which I am thankful. Carl W. Scarbrough, designer par excellence, brought his refined touch to the beautiful physical book.

Greta Rybus not only made the photographs for the covers of all three new volumes of this project, but went above and beyond, reading and re-reading Dubus's story, and offering thoughtful, caring, and deeply felt creative ideas about how the photographs might speak in conversation with Dubus's complex stories. We should all be so lucky to have the opportunity to work with collaborators as gifted and generous as Greta.

For too many reasons to note here, I will be forever indebted to the generosity of the author whose words introduce this volume: Ann Beattie. It seems incredibly fitting that Ann introduces this first volume, as it was our mutual affection for Dubus's writing that first ignited our friendship a decade ago. It is an honor to have Ann's words here.

Finally, the last two people to thank are the first two people I reached out to when I conceived of this project: Andre Dubus III and David R. Godine.

David first published Andre Dubus's short stories and novellas more than four decades ago, and for that reason alone, this book simply would not exist if not for the unflagging support of Dubus's work. After every turn, David's enthusiasm and considerable knowledge was invaluable.

Andre III's generosity and big-hearted embrace of this project girded my confidence to proceed. He quickly invited his sister Suzanne Dubus into the process, and both became steady sources of ideas and support. In a world that sometimes seems stymied by a dearth of good men, Andre is one of the very best men I know. *Thank you, brother.*

# AUTHOR'S BIOGRAPHY

ANDRE DUBUS (August 11, 1936–February 24, 1999; pro-
nounced da-byüs) was born in Lake Charles, Louisiana to a
Cajun-Irish family and educated in Catholic schools. After
peacetime service in the U.S. Marine Corps, Dubus attended
the University of Iowa Writers' Workshop, where he earned
his MFA in 1965. In 1966, he moved north, settling in Haverhill, Massachusetts to teach literature and creative writing at
Bradford College until his retirement.

Dubus's short stories and novellas appeared in distin-
guished literary journals such as *Ploughshares*, *The Paris
Review*, *The Sewanee Review*, and *The Southern Review*, as
well as national magazines such as *Harper's*, *The New Yorker*,
and *Playboy*. In addition to his many short story collections,
he published two collections of essays: *Broken Vessels* and
*Meditations from a Movable Chair*. The award-winning films
*In the Bedroom* and *We Don't Live Here Anymore* were adapted
from his stories.

His prose earned him a MacArthur "Genius" Award, the
PEN/Malamud Award for Excellence in the Short Story, the
Rea Award for the Short Story, the Jean Stein Award from the
American Academy of Arts and Letters, and nominations for a
National Book Critics Circle Award and Pulitzer Prize.

Andre Dubus published just one novel during his career:

*The Lieutenant* (Dial Press, 1967). After falling under the spell of Anton Chekhov, Dubus would consciously devote himself to the short story and novella for the rest of his life. While his stories were revered when they appeared in literary journals and magazines, after the publication of his novel, Dubus received rejection after rejection when it came to publishing a collection of his stories.

Literary agent Philip G. Spitzer became one of Dubus's earliest and most loyal supporters. During a casual lunch in New York City, Spitzer handed David R. Godine a plain manila envelope with the manuscript for *Separate Flights*. Godine called Spitzer the next day and offered to publish the collection. In the end, Dubus waited seven rejection-filled years between the publication of novel and his first short story collection.

In a 1998 interview with *Glimmer Train*, Dubus recalled "The rejections that really hurt during that period after I published *The Lieutenant* were not the rejections slips that said 'I don't like the collection of stories,' but the ones that said, 'We'll publish this collection of stories if you write a novel.' That hurt. I thought I was being told to be somebody else."

Neither Spitzer nor Godine insisted Dubus write a novel but instead supported his devotion to the short story. Godine quickly realized "there was more punch contained in one Dubus short story than in 99.98% of all the novels being published. I still feel that way."

"I'm one of the luckiest short story writers in America because of Godine," Dubus told the *Black Warrior Review* in 1983. "How many publishers would publish four collections of stories by a writer, without *one* novel?" Indeed, the closest Godine ever came to publishing a novel by Dubus was issuing the long novella *Voices from the Moon* as a gorgeously designed standalone book in 1984; the novella appears in full in volume three of this project, *The Cross Country Runner*.

Dubus's devotion to the short story form—the novella bears a much closer relation to being a long short story than being a short novella—fit him not simply as a prose form, but from a philosophical stance. "I love short stories because I believe they are the way we live," he once wrote. "They are what our friends tell us, in their pain and joy, their passion and rage, their yearning and their cry against injustice."

In 1986, while attempting to aid two motorists on a highway in Massachusetts, Dubus was struck by an oncoming car traveling nearly sixty miles an hour. Dubus stopped at what he thought was a car broken down in the travel lane. The car, it turned out, had become wedged on a motorcycle abandoned in the middle of the highway. As Dubus helped the two motorists—Luis and Luz Santiago, a brother and sister from Puerto Rico—to safety, another car approached. Dubus pushed Luz out of the way. Luis, a young man of only twenty-three, was hit and killed instantly. Dubus was struck, thrown over the car's hood and landed in a crumpled, bleeding mass; a quarter found in Dubus's pocket after the accident had been bent in half by the impact.

While it's startling that Dubus somehow managed to even survive the blow, the accident left him with thirty-four broken bones. He lost his left leg below the knee and his right leg was crushed to the point of uselessness. He would be confined to a wheelchair for the rest of his. After the accident, Dubus was unable to write for some time. He eventually found his way back to writing fiction, in part, by writing a series of powerful essays. In need of money for medical and living expenses, Dubus finally—with the blessing of his longtime publisher, David Godine—accepted an offer from a large New York City publisher. A full decade after Dubus's accident, *Dancing After Hours* appeared in 1996, published by Alfred A. Knopf, and went on to be named a finalist for a National Book Critics Circle Award; the fourteen stories in that collection are his only stories not included in this three volume collection.

On February 24, 1999, at the age of sixty-two, Dubus suffered a fatal heart attack. He was laid to rest in Haverhill, Massachusetts in a simple casket handmade by his sons.

## A NOTE ON THE TYPE

WE DON'T LIVE HERE ANYMORE *has been set in Jonathan Hoefler's Mercury types. Originally created for the* New Times *newspaper chain and later adapted for general informational typography, the Mercury types were drawn in four grades intended to be used under variable printing conditions—that is, to compensate for less-than-optimal presswork or for regional differences in paper stock and plant conditions. The result was a family of types that were optimized to print well in a vast number of sizes and formats. In books, Mercury makes a no-nonsense impression, crisp and open, direct and highly readable, yet possessed of real style and personality.* ♦ ♦ ♦ *The display type is Quadraat Sans, a family originally designed in 1996 by Fred Smeijers for FontFont, and subsequently enlarged and expanded into a much larger constellation of types.*